Detective Maddie Ives Book 4

HE KNOWS YOUR SECRETS

An absolutely gripping crime thriller with a massive twist

CHARLIE GALLAGHER

First published in Great Britain 2019
Joffe Books, London

Please join our mailing list for free Kindle books and new releases.

www.joffebooks.com

ISBN: 978-1-78931-271-3

AUTHOR'S NOTE

I am inspired by what I do and see in my day job as a front-line police detective, though my books are entirely fictional. I am aware that the police officers in my novels are not always shown positively. They are human and they make mistakes. This is sometimes the case in real life too, but the vast majority of officers are honest and do a good job in trying circumstances. From what I see on a daily basis, the men and women who wear the uniform are among the very finest, and I am proud to be part of one of the best police forces in the world.

Charlie Gallagher

CHAPTER 1

Saturday

The young woman pulled open the front passenger door of the taxi, flung in her rucksack and slid into the seat almost in the same movement. The driver jerked towards her as if caught out. He moved his head back and forth, then tutted and fussed over a tablet held against his steering wheel. He managed to pause whatever it was he'd been watching.

'Hey, you need to go to the front of the queue. They get angry!' An accent accompanied olive skin — Middle Eastern maybe.

'I chose you,' she said.

'Taxi cab! Take from the front!'

'Break the rules for once. It won't hurt now, will it?'

'I am new here. These people, they already don't like me.'

'You want me to tell them? I can. I'll go and speak to each one, tell them that I don't want any of them fucking *pricks* to drive me, that I want you, because you are new, and that you told me to make sure they knew. Or do you think that might draw attention to you even more? You choose.'

She could feel her anger rising, and knew she needed to control it. She just needed to stay calm. Her rucksack had fallen between her feet. The zip was open, revealing some of the contents. She resisted the urge to check it all again; she must have done so ten times already. She reminded herself that she had everything she needed. She felt a little calmer.

The taxi driver was still shaking his head but he had put away his tablet and was now pressing at his phone. He fussed with his seatbelt but abandoned his attempt to fasten it when it didn't clip in straight away. He tutted again. 'Where do you need to go?'

'Capel. There's a café on the top. It looks out over the sea. Do you know it?'

'I know this. Breakfast?' He grinned now. The engine fired. The car was an automatic, she felt it rock forward when he pushed it into *Drive*.

'Near there. A bench — it's a memorial bench. It has the best view.'

The taxi pulled out. She looked out of the passenger window as they moved past the rank of taxis. The drivers all glared at her. She aimed her best daggers back.

'Memorial? This is not a word I know,' said her driver.

'Memorial . . .' She ran the word over in her mind, saw the faint reflection of her lips in the window as she said it. Maybe it wasn't a word she knew either. 'I guess it means, *in memory of*. Yeah, that's it. People pay for them to be there and they stick a plaque with a few words on them — some pretty words or something. Most of the benches up there have them. It's a good place. A lot of people go there to stare out to sea. It becomes their favourite place, then they die and maybe their family think it's a good idea. Fitting, like, you know?'

'So you have someone to go up there and think about?'

'I guess I do.' She could still see her lips when shadows fell over the windows, dimming the light within. They ran under a bridge and she saw her expression was one of subtle surprise.

'Someone you loved?'

She considered this. 'It never stops does it? It doesn't for me, at least. You either love someone or you can't anymore. There is no *loved*.'

'Okay then, this is good. Good for you and also good for person you think about, I say.'

Another dark building swept past her window. In the reflection this time she could see the driver; he was looking over at her with a smile. She didn't return it. She wasn't looking to make a friend, didn't need to be told she was doing the right thing. She just needed to get up there. He must have got the hint; the next dark background showed his focus was back on the road ahead.

They were in the coastal town of Langthorne in the south-east of England. Capel, her destination, was a village between Langthorne and Dover. They shared the same expanse of white cliffs that had somehow become synonymous with Dover.

The man pulled off the main drag. The sun was still low in the sky and they now drove right towards it. He stopped at a junction, his head moving left to right. She dropped her window a little. It was just gone seven in the morning but it already felt warm. It was late August but not yet feeling like late summer.

The man squinted as he peered over at her. 'Where is memorial?'

The road in front was close to the edge of the freshly cut lawns that covered the clifftop. The grass was only left to grow wild when you got closer to the edge and her eyes were dragged to its movement in a light breeze.

They had come out too far up, so she directed him back in the general direction of Langthorne. They passed several benches on the left but she knew what she was looking for. She stopped him a hundred metres short of the café. There were houses to her right, most with big windows to the front to take advantage of the breath-taking view. The car still ticked along. Here the flat expanse of green grass was at its widest point and there were two benches, ten metres apart, both angled slightly to face in the direction of Langthorne's harbour arm. Visibility was so good she could see the white cliff faces of France, like a reflection in a distant and hazy mirror.

'Which one is your bench?' The driver's voice cut across her focus. She was aware that her heart was racing and her breathing shallower — quicker, too. This was it . . . she had arrived. She took her phone out. Her hands shook. She had to take in a deep breath to steady them. She managed to get a message away. She waited, her stare fixed on the screen. She saw a grey tick appear next to her words confirming it was sent. A moment later and a second tick appeared and she knew it had been received. She sucked in another lungful of air then ran her thumb gently over the name of the recipient. But there was no time for sentiment. She switched the phone off.

She bent over and reached down into her bag. Her fingers wrapped around a glass ashtray. It was thick and heavy and cold to the touch.

'It's just a little further on . . .' Her own voice sounded husky. She was still bent over, her hand near the bottom of the bag. She waited. Her eyes flicked right. The driver pushed the shift into *Drive*. She saw his leg move, his foot stepping off the brake. The car rolled forward and he leaned towards her slightly to ask her to speak louder.

It had to be now.

She snatched her hand out of the bag. The ashtray felt heavier than she was expecting as she turned it in the air and swung it in an arc towards the driver. The cold glass smashed into the side of his head. His head jerked away from the force and there was a thud where he collided with the solid metal pillar. The severity of the blow caught them both out, knocking the ashtray from her hand to thunk off the handbrake.

Then there was a moment of pause, the man's expression turned to shock, his eyes flared wide but he didn't look in control, his whole head seemed to wobble. Then came the blood. It ran in a thick slather from the side of his head and she could only look on. He reached down to his lap with his hands but his eyes didn't seem able to follow, he scrabbled around like he was searching for the dropped ashtray. She panicked . . . *she couldn't let him get a hold of that!* It wasn't finished yet.

She threw her right hand out again, this time in a punch. It wasn't very firm but it worked as a distraction and he raised his hand to protect himself. The ashtray came with it but his grip was awkward. She lashed out again, this time aiming for his forearm. It worked. The ashtray fell back to his lap. She scooped it up. It felt instantly clumsy but she was able to move it back so it could have momentum going forward. She held it tighter and pushed it towards him with all she had. Again it was a firm hit to the side of his head, again he could do nothing to protect himself. He collided with the seatbelt housing that stuck out from the side of the car with a solid clunk.

The car lurched as his foot found the gas pedal. His legs shook and his hands pushed out towards her, but with no coordination, as though he was losing his functioning.

The car jerked to a halt. Her body took an impact from the dash down her left side. The heavy ashtray crushed her hand against solid plastic. The blood on the side of his head kept coming — enough to coat his entire ear and run down his neck. She lifted herself up a little to put one knee on the seat. She pushed herself forward, her eyes searching the driver's footwell. He was murmuring, his hands lolling in his lap, and his face was now facing down, saliva hanging from his lips. She dropped the ashtray and leaned forward to reach for his right leg. It was stuck out, locked against the brake pedal. That was no good. She needed to get the car rolling. She took a firm hold of his right thigh and tried to pull it backwards. It did nothing. There wasn't the room. She leaned further forward to hook her arms behind his knee and yanked it back. It worked; the car started to roll gently forward. She sat back up. The man was still murmuring but his eyes were shut.

She pulled the steering wheel hard left and the reaction was instantaneous. The front wheels met with a lip and bumped up onto the grassy expanse. She peered out of the front, adjusting the steering enough so that they moved onto the grass and started across it. They were heading directly between the two benches, towards the cliff edge and the warming sun beyond it. She bit down hard, on her face the beginning of a smile. This was it.

Everything suddenly jerked forward. She got her hands out in time to stop herself crashing into the dashboard. She glanced at the man. His leg was locked back out, his neck looked to be stiff, as if he couldn't turn his head, but his eyes peered across at her and they had focus now. His mumbling was louder, there was intent in the words he was trying to form — he was fighting for his life. She leaned across again to take a hold of his leg. She could feel blows on her back as he struck her but his blows lacked any power or accuracy. His leg was stronger; it was as if he knew that he needed to put all of his energy into keeping it locked out, no matter what. This time she couldn't move it. She sat back in her seat and picked up the ashtray again. He was staring at her, his eyes wide enough that she could see white all the way round the outsides. His voice got louder as his eyes flicked to her raised hand. His speech was nonsense.

'This has to end. I'm sorry.' She smiled. She knew he didn't understand now, but he would. In the next life.

She clasped the ashtray in both hands and threw it forward with all her might. She got a clean strike to the side of his head, and the man slumped over, unconscious, against his driver's door. It was as if she had found his *off* switch. The car started rolling again.

She sat back in her seat and threw the ashtray down. The car bumped slowly across the grass. She lifted her rucksack and put in on her lap then pulled the seatbelt across and clipped it in, being sure to trap the bag against her. She wrapped her arms across it too. Nothing was more important to her now.

Satisfied, she sat back in her seat. The car seemed to be picking up pace where the ground now sloped gently downwards. Then the vivid green grass in front seemed to run out and all that was visible ahead was the glorious blue of the sky tinged with the golden warmth of a sun that consumed her entirely in a flash of light. She had a moment to consider that maybe it was over already, that this was the afterlife.

Then the sun was gone. The car scraped, she felt a violent thud then a shudder on the underside of the car that vibrated through her feet and buttocks — and the sea lurched into view. There was a loud bang and the car bucked crudely. But then it was free.

She closed her eyes to this bit, so the warmth of the sun and the sight of that beautiful, deep shade of blue would be earth's final embrace.

CHAPTER 2

Kelly Dale swept open the curtains and flinched at the sunshine. It was bright and low. Just a few days earlier it had been the same and she could recall smiling at it before stepping aside to let it flood the room and her mother's pale face. Her mother had smiled broadly. She always did at the sunshine, no matter what else was going on. But that was two days ago. Everything was different now.

There were two dirty teacups. The kitchen sink was under the window and her mother's bed was directly opposite. It was a small place and the bed took up most of the open-plan living area. The one bedroom was down a short corridor past a bathroom that was so small you could wash your hands while still sitting on the toilet. In the kitchen area, her gaze lingered on a wooden ornament: a wooden duck wearing bright yellow wellies. Its head bobbed forward like it had something to say from its place on the windowsill. She put the cups down and turned away from the sun. She saw the hand-stitched doilies her mum had made to pass the time and that were now cheering up the only armchair with a smudge of colour. Yes, her mum's home was small, but there was such warmth. Her mum could make anywhere feel warm and cosy — safe, even.

She turned back to the sink and picked up one of the cups. Bone china, with a gold rim and an illustration of a young woman, finely dressed for an era where the horse and carriage she was sitting in made sense. Kelly studied it closely, longing for a hint of her mother's lipstick caught on the rim — some sign of her at least — anything. But there was nothing beyond the dregs of her final drink. Their last cup of tea together had been supped between frail, thin lips. It had been a long illness and some time since her mother would have had any cause to apply lipstick. The police officer had told her that she should take solace in the fact that the pain was over for her mother now. What he didn't say was that hers had only just begun.

She plunged the cup into soapy water that was hot enough to scald her hands. There was a knock at the door. She looked up at it and then at her hands, covered in foam. She held them just above the bowl as if she were frozen in time. It took a second knock for her to move. She picked up a tea towel on the way to the door.

'Hello?' Kelly recognised the voice through the door as Joan's. She lived in the flat opposite. Joan and her mother had been friends, good friends once, never apart, but since the illness her mother had pushed everyone away. She said that she needed to, that she thought she looked weak — *'pathetic'* was her word — and she didn't want that as the lasting image people had of her. Kelly had long since given up trying to convince her otherwise.

Kelly pulled open the door. Joan was holding a dinner plate with a plastic lid covering it.

'Hey, Joan.' Kelly's voice came out as a croak. She hadn't spoken a word since a stunned *thank you* at 10 p.m. the previous night — when they had finally taken her mother away.

'I thought you might want a breakfast. I mean . . . I know you probably won't want to eat anything, but you should.'

'You know, then.' Kelly was a little relieved. She didn't think she could say it.

'I saw them come and go. I was going to come round. Say my dues . . . but . . .'

'You should have.' Kelly's response was automatic; actually, she was glad Joan hadn't.

'These are private times. For family. I didn't want to interfere.'

'Okay.'

'I'll come to the funeral, though. Just you try and stop me, girl!' She laughed. 'Me and your mother . . . the terrible twins we were. I've never known a woman like her. She was wonderful.'

'She was,' Kelly said. The words hung in the air as if both of them were considering the first use of the word *was*.

'You should eat.' Joan held up the plate. Kelly took it, still on autopilot. Eating was the last thing she wanted to do right now but she saw it for what it was, an excuse for Joan to come around, to signal that she knew and to offer her assistance.

'Anything you need . . .' Joan continued.

'I know.'

'Don't even hesitate, no matter what. Are you organising the funeral?'

Kelly nodded. It was just a reaction. She hadn't really thought about it. Her mum had talked about it: she'd hinted that she was going to make some arrangements. But Kelly knew she wouldn't have done. Her mother wasn't very good at *arrangements*; there was no way she had ever sorted anything. The undertakers who had come the previous night had left a leaflet somewhere. Joan still lingered. Kelly realised that she was waiting for an invite to come in. She couldn't cope with that, not right now. She waited her out. Joan got the hint.

'I'm just across the hall. It's a lot for a twenty-two-year-old. You're still a kid, Kell. Don't be a martyr, okay?' Joan reached out. The hug was awkward. Kelly didn't have any strength to hug her back; she could barely lift her arms. Kelly's phone wolf-whistled her from somewhere behind

— her message tone. She managed a reassuring smile back to Joan but it had already dropped away by the time she had turned from the closed door. She sighed. She was back on her own.

She pushed the plate onto the table and walked to the phone. It was face down. She considered leaving it like that. She knew how fast word would get out and that the messages would start. The last thing she needed was empty messages from people telling her they were *sending hugs*.

She spun it over. The screen only showed the sender: Holly. She sucked in a breath. Nothing for a week — she had almost stopped hoping — and now a message from out of the blue. Maybe she had heard. She felt her heart quicken, and hated that Holly still had that effect. She wanted to not care, to put the phone back on its face and get on with her life. After all, Holly had told her to do that, to forget about her, to go and find love with someone who deserved her.

But she *did* care. Like she had never cared about anything or anyone else. She unlocked the phone. Holly's message appeared under a long list of sent messages from Kelly pleading with her to get in touch, to say something. She had said something now.

I know you'll be angry, I know you won't understand, not now. But I did this for you. You have to make sure they know. You can be free. We all can. I love you, more than I ever thought I could love anyone. Make sure they know . . . I always promised . . . I'll be the sky and you be the bird . . .

Kelly's chest tightened, her lips bumped and mumbled over the words as she read them again.

'Oh no, no, no! *Holly*!' She fumbled to dial Holly's number. It went straight to voicemail. She hunted the room for her shoes. They were pushed up against the wall beside the door. She couldn't move towards them, she had to stop — her chest was so tight, her heart beating as though it was knocking to get out. She reached out for the back of the armchair. Her vision was closing in, the blackness creeping in from the edges. She slammed her eyes shut and focused on her breathing. This wasn't the time to panic; she needed to go and she knew exactly where.

* * *

The hill to the village of Capel was steep. Kelly's old car shuddered as she neared the summit. She had to change down to first gear. The car shook on its suspension and the engine coughed. She pressed the accelerator; it coughed again then cut out completely. She swore and reached for the keys as her other hand guided the car over to the left. A blaring horn swept past her right side as she limped out of the way. The road levelled out, with Capel now in front of her. As the car rolled slowly forward, the nearside wheel bumped into a raised, muddy bank. Her foot pumped the brakes and she rocked forward. She turned the keys and the aged motor turned over but the sound was all too familiar. It wasn't going to start.

'Not now! Not FUCKING NOW!' She thumped the steering wheel. Suddenly every reflective surface seemed to pulse blue. Her mirrors were the brightest. A police car swept past her, seeming to drag the noise of its siren along behind it. It surged along the main road into Capel then braked hard, almost overshooting a right turn. Kelly knew that turn well: it cut through a block of houses then came out onto a road that ran directly along the clifftop close to a café, close to where she and Holly had last talked of *freedom*.

She tried the car again: the same sound. It was no use. She shouldered the door open. When she put a foot down and stepped out, she could feel the car was now slowly moving backwards, and it set her off balance. She fell back into the driver's seat and yanked on the handbrake. The car jerked to a stop. She leapt out and slammed the door behind her. The car was at an angle now, pointing back out into the road. She didn't bother to lock the doors before she broke into a run.

She sprinted the two hundred metres or so to the junction where the police car had turned. Now her breath was gone, her legs too. She had to stop. She gasped for air, still pushing forward in a fast walk, breaking into a jog every few steps, her eyes narrowed to the sun. She spotted the police car. It was facing away from her, pulled over roughly but angled so that it was across the road enough for no one to be able to pass. Beyond it she could only see a hint of green under a blue sky. But she knew this place. She also knew there was also a 600-foot drop and then an endless expanse of sea.

The emergency blue lights still flashed at her from the top of the car. As she approached, a police officer walked over to it. He pulled a phone from his pocket, swiped the screen a couple of times with his thumb, then lifted it to his ear. He began what seemed like aimless banter. She moved a little closer. The policeman was lost in his conversation. He laughed; it was booming. She could make out his words now.

'We can see the marks where it's gone over. It's definitely from here. We can't see the bottom, though . . . yeah, that's right. We'll just hold the scene. No, I agree, there's no chance of a rescue. It's a body recovery job, and probably a long one. Yeah, yeah . . . No, I know . . . a fucking long way down, sarge! If you need something more specific then I suggest you send a lanky probationer up here with a tape measure!'

His booming laugh was back but the force of his words hit her before she had even processed them. She dropped to her knees with an impact. When she lifted her head, the officer was looking towards her and had stopped talking. She suddenly flushed with panic. It snapped her back to her feet, and she spun on her heels to walk away. She heard him call out. She kept walking. He called out again. His voice carried but it sounded more distant; he wasn't following. When she heard his voice again, it was at a level that suggested he was back to talking to someone on the phone. She could no longer make out the words. It didn't matter; she had heard what she had needed. There was nothing more he could say that would make a difference.

She almost made it back to her broken-down car before she broke down, too.

CHAPTER 3

Kelly managed to get the door shut. She leant on it with all her weight as if the world outside was likely to try and push its way in. Her mind swam and she felt dizzy trying to make some sort of sense of it all — put it in some sort of order. She stumbled against the work surface of her mum's kitchen as, for the second time that day, her vision closed in. She heard the smash of something falling to the floor. She could focus enough to see a cooked breakfast now intermingled with broken pieces of crockery. She waited. She knew it would pass. Finally the throbbing in her head abated, enough for her to stand up straight and to push away from the unit that had been her support.

There was a knock at the door, the same pattern as before. She knew it was Joan. She had probably heard the smash. She'd probably been standing at the door listening from the moment Kelly had come back in. Joan had been a good friend to her mother, had done a lot for her, but she was a nosy cow. The knock came again, this time more urgent.

'Yeah, hang on a minute!' Kelly called out. 'Who is it?'

'It's Joany, love. You okay in there? I thought I heard a noise?'

'I'm okay, yeah. Clumsy. I think I might have broken your plate!' She forced a chuckle from somewhere. She was under no illusion that it sounded natural.

'Don't worry about that, love. You're okay though?'

'Fine. Just clumsy is all. I can't seem to function well this morning.'

There was a pause as if Joan was considering her response. 'You want me to come in? I could help you clear up? Maybe put the kettle on?'

'Very kind, Joan, but I'm okay. Honest. Just an accident.'

Another pause. 'Well, okay then. As long as you're sure. I'm just over the hall.'

'So you fucking said,' Kelly muttered then raised her voice to answer. 'I know where you are, don't you worry. I appreciate it too.'

Kelly held her breath to listen. She heard the sounds of someone moving away. She moved to the sink to run water into a bowl so she could clean up. She hung over it, suddenly feeling nauseous. She waited for it to pass.

The door knocked again.

'That woman!' Kelly muttered. She stayed still. She had no intention of even talking to her this time, let alone going over to open the door. She silenced the running water and twisted her head towards the door. This time the thump on the door was hard enough to make her jump. It didn't sound like the knock of a fifty-something woman from across the hall. Then she heard a voice that definitely belonged to Joan, and confirmed that the knock didn't.

'Can I help you?' Joan said. She sounded more distant than before.

'No.' The response was gruff, deep and bassy.

Kelly recognised the voice even from that one word. She rushed a breath and whispered, 'Not now!'

'She's just lost her mother in there,' Joan persisted. 'She might not even be in. Maybe I can take a message? I don't think she wants to see anyone right now.'

'How about you keep your nose out of my business? Nothing here for you. Get back in your little flat and shut your door.'

'Dammit!' Kelly cursed under her breath. She moved to the door and swung it open. A man stared in. His broad shoulders filled her doorway his piercing eyes looked out from a face that was scratched red, as if he had just this minute put his shaving razor down. Somehow he always managed to have that look. He was in smart trousers and a shirt done up to the neck, with no tie. It looked expensive. He lifted his arm to grip the top of the doorframe. His tongue rolled behind his bottom lip, pushing it out towards her.

'Kell,' he grumbled. He didn't look her directly in the eyes; she didn't think he ever had. Through a thin gap between her visitor and the doorframe, she could see Joan was still standing in her doorway.

Kelly spoke through the gap. 'It's okay, Joan. He's a friend.' She hoped she sounded convincing.

Joan lingered, staring at the man's back. It was all he was showing her. Finally, she nodded. 'Well, okay, love, I'll be just here.' She closed her door.

Kelly stepped backwards into the flat. The man stayed at the doorway. It wasn't hesitation; this wasn't a man who hesitated. His delay at the doorway sent out a message: that there was no way out past him. Not unless he allowed it. She moved slowly backwards, stopping only when she bumped into the edge of the work surface. A piece of crockery crunched under her shoe.

Finally, the man ducked under the doorway and moved in. He closed the door firmly with a flick of his elbow. He wasn't looking at her at all now. Instead he seemed to be looking around. He took in the smashed plate on the floor, before his eyes rested on the empty bed that dominated the room.

'She's gone, then?' he said.

'What do you want, Freddie?' Freddie Rickman. She had been told that was his name a couple of times, but never without the person adding some caveat or other: *Freddie Rickman, yeah, you wanna be careful round him* or, *Freddie Rickman — that's someone you don't want to get on the wrong side of.* She had no intention of being on any side of Rickman. She didn't want to be around him at all and had always made that clear. She certainly didn't want him at her mother's home.

'Want?' He was still searching the room. He moved to the sink and picked up a picture from the windowsill. It was one of Kelly and her mother a few months before, not long after the diagnosis had changed — when she had been told that, this time, the cancer was going to get her. Her mother was smiling with a brightness she had no business having.

'I assume that's why you're here. You want something.'

'Are you coming to work today?'

'I lost my mum.'

'And if you hadn't?'

'What do you mean, if I hadn't?'

'Don't play silly buggers with me, Kell. You know what I mean. Did you intend on coming to work today?'

'No.'

He leaned back onto the windowsill, still holding the picture. His gaze lifted just enough to look over the top of it and settle around her midriff. He didn't speak.

'I spoke to Benny. I told him I was done. We both told him we were done with it.' Her voice quivered a little. She had been stronger when she was speaking with Benny. He was who they usually dealt with; there was rarely a reason for Freddie to speak with her directly. Benny was someone she knew even less about. She didn't even know his real name, just that 'Benny' wasn't it. Whatever his name, he was easier to refuse, nowhere near as physically intimidating. But she'd been angry then, too — appalled even. She'd stood her ground, made herself clear. And Holly had been standing next to her. She was always stronger when Holly was with her.

Freddie didn't react. He fixed his gaze back on the picture frame. It somehow looked smaller in his grasp. His big shoulders were rising and falling as he breathed, their movement seeming to increase in speed, while his cheeks rippled like he was biting down hard. The sound of the frame dropping to the floor made her jump. His head snatched up, his gaze was resting somewhere around her lips.

'You don't *tell* Benny anything! You hear me?' His voice was quiet, whispered almost, but so laden with rage that it was more effective than a shout. She had seen him angry with people before, but he hadn't shouted then either. He was more measured than that — colder.

'I *am* done,' she said. She tried to step back further, and the work surface dug deeper into her backside.

He looked away, back to the floor, his attention seemingly back on the picture.

'I lost my mum. Last night. Right now I can't do anything. I can't even think—'

'Holly.' Freddie cut in with venom, his voice still quiet and down towards the floor. 'And I swear, if you lie to me you will be buried at the same time as your whore-mother . . . Did you know?'

'Know?'

'Don't fuck with me!' That same hiss. Now he leaned forward and stared at her mouth as if waiting for it to move in reply. His whole face was a snarl, the skin of his cheeks seemed ever more flushed. 'I hear she's going to the cops. She thinks she can run her mouth and get into my business. Did you know?'

'She never told me nothing about that. Who told you that?' Kelly's voice was breaking. She feared he would see it as a sign that she wasn't telling the truth. She coughed to clear her throat.

'Where is she? She's not at her place — but then she's always with you. Is she here?' He was back to looking around the room. 'In there perhaps?' He walked across the living area, right past where Kelly was still backed against the units. He stomped down the short hall while she stayed facing away. She jumped when she heard the bedroom door bounce off the wall as it was opened roughly. She heard another thud, then a squealing sound like he was moving the hanging clothes around in the wardrobe. The next sound was the ceiling fan. It always started with a squeak. He had to be searching the bathroom. It was tiny — certainly there was nowhere for someone to hide. He would be back any moment.

When he stepped back into the room he came to her shoulder, just out of sight. She could sense him staring at her. She didn't turn. She cleared her throat again.

'Did she speak to the police, Kelly? And before you answer, you should know that this is about her . . . She made her decision and I won't see you as part of that. But this is the only time. If you tell me no and I find out you're lying . . .'

'No.' Kelly was quick to reply, no hesitation. 'I reckon I would know if she did and I don't know nothing about speaking to the cops. I don't know what you've heard — where any of this is coming from. She's cleverer than that. Why would she?'

'She wants out, doesn't she? You just said that.' He moved to face her directly. 'You both do!'

'People get out, Freddie. We know that. We've seen them go and you let them. You won't see or hear from us again. We've done our time and we've been good for you. I've got no intention of talking to anyone about your business — I just want out.' She straightened up suddenly as Freddie stepped towards her. He stopped so close they were almost touching at the hips. She leant away, her back aching instantly as the work surface still pushed into her. He was close enough for her to feel his body heat and smell the sickly scent of his aftershave. 'I don't know what you're talking about. She wouldn't talk to anyone. She knows better.' She was dead, too. She couldn't tell him that though; there would be questions that she couldn't answer.

He lingered on her. He seemed still focused on her mouth. He lifted a hand slowly and rested it on the side of her face. She tried to move away but she couldn't. He moved to trap her against the bench with his hips. His other hand flashed up to grip both sides of her mouth, squeezing to make her lips pout. He was so close she could only see his bright blue eyes. They were still turned downwards.

'There's nothing more beautiful than a woman's mouth . . . her lips . . . the things she can do with them. But when they tell me lies or when it's my top-earners telling me they don't want to work no more, they're ugly. *Useless.* Do you understand?'

She couldn't speak. She couldn't even make a noise. She managed to twitch a nod into his hands. He pushed her head back further; the strain on her back was agony to the point where it felt like it might give.

'You have work. Today. *Both* of you. Midday. And I got other people to talk to about you — about that bitch girl-friend of yours. And if I find out those lips have been telling me lies, they *will* turn ugly real quick.'

He pushed off her. She groaned in pain and he moved away.

'I can't!' she breathed. 'I . . . I don't even know where she is! What if I can't find her?'

The man snorted, his focus still on her mouth. 'I have a feeling you'll be able to find her just fine. If not, there's a big market for solo girls. Or maybe we pair you up with someone new. Put those lips to good use maybe!'

'I can't — not without her.'

'Then make sure you bring her along. For both your sakes. And don't be late.'

CHAPTER 4

Detective Sergeant Maddie Ives gave a stretch as she stepped out of her car. The marked vehicle in front pulsed in blue while a uniform officer seemed to be pacing around with a phone held to his ear. She recognised him: PC Vince Arnold. He ended his call as she approached.

'Morning, Mads!' he grinned wildly. 'A little late for the sunrise, I'm afraid, but I'll do my best to make it romantic.'

'I daren't even ask what the word *romantic* means to you, Vince. And I'm beginning to think you're the only officer working your section. How did I know it would be you up here?'

Maddie was drawn to the noise of another officer approaching from the side. PC Sharon Jones. She was smiling too.

'He was so keen to get here, sarge, he nearly overshot the junction! He only goes to calls that might prompt a Major Crime appearance. I reckon it's something to do with you coming out.' She winked over towards Vince, who laughed.

'Works both way, ladies. I was thinking that DS Ives here comes out to a lot of calls where I'm already in attendance. Maybe that's part of her decision to turn out in the first place?'

'Had I known you were here, it would definitely have been a factor, Vince. You would have got Harry Blaker instead!'

Vince's laugh this time was somehow even louder. 'Where is the miserable old bastard?'

'Suspected suicide, would you believe.'

'Another?'

'Yeah.'

'Two in at the same time?'

'Yeah. If it wasn't such glorious weather I would be checking to make sure it wasn't Christmas Day.' Maddie wasn't sure the age-old assumption of suicides being more prevalent at that time of year was actually true; certainly she hadn't seen any stats to back it up. Maybe turning up to a suicide on Christmas Day just stuck in the memory more. She shrugged. 'It can happen.'

'It can. You wouldn't think people would want to go on such a beautiful day, though, Mads. Sun's up, birds are singing . . . that view. I can't promise a picnic basket but I have got my scran on me. You fancy going halves on a peanut butter sandwich, a KitKat and a packet of crisps? I'll even put my coat down for the lady.'

'So there we are, Vince: half a KitKat on an upturned police coat at the scene of someone's tragic death — we found your romantic. And you couldn't even have a shave this morning. You're lucky it isn't the boss up here. Is that *stubble?*'

'Cheeky cow! This is almost a week's growth!'

'It's a five o'clock shadow at best.'

'I'll leave you two to it, shall I?' Sharon said over Vince's laughter. 'You really do sound like a married couple!'

'I'd much rather you didn't. I was hoping someone might give me an update and maybe someone with a little professionalism. So, *Sharon* . . . I assume I should be looking to you for that?'

'I think you're right. We had an immediate call come out as a broadcast — nearest patrol to make their way to this location. One of the residents called it in — said they had heard a car go over the cliffs at this point.'

'Heard?'

'Yeah. Didn't see it. I've done some door knocks for those directly opposite and no one else has anything to add so far. You can see where it went over, though. There are clear tyre tracks up to it and then a chunk's missing. The skipper's down the bottom at the landing site.'

'Skipper?'

'Tim Betts. They *think* they've found the landing site at least. It's not somewhere they can get to easily, apparently. The coastguard have scrambled their chopper to come out as part of the search, but we're not expecting a rescue effort.'

Maddie turned to where she could indeed see two clear tyre tracks reaching out towards where the land ran out. She walked alongside them, keeping a metre or more distance. There was no sign of the car having braked at all. The grass wasn't long. The ground underneath would have cut up easily as a soft layer on top of the solid chalk. She looked back at the distance travelled; it was enough for a final contemplation.

'Doesn't look like they tried to change their mind. It's a straight run, too.' Maddie was voicing thoughts out loud. Sharon was still standing close to her, close enough to reply.

'I agree. There is a mark on the bank, sort of where the road meets the grass. Could be a skid but it could just be where the car changed direction. I guess that's something we may never know.'

'Not something you should ever say to a detective . . .' Maddie said. She was now at the edge. The damage here was obvious. The cliff had a gentle slope until right at the end, where a ledge rose up to jut out. A chunk of chalk had been gouged out, probably dragged along by the underside of the car when the front wheels ran out of ground. She stepped immediately back, making sure her colleagues knew to do the same. There was no way of telling if the rock had been weakened, and there might be another slip yet so she would rather not be standing on it if there was. There was a working-at-heights team on their way. They had all the equipment necessary to go right over. In previous cliff jumps they had performed remarkable rescues where abseiling down the face from the top was the only way.

'Long way up,' Maddie mused. This wasn't going to be a remarkable rescue; this was a recovery at best.

'Long way down, you mean.' Vince said.

'And Tim's found the landing site, you say?'

'Rough area. He could see my hi-vis when I held it up, so not exactly scientific. Looks like it went off in a straight line, though. He said he can't see nothing down there. There's a whole load of brambles and rocks in the way. Couldn't have gone off at a worse place, apparently.'

'Of course it couldn't! No chance of identifying the car, then?'

Vince shrugged. 'The chopper might manage it but we've got nothing yet.'

'Well, then, there's nothing much for me to do up here. Are you two happy to do the search? Just this patch — say, twenty metres either side of the tracks for now?'

'Can do, Mads. Ain't nothing else to do.'

'Thanks. And not too close to the edge. Your ego alone would be enough to trouble any cliff edge, let alone a weakened one.'

'Ouch!'

Maddie looked away from the drop and over towards the row of houses on the other side of the road. Their activity was attracting attention: there were curtains twitching and some other occupants were watching from their doorways and top-floor windows. Maddie always had to resist the urge to wave in these circumstances. She turned away instead, reminding herself that she would be doing exactly the same if it were her street. Her eyes followed the cliff edge as far away as she could see. Policy stated that the investigating officer should go to the jump site first and for good reason: nine times out of ten there would be some property to find such as discarded clothing, a mobile phone or, often, empty alcohol vessels or pill blister packs. And very rarely did someone reach a point this low in their life where they didn't try and put their reasons into a final assembly of words. Here, there was nothing. Death was always sad, it never seemed to hit Maddie any the less hard, but a desperate act like this and with nothing left behind? It seemed so much harder. It was as if someone just wanted to disappear without leaving a single trace of their life. No one should ever do that.

'Has anyone spoken to the informant yet?'

'The FCR spoke to her on the phone,' said Vince. 'They put quite a bit of detail on the CAD. I heard Tim on the radio sending a patrol up to speak with her but they got diverted to an immediate. It's still pending. Shazza did a few houses but we were told not to go to the informant for now — the skipper didn't want us tucked up when we need to be manning the scene. That one will need something written down.'

'And you didn't bring your crayons?' Maddie couldn't keep a straight face.

'Very good, sergeant!' Vince's eyes twinkled with his reply.

'Okay. You can tell Tim not to worry. I'll go and speak to her. Do you know which one it was?' Maddie scanned the row of houses.

'The one with beige double doors, and deck chairs in the porch. She was a bit *anti*, the call-taker said. Probably interrupted her day . . .'

Maddie fixed on the house described. The 'porch' was actually a long slab of flat roof jutting out from the front of the bungalow. It incorporated the front door and a strip of glass windows for making the most of the sea view.

'Get the search here done for me, please and then hold tight. I'll try and get the scene stood down as soon as possible.'

Sharon shrugged. 'There are worse ways to while away an early turn!'

Maddie nodded and then set off to cross the road. She heard Vince call after her.

'And it's getting closer to lunchtime, Maddie! The offer still stands, yeah? Half a KitKat, I said. That's two fingers each!' Maddie looked back to find Vince laughing, while Sharon had the expression of someone who didn't know how to react.

'You just can't help yourself, can you, Vince? There's a fine line . . .' His laughter stopped, but started up again when Maddie couldn't keep a straight face herself. '*Bastard*,' she muttered under her breath as she turned back towards the informant's house.

CHAPTER 5

Margaret Thoroughgood bristled the moment her door opened to Maddie holding up her warrant card. Maddie hadn't known what to expect, but a stern look and a refusal to let her enter would have been low on her list.

'I just wanted to talk to you about this morning — about the report you made.'

'I've talked all I need to about that. Some lady on the phone . . . she wanted to know the ins and outs of a duck's posterior! A man goes over a cliff and rather than rushing to his aid you want to know when my birthday is?'

Maddie was straining to hear the woman. Some small dog was providing a yapping soundtrack from behind her. 'I can assure you the call-taker would have already set the wheels in motion for us to respond when she was taking your details. I apologise, though, if it seemed a bit much.' She paused. Then, '*Man*?'

'What?' the woman snapped. She was still standing in her doorway, most of her concealed by her front door. Maddie had been able to push open the first door that led into the slim porch and it had immediately felt warmer in there than outside; stuffy, even, and the muggy air was tinged with the earthy scent of potted plants. There were two armchairs, a pair of women's slippers neatly laid out in front of the closest.

'You said *a man* went over the cliff. I was told you only heard the incident?'

'Well, yes, I did. But it has to be a man doesn't it? Causing all this fuss just to be selfish. Typical.'

Maddie smiled, she hoped it might break down the frosty barrier. 'You may well be right but unfortunately, depression can affect anyone.'

'I'm sure. I told your girl on the phone all that I know. I'm afraid I can't be any more help and have rather a lot to attend to this morning.'

'Loud and clear. Could you just help me understand one detail and then I'll leave you alone?'

The woman huffed. She turned to look behind her where the yapping sound was still incessant. She huffed again, making it obvious that she would rather be anywhere else.

'I really am rather busy.'

'The fall is quite dramatic from up here. It's a long way down and I think the vehicle would have landed some distance away and behind all that rock — and yet you say you heard it?'

Margaret hesitated. 'Well, I . . . I mean . . . I had heard a surging engine, you know? It was obvious what had gone on!'

'Mrs Thoroughgood—'

'Ms!' the woman cut in curtly. Her nose twitched. She plainly didn't like being challenged.

'*Ms* Thoroughgood . . . I believe you may know a little more. Maybe you even saw what happened this morning?'

The woman huffed and rolled her eyes, but she didn't deny it.

'I would expect that the person who went over the cliff today will be very seriously injured or worse. It will be my job to tell the family of that person just what happened. When I do, I would really like to be in full possession of all of the facts. If you can help me with that, if you can fill in any gaps, then I would really like to know. If not for me, for the family.'

'It really changes nothing!'

'What doesn't, Ms Thoroughgood?'

'I was sitting out in the front here, where I always have my morning coffee — as long as the weather's good. I saw a car pull up at the roadside. Then it moved off the road, onto the grass and just kept going.'

'And you said before that it *surged?*' Maddie took a notebook out of her bag.

'Well no, it didn't actually. It was very slow. It sort of jerked a couple of times, like it was braking. It seemed to roll on the road then stop — then it rolled a bit more, then stopped for a little longer. Looking back, I suppose he might have been battling with himself. But when he turned onto the grass there was maybe one more stop but then it just sort of . . . well, rolled off.' The woman suddenly pursed her lips as if she was fighting emotion. It caught Maddie out a little. 'Would you excuse me a moment.' The door was pushed closed.

Maddie stepped back to let it click shut. She left it thirty seconds then tapped lightly on the glass. Another thirty seconds passed before the door opened again. This time it was pulled open fully.

'Would you like to step in, perhaps?' Ms Thoroughgood backed away and opened the door wider. The sound of the dog was now muted. A little white dog of some toy breed or other was on its hind legs behind a patio door at the rear of the house, its front paws resting on the glass, head jerking in near silence like a furious mime. Ms Thoroughgood led Maddie into her living room. She sat on the edge of an armchair and gestured at a sofa next to it.

'Thank you,' Maddie said. 'Who's the dog?'

'Molly. She's my Bichon Frise. And my best friend of course.'

'Of course.'

'I must apologise first. You should know . . . I have seen this before. I stopped sitting out there for a long time — it's only really been the last year or so I've been out again. There was a young man. I told my ex-husband to call the police immediately. We could tell he was distressed . . . the pacing — well you can just tell, can't you? The operator on the phone, she said they were on their way but they might be a while. I thought it might help to go over and speak with him, just to see if he was okay. It was a freezing cold morning. I even made up a cup of coffee to walk over to him.' Margaret's harsh exterior was gradually slipping away. She seemed to have rushed a breath. 'He took one look at me and then he was gone. Just like that.'

'That must have been awful.'

'From that moment I said I would never get involved again. It's not my place. This is a well-known site for this sort of thing — right opposite me. It's like a platform, you see, that sticks out away from the edge and there are rocks below . . .' Another wave of emotion seemed to pass over her. 'But people are going to do what they are going to do. They don't want me sticking my nose in and I certainly don't want to be there to see it.'

'But this morning, you still called us.'

'I did. I guess I couldn't help myself. I saw the car and I just knew I had to call — I mean it's hopeless isn't it, that someone might . . . but you have to call.'

'You do. Thank you for that.'

'But not for the fibbing, right?'

'I won't hold it against you, Ms Thoroughgood. In the circumstances I appreciate that you took any action at all — and I have been told far worse fibs.'

Margaret waved her away. 'Margaret. Please. Only people who are trying to sell me something call me Ms Thoroughgood these days.'

'So tell me, Margaret . . . what did you see?'

'I saw a man. It looked as though he was arguing with himself. He was agitated. The car jerked a few times like I said. I was just sitting out there with my coffee. I thought maybe he was on the phone. He was going along the road to start with. Then he just turned up onto the grass and slowly rolled forward. I was sitting out the front, in my chair there. I just about had the time to stand up as he went over. I remember seeing the back of the car lift. It sort of tipped over and that was it. Gone.'

'Okay, thank you. Do you remember anything about the car at all?'

'You mean like the make? I'm not good at cars — I've never had the slightest interest.'

'Big or little, maybe a colour?'

'It was white. And big. Not one of these big off-road things you see so much of now — a *car*, you know? Like a normal car shape. Sticky-out boot. I'm not describing it very well, am I?'

'Sticky-out boot. I think I know what you mean. Maybe like a saloon car?'

'A saloon car! That's it. We had a Rover once. I remember that was a saloon and, yes, it was the same shape as that.'

'But not the same car?'

'No, goodness no! That was quite some time ago. This seemed to me like a much more modern car. Oh! There was a plate on the back!'

'I was going to ask you about the regis—'

'Not a number plate! One of those plates they have to have when they're a taxi!'

Maddie looked up from where she was writing her description. 'It was a taxi?'

'I thought it was. My eyes are not what they used to be but they have those square plates on the back — the white ones. I get one once a fortnight for the food shop. It had a plate like that.'

'Okay, that helps a lot. *Did* you see the actual registration at all?'

'I'm sure it had one but I would have had no chance at making out any letters or numbers from that far away. If I'd been reading the newspaper I would have had my glasses, but I wasn't today. Sorry.'

'Don't be. You've been a great help. Do you remember what this man looked like?'

'Tanned. Very dark hair. Foreign, maybe — that was the feeling I got. I couldn't really see details. He was wearing a white shirt with a collar. I remember that; it stood out against his skin.'

'What age would you say?'

'I have no idea. I am sorry. I couldn't see him well.'

'And he was the only occupant? Just to be sure.'

'I couldn't see anyone else. The back windows were darker.' She lifted her hand suddenly to her mouth. 'Oh, goodness! Could there have been someone else in that car, do you think? Someone in the back? I didn't see anyone. I just thought he was on the phone.'

'Was he turning around? Like maybe he was talking to someone in the back?'

'No! I mean I'm pretty sure he wasn't . . . No, he didn't look in the back. I would have remembered that.' Her hand fell away from her mouth, she looked a little relieved.

'Okay then. Before I go, may I check I've got your account right?'

'Sure.'

'You were sitting out at the front of your house this morning. You saw a white, saloon car pull up with a single occupant who looked animated and may have been arguing on the phone.'

'That's right.'

'Did you see a phone? I mean, was he holding one?'

'No. I would have been able to see if he had his arm raised from that distance but they don't hold them anymore, do they? Driver's, I mean. I assumed he was on one of those hands-free things.'

'Okay. And the car was moving left to right as you watched from your house?'

Margaret fidgeted with her arms. 'Yes.'

'So he was on the side of the car closest to you?'

'He was.'

'And the car was jerky to start with — like he was braking. Then it turned up onto the grass and moved across it to the cliff edge. And you didn't see any more braking?'

'It turned onto the grass and stopped. I saw the lights. But that was the only time — it just rolled from there.'

'And it moved slowly until it tipped over?'

'Yes. Just like that.'

Maddie closed her book. She stood up and lifted her card. 'Take this. If you think of anything you think might be relevant, please give me a call. Anything at all.'

Margaret stood too. She looked a little uneasy, unsteady even. The eyes that fell to the card were a little glazed.

'And if you want to talk to someone, about what you saw or have seen up here, you can call me, too. Anytime. Even if I'm not the right person to help you with it, Margaret, I can put you in touch with someone.'

'Talk about it?'

'It helps. I've seen things in this job that have upset me and I made sure I talked about it with the right person. None of us is immune. What you saw wasn't pleasant. Don't feel like you need to keep that in.'

'I've seen a lot worse I can assure you, DS Ives!' The harsh front seemed to return, her eyes snapped back to focus.

'Life isn't a test of your resolve, though, Margaret. It can all add up. Talking can help.'

Margaret looked back down at the card. 'Thanks. Like I said, I just need to learn to keep my nose out. Maybe I'll sit in the back garden from now on.'

'Be a shame to deny yourself that view . . .' Maddie lingered. Margaret responded by moving them back to the front door. Maddie took the hint. 'Right then, I need to get back to work and I think you have a little friend who is rather desperate to get back in here!' Maddie nodded towards the dog who was still smearing her paws against the glass.

'She's my little protector now. A good listener, too.' Maddie noted the first hint of warmth in her expression.

'I bet. As long as you have someone who will listen. We all need that.'

CHAPTER 6

'What've you got then, Harry?'

'A busy Saturday is what I've got.' Harry growled back. Maddie knew what he meant. A weekend was a busy time for the inspector left covering. The area had four towns in total. It wasn't even the relatively good bits of dealing with incidents that would take up time either; the Senior Management Team would be back at work on Monday morning and would expect a full report of all activity, meaning that the weekend inspector could end up spending all their time writing up what everyone else was doing. This was not something that played to Harry's strengths.

'I can imagine. I'll write up the cliff job best I can so you can just copy it over. I've made a start but I can't do the big finale yet.'

'Big finale?'

'The victim. We can't get anywhere near the car. I've just seen the pictures from the helicopter and it looks like it's been sucked in by the undergrowth! The rescue and recovery team are hoping to get to it today but no one's sure when they might be able to pull it out. I do have a lead on a missing taxi however.'

'Missing taxi?'

'The witness who saw it go over, she could only give the description of a white taxi. I called around the firms. Langthorne Taxis can't get hold of . . .' She looked down at her notes, *Taruc Mardin*, a Turkish national. He's only been working with them for a few weeks.'

'And he drives a white taxi?'

'He does. A white Skoda Octavia. Which would fit with what she saw. They couldn't track his GPS either, seems his phone is switched off.'

'Switched off?'

'Well, it's off, anyway. More likely smashed to pieces. Taxi drivers run everything from their phone, you can't work with it off.'

'Sounds like our man, then.'

'It does. I'm just going out to the next of kin. Who knows, maybe Taruc will open the door?'

'That would give us a problem,' Harry said. He sat back in his chair now with a subtle grunt. Maddie thought he looked tired. He ran his hands over his closely cropped head and grimaced enough to make the scarring on his face twitch and lift. She decided against pointing it out.

'I guess it would. I'll try not to act disappointed if he is there.'

'Are you going on your own?'

'I'm meeting uniform outside. That way I can leave them there if there are any welfare issues. I need to be able to pull away. I'll need the place searched, too, assuming his family allow it.'

'Want company?'

Maddie shrugged. 'Sure. This is a job that requires a sensitive and sympathetic approach. I can't think of anyone better!'

'Thanks, Maddie. I could do with a break from typing.'

'Do you not have anything from your suicide this morning?'

Harry sighed. He slid a clear plastic evidence bag across the table towards her. The description label on the front, filled out in Harry's scrawl, read *Handwritten Note*. She flipped the bag over, to see through to the letter inside. The large, flamboyant handwriting immediately struck her as that of someone older.

When it comes to writing a note of this type, of this grandeur, of this importance, and one realises that there is no loved one left to address it to, then perhaps one can understand the reason for the writing in the first place.

There is only one element of my personal affairs I could not resolve. Please, please look after my dog. He is a wonderful companion. My reason for making it this far.

But for now, I need to be with her again. It aches every day.

And to the person(s) who find me. I am truly sorry. I hope it has no impact and that you can take comfort from the fact that I am where I wish to be.

I made this decision of sound mind.

The dog answers to the name Jock. He enjoys long walks, and titbits sneaked to him under the table.

All the very best,

Ronald

'Ronald?' Maddie said.

'Yeah. He could have helped me out a little more and included his surname, maybe even a date of birth, home address and next of kin, too.'

'Reading this, I'm not sure he has a next of kin.'

'He doesn't. He did, but she was already there.'

'Already there?'

'He was found on a bench opposite his wife's grave. We found a wedding ring on top of it. It didn't take much detecting to put two and two together.'

'I see.' Maddie hesitated. 'Are you okay?' She curled her toes in her shoes, suddenly very aware of what she had said, unsure how he might react.

Harry lifted his head. 'Fine.' He said, his tone suggesting that he had understood the sentiment. Maddie felt like she had got away with that one. Harry had lost his own wife not that long ago and it had taken him more than a year to even mention it to her. Recently, however, he had disclosed that he wasn't coping very well and mentioned seeking out a professional. She considered now as the time to ask how that was going. She disregarded it quickly. Harry was not the sort to discuss something like that when prompted; he would bring it up when he was ready.

'Okay then. So yours is open and shut?'

'Pretty much. Just one outstanding issue.'

'Go on?'

'Any chance you would like a King Charles spaniel called Jock?'

'No!' Maddie chuckled, 'Although I do like his attitude towards titbits under the table!'

'That's what I thought.'

'Poor Jock.'

'Indeed. His name seems to be all he has left. He responds to it too.'

'He responds to it? Have you been playing with your new furry friend, Harry?'

'I merely transported him to the kennels downstairs. I had to empty a lot of the tactical team's equipment from it first, I should add. I was quite tempted to let the little fella mark his territory all over it — teach them a lesson.'

'Enough time to get attached?' Maddie laughed.

'There isn't enough time in the world.' Harry replied, but it wasn't instant. 'Are we going out to deliver this message or not?'

'Yes, definitely. It's just an enquiry for now, though. We need to ask a few questions first. I want to be sure it's Mr Mardin at the bottom of that cliff before I go in there and break the news.'

CHAPTER 7

From the outside, Truro House was nondescript, a grey-fronted block of flats with squared edges and equidistant windows. There was a flash of faded orange under the larger of the two windows of each flat, to stop one property running visually into the next. But to Kelly Dale this building stood out. It prompted dread in her like none other could. Specifically Flat No. 12, where she was due to work for the next hour or so.

She checked her watch: it was just before midday. The fact that she dreaded this place so much and yet she was right on time showed the pull this square of bricks had on her — or at least the pull of the people who would pace along its corridors while she completed her shift.

At least they were not insisting on hotel rooms anymore. For a time they had moved around the same three hotels, their destination for each day based on availability as well as who was taking cash payments for the room while also asking the fewest questions. Kelly had hated it. Entering hotels meant interacting with people; it meant picking up on the looks, the knowing looks, she received — when they actually knew nothing at all. It had made her angry at first and it was always Holly who had talked her down. She had told her that it didn't matter what people thought they knew; all that mattered was the truth. And then she wasn't angry anymore — just like that. Holly had that way about her. Kelly wasn't angry now, either — her anger had waned since she had realised Holly was gone, but only to be replaced with something far stronger: *fear*.

Somehow, she moved forward, her steps laboured as she looked up to Flat 12's window. The communal door was insecure. She was supposed to buzz to let them know of her approach. She didn't. It didn't matter, because the second she stepped through into the echo of the bare corridor beyond, a figure stepped from the shadows: Benny.

Benny was tall and thin and managed to look both young and worn out at the same time. Skulking in the shadows suited him. Now he was in the light, she could see his familiar leering look, the furtive movement of his eyes, which seemed to flicker all over her, never settling.

'You're late. I was just gonna call the boss. He told me to call him straight away if you didn't come.'

'And of course you do exactly what he tells you.'

Benny sniffed. 'I do my job. You will too if you have any sense.'

Kelly was focused on sounding strong. 'Anyway, I'm right on time.' The last thing she wanted to do was show her fear to this man.

'*You* might be. Where's Holly? You two are a package. One late, both late.'

'I don't know. I told Freddie I didn't know where she was.'

'Like fuck you don't! You know what this means for her, right?'

Kelly shrugged, 'Maybe she doesn't care anymore.'

Benny leered back, his expression now carrying genuine glee. 'You know what this means for you then, right?'

'Solo. A big market apparently. So, yeah. Freddie said.' Kelly did her best to sound flippant, like it was all arranged with his boss and he shouldn't worry.

'Solo? Oh no. *I* spoke to Freddie today, too. He said he wanted to shake it up with you two. Said it was getting a bit stale. Seems like now you'll need to do the shaking all by yourself!'

'What are you talking about, Benny? I've had a rough night. I'm not in the mood for games.'

'You'll see what I mean. *He's* waiting!' Benny laughed by forcing air through his nose.

'Who's waiting?' She bit down on her lip, that feeling of fear suddenly peaking.

'We got you a new playmate! It was gonna be for the both of you but now you're gonna have to manage him all by yourself!'

'Solo . . .' Kelly was suddenly fighting for breath. 'He said *solo* . . .' She was fighting off a full-on panic attack. Her eyes flicked back to the door she had just stepped through. Benny must have read her thoughts.

'Don't you go thinking about that, now. You know how this ends if you don't go up there and do your job. He told you to bring her along. Maybe he knew you weren't going to and got a Plan B sorted.' Benny leaned in and lingered on her horrified expression, obviously enjoying himself. 'You might even like it.' The leer was back. He licked his lips then stepped back to allow his eyes to run down her body. They lingered on her chest. 'There's been a lot of call for you to move back over. You don't want to be upsetting Freddie either — no more than you have already. He's not a happy man.'

'But he said, earlier . . .' Kelly was having to squeeze the words out. Her throat felt like it was closing up. 'I've lost my mum, I've lost . . . Holly . . . I can't . . .'

Benny stepped in closer, his eyes still flickering over her chest. Then he leant in to force her to look at him. 'I really suggest you do,' he hissed. 'You're already late. Don't go making it worse. You know he'll be watching!'

He stepped out of her way. She had her head dipped, her gaze now to the floor. She heard a scuff behind her. Benny had moved to where he would be blocking the door.

The stairway was directly in front of her. She knew there was another door to the outside on this level but making a run for it was not really an option. Running out of this building would be just the start, she would have to keep running and there was no way she could do that. Not on her own. She didn't think she had the energy.

The moment she felt the bottom step under her sole she heard Benny call out from behind her. 'I'll be watching, too!' His voice filled the space as it echoed off the concrete steps and walls.

She didn't answer. She didn't even look back.

She dragged her feet along the corridor of the first floor. Her legs still felt heavy. The numbers were counting up as she went with the evens on her right. She passed the door marked 10 and slowed further; No. 12 was just a few more paces. The number was missing from the door but it didn't matter; she knew it well enough. She could see the door was ajar. Artificial light leaked from behind it to reveal dust motes in the corridor. She rested her palm flatly against its surface, absorbing some of the cold from the wood. She already knew the scene behind. The curtains would be closed — the lighting was too important to leave to nature. A large, directed lamp would be on a rig, angled over the centre of a bed with a yellow filter stuck over it to soften its harsh edges. It would be hot under its glare. The bed was usually the only furniture. There was sometimes a chair with a coarse towel thrown over its back and bottles of water lying together in the middle where the seat dipped inwards.

She closed her eyes. She always paused here with Holly. They'd stand on the threshold with their hands tightly linked. For just a moment, Kelly could almost pretend that Holly was with her, that they could still embrace like they always did. She could almost smell Holly's scent and hear her whisper that it was okay, that they would do something nice later and how she should focus on that. And that repeated promise: that she was going to set her free.

Kelly choked back the tears and pushed the door open. The light was bright and she could instantly feel the heat from the lamp. A man jerked upright from where he had been leaning forward. He was early thirties with a strong build, in tight jeans. He was already shirtless and he put his hands on his hips. The bed sheets were as she remembered: an off-white with a faded floral pattern. The webcam was set up on a stand and pointing directly at the bed. It was what the man had been bending over. Beyond it a laptop glowed white, propped up on the second chair. She could already see text filling the screen, each line appearing with a *ping*. Each *ping* was another typed demand from the 'members', filthy men who would be controlling her next hour with their typed requests.

The man stepped away, he seemed to check that he was off camera then he gestured furiously for her to step in. He tapped his wrist where a watch might be then tugged at his belt and started pulling at his jeans. He wasn't someone she had seen before. She had no idea who he was but she knew that didn't matter. She could do nothing to choke back the tears now.

He reacted, his jaw seemed to crease, his face a mask of fury. She felt a firm shove from behind. She stumbled into the room and, before she could turn, she heard the door pulled shut. There was a click — the sound of it locking. There was no getting out of that room, not until she had done what was required of her. She turned back to where the man stood, still furious. He gestured again, then pulled his trousers down as the laptop behind pinged with demands.

CHAPTER 8

Maddie closed the door of her unmarked Ford Focus and paused. The semi-detached house that they had come to in the East Cliff area of Langthorne was just a few hundred metres short of the entrance to a primary school and within walking distance of an area known as 'the Warren'. This was a winding trail that commenced on the clifftop and finished on the beach below. It was a good area where you might expect good people. It made the news she was about to break all the more difficult.

Harry stood up out of the passenger side. He must have seen her hesitation. 'Do you want me to do the talking?'

'No, it's okay. I'm just trying to get it straight in my mind.'

'They may already know. It's on social media isn't it? And local news.'

'Not really. They've reported a car going over, but that's about it. The press don't have any other details. We don't have much more.'

'Time to get some answers, then.' Harry walked up the drive to the front door. By the time Maddie joined him it was already being answered in response to his firm knock.

'Hello?' A young woman answered. She wore a light brown hijab and seemed wary of Harry. Maddie was aware of the etiquette around male strangers among some Muslims. She pulled his arm gently to stand in front of him. It got the woman's attention.

'Hey,' Maddie said. 'I am looking for the home address of Taruc Mardin. I'm a police officer. We both are. I was hoping to speak with his family.'

'Taruc?' The woman had big, brown eyes that Maddie thought were quite striking. They seemed to widen even more. 'My husband? Is he in trouble? Is he hurt?'

'Can we come in — just for a few moments?' Maddie stepped forward. The woman hesitated but then bowed her head slightly and gestured for them to enter. Maddie immediately knelt to take her shoes off. She made eye contact with Harry to make sure he did the same. She could tell he was grumbling under his breath.

The living room was just off the hall. The woman led the way. She gestured to a long sofa but stayed standing herself. Maddie took a seat.

'Tea?' the woman offered. She backed towards a second door that led to the back of the house.

'No, thank you,' Maddie said. 'You may want to sit down. There are some questions we need to ask about your husband. Have you heard from him?'

'Heard from him? He is at work.' She sounded a little panicked now.

'He's a taxi driver, right?'

'Taxis yes, he drives.' Her attention flicked back to Harry. She was still standing and she gave the impression of being on the verge of backing out of the room.

'A taxi was involved in a serious incident today, and the driver . . .'

'Taruc?' she breathed.

'We can't be sure. We have a rescue team with the vehicle now. There are . . . complications. With getting to it, I mean. We are trying to determine if it is your husband's car. His taxi firm haven't heard from him since earlier today and the type of car fits with what your husband was driving.'

'A white Skoda, this is the car? He drives this!'

'That's right.'

'Oh . . . Taruc! Is he . . . is he dead?' She lifted her hand to her mouth and those deep brown eyes were now brimming with tears.

'We cannot be sure. I am so sorry to come here without answers but if it is his vehicle then the chances of us finding someone alive are very low. I am so sorry.'

Mrs Mardin pitched forward with her hand still over her mouth. Maddie rose to stand. It looked for a moment as if the young woman might keel over but she reached out to take hold of the doorframe. Suddenly she spun on her heels and moved out of the room. Maddie and Harry exchanged glances but didn't speak or move. Just a few seconds later, Mrs Mardin reappeared holding a phone to her ear. Maddie could hear the dialling tone through the silence of the room, then the sound of it cutting straight to voicemail. The woman dialled again. Her eyes had lost all focus and her hands trembled. When the phone cut out again she looked at Maddie. 'What happened?'

Maddie took a moment to consider her response. 'We are still trying to work that out, but it might be that Taruc set out this morning to hurt himself. Would that be a surprise to you?'

'Hurt himself?'

'Is there any suggestion that Taruc might look to take his own life? Has he been suffering with his mental health?'

Mrs Mardin flushed, her whole demeanour suddenly of someone angry. 'He would never do this! Not to his family. This is not him. We have nice life . . . we have nice home . . . we are people of God.'

'I know this is difficult. I am so sorry to be asking these questions. We do not know your husband. We do not understand what has happened so we must ask.'

'Ask your questions . . . but I will tell you this . . . this is not a man who will take his own life. It is not for us to decide when we die, or how. This is for a higher being to decide.

This is great shame on our family! You must not share this,
our community . . .' She broke down again.

Maddie was still standing. She gave the woman a
moment. 'We have no intention of sharing anything. We're
just trying to understand. From what we know right now, it
is difficult to see how this could have been an accident. Has
he made any contact with you today? Did he leave you anything to read or say anything that might suggest he was not
intending to come home?'

'He *WAS* coming home!' Her raised voice seemed to
catch her out as much as it did Maddie. She seemed to check
herself. She was wearing a long, elegant dress at which she
now tugged as if to straighten it. 'I am sorry — this is a
shock to me. We have children. Two children. They are just
at school. I will need to speak with them, I do not know how
I can tell them all of this.'

'I can't imagine.'

'But it may not be him? This is what you say?'

'We have not been able to get to the vehicle just yet. But
we are as sure as we can be. I think you need to be prepared
for it to be Taruc. I know this is hard.'

'Cannot get to him? What has happened that you cannot
get to him?'

Maddie hesitated again. Harry cut in. 'The vehicle was
driven over a cliff. No sign of braking, no deviation. it would
appear to be a deliberate act.'

Mrs Mardin fixed on Harry as if he was speaking a different language. Her eyes glazed, her head started to shake
slightly.

'I know that the thought of Taruc taking his own life
is not easy to talk about, but if he left you something . . . if
he hinted at this . . . if you know something about why he
might have done that then you need to let us know now. We
are not looking to share what happened or the cause of it
with anyone else but the less we know the more people we
may need to speak to — to get our answers. Then we start
to lose control of the information.'

'He does not do this. This is not him. We have nice life — happy life! He loves his two boys . . . they are everything. He loves me! We talk, two nights ago . . . we are moving house. We rent here but we will buy in the area. We are happy here. We make plans like normal family!' She leaned back against the doorframe.

Maddie's phone rang out.

'Would you excuse me?'

She was glad to be able to step away and the woman didn't look up. Maddie moved into the hall, but she could hear Harry's rumbling tones. She guessed he was trying to comfort her. It wasn't really Harry's strength; she should hurry her call.

'Maddie, where are you?' It was Mitch Evans, a civilian investigator who worked with Major Crime. His role was largely the collation of information and most of the time he was based out of headquarters. He was mainly desk-bound, a good single point for all information to go through when a team of detectives were working a case.

'At an address in Langthorne. The wife of a taxi driver.'

'Taruc Mardin by any chance?'

'Yes. Do you have something to add?'

'The rescue team have made it to the car. We're pretty certain it's him.'

Maddie sighed. 'Pretty certain? His wife might want a little more than that.'

'It's him, Maddie. How's that?'

'Okay. Deceased?'

'Yes. Both of them. Very.'

Maddie's thoughts had been on what she was going to say when the call finished and she had to return to the living room but her mind now snapped into focus. '*Both?*'

'I thought that might get your attention! Taruc had a passenger on board. We've been able to use a roadside lantern and we got an instant hit.' Maddie had seen the 'lantern' used before. It was a bit of kit issued to Traffic, effectively a mobile fingerprint device.

'Okay?'

'Seems Holly Maguire was along for the ride. She's still in the passenger seat. Our driver was thrown clear. They've pretty much retrieved him already. Maguire and the car are going to take longer but it should be in the next few hours.'

'Holly Maguire? Is that someone I should know?'

'You would if you worked vice. Thirty-four-year-old woman who's been linked to prostitution in the town for some time. She's turned up a few drug warrants, too, but only suspected to be an occasional user. Last intel is two years old, though, so nothing recent.'

'Do we have an up-to-date address . . . next of kin, that sort of thing?'

'I've had a quick look. We have an address. Again, it's a few years old. I'll see what I can get for next of kin and anything else I think you might need. I know the uniform skipper is tasking out the death message once we have someone to deliver it to. Did you want me to put the skids on that?'

'Not necessarily. I'll talk to the boss, though. He's here with me now. This changes everything.'

'It does. It's not just a simple suicide anymore, Maddie, is it?' Mitch chuckled like this was *so typical*. Maddie felt a sudden surge of anger. She was standing out in a hallway, opposite a cluttered shoe rack. The shoes were seemingly arranged from big to small. Several coats hung over it, too. The one closest was a small, blue rain jacket with a Paddington Bear print, all evidence of a rich family life. Mitch Evans's chirpiness grated, as did his turn of phrase. *Simple suicide.* She swallowed her first response however, reminding herself that while she was looking at the shoes belonging to the children of their victim, he was some way removed.

'It's not, if such a thing exists. Find out what you can about both our victims. We'll head down to the scene. First I need to break the news to his wife.'

'Have you not done that already?'

'Kind of.'

'Kind of?' Mitch chuckled again.

'Kind of. When I first stepped in here, there was hope. I can't offer that anymore.'

'I guess not. Rather you than me!' That chirpiness stayed. This time Maddie just hung up the phone.

CHAPTER 9

As Maddie stepped out of the car, the sea air was an immediate assault on the senses. The breeze still carried warmth, along with enough salt content for her to taste and smell it at the same time. The sun was bright against the cliff's white face more than a hundred metres away. She could see an area of hard standing then a high fence that marked the edge of a railway track passing under the cliffs. From here there was an area of greenery that looked thick even from this distance. Suddenly she could understand why it had taken all morning just to reach the stricken vehicle.

She stepped under a length of largely pointless police tape that flapped in the breeze; she didn't imagine this to be somewhere that members of the public were at risk of strolling through. Access to this point was impossible on foot and via vehicle only when granted by railway staff. She paused to hold the tape up for Harry, who grumbled a thank you. She could see marked vehicles from the police, ambulance and a local search-and-rescue charity that worked with police regularly on misper cases. A coastguard pickup also came into view as she walked to the scene.

'Anyone for a game of emergency services bingo?' Maddie said. Harry didn't react. A huddle of police officers presented as black silhouettes against the white of the looming cliffs. The first to break away was a man she recognised as Sergeant Tim Betts. He was shaking his head while he walked towards her.

'Been here all day,' he said. 'Can't say it's been an easy one, this one. Literally couldn't have gone down in a worse place.'

'So I see. Where are we?'

'In the middle of a shitload of brambles. We've beaten our way through to the car. Now it looks like the way to go is to just drag it out. There's not much that we can do otherwise. Recovery vehicles are en route. CSI have done what they can in situ. We're just waiting for you to give us the okay to move it, really.'

'They're here, then — CSI, I mean?'

'Nope. Been and gone. Coming back, though. Charley had to pop back to the nick for something she was missing. She did say what it was, but it was a long word and I've forgotten it.'

'I see. And they agree with the dragging idea?'

'It was CSI's idea. Charley herself said to "sell it" when Major Crime got here.'

'Okay then. We would generally take the lead from them anyway, so if she says to move it, I suggest we move it.'

'She did say she was in charge! I think she just wants to be able to record that Major Crime okay'd it. She's managed to get photos of the interior and the surrounding area. Up top has been done as well. The helicopter's taken some more general ones and I already have those on my email. They show it up the best to be honest — you get a better idea of what's happened. The car's come to a rest upside down so we will be dragging it out on its roof. The brambles are sort of holding it up.'

'Has Charley done anything inside?'

'Not with the car. From a risk assessment point of view, we shouldn't have gone anywhere near it, really. I had to lean in to take a fingerprint on the lantern, but I shouldn't have done that to be honest. The car's just about ready to fall and it still has a way to drop. You'll see what I mean. You wouldn't want to be stood in front of it.'

'So body recovery will be when the car's out?'

'Definitely. The driver was thrown clear. Charley has processed him and he's gone already — she took a lot of photos so you wouldn't moan. He was quite a mess, as you can imagine, but better preserved than his passenger. Neither of them has much left to recognise. A lot of us know Holly from old — *knew* Holly, but none of us would have been able to positively ID her if we hadn't got that fingerprint hit. Again, you'll see what I mean. I guess a six-hundred-foot drop will do that.'

'So what are your thoughts, here, sergeant?'

Tim smiled. 'I don't think I've ever been asked that! We normally hand over to the detectives and keep our thoughts to ourselves.'

'We're all detectives, Tim. We just handle different parts of the investigation. What's gone on here? In your expert opinion?'

'Like I said, we all know her as a local Tom. So me and the rest reckon she was up on the top, maybe engaged in what she knows best and things got a bit out of hand then the earth quite literally moved, if you know what I mean.' Tim was smiling. Maddie did the same. It seemed easier now she wasn't in the victim's family home.

'So an accident?'

Tim shrugged. 'Maybe the handbrake slipped and no one noticed in time. I dunno how you would prove that. Maybe that's why I'm not the official *detective*!'

'It's a good theory. I hadn't considered that.'

'Did you know Holly?'

Maddie shook her head. 'Never had the pleasure.'

'And she would have been active when you were elsewhere.' Tim now spoke to Harry. 'How long have you been on the East, boss?'

'A couple of years. I've not heard of her either.'

'Might explain why that wasn't your first thought. Don't get me wrong . . . nice enough girl — never gave us any real issues — but she was prolific for a while. We were more worried about keeping her safe than anything. She got into the scene quite young. All quite sad, really.'

'Scene?'

'Selling herself for sex. There were rumours about her a good few years before she turned eighteen even. Broken home, moved about a lot — the standard story. She didn't deserve this, that's for sure.'

'I'm sure she didn't. Can I get closer? I'd like to have a look.'

Tim looked over at Harry. 'Well, I've just been outranked so the scene now belongs to Major Crime. That means that all health and safety considerations go with it. You can certainly get to it but I am telling you that it's dangerous to do so.'

'Thanks Tim, I'll bear that in mind!'

'No you won't!'

Maddie moved forward, acknowledging nods from the throng of officers. Normally she would expect some banter, someone calling out about shiny-arsed detectives, but it was noticeable how much Harry's presence could be a silencing influence. It was always in good fun, each department liked to mock the other, but Harry's reputation was not of someone who liked to be part of *good fun*.

The brambles were thicker than she had expected. Probably undisturbed for many decades before that morning when a path had been so crudely hacked through them. The thicket wore it like a fresh wound. She still couldn't see the car, even though the ground was starting to slope upwards. It soon became steep and she had to lean forward to move up what changed from compacted mud against chalk to white boulders. She looked up at the cliff face. From where she stood, she could see there had been a collapse at some point, and she was climbing the debris. Looking directly up made her dizzy. The clifftop jutted out as a lip a long way above.

The cliff fall looked to have been a slip from the bottom two-thirds, leaving the top clinging resolutely to the face — for now at least. She suddenly felt a lot less safe.

'I can see why this is a popular place.' Maddie called back to where Harry was following.

'Popular?'

'The woman who lives at the top — the witness . . . she said this was a popular place to do it. I can see why. It's almost like a diving board.' Maddie cast another glance up. 'Maybe we should have waited for them to drag it out?' She could see Harry was looking up too and must have been thinking the same thing.

'Looks to me like it's been like that for a long time.'

'To me too, but it just had a car run over it.'

'It did. No need for us to linger, then.'

Maddie could now see the car. It was as described: upside down and with its underside angled away from the cliff edge. What was left of the front was embedded in rock and bramble. There looked to have been some attempt to cut it away. She could see a rope wrapped around the rear wheels that trailed out of sight to be connected to the recovery vehicle when it arrived. She wasn't so sure it would be possible to drag it out, though, as it would have to be up and over the chalk boulders it had come to a rest on.

She stepped up onto a rock that brought her level with the front window on the passenger side. The glass was missing, seemingly entirely smashed out. She braced herself, then leaned to look in.

At first, she couldn't make out much. The sunlight was even brighter this close to the cliff face and it took a moment to adjust to the change in light. There wasn't much room in there either; the car had been crushed so the roof was just a few feet from the underside. The only real space left was in the footwell and Maddie could see that this was into where most of the young woman had been pushed. She was bent forward but far beyond what was possible without catastrophic injury. Her back must have been snapped in two.

Her head was almost between her feet, faced towards where Maddie had her hand over her mouth. Her seatbelt was still in place and she could see it was wrapped around a yellow rucksack pressed into her lap. Her arms seemed to be locked tightly around it as well.

Maddie was glad the woman had her eyes shut at least. It was always the eyes of the dead that left the biggest impact on her. She stepped away, casting a careful look back up to the chalk ledge above. A step away meant a step down and Harry took the opportunity to take her place.

'Well, she doesn't look like someone who was in the middle of a sex act,' Maddie chuckled nervously. 'Fully dressed, seatbelt on and a bag on her lap. I'm not sure what you could get up to, really?'

'Fair point.' Harry's voice was muffled. She looked up to see he seemed to be leaning much further in.

'You okay up there?'

'Yeah.' His voice was suddenly clearer as he peered back at her. 'I'll be interested to know what's in that rucksack.'

Maddie's attention was drawn to Harry's bright blue glove that was gripping the door.

'Can you get it?'

'No. I can reach it but she's got the death grip. It'll take some doing.'

The death grip was well known to investigators. Victims meeting a sudden or violent end often experienced a muscle spasm that ensured anything held in the hand at the time of death was gripped like a vice. Prizing dead fingers apart was just about impossible without the inevitable *crack* of breaking bones. Maddie had been there for it once; she vowed never to be there again. It was on her long list of reasons she could never be a CSI.

Harry was back leaning into the car. When he re-emerged he was scowling.

'This was loose, though.' He held something up. Maddie stepped up to inspect it closer. She wasn't wearing gloves and was careful not to touch it. She could see now it was a glass ashtray. It looked to be smeared with blood, but she could make out a name and logo.

'*NH Cars*?' She read from the side. 'Isn't that a bit out of place?'

'No idea.' Harry replied. The lettering was faded. The design of the thing as a whole seemed dated. It reminded Maddie of the solid, chunky ashtrays you used to find in working men's clubs or snooker halls before the smoking ban made them largely defunct.

'Taruc drives for Langthorne Taxi's, but. *NH Cars* sounds like another taxi firm,' Maddie said.

'It does.' Harry stepped down next to her. He was still holding the ashtray. He turned it over and studied it intently. It was cracked at one of the corners but still whole. 'They really don't make these anymore,' he mused. 'I'll ask CSI to seize it. It'll need swabbing then bagging and tagging here.'

'Swabbing?'

'For the blood.'

'Everything's covered in blood! The car fell off a cliff.'

'Still worth it,' Harry shrugged. 'You might also want to get loose items assessed so they can be attributed to whichever one they belonged. That won't be easy.'

'Might want?'

Harry shrugged again. 'You might not. It's probably a waste of everyone's time and of taxpayer's money.'

'Waste of time? This isn't a simple suicide anymore, that's for sure.'

'Not a simple suicide, no, but a simple murder-suicide maybe.'

'Simple how?' Maddie said.

Harry was back to looking up at the ledge. 'Tim Betts might have hit the nail on the head you know. You could make this complicated or it is a simple sex act gone wrong.'

'Whenever you talk about your cases, you're the first one to say *there's no such thing as simple*!'

'I am. But this isn't my case.'

CHAPTER 10

Kelly fumbled over the door handle; her shift was over, she had to get out of there and it had to be now. The door didn't come instantly and she was starting to panic. She twisted the key in the lock until she heard a *click*. She cursed her own stupidity. Finally the door pulled open and she stumbled out only to have to stop suddenly. Her eyes were down, her mind a whirr and focused on just one thing — getting out of that room — but there was a figure in her peripheral vision. He was standing in the hall, right in front of the door.

'Benny!' She couldn't hide the shock in her voice.

'Leaving so soon? That's what I like about you, Kelly . . . in and out!' He chuckled. Kelly didn't.

'I'm done,' she said.

'For today.'

'No. I told you, Benny . . . I'm not doing this anymore. I told Freddie, too. He can get angry, he can come and see me, whatever he wants.'

She fixed her eyes on him, doing her best not to break off, not to show her fear. She wasn't scared of him — never had been. It was what he represented that scared her. But she didn't want her fear to show. Not for a second. He would interpret it as fear of him and he would be delighted.

'You did. And what did I tell you? No good telling me nothing. You need to tell Freddie in person if you think you can just stop working for him. But I'll tell you again. Freddie decides when people don't work for him no more. You don't want to be forcing his hand, Kell. Not now. He's already got the hump with your ex.'

'I told him this morning.'

'And yet here you are! He told you to come, right? Until he stops telling you to come, you need to be doing what he says.'

'She isn't my ex.'

'Whatever she is — or isn't — she's putting you right on the line, Kell. You would do well to stay away from her for now. We didn't think you were gonna show today. We figured she might get in your ear enough to have you making silly decisions. You made the right choice today . . . don't go and fuck it up.'

'I've got to go and bury my mum. I can't deal with this right now.' She pushed past him while he stood fast. She marched down the hallway, trying to ignore her own physical discomfort and the sudden urge to vomit.

'Do whatever you need to do! Just be back here on Monday, yeah?'

Kelly kept on walking. The corridor was long and dimly lit, like a tunnel. The only natural light was provided by a window at the end. She fixed on it and quickened her pace.

She needed to get out of there.

CHAPTER 11

The girl fell onto the back seat of the taxicab with a scream that turned into a piercing laugh, which ended with a snort. A man laughed too but he stood outside, next to the door she had just fallen through. The driver angled his mirror. He could see the girl was lying on her side, her face twisted in laughter. She scrabbled to try and reach a sitting position. Her black dress had ridden up enough to reveal dark underwear and her long legs moved without coordination.

'James, you idiot! Don't push me! I've had too much to drink for you to push me!' Her voice was piercing too. 'Look, I've got my short dress on! You can't go pushing me over.' She was sitting up now. She lifted her bum to pull her dress down and clamped her legs together. She was still sat in the middle. The driver moved the mirror back so that it was at head height. The boy slid in next to her.

'Move up, Libby! Your fat arse is taking up the whole seat!' He was slurring too.

She thumped him on the arm, laughing. The boy reached out to close the door.

'Where are we going?' the girl demanded. Her volume control was broken, like so many drunks he had picked up. She struck him as well spoken, probably softly spoken usually, but not tonight. Tonight she was loud and brash. The boy took a moment.

'I don't know. We can't go to my place. I'm not allowed.'

'We definitely can't go to mine!' The girl snorted again. 'My mum would kill me! And you!' She laughed again.

The driver moved away from watching their interaction to check his phone. It was clipped in on the right side of the dash. He typed in a code to declare himself off duty then powered the unit down entirely. The young couple in the back were still involved in a slurred conversation. He spun around and grinned.

'Had a good night?'

'Yeah, been good, mate. I was hoping it might get even better!' the lad beamed back at him. His hand rode up the girl's thigh. She slapped it away.

'Not in here it won't!' she giggled. 'I have a friend. She lives in a flat. She has a spare room and might let us crash.'

'I might know a place,' the driver cut in. The woman was struggling to work her phone. She looked up at him. She was pretty: big doe eyes with long, straight hair either side. Slim, too. Young-looking. *Perfect.*

'A place?' the boy said.

'Yeah, you know . . . for adults that want to be adults after a night out.'

'That's okay,' the girl said. 'I'd rather go to a friend's house.' She turned to the boy. 'I want you to stay, James, but maybe just *stay*, you know?'

The boy grinned. 'Sure, babes.'

'A hotel isn't the right place . . . I'm not a hotel kinda girl . . . yet. Is that okay?'

'It's okay. I can take just waking up next to you anyway. I've not had the pleasure of that even. Just don't be looking at my nipples!' he giggled. She smacked his arm again.

'This place . . . it's not a hotel. It's just a spare flat. Runs like an Airbnb. But it's not booked up that much.'

'Ah yeah, you need to pay, though, right? Only tonight kinda wiped me out, man. Maybe your mate's house is the best bet, Lib?'

The girl shrugged. 'She's not picking up. She might be in bed. She's got a kid.'

'A kid! I don't want to be waking up a kid. I thought you said she lived on her own?'

'Well yeah, but with a kid!' The girl emitted another snort and her head lolled forward. Whatever she had consumed that night, the effects seemed to be worsening.

The boy turned back to the driver. 'What's this place?'

'Like I said . . . it's like Airbnb. I know the guy who owns it. Sometimes when I work late I call him and he lets me stay if it's not booked up. I know it's free tonight. I was going to stay myself but I'm thinking I'll knock off early and go home now. I don't have to tell him it's not for me. Won't cost you a penny.'

'Okay. That sounds okay. So it's a flat, right?'

'Sure, a flat. Clean. Always ready for guests. Be tidy and respectful, that's all I ask. You won't be bothered.'

'Do I need ID or anything?' the girl called out. 'I mean I've got ID but it's not exactly official, you know? Sixteen-year-olds can't book on Airbnb . . .'

'I thought you said you were seventeen, same as me?'

'I'll be seventeen next month, okay? That's close enough.'

The taxi driver was starting to lose patience. He needed them to focus.

'You don't need an ID — you're not booking anything.' The driver smiled at them both in turn. 'It's not far.' He spun away from them and engaged first gear before the conversation could continue.

Ten minutes later, he pulled up and turned off the ignition. The flat was in a block with the entrance just a few metres away. At just gone 2am, it was quiet. The windows were mostly black squares blending into the façade but a few showed slits of dirty yellow where lights leaked out from between pulled curtains. The exception was Flat 12. Not only was the window to this flat lit but the light was harsher, a bright white that would need dimming down and controlling. They should have received his message; they should have had enough time to prepare the room by now. He stepped out of the car and, while he was still looking up, a stark, black outline appeared at the same window. The curtains were tugged shut. His eyes dropped to the couple in front of them, they had their arms interlocked but he could see that some of their enthusiasm had gone — the girl, in particular.

'I don't know . . .' she said. She was looking up at the block then her eyes dropped to where some bins were pushed against a brick wall under a streetlight.

'Come on,' the boy said. 'Let's just have a look. We'll stick our head round and if we don't like it we can walk away. I'm sure my man here won't mind dropping us somewhere else?'

'Sure, no problem!' The driver grinned. 'But you will love it, I know you will.'

The girl stumbled on her heels as she was led towards the communal entrance. It made her giggle again and she had to stop to adjust her footwear. The driver hung back a little. By the time the kids started walking again, he could see that someone was waiting for them at the entrance, albeit off to one side, using the shadows to stay concealed for now. He needn't have bothered. The young couple were oblivious, lost in each other. They bumped shoulders playfully, their arms entwined. When they reached the door, the boy turned back to speak to the driver.

'Sorry, mate. I just thought about your fare!' He plunged his hands in his pockets and scrabbled around.

The driver held up his hands. 'Don't worry about it. I'll leave you here. My friend will show you up.' He gestured as the door now pushed open and a figure stepped out of the shadows. The young couple turned to a tall, scrawny man with a leering smile and an oily exterior reflecting the weak light. The girl's giggle fell away.

CHAPTER 12

Sunday

DC Rhiannon Davies was getting quite adept at knowing when someone was lying to her — or at least not telling her the whole truth. And Wendy Battle was not telling her the whole truth. Rhiannon had a uniform chaperone, PC Rob Hills, and exchanged a quick glance with him. It was clear he was thinking the same.

'So your daughter isn't here and you don't have any way of contacting her?' Rhiannon repeated back what she had been told to demonstrate how ridiculous it sounded. Mrs Battle did not strike her as a woman used to lying and certainly not as someone who was comfortable with it. She blushed while stumbling over more words as if trying to choose them carefully. Then she abandoned what she was trying to say altogether.

'Look, she said she doesn't want to talk to you.'

'Do you know why that is?' Rhiannon said.

'No. She was very insistent. I couldn't even get her to come out of her room.'

'You must be very worried about that. A police officer comes knocking on your door to speak to your daughter and she refuses even to come out of her room? Something has gone on, Mrs Battle. We both know that. I know you want answers just as much as we do.'

'And you can't tell me anything more?'

'I can only tell you what I know. I'm looking for answers myself. That's the reason we came here in the first place.'

'And this boy . . . you say he's her boyfriend?'

'According to his mother. I can't get confirmation from him right now, as you can imagine.'

'No, I suppose you can't. You say he has a fractured skull?'

'Yes. And it might get worse . . . they can't be sure of the extent of the damage underneath. He's taken a real beating, Mrs Battle. He's seventeen.'

The woman was still standing in her doorway, still hesitating, but her resolve had weakened to the point where Rhiannon sensed she was about to fold.

'And you think my Elizabeth had something to do with it?'

'I think she might know something about it. I don't think she beat a boy to the point where he's fighting for his life — not for a moment — but, from what I can tell, your daughter was the last person to be seen with him last night. It really is critical that I speak with her.'

'She doesn't even have a boyfriend. She would have told me. We would have talked about it. She told me she was staying at a friend's house, a *female* friend from school — her father is on the council. Have you checked with them? Asked them if she was there?'

'No. I was really hoping to just cut all that out and ask Libby — sorry, *Elizabeth* direct. We need to start making progress. Whoever inflicted those injuries on that poor boy could be using every minute to get further away.'

'She said no.'

'So you said, and through her bedroom door. How about you let me try?' Rhiannon stepped forward, applying a little more pressure. It seemed to do the job. Wendy finally stepped back and Rhiannon was in. The woman sighed a gesture at the stairs. Rhiannon accepted the invitation.

'Do you mind . . .' Rhiannon spoke to her uniform colleague. His stance and uniform was oppressive and that was the last thing she wanted. PC Hills didn't argue. He nodded and stepped to one side, his hands held tightly behind his back, seemingly happy that Rhiannon would not come to any harm. That was the reason for his presence too — to look after her. She had been injured recently at work. Though there hadn't been much her colleagues could have done about it, some of them had overreacted a little and now she couldn't step out of the station without a babysitter of some sort. She should be grateful perhaps; the gesture came from the right place even if it was starting to get a little tiresome.

The stair carpet was thick underfoot and her approach was in near silence. At the top were three doors facing her: straight in front was a bathroom; to the right, a room that looked to be in use by a young boy; to the left was the only door that was closed. She turned to where Wendy had followed her up.

'Maybe you could give us a moment? Sometimes I find that people can be a little more comfortable away from their parents.' Rhiannon tried to look reassuring. She had also raised her voice in the hope that Libby had heard the request, like now they were on the same team.

Wendy hesitated, but then did step backwards.

'Well, I'll just be right . . . I'll be in the kitchen. Tea?'

'Lovely, thank you.' Rhiannon waited until she was out of sight then faced the closed door. Rhiannon knocked gently. She left it a full minute before she knocked again. There was no response.

'I know you're in there, Libby. Don't blame your mum, okay? I don't think she's had much practice at fibbing to the police!' This time an answer came.

'Go away.' Instantly it was clear it was the voice of someone upset.

'I can. You don't have to talk to me now but you will have to talk to me sometime. Or my colleagues in their uniform — maybe at your school.'

'Just leave me alone, please.'

'Don't you want to know how he is?' Silence. But Rhiannon wasn't leaving until she had spoken to Libby. She considered her options. Libby was the last person known to have seen this boy prior to his being seriously assaulted. Technically that made her a suspect. Her refusal to talk to the police added more grist to the mill; Rhiannon could arrest her. She shook her head. That would need to be a last resort, talking to someone under arrest presented more obstacles even than talking to a teenager through a closed door. She tapped the door again.

'It's just me. I've sent your mum away. I'm not much older than you actually, Libby. Just a few years, really. So I remember exactly what it's like when you're sixteen, when you have a boyfriend and maybe you tell a lie to get some time together. I don't care about any of that. I just want to know what went on?' She paused for a reaction. This time there was none. 'And I want to know why James Miller might die in hospital, as he can't tell me himself.'

The door scraped, then pulled open. A slip of a girl peered out, her eyes wide and puffed with moisture. They were red too.

'He might *die?*'

'A fractured skull, Libby — that's serious stuff. The skull is what protects a lot of the really important bits. He's young and he's strong so he has a good chance but he is certainly not out of the woods just yet.'

The girl stepped back. Her leg gave and she stumbled. Rhiannon was quick to react; she reached in and grabbed her flailing arm for support. The girl steadied herself then threw Rhiannon's arm off.

'Don't touch me!' she hissed. She moved backwards. There was a large bed against the far wall. She jumped up onto it and sat in the middle, pulling her legs up to her chest. She was wearing a nightie that was more like a long t-shirt. She pulled it tight over her legs.

'Are you okay?'

'I'm not the one with a fractured skull, am I?' the girl snapped.

Rhiannon took a moment to look around the room, giving the girl time to calm down a little. It was a big room. The blinds were shut but there was still enough light to make out a few details, like the clump of clothes heaped under the window. She could just make out a lacy edge to the black material of an evening dress. It looked to have been thrown to the furthest point from where she sat. Otherwise the room was neat and tidy; nothing else seemed out of its place. Rhiannon studied the girl closer. She was still hugging her legs and had her head down to avoid eye contact. She wore a sulky pout that Rhiannon guessed to be well practised for use on her mother downstairs. Her hair was long. She was wearing it down and it looked to be unruly, like how it might be if it had been left to dry on its own. She couldn't think of a situation where a pretty girl of her age might wash her hair and not instantly dry it — and straighten it, too, even when she was just sitting in her own bedroom. She was pretty, too: high cheekbones that shaped a pleasing face with big, brown eyes and full lips.

'That doesn't mean I'm only worried about him. I'm worried about you, too. So, are you okay?'

'Not really.'

'What happened, Libby?'

'When?'

'You know when.'

'I don't know. I don't know what you're talking about.'

'Last night . . . what happened?'

'I don't know what you're talking about!'

'How did you get that bruise?'

Libby looked over at her. Rhiannon made sure she kept eye contact until Libby broke away to the fresh-looking bruise on her right upper arm. She snatched her gaze back up. 'What bruise?'

'Did James do that?'

'He would *never* hurt me!'

'Okay then. Did someone else? Did he try and protect you and he was set upon? I know you're scared, I can see that, but I can help you. We will keep you safe.'

'You have no idea.' This last sentence was so quiet Rhiannon almost missed it. She stepped forward to ask her to repeat it.

'Say again?'

The girl suddenly swept to her feet. She paced across the room, her eyes dropping momentarily to the clump of clothes before she gave them a wide berth.

'I don't know anything. We got a taxi. He dropped me here and then he left. He was supposed to be going straight home. I don't know what happened to him after that.'

'Did he text you after you left? Or have any contact?'

'No.'

'Did you text him?'

'No.' She spun from where she had been inspecting the blinds, running them through her fingertips.

'A couple of sixteen-year-olds after a night out together who don't even send a *goodnight?* Did you argue? Fall out?'

'He's seventeen.'

'So you did argue?'

'No!'

'Convince me. Tell me why you're different to every other couple.'

'We might have done.' She shrugged. 'I'd been drinking.'

'Can you check your phone?'

'I have, okay? No. There were no messages. I must have just got in and collapsed. I thought he had done the same.'

'Where were you drinking?'

'Langthorne.'

'Where did you end up?'

'The Party Bar. It's the only place that stays open late.' Her anger was starting to slip. Rhiannon could see her eyes were filling again, and glazing over, too, her emotion brought on by being forced to remember.

'Who were you out with?'

'A couple of his mates for most of the night but the last hour or so it was just us. We were drinking and dancing. I like dancing.' She flickered a smile. The upward curling of her lip was met by an errant tear. Rhiannon waited for her to continue. 'The lights in the club came up. I didn't know it was so late. We walked outside. It was busy — people everywhere. I managed to blag a taxi, I think it was for someone else but he didn't seem to mind.'

'He?'

'The driver.'

'So you didn't call a taxi?'

'No. They just line up right outside. It was kicking-out time.'

'Do you remember what firm it was?'

'No. I don't remember much after that. The air you know, it always hits me!' She held the smile a little longer this time but Rhiannon could see it was empty.

'Did you come straight home?'

'He dropped me here.'

'Straight here?'

'I told you I don't remember much after I left the club, but yeah, that was what happened.'

'And he was going straight back home?'

'That's what he said. Nothing was open at that time of night.'

'And he lives in Dover, right?'

'Elms Vale, yeah.'

'Has James got any issues with anyone at the moment, is there any reason that someone might want to hurt him?'

'No.' Libby wiped away another tear.

'What about you?'

'Me? Why would I want to hurt him?'

'I meant is there anyone that would want to hurt *you*? The bruise . . . your hair . . . your room here . . . it looks like you got in after a bad night.'

'What do you mean?'

'That looks like an expensive dress you've thrown down over there. I assume that was the one you were wearing? And then you showered, too. I've been on many a night out where I've come back worse for wear — a shower was the last thing on my mind.'

'I was drunk! So what if I left my dress on the floor? And who said I showered last night? I might have this morning.'

'You didn't though, did you? That bathroom is bone dry in there. And your hair was still wet when you went to sleep last night.'

'Well, aren't we the detective. You got me! I got in from a night out and had a shower. Well done!' The anger was back and it was now the overriding emotion. Rhiannon assumed it was because she was challenging her in the right areas. Wendy Battle had lied to her at the front door and now Libby Battle was lying to her in her bedroom.

'If you know more than you're telling me—'

'I've told you everything. Now I want you to go!'

'I'm not here to upset you, Libby. I just want to be sure you're not in any danger — and I want to catch the people who did that to James.'

'Then go do that.'

'Everything okay in here?' The door pushed open, the thud suggesting Wendy had used her foot.

Libby moved immediately back to her bed, her legs pulled back up for her to hide behind. 'Fine. We're done.'

'All sorted?' Wendy put a cup down on the bedside table. 'Did you find out what happened?'

'I don't know anything!' Libby squealed. 'Can you both just leave me alone? I haven't done anything wrong, okay? That's it! That's all I have to say. I didn't do anything wrong and I don't know what happened. I wasn't there. Now get OUT!'

Rhiannon held her ground. She knew her next question was pointless but she didn't want to leave without asking. 'Libby, can you give me consent to download your phone? It might help me—'

Libby swept open her drawer. She grabbed a black handset and threw it at Rhiannon's feet. Rhiannon looked at it in surprise. She hadn't expected that.

'Keep it for all I care! Now, leave me alone.'

Rhiannon bent to pick up the phone. She met Wendy's questioning look. 'I should be able to bring it back out tomorrow, maybe. It doesn't take long. It's quicker with a PIN, though?' She turned back into the room.

'Two-five-eight-zero. There, you have everything you need. You'll see I was telling you everything.'

'I'm sure you are. Can you just tell me his name? Your boyfriend, I mean.'

Libby looked up at her, her expression confused. 'You know his name? You *said* it like a hundred times!'

'I did. You're right. But you couldn't bring yourself to say it once. This is your last chance, Libby, if you know something, something that can help?'

'Just get out.' Her voice was lower, her tone resigned.

'Thanks for your time. You know where I am, if you want to talk about anything.' Rhiannon didn't get a reply. 'I'll see myself out.'

Maddie didn't like these places. She had been to vehicle recovery yards just a handful of times in her career but each time she had felt a real sense of trepidation. They were places of misery, of crashed and broken cars; a waiting room for the crusher.

From the parking area out at the front, she was able to glimpse through the high fence to what awaited. She was led through, hanging back behind Harry, hoping he wouldn't notice her hesitancy.

'You okay?' His voice made her jump. It snatched her away from staring at an SUV with a bonnet that was bent back, its surface arching away from the point of impact, exposing the grill and engine bay as if it was trapped in a silent scream. She should know better; Harry didn't miss a thing.

'I'm good, yeah, I just hate these places.' She gave a tense chuckle.

'Me too.' Harry's smile was warm, but he was quick to move on. Maddie was suddenly very aware of the sensitivity with Harry and car accidents. She hadn't considered that this was a far worse experience for him. He had quickened his pace across the yard, catching up with the overweight employee who was leading the way. He had a pair of filthy overalls tied off round his waist while the cuffs dragged on the dusty floor. Maddie was left with her mouth flapping where no words seemed right. She got her head down and followed.

'Well, good afternoon! I do apologise if you were promised a car to look at. All I can really offer you is a sort of flat, metal box. Is that gonna be okay?' Charley Mace had given the cheery greeting. She was Maddie's favourite CSI officer, not least because she liked to wind up Harry where no one else seemed to dare. She stood in front of them in a forensic suit. She turned to Harry and her smile dropped away, although the sparkle remained in her eye. 'And I assume you are the reason I am dressed in all this get-up?' Her blue gloves flashed a gesture down her front.

'Not my job, actually,' Harry said. 'DS Ives here is the one who isn't happy with the circs.'

Charley turned her playful eyes to Maddie. 'Meaning you're the reason I'm sweating out in this?'

'I guess so!' Maddie's mood lifted now her focus was on the CSI officer in front of her rather than the metal corpses that had them surrounded.

'I hear this is a case of a bit of adult liaison gone wrong?' Charley said.

'It could be,' Maddie conceded.

'Well I for one hope it isn't. If you've got me going to all this effort, I hope it's for something!'

'It's always for something, Charley. And you know I appreciate your efforts. How are we getting on?'

Charley turned back to her workspace. Maddie looked beyond her to the white Skoda. It was pretty much as Charley had described: a flat, white slither of metal. She could see where the supports holding up the roof had buckled on one side and snapped completely on the other. The gap where the windscreen would have been had almost closed up completely. The driver's side was closest to her and both doors on this side were pointing outwards. The passenger door had seemed to be in better shape when Maddie had leaned through it at the scene. The car in a worse shape than she remembered but, now it was the right way up and sat on buckled wheels in front of her, she could get more of an appreciation of how a steel-framed box had been crushed in an instant, like a blown egg. It was hard to imagine the forces at work.

'I'm almost done, there's not actually that much to do. I got your brief and I didn't see any need to deviate. No forensic work on the exterior of the car, and on the interior only if there are any tell-tale or suspicious stains. It being a taxi, I was a bit worried about that one! And forensic capture of any items of personal property only.'

'That's right,' Maddie said. 'What about our victims?'

'I was able to process them both at the scene. We talked about keeping the girl in the car and doing it elsewhere, but it's always my preference to get the work done on victims where they are found. It wasn't one of my more pleasant jobs. I got swabs from all the places that might back up the theory of a sex act with an unhappy ending. I'm sure you don't want me to explain what that means and you definitely don't want me to describe how I did it.'

'You're right about that. Again, thanks. That can't have been pleasant.'

Charley waved her away. 'You can't sign up for CSI work without understanding that someday you may have to rub a dead man's penis with a cotton bud at the bottom of a cliff. It's not all glamour, you know.'

Maddie laughed, and the rest of her tension went with it. 'And the girl?' she said, eventually.

'It took a while to get her out. Our driver was thrown clear, as you know, so he was quite easy. The girl was still strapped in her seat, holding tight to her rucksack. I'm just sorting the contents of that now.' She pointed down to where she had laid a white sheet out on the floor. Maddie hadn't noticed it until now. She stepped forward. The rucksack was lying in the top left corner of the sheet with a yellow plastic sign stood next to it displaying the number 14. Smaller exhibits ran from left to right, Maddie assumed in the order they had come out of the bag. Nothing jumped out at her as being particularly significant. A jumble of handwritten letters, a scrap of paper with a web address noted down. A couple of photographs, one of a black-framed door with a glass panel at the top, taken at close enough range for her to see a mesh running through the glass to reinforce it — albeit blurred. The other picture was of the interior of what looked like a sparse flat, where she could only make out a bed as furniture. Neither looked to have been taken with any care. The shot of the door looked rushed overall while the interior of the room was at an angle, almost as if it had been taken by accident. They were both printed on A4 paper that had started curling at the edges as if it had been in the bag for a while.

Maddie's eyes continued along the line. Next was a small plastic fob, bullet shaped and attached to a key ring. Next to that was the number twelve, beaten out of thin metal, and then a small book that looked new. Brightly coloured with a picture of a bird on the front, it was labelled *Addresses.*

'Anything in there that might assist with next of kin? I've been told we've got nothing so far.'

'There are a few addresses written out. No clue as to who lives in them, nothing else that I could see but I only flicked through it briefly.'

'No problem. I'll have a look later.'

'There are still a few more bits that came out of the bag that need seizing. There's a handwritten list of something on some lined paper — looks like initials to me but, whatever it is, it's not going to answer any questions. If anything you're just getting more questions here.'

Maddie was drawn back to the car, her interest waning in the random items that Holly Maguire had in her possession in her last moments. Maddie found herself considering that if it was all that she owned in the world, that might fit with the picture other officers had painted of her: a drug-taking prostitute leading a chaotic life. But whatever she had been in life, she didn't deserve this as an end. Maddie's mind flashed with the unimaginable fear of going over that cliff, of the car rolling forward, of the tipping point playing out in near slow motion so the occupants could see what was coming and how they would know it was too late to stop it. Charley's voice pulled her back.

'There's nothing that stands out from a forensics' point of view I'm afraid.'

'Okay, then.'

'The rucksack itself, too . . . It looks like a kid's one to me. It just doesn't strike me as the sort of thing an adult might choose?'

Maddie looked at the rucksack for the first time in any real detail. It was pale yellow with a rounded pocket on the front, the top half of which was covered in glittery sequins, while the bottom half had a small image that looked like an ice cream cone with a rainbow on top. The word 'Smiggle' was written on a pendant that hung from the zip. Charley had a point. Maddie took her book out to make a note of what she could see.

'Don't worry about that,' Charley said. 'I'm running an exhibits register. I'll scan a copy across when I get back to the office. I'm nearly done here.'

'I can book them in, if you like? Just leave them with the register on my desk. I should probably have a proper look. Anything else loose found in the car?'

Charley shrugged. 'It's been searched as well as I can. I did speak with a PolSA who said he could put search-trained officers into it but it's a lump of twisted metal . . . we're not going to be able to say there isn't something tucked up in the rear footwell, for example, or thrown a hundred metres from the car as part of the fall. I've searched what I can. I've dug out an air freshener and I think I've got the mobile phone that belonged to the driver. Holly's mobile was in her pocket. I seized it but it looked pretty broken. I guess it's down to you how far you want to go with searches beyond that.'

'I don't see the need for a search team,' Harry said. 'Sounds like it's all been covered.'

Maddie turned to him. He was looking away from their scene, his hands pushed into his pockets. She could tell he was lacking enthusiasm. 'It does,' she agreed. 'We did see an ashtray at the scene — it had blood on it. Not a great surprise, I appreciate, but that isn't here?'

'It's in the CSI office. I swabbed it at the scene but had to book it in separately to send the sample off. When I got it on the table in the office I picked out a hair from one of the cracks, too.'

'Meaning?'

'Meaning it must have hit one of them — the driver, I would say, from the colour. But an object like that loose in the car would have been flying around the interior for sure. No way of saying it didn't strike him then.'

'Or it could have been used as a weapon? Before it went over the cliff?'

'If I found it in another scene, I would be pointing it out as a possible weapon. Not here, though. I've sent it away to make sure the blood and the hair matches one or both of the two victims. I don't want to be red-faced when you search their homes and another body turns up! Not much else I can tell you, though.'

'I guess not. And no signs of any other bodies, thankfully.'

'A sex act gone wrong would make sense, then. Like uniform were saying?' Charley shrugged again. 'Not that it's my job to talk about what makes sense.'

'Well, I suppose it does. I was hoping for something else from the car, though — a used condom . . . some sort of sex toy or a restraint . . . Anything, really.'

Charley was clearly battling laughter. 'Sorry . . . there are too many obvious jokes!'

'Obvious means not necessary,' Harry growled. 'Right, we need to go and see a taxi firm about a driver. Are we done here, DS Ives?'

Maddie was doing her best to stifle her own laughter. She nodded. 'Yeah, I think we should stop now, before we continue with my wish list for a Saturday night.'

'Let's get going, then.' Harry's straight answer seemed to be the final word. Maddie shot a hurried glance at Charley, and both squealed with laughter.

* * *

Maddie surveyed the occupants of the taxi office from the threshold. Old habits, perhaps. In a previous life, it had been essential to know who was in a room before she entered it. There were only two people. The closest was a young lad with a Staffordshire Bull Terrier without a lead, leaning so far back on the plastic seating he was almost lying down, despite being in a deep conversation with a young woman in the seat next to him. She was bowed forward as though she was about to be sick, but she snapped up when Maddie and Harry moved past. Maddie was greeted at a glass window by an employee who had an instant air of impatience about her. The term 'greeted' had to be applied loosely. It was more a toothless attempt at a smile, with no real commitment. When Maddie identified herself as a police officer and asked who was in charge, she only got a shrug. Maddie was aware of the two occupants in the background getting to their feet and filing out. It seemed to take the woman another few minutes to realise that Maddie and Harry were not just going to go away. Finally she said she would *go and get someone* but gave no idea who that might be. Maddie didn't think it was going to be the owner of Langthorne Taxis as she had asked. She was quickly proven right.

'Yeah?' A large man loomed against the glass. He had to bend down to where the small holes were cut to allow for voices to be heard, adding to the overall impression of a caged beast.

'Afternoon. I'm DS Maddie Ives, this is DI Harry Blaker and we were hoping to speak to the owner of the firm here. It's about what happened yesterday.'

'Yesterday?' The man's spoke slowly, his tone suggesting apathy. He wore an off-white t-shirt with the sleeves cut off. He was overweight and his excess fat seemed to be pushing up, flaring his neck out and flushing his face an unhealthy-looking shade of red.

'Yesterday. There was an incident on the clifftop with one of your drivers. I'm sorry—'

'At the bottom I heard.' The man spoke over the bit where she said how she was sorry for the loss of one of his colleagues. She abandoned that tack; he could hardly present as less bothered.

'Quite. So you know what I am talking about, then.'

'I don't know nothing. I just drive here.'

'Okay then. I did ask to speak to someone in charge. Who runs the place?'

'He ain't here.'

'Okay then, who's running the place today?'

'I am.'

Maddie wasn't getting anywhere. Harry had detected it too.

'Where's Freddie?' Harry said. He stepped closer to the glass. The man stepped back and shrugged.

'Don't know no Freddie.'

'Funny, that. He owns this place, I heard. You sure you work here?' Harry did nothing to hide the sarcasm in his tone.

'Sure I do. Guess we can't help you.'

Maddie took out her business card. There was a gap at the bottom of the glass. She pushed it under, keeping her fingertips on it until the man looked her in the eye.

'Whoever runs this place, can you make sure he gets my card. And ask him to get in touch straight away, I'm sure he doesn't want us sniffing around.' She jutted her thumb in a gesture behind her. 'It seems to be bad for business. He just needs to call. I might even be able to do this over the phone.'

'Alright, love. I'll do my best, yeah?'

Maddie waited until they were back in the car before she spoke to her colleague.

'Freddie?' She was in the driver's seat. She sat back to make it clear that they weren't moving until she got an answer.

'Freddie Rickman.'

'First time I've heard his name.' She stared over at him now. He stayed looking forward.

'Mitch sent an update through. They did some digging around NH Cars. It was bought by Freddie Rickman five years ago. That's when it was changed to Langthorne Taxis. He's the owner.'

'You didn't think to mention that before we went in there?'

'Mention it? What for? We need to find out what they knew about their driver — like if he had been acting oddly. Then maybe ask for an opinion on why a ten-year-old ashtray was in the car when they died. Rickman isn't going to be the right person to ask those questions. Day to day, he won't have anything to do with running the place. It's just a place to attach his name to.'

'You know that?'

'I was told a bit about him. There's plenty of intelligence around him. Seems he's a career criminal with links to drug supply and prostitution. He's been arrested five times or more, mostly for violent offences, but he's always released without charge and really quickly. This place will be one of the ways he tries to make himself look legit. A place to wash his money.'

'Prostitution?'

'He was the owner of a few places that were raided as brothels a few years back.'

'What happened to him?'

'To him? Nothing. As always. He's just the landlord, don't forget. He just rents the place out. According to his account, he had no idea what was going on in the building.'

'Of course he didn't. And you didn't think to tell me this?'

'Which bit?'

'Jesus, Harry! A suspected sex worker dies in a taxi and you know that the owner of the same taxi firm is involved in prostitution?'

'I don't *know* that. There's nothing recent.'

'You know what I mean!'

'Mitch sent me a brief update as he was finding bits out. He's going to present a fuller picture to us both. I didn't see the point in telling you something when you're going to get it all anyway.'

'This is my job, Harry. I need to know everything. If the DCI calls me with questions and I don't have the full picture, how does that make me look? Especially if you can tell him more?'

'I'm still the boss, last time I checked at least. I have the overview while this is a major crime enquiry. Which may not be much longer.'

'Not for much longer?'

'That's what I said. If CID had a skipper covering the weekend like they should have, they would have come out with you. And from what I've seen, they would have been left to run it. We don't investigate misadventure. Or suicide for that matter.'

'Murder-suicide is always attended by Major Crime.'

'And pretty quickly dropped by Major Crime. I know the policy, I also know they're a waste of our time. We'll go out with CID . . . we take it if it's clear it wasn't a suicide. You can't tell me we're clear on anything at the moment.'

'This is my job, however that came about.'

'Until I say it isn't.'

'So do I not have an input on whether I think it's *misadventure* or not?'

'We have a lot of work on at the moment. The Harnett case file — how are you getting on with that?'

Maddie huffed.

'I take it that means you're no further along? CPS will lose their patience, Maddie. They've already given you two extensions.'

'They keep changing what they need! We both know that case file is a waste of time. I'll spend the rest of my life getting a bulletproof case together with all defences negated and Justin Harnett will turn up and plead guilty. Why wouldn't he?'

The Justin Harnett case was one of Maddie's more frustrating — and upsetting. Justin Harnett killed his brother but in circumstances that most people who were involved felt was tragic. The two brothers had fought their whole lives — nothing serious, not much more than most brothers who were close in age. On Justin's thirtieth birthday, he had argued with his younger brother Michael over his plans to go travelling. It was petty. Michael thought Justin should be taking his girlfriend. He called him disrespectful for expecting her to wait for him for six months. Justin lost his temper. He punched his brother once to the face and the combination of that blow and the one to the back of his head as he went down was enough to kill Michael instantly. Justin Harnett had not intended to kill his brother and certainly had not wanted that outcome, but the offence was complete. Charging him with the murder and watching a close family tear itself apart at the seams was one of the darker days in her career. Her motivation to complete the work that would determine Justin's sentence was very much missing. Part of her thought he had already suffered enough.

'I'll tell you why he wouldn't — if he or his brief get a sniff that we are unprepared. The media interest alone should be enough to sharpen you up. This job has the ability to make us look very silly.'

'By *us*, I take it you mean *me*.'

'Same thing. The press don't see us as separate entities. We're just the police.'

'But we are separate entities. Hence I don't automatically know what you do — you have to tell me.'

'Noted.'

'What does that mean? Misadventure or not, I'm an investigator. I can't do that without all the information.'

Maddie twisted the car keys roughly. Her anger was starting to spill over.

'And now you have it. You really think we have something here? We go after bad guys — murderers. There's no one here to chase.'

'You don't think Freddie Rickman changes this? Maybe a man who runs a taxi firm to launder his money, a pimp with a penchant for extreme violence, might have a motivation to run that car over a cliff.'

Harry didn't answer straight away. 'I'm not sure I'm seeing a motivation.'

'That's our job, though, isn't it? We need to find it. Or at least be sure there isn't one. So we need to speak to this Rickman fella.'

'If it makes you feel better. Don't expect to get anything out of him, though.'

'We'll see. I'm getting a lot of practice at getting information out of people that would only give you half the story.' Maddie was still fuming, but she cut it there before she overstepped the mark. She pulled out into the traffic.

'You're right,' Harry said. 'It is relevant. I should have told you earlier. Let's go back and get this full update and we'll work out where we go from there.'

'We? I'm quite happy to do this on my own.' Maddie spoke a little softer. 'I'm the one who needs to be convinced. I'm just not yet.'

'I know. But you don't go and see this man alone. He's a nasty piece of work, from what we do know.'

'All the more reason to go and speak with him, then. And throwing someone over a cliff? That would be pretty nasty, Harry.'

CHAPTER 14

Kelly stopped a few paces short of the communal door to Truro House. She knew she was going to have to go in, but she always felt better for taking a moment. Previously it was always Holly who would lead the way. She had her own fob to open the door and she would hold it open while Kelly took her moment, her face a reassuring smile the whole time. How she missed that! How could anything ever be okay now? She suddenly felt a surge of anger towards Holly for leaving her to do this alone.

'How could you?' she hissed at the door. It instantly clicked and flexed in its housing as if it had unlocked to the sound of her voice. But she knew better, she knew that someone was watching the camera that was concealed in a glass dome above the door. She stepped forward and pushed through it, stopping again on the threshold, waiting for Benny to detach himself from the shadows. There was nothing — no movement, no sounds. Nothing — just the scuff of her shoe leather as she started up the stairs. The anger was fading now to be replaced by that familiar knot of fear in the pit of her stomach. She didn't know what to expect. She mouthed words of a prayer that she would at least be working on her own.

She made it up the two flights of stairs to the corridor
that would lead her to Flat 12. She took in the passing numbers like she always did, slowing as she passed Flat 10 — like
she always did. The door to Flat 12 was shut this time. She
dipped the handle. It was locked. She stepped back, confused,
her eyes running over the door, resting on the spy hole that
was just above where she could now see a faint outline of the
number 12 that was seemingly written in dust. She put her
hands on her hips, staring at the spy hole, waiting for someone
to open it. She wasn't in the mood for games. A door opened,
not the one in front of her, but of the flat to her left. Benny
stepped out from it, his usual leering smile plastered across
his face.

'What's going on?' Kelly asked, keeping her voice down.
She couldn't believe that the other residents had no idea what
was going on but she had been warned always to be quiet
when in the corridor. Now it was force of habit.

'Upgrade,' he grinned.

Kelly shrugged. She pushed past him. They bumped
shoulders as she stumbled into the room. The layout was
identical: the bed was the same, as was the lighting rig, the
laptop setup and the webcam. She looked for a place to put
her bag down. That was when she realised she wasn't alone.
A young girl flinched on the other side of the room. Her
eyes were flushed red and tears ran down her face. She took
a sharp intake of breath as their eyes locked.

'Who the hell is this?' Kelly said.

'Fucked if I know,' Benny said.

'She's a kid. What the hell is a kid doing here?'

Benny's leer remained. 'Old enough.'

'Surely you don't . . . No way! You think I'm working
with her? No way!'

The girl sniffed. Her eyes shed fresh tears. She looked
to be battling with her breathing.

'Like I was saying to her, Kell. You ain't got no choice!
How about I let you girls get acquainted? You got four minutes by my watch. Ain't a lot of time, granted. Best you tell

her what's what.' He walked past her this time, but he made sure their shoulders collided again — harder this time. 'Pretty, ain't she? Don't say I don't give you nothing!' The slamming door cut off his chuckling.

Kelly turned to the girl. 'What's your name?' she snapped.

The girl's voice just came out as a wail.

'You need to calm down, okay? I'm not going to hurt you. But there are people here who will if we don't calm down and sort this out. So, what is your name?' She softened her tone as best she could. It still had an edge, though — nothing she could do about that; she was trying to conceal her own panic.

The girl's head slumped forward and shook rhythmically from side to side. She was talking again but it was through tears, it was more like a constant sound than individual words. Kelly walked over to her, careful to hang back a little and to give the girl space. Movement on the laptop monitor caught her eye: the camera had captured her moving across the front of it; the monitor had a second or so lapse. She could tell from the display that they were already live. This exchange was already streaming out via the internet to a million voyeurs. Lines of text were appearing thick and fast, each one accompanied by the chime sound she had come to hate so much. Already the comments were enough to make her feel nauseous. The girl might be off camera now but the watching members had certainly caught sight of her. She was already popular, the comments suggesting that they liked the fact she was young but, more than that, they liked the fact that she was crying. The punters were baying for the performance to start. Kelly knew from experience they were not patient people. She also knew that Freddie and his crew were even less so.

She moved so she was off camera too and close enough that they should be able to talk without the microphone picking it up. She knew there were other cameras, too — at least two in the corners that were solely for Benny to monitor them constantly. She couldn't be sure where he was doing this from today but she knew he would be close.

'Listen to me. You need to calm down, okay? We need to work this out. You're going to be okay but you need to talk to me. Have you been here before?' Kelly certainly hadn't see her and she was young, definitely *too* young. She had long brown hair tied back from a face that would be pretty if it wasn't puffed red, with make-up running down it.

'They . . . they made me . . .'

'Okay . . . listen to me,' Kelly leaned in. The girl was still looking down. Kelly touched her lightly on the shoulder and she stepped back so quickly she almost toppled over. 'Woah! I'm not going to hurt you, okay?'

'They hurt me.'

'I know. They hurt me, too — before. But I learned how to get through this. You can, too.'

'Get through?'

'What's your name? And say it quietly.'

The girl sniffed and then breathed her response, 'Libby. My name is Libby.'

'Okay, Libby, that's good. So you've been here before? And you know why? What's expected?' The girl's eyes were dragged to the monitor. The chime sound was going off almost constantly now, the lines of text coming through so fast they were merging into each other. Kelly had never really taken much notice before; she did her best to ignore the words, the requests. Holly always took charge of that and she would do her best to shield Kelly from them.

'Expected?'

'Yes. The reason you are here. Do you *know* why you are here?' She was angry now; she couldn't keep her voice low. This girl needed to snap out of it. They were going to have to do something soon. 'You need to answer me. This is not something that is going to end just because you're crying, okay? It only gets worse.'

'He told me! He told me, I thought he was joking. I thought last night was it!'

'Last night? What happened last night?'

'I was out. With my boyfriend. Someone brought me here. I was drinking a lot. I don't really know how we got here. We were looking for somewhere to stay. The driver said he knew a place. When we got here . . . They beat him. My boyfriend, he's in hospital. Then they made me . . . in front of the camera. I don't remember it so well. I had to take my clothes off. There was a man here too . . . I don't remember what he looked like!' She started to cry again but Kelly could see she was fighting it this time. When she spoke again her lips were soaked in her own tears.

'There was more drink here. I didn't want it but they made me. When it was finished . . . when it was finished, they said they would send it to everyone in my phone if I didn't come back, send out what I had done. They held onto my phone. I only came back for it and then he tells me that I have to do it again . . .' She had to fight her sobs again. Kelly waited.

'I should have told the police. They came to my house but I just lied. I said nothing happened. I could have just told them! But my mum . . . If she knew . . .' She was working herself up again, Kelly needed her to stay calm. She touched her shoulder again, this time Libby didn't pull away.

'Do you know what they need from you today?'

'Strip . . .' She said it so quiet that Kelly almost missed it. 'That's all?'

'He said that was all I had to do to start with, but he said I would be working with a girl who would show me the rest. She lifted her eyes. Kelly could see they were filling with panic. 'Please . . . just let me go!'

'Let you . . . You think this is me? I don't want to be here anymore than you do!'

'I can't do it. Not again. Not now!'

'I know — I know how you feel. I remember when . . . I remember when I first came here. They got me the same way, but you can get past it — you have to. These are not people you can say no to. Not right now. We can figure this out, but right now we don't have a choice, okay?'

The girl's eyes moved to the sound of a chime from the laptop and they flared wide. 'People are watching now, aren't they? Oh God! Look what they are saying!'

Kelly turned to look back at the monitor. The bed was pictured in the centre and she could just about see Libby's back now — nothing else. The text was in three lines along the bottom. It kept to three lines; each time a new request came through it replaced the one at the bottom. They were coming through almost instantaneously, members demanding what they had paid for, working themselves up into a frenzy and most seemed delighted at the prospect of the *fresh meat* they had seen for just a tantalising amount of time. Already the requests were getting perverse.

Libby suddenly straightened. 'I have to go! I don't care where they send it — I can't do this!' Kelly tried to grab her but she was already too far away. She followed her to the door.

'Libby!' She called out. 'Libby, don't be silly. Trust me, you won't get out of here! This isn't about them sending videos to your friends! Don't be so naïve. I can help you but we're going to have to get through the next hour or so. It's easy, okay?' Libby stopped at the door. She looked like she was going over her options. Kelly heard a noise from the laptop she had heard before: it was a warning that the feed had been cut. Someone was coming. Libby wrenched the door open.

'LIBBY!' Kelly shouted.

'I'm going to the police!' She stepped out of the room but stopped immediately. Libby's head suddenly jerked down to the right and she stumbled back. Benny came into view. He had a fistful of Libby's hair. He pushed her further into the room, her hair still wrapped up in his fist, her legs bowing like she was off balance but unable to fall to the floor. He threw her onto the bed, his face a snarl. Kelly stepped in front of him to try and break his focus. He leaned to try and see around her. She could hear Libby screaming. Benny lashed out and Kelly didn't have time to react. The blow connected firmly with the side of Kelly's face and knocked her sideways. He moved past her and grabbed another fistful of Libby's hair. He wrenched her head up to where he was stooped over her.

'Day ONE!' he raged, his face now an inch from hers. He seemed to check himself, his eyes glancing to the walls before he fixed back on her. His voice was now a hiss but his anger just as prevalent, 'I was going easy. A dance . . . strip off — each give yourself a little fucking rub and then you could fuck off. But if you wanna cause me trouble I'll fuck you myself. Right now. On that bed. You gonna cause me trouble? ARE YOU?' He wrenched her head up closer to his. She moaned, her face contorted in pain.

'No . . .' she managed.

He threw her head back to the bed then picked a clump of torn hair out from between his fingers as he straightened up and stepped away. When he stared over at Kelly his eyes were still wide. He jabbed towards her with long fingers. 'Sort her out, Kell. Show her the fucking ropes before she gets herself seriously hurt, you understand me?'

Kelly snatched a nod, her hand over her mouth.

'I was trying to be nice. I have to come back in here again and I won't be nice, you hear me?'

Kelly nodded again. Libby was now sobbing silently on the bed, her hair a mess and covering her face.

'Look, Benny . . .' Kelly's voice was soft, pleading. 'Look at her, mate. She can't perform. Not now. How about she stays but she watches, yeah? That way I really can show her what she needs to know. I'll do a solo like we agreed. Then she knows what's expected. It's not fair for her to come here and just—'

'FAIR!' Kelly flinched as Benny charged at her, stopping inches short to hiss in her face. 'I've been as fair as I get. This ain't just you on the line! I ain't the only person watching this feed, you get me?'

Kelly did. Benny was just the man who opened the door and ran the rooms. There was anger in his voice but there was fear, too — desperation even. For his own sake, he needed them to do what they were told and that made him even more dangerous.

'Okay, Benny, I understand. We're cool in here, okay? Just give me a few minutes.' She turned back to the bed. Benny moved away. She waited for the door to pull shut. It was so firm it rattled the walls.

'Libby, you still with me, hun?' Kelly squatted down, closer to where Libby's hair flickered as she still rushed her breaths. 'It's just a little dance, we take our time, take off some clothes. It's easy, okay? Just like in the shower, that's all. Or you're boyfriend's birthday!' She tried a chuckle. 'Don't worry about anything else. Don't worry about the laptop. You let me worry about that. Everything is going to be okay . . .' Kelly's own tear caught her out. Through the fog of her own panic she suddenly recognised this speech: it was the exact same one Holly had given her the first time they had met in the room next door — when she was seventeen. Holly had promised her that, too: that everything was going to be okay. More times than Kelly could remember, Holly had promised that she just needed to do as she was told for now and that soon she would be free. And she still wasn't.

'Please, Libby. We both do this or we're both in trouble . . . these people . . .' Kelly ran out of words. The desperation in her voice must have had an impact. The girl rose to a sit. She swept her hair aside. She was biting down on her bottom lip.

'Just a dance,' she sniffed.

Kelly smiled, she felt another tear spill down her cheek, this girl was breaking her heart. 'Just a dance. Just block everything else out. It's just a dance — and I'll be right here with you.'

'And everything will be okay?'

Kelly nodded, 'I promise.' The words fell out of her mouth before she could stop them. Maybe this was how Holly had ended up promising her.

Libby looked beyond her. The chime sounds had started up again, the feed was back up. There was a thump on the wall, the side that would be Flat 12. Their time was up.

'I'll make a start. Watch what I do. But you can't be far behind me, okay?'

Libby nodded.

Kelly wrapped her up in a hug then held her by the shoulders. 'Just a dance.' Then she turned away and stepped out in front of the camera.

CHAPTER 15

Monday

6:30 on a Monday morning was always going to be a time
to scowl at a ringing desk phone. No one should have even
known Maddie was in the office. Lord knows, she wasn't
due to be but she couldn't sleep and had abandoned bed for
an early start. She had every intention of coming in to work
on the Harnett case file but her mind was still on Freddie
Rickman and she simply couldn't shake him.

Mitch Evans had given an update on the collated information just before she had gone off duty from her previous
shift. It wasn't much; she hadn't really learned anything new.
Certainly there was nothing new about the man behind the
taxi firm for whom Taruc Mardin had been driving and there
was still nothing to explain why Taruc's car had gone over
the edge to a six-hundred-foot drop. The woman sat next
to him at the time of the tragedy was linked to prostitution
on police intelligence systems, but that intel was two years'
old at best. And even then it wasn't confirmed. Mitch had
managed to find a reluctant informant at Langthorne Taxis.
They refused to give their name or contact details but they
did say that Taruc had worked for them for less than a month

and his reference from his previous job was in the north of the country. That tied in with what his wife had said about them moving to the area recently. Taruc had no links to sex workers and there was nothing about him on police systems at all. The only information she could get about him was that he was a devoted family man who attended Mosque for prayers every Friday, generally kept himself to himself and had an unblemished record driving taxis in different parts of the country for the previous eight years. That, in itself, was no mean feat.

To add to her frustrations, Maddie hadn't found a single link between Taruc and Holly Maguire either. Harry had used that to back up his theory of a family man engaging in illicit sexual activity with a sex worker. *He would have worked hard to make sure there wasn't a link* he had said. *It makes perfect sense.* Harry was so matter of fact about it and it grated on her. She didn't argue with him at the time but she couldn't shake the feeling that something just wasn't right. Her early morning start, then, had not seen any progress on her case file — rather, more quiet contemplation that led to the conclusion there was nothing here at all and it was now just about her not wanting Harry to be right. Maybe she was looking for a complicated solution when there was a simple one staring her in the face. But even Harry couldn't answer her question as to why a prostitute performing a sex act in a car that slipped over a cliff would be clinging tightly to a rucksack, the contents of which seemed to be a mishmash of worthless scribbles and blurred photos. She had called Charley, too for another of those conversations that you could only ever really have with a CSI.

'Charley — the dead girl in the car . . . was she wearing nice underwear?' Of course Charley had been a little caught out — she had been just about to go off duty. But after she had finished her incredulous giggle she had confirmed that Holly had been wearing mismatched underwear: off-white Sloggi knickers and a black bra. Hardly the choice of a woman with a pre-arranged sexual encounter.

Maddie was missing something.

And now her phone was ringing when no one should know she was there. She looked down at the screen. Someone had dialled the hunt number for Major Crime, which meant the call was to the department rather than her direct. She was relieved momentarily, until she saw who was calling her: Custody.

'Morning . . . Major Crime.' She managed to sound far more cheerful than she felt.

'Oh! Sorry, I wasn't expecting anyone to actually pick up!'

'You called a phone not expecting it to be answered?'

'Well, yes, I mean we do it sometimes out of hours. We know you lot have a voicemail that kicks in. I was going to leave a message for a more earthly hour, see?'

'Well you can still do that if you want. I can just listen, not answer back, pretend to be a dumb machine?'

'Is that DS Ives by any chance?' A male voice now had a chuckle.

'It is.'

'Daryl Chambers. Down in the dungeons.'

'Ah yes! How are you, Daryl?' Daryl was one of the custody sergeants whose day shift often overlapped with hers. A nice enough bloke but a bit of a walkover she reckoned. A few of the prisoners had commented to her how they liked seeing him behind the desk when they were brought in.

'Ask me again in about half an hour!'

'This is going to be a long conversation, then?'

Daryl snorted a little now, as part of his laugh. 'Not that long, I hope! It's all a bit odd, really. We had a message come through on the bat phone. Some girl. Sounded young. Said her name was Libby. She said she was visited by a female detective about a nasty assault but she wouldn't say any more. She said she wanted to talk to the same officer again. We assumed it might be you up there in Major Crime.'

'Not me. I don't know a Libby. Did she give any more details? I can look her up on the system, see who's investigating her.'

'No. I did ask. We were going to do that. She said not to worry about it and hung up. I did call up on the radio for a patrol to go and intercept and get her details but there's no one left at the nick.'

'How long ago was it?'

'A good ten minutes by now, I suppose. I'm sure someone will know what it's all about. I wasn't going to call, I assume she'll come back when the front counter opens but she sounded a little upset.'

'Well, nothing to do with me. I'll go and have a look — see if she's still hanging about outside. I could do with stretching my legs anyway.'

'Great. Thanks for that. Sorry to bother you.'

Maddie stepped away from the phone and strode to the window. The 'bat phone', as it was known, was by the public entrance to the police station and provided a direct line through to the custody block out of hours as this was the only phone manned twenty-four-seven. She couldn't see it from her vantage point but she would be able to see if anyone was walking away. There was no foot traffic at all.

When she stepped out of the police station, the vehicular traffic was already starting to build with a familiar and constant dull roar. The phone was a sharp left out of the gate. There were a couple of parking spaces for visitors at the front but they were empty. She walked out onto the street. She could see some people on the other side of the road but they were walking with purpose, their heads bent, not looking like they were paying her or the police station any notice. The approach to the front counter was empty too, the phone pushed into its receiver. Whoever this Libby was, she was gone.

* * *

Kelly woke up to the usual radio station then rose from her bed to the same cheery sun that flooded her face as she tugged back the curtains. She had even slept well and for a moment, it was almost like a normal day. But when she walked into the main living area, suddenly nothing was the same. Her mum was gone. Holly was gone, too, and the ache in her heart returned. She sighed in acceptance that this was becoming the new normal. She had never felt more alone.

She pulled open cupboards, aware that she couldn't recall the last time she had eaten. She had nothing in. The sink was cluttered with full mugs of cold tea where she had made them to keep herself busy, only to disregard them immediately. She leant over them while her mind raced with images of the night before, of the poor teenage girl who had finally found the strength from somewhere to strip in front of a live-streaming camera. Kelly had known that every minute Libby was in there she was making her situation worse, tightening the hold others had over her and there was nothing either of them could have done about it.

They had spoken briefly after. Kelly had taken the time to make sure Libby knew what she was involved in, what was expected of her and what might happen if she didn't toe the line. Libby might have been listening but her eyes looked empty and without focus, her body had hung off her slim shoulders as if all her strength and fight were already gone. The expectations of her would only increase. She was going to be in demand. And the demands would soon be exceeding a striptease. Kelly already knew that she wasn't going to be able to cope.

She needed to blot Libby from her mind for now. Both girls were expected back for midday today. Kelly had told her to be early so they could meet outside the building. Kelly knew how difficult it was walking into that place on her own; she didn't want Libby to have to do that.

The thought of it was making her anxiety worse. She had her own problems, her own demons, too. The last thing she needed was to be worrying about someone else, to have to be the strong one. She had realised that this must be just how Holly had felt when they first met, when she was the scared little girl having to turn up on her own and Holly had insisted on them meeting first. She remembered how much stronger it had made her.

She opened the fridge. There were eggs and some milk, nothing else. She shook her head and slammed the door shut. She wasn't sure she could eat anyway. Her eyes moved to the windowsill, to the white envelope that contained the money she had been given last night, her weekly pay for *working the camera* as Benny called it. She hadn't even looked at it; the envelope was still sealed. She never did. Holly used to deal with all that. She knew she was going to have to deal with it now. She had put life and bills on hold for the last couple of days but she wouldn't be able to do that for long.

There was a knock at the door, light — tentative almost, but Kelly still jerked towards it. She wasn't expecting anyone. It could only be Joan. She wasn't usually hesitant when knocking the door but maybe meeting Freddie the previous time had had a lasting effect. Kelly moved to the spy hole. She could only see blackness. When she pulled the door open it was obvious why: Marlie Towers's arm dropped from where she had been holding it up to push her finger over the hole. She had good reason: if Kelly had seen her through the spyhole she would never have opened the door. As it was, she pushed it back to close. The door bounced off something trapped in it. Kelly looked down to where Marlie had stuck a brown leather boot in the doorway.

'I just need two minutes. It's important.'

'For what?' Kelly snapped.

'I got a message. I was told to deliver it two days after.'

'Two days . . . after what?'

'After Holly went. After she did what she did.'

Kelly took a moment. 'You knew?'

Marlie was chewing gum. 'Sorry, kid.'

Kelly pulled back the door to try and slam it again. This time Marlie stepped into it, pushing against it with her chest as well as her hands.

'Look, we can play this game . . . you can kick me out and pretend you don't want to hear what I got to say and I'll just stand out here until you're done with your silly game.'

Kelly stepped back. She could feel herself getting upset. She turned away, desperate that Marlie wouldn't see it. She heard the door knock against the wall where it was pushed right open. She moved to the other side of the room.

'Two minutes.' Kelly turned to face Marlie.

'Fine with me.'

'Well?'

Marlie smiled. 'I'm not your enemy. I know you think I am, but we're all just trying to survive.'

'There's more than one way to survive. You would have had me and Holly on our knees in back alleys or doing in-calls to strangers' houses if you'd had your way. How much of a cut were you going to take again?'

'It wasn't like that. Holly knew that.'

'You nearly had her convinced, you mean.'

'She trusted me. That's why she trusted me with this. You think what you're doing is any better or any safer? You might not be walking into a stranger's home but you're still walking into Freddie Rickman's place. You don't know what he has planned for you or what happens when he doesn't need you anymore. You won't be his top earner forever, you know. Then what — when you don't bring the money in?'

'Freddie Rickman's place? Remind me again who owns the house you run?'

'Exactly. The house *I* run. He doesn't have anything to do with it day to day.'

'Until he decides he wants to. I've heard all this rubbish before when you were telling Holly how you protect your girls. It was bullshit then, too. Your two minutes is just about up. I have no interest in speaking to pimps.'

Marlie huffed. She looked like she was taking a moment to calm herself, to suppress her first reaction. 'Holly came to see me, the beginning of last week. I didn't know, okay, what she was planning — I mean, not for sure. But she was talking about crazy stuff, about doing herself in and taking one of the drivers with her. I didn't want to come here anymore than you want me here.'

'Drivers?'

'Langthorne Taxis. We all know their drivers are the ones doing the recruiting for Freddie. They've been tapping up young girls and they're getting younger — I mean kids, really. They get hold of someone pissed up or vulnerable or both and they force them into a mistake they can use as leverage. These kids will do whatever they're told. Freddie don't give them no choice.'

'Why are you telling me this? I think I know that better than anyone.'

'Of course you do! You know most things better than anyone, ain't that right?' Marlie didn't manage to suppress her anger this time.

'Did you come here to tell me anything new at all?'

'Holly came to me talking about setting you free. You were all she ever talked about. She told me how much she loved you — how it was killing her to see you every day doing what you were doing. She felt responsible, like she should have got you out a long time ago. I don't think she saw no other way. She was upset — like *really* upset. I ain't seen her like that since she got sober and she *was* sober, too — not a thing in her.'

'It wasn't her fault.'

'I said that, but it didn't matter what I said. She weren't having none of it. She said she had this plan. That was when she started talking about doing herself in. She said when it happened that she wanted me to come and see you. I had to leave it two days and then I was supposed to come and tell you what she came to tell me. I told her to stop being silly. I said she was scaring me. She seemed dead serious but I guess I still laughed it off. I didn't want to think she would go through with something like that . . . But then she did it. I wasn't gonna come around, I know we don't see eye to eye, but it played on my mind and it was her dying wish.'

'And you didn't try to talk her out of it?'

'Of course I did! I told her not to go and do anything stupid. But I didn't really think she would anyway, you know?

I spent ages telling her to think about it. I said there had to be another way. Then she asked me what and I guess I couldn't think of nothing. I just said *something will come up*.'

'And then she told you to come and see me?'

'Two days after, she said. She made me give my word. I still didn't think it was serious. No way I thought she was going to do it within a week.'

'What did she say? Why two days?'

'She said it had to be two days. That was the right time, apparently. By that time the cops should have done their bit. When she went, she said, she was going to make sure she had some stuff on her — some stuff for the police to check up on. I think that was the big plan . . . she was giving them enough to start sniffing around Freddie — Benny, too, maybe and then you could walk in there to fill in the blanks and it would all come crashing down around their ears. You're supposed to go see the cops. To tell them what you know. That's what she wanted. I've got some wheels now. I can take you down there. I feel like I should.'

'I'm not going to the police. Why would I? This is ridiculous! You could just be here to stitch me up. Freddie's got wind that someone's been talking — he's looking to take it out on someone.'

Marlie angled her head a little and her eyes narrowed. 'So this is totally out of the blue to you? Only she said she was going to get a message to you . . . just before. She said that you had talked about it before, too. That you wouldn't listen . . . this ringing any bells?'

'No!' Kelly tried to be as strong as she could but she knew her voice was betraying her. Holly *had* talked about something like it before — a long time before. Kelly had dismissed it as just talk, the sort of thing you said when you were feeling desperate.

'Well, okay then. So you'll be just as confused as me. She wasn't making too much sense and it was all a bit rushed. I kept trying to get her to slow down but it was like she was excited, you know what I mean?'

Kelly did. Holly had been exactly the same when she had talked to her about it. She kept quiet as Marlie continued.

'She said about how she was going to take a driver out so they would go and visit the firm. It's one of Freddie's. She said she would have stuff on her that would show what he was up to, with the girls on the cams, with you and her, right down to how he took over the business in the first place. But she said they would have blanks. They would need some more detail and she wanted you to go down there two days after to fill it all in for them. She wanted to give them enough to be interested so they would listen. The last thing she said to me was that she was worried they wouldn't even investigate it, that she wasn't worth their time. That was another reason why she was going to take out a driver with her . . . she didn't think anyone would blink an eye if she just offed herself but they would look for answers if there were two of them. She made me promise I would get you down there.'

'And how are you going to keep that promise?'

'I said that. I asked her and she just laughed, the bitch!' Marlie broke into a smile that seemed like a genuine reaction to a memory. Kelly couldn't see why she wouldn't be telling the truth, couldn't see what angle Marlie could be coming from if she was playing her. And Marlie was well known for always having an angle. She was probably the most streetwise person Kelly had ever met — even more so than Holly. She knew every trick and she never did anything she couldn't benefit from.

'What's in this for you?'

'For me?'

'Why do you care?'

'That ain't fair, Kell. We may have had our disagreements, the lot of us, but I never stopped loving that girl. Not like you, I get that. But people like us don't last long if we don't have each other's backs. She asked me to do something — a dying wish. I didn't know that at the time but that's what it was. You don't fuck about with people's last wishes. That's some proper bad karma right there.'

Kelly rubbed her face. She didn't know what to make of it. 'You should have told me.' But her voice lacked conviction.

'Told you what? That Holly had turned up all excited, talking about how she was gonna die for you? Then you would've fronted up Holly and she would know she couldn't trust me either and then you'd both have the hump with me. Like I said . . . in this game you need friends.'

Kelly took a moment and she sucked in a deep breath.

'This ain't all news to you, is it?' Marlie said.

Kelly let her breath go in a sigh. 'No. She said something like it once. I dismissed it — all of it. Maybe if I hadn't . . .' Her hand moved to cover her mouth and stared down at the floor, too. Then, she felt Marlie's arms wrap around her. Kelly didn't push her away.

'We're not so different you and me,' Marlie said. 'I know that. I think that's why we clash. You must be hurting — I heard about your mum, too. Holly talked about her, said she was the only thing keeping you in the area. I think she thought that when she was gone you could move your life somewhere else, somewhere better. She just kept saying she wanted to get you out of all this, get you free. I honestly don't think I've ever seen love like it.'

Kelly lifted her arms to squeeze Marlie back. 'Set me free? If this is freedom then I don't want it. How can it hurt so much?'

Marlie unwrapped her arms, took hold of Kelly by her shoulders and leaned in with intensity in her eyes.

'I know it hurts. I know you feel let down and abandoned. She will have left bruises, of course she has—'

'Bruises? That isn't it at all. The bruises aren't what worry me, it's when they heal, when they fade . . . what then?'

'You'll always have the time you had. Now you have to move on with your life and that means getting yourself out. Just like Holly wanted for you. I'll take you down the cop shop. Go in there and tell them everything you know. They'll keep you safe — they have to. But not just you, there are other girls. Lots — a lot more than you know. Holly said the cops would already have the addresses — they just don't know it yet. And when you get him nicked, there are people ready to come forward to back you up. But this has to happen first — *you* have to happen first!'

Kelly shook her head. 'The police? Do you know what Freddie will do if he finds out I've talked to them? He's already been here to threaten me. He thinks Holly spoke to them, although I don't know where he got that from. He's got ears everywhere. He'll find out.'

'Holly was digging around. That's what he's heard, I bet. She ain't been to the cops. Like I said, she didn't think they would give her time of day. He will find out quickly when you talk. You have to make sure the police know that. You have to tell them that they need to keep you safe. And they will. I've seen it before. I've seen girls who got assaulted when they were working, badly beaten and by important people — bigwigs and all sorts. These blokes would do anything to protect their reputation, and I mean *anything*. The cops were good, true to their word. You know me and cops . . . there's no love lost. But they did their job. Even when they didn't nail the blokes responsible they still kept those girls safe. You can trust them to do that.'

'So why *didn't* Holly walk in there and tell them what she knew?'

'Don't you see? She *has*, just in her own way. She's got quite the rap sheet. She knows that. Ain't no one there who was gonna take her seriously, not until it was too late. She said that. She was terrified of that. Of going down there and giving them everything and them not taking her serious. It would have put you at risk — her too, but she only ever talked about you. She knows that you're different . . . the cops don't even know who you are. And Freddie's gotten bold, *reckless* if you ask me. His drivers used to pick up druggie girls from broken homes — them that already know the rules about squealing. Now he's recruiting young girls with no police records, no idea of this world at all. Little posh girls living at home with mummy and daddy. It's a big risk, but Freddie's full of himself now. He's got himself convinced that no one will ever talk. And you know why he's after scared little posh girls? They're big earners, plain and simple. Them sad fucks sat at their computer screen with their cock in their hand are nothing but a fucking blur when they see some posh eighteen-year-old white girl totally out of her depth. Maybe even crying in fear wondering what the fuck's going on. Gets them right off and they'll pay whatever you ask them to. The world's a sick place.'

'Sixteen,' Kelly said quietly.

'Sixteen?'

'I met a girl. A new girl. She's sixteen years old and utterly terrified.'

Marlie linked her hands together and lifted them to rest on the back of her head. 'Jesus, Kell! You gotta get in that cop shop. You gotta tell them. This has to stop! Time was, there was rules. Time was, this was a way to earn a good living for those that wanted it — but *grown-ups*, though! Girls old enough to know what they were getting into. These kids, they don't want to be there, do they? I'll run you down.'

'What about you? You can come in with me. You can tell them what you know, too?'

Now it was Marlie who was shaking her head. 'Can't do it. I can't be the solution and the problem at the same time, love. The cops know me, they know what I do. I turn up to talk about sex workers like I'm all high and mighty and they won't hear a word I'm saying. More than that, though, I gotta be looking after those girls. When you go down there today you're gonna cause a stink. It should all go just fine — but say they let Freddie out? Or they don't round up his foot soldiers? They'll leave me and my girls alone. No way they'll think I've got anything to do with it — not for a few days at least. That's why she came to me first. I've done my bit. I gave her some stuff from the house and I came here today. And besides, the only person with a longer rap sheet than Holly round here is me. I wouldn't get through the door, love. You, you're different. We all know it — that's probably why I never liked you! You got no history with the cops. Holly said they don't even know you exist. You walk in there talking nice like you do and you tell them a story, they'll sit and listen. I'll take you down. I'll drop you near, but then I gotta get out of there. But when the time is right, when you got that piece of shit on the floor, we'll all be there to twist the knife.'

Kelly stepped away. There was so much to take in, so much to consider. 'I can't . . .' she said, finally. 'Libby, the girl from last night . . . I'm meeting her tonight for work. I need to get her safe first. If I don't turn up it'll just be her . . . and he might already have a sniff that I've gone to the police . . . Other than a name, I don't know anything else about her to warn her.'

'This is your chance, girl. Tell the cops she's in danger. They'll meet her.'

'There isn't time! Not to be sure!'

'This Libby needs to look after herself. You've been long enough worrying about other people. This is your chance to be free. Holly's given you that. *Fuck!* Holly died for that!'

'It's so much. Too much! It's not fair. Holly should have talked to me before she decided the next step in my life. Now there's all this pressure . . .'

'The cops, they can take that all away. Put it on them to keep you safe — that's what they do. This ain't for you to bear. I think she thought this would be easy, that you would walk in there and they would take over. It's not like that, I can see that, but they *will* listen. That should be all you need.'

'I need time to get my head sorted — to get it all straight in my mind. Then I'll go and see them. I'll tell them what I know. I'll ask them to get me safe. But I can't go now. I need to work today. I need to talk to Libby — she's just a kid. I'll need to take her with me. She's the little posh kid you were talking about — they'll listen to her, too! I have to get her first — I can't just abandon her. Holly wouldn't want that. She never abandoned me. I never wanted to be responsible for anyone else . . .'

'Nor did Holly. I guess she took you under her wing, right? I know there was more to it with you — I know you gave it all back — but she took a punt. In this game, caring for other people can get you hurt. It got her killed.'

'She made that choice!' Kelly snapped. She backed down immediately.

So did Marlie. 'You're right, love. I'm sorry. That came out all wrong. This is your last chance, though. I gotta get going. I've been here too long already.'

'I *will* go. But after. I need to turn up today and I need to get everything straight. Then I'll go.'

Marlie locked onto her as if satisfying herself that there was no chance of changing her mind. 'Tomorrow, then.' Marlie wrapped Kelly back up in a hug and whispered into her ear. 'Holly's looking down on us right now. Your ma, too. And they're both proper proud!'

Kelly's eyes filled with tears. She embraced the hug to the point she was disappointed when Marlie pulled away and spun for the door. She didn't slow or look back this time. The closing door brought the silence back but it seemed different: thick, like a blanket wrapped around her too tightly. She cast a glance at her mother's empty bed, the duvet still pulled back from where they had lifted out her lifeless body. Her head swam. She had to get out of there. She moved to the door. Her mother's coat still hung on a peg on the wall. Its scent was disturbed as she wrenched the front door open — her mother's perfume. It stopped her dead. She reached out for the sleeve and pushed it to her face, rubbing it against her cheek as she inhaled gently. She pulled it right off the peg and hurriedly slipped it on. She turned back for her car keys. They were on the side, and she fixed on them, not wanting or daring to lift her gaze to anything else.

CHAPTER 16

Maddie swept past the untidy queue to make straight for the back of the coffee shop. It was established as her usual haunt by now, a place she had visited countless times as a way of stepping away from the police station and the intensity of investigations, to take a moment to breathe. Today however, she could do without it. She had finally given the Justin Harnett case file some attention but that had only served to remind her of just how much work was required. But today's meeting was not one she felt she could postpone. It was not for her. Today was about Rhiannon Davies.

Rhiannon was still working CID, despite Maddie making a couple of attempts to poach her for Major Crime. She'd come close, too, but Rhiannon had suffered a recent setback when she was seriously injured in the line of duty. Maddie had blamed herself, but the fallout had been a crisis in confidence for both women. They had met up fairly regularly almost since Maddie's move to the force but had become very aware that the tone of the meetings had changed since that incident. Where previously they had been chatty, jovial and a welcome break from the day-to-day running of investigations, they could now be awkward and unnatural, with both parties careful over their words.

Maddie sat down opposite Rhiannon, who leaned back in greeting.

'Hey!'

'Hey yourself. Thanks for getting them in.' Maddie gestured at the coffee waiting on the table.

'No problem. I think it was my round anyway.'

'Well, this was my idea, so that probably means I should be buying.'

'You can get the next ones.'

'Deal.' Maddie leant on her elbows and tried to work out where to start. It never used to be like this. Rhiannon had been the first person she had spent any time with when she had first arrived in Lennockshire. For Maddie, it had been a new force, a totally different role and in circumstances where she couldn't help but feel sorry for herself. Rhiannon had managed to make it better almost instantly. Her enthusiasm was contagious and she had pulled Maddie along with her, rekindling her passion for policing and reminding her what she was there for — catching bad guys.

Now their exchanges were staged and clumsy. Maddie fidgeted with a sugar sachet, then watched the swirl as she stirred it in.

'So . . . this *was* your idea. Which means you have to talk!' Rhiannon chuckled but it sounded forced.

'I guess I just wanted a catch-up. It's been a week or so, you know. I was just wondering how you were?'

'Fine. Nothing's really changed since last week.' Her face hardened a little.

'You know, this is getting ridiculous.'

'What is?'

'This. Us two. Meeting up time after time and just sitting opposite each other. It's like we've fallen out!'

'Well, we haven't. I think you fell out with yourself.'

Maddie leaned back, looking down to where the liquid in her coffee was starting to settle. 'You might be right. What else do you think?' Rhiannon eyed her with a little caution, enough that Maddie felt she needed to prompt her. 'And you can be as honest as you want. Off the record, see.'

Rhiannon shrugged. 'You don't like yourself very much sometimes. You blamed yourself for what happened to me — maybe you still do. It's like every time you see me, I'm some sort of reminder of some weakness or a failing and it means you can barely talk to me.'

'Okay, then. And what about you? How come you can't talk to me?'

'I did. I told you this wasn't your fault. I told you that in hospital straight after. You came for me — you and DI Blaker. I've never been so happy to see two people in all my life!' This time her smile was more genuine.

'Harry carried me for that whole investigation — that's what it felt like, anyway. I *do* blame myself. I try not to work with Harry as much anymore. I feel like he knows it — he must do. I don't know if he has confidence in me and I'd thought he was just starting to get some.'

'Have you said that to him? Asked him if that's how he feels?'

'No. He would spare me that anyway, even if it *was* how he was feeling.'

'Harry Blaker? He doesn't spare anyone anything!'

'I might have agreed with you a couple of months ago, weeks even. But I saw some vulnerability in Harry. It was nothing to do with the job — his home life crept in a little. I think if he were to have a go at me he would have to face up to his own issues.'

'So, there you are . . . we're all vulnerable. We all have good days and bad days and I don't think anyone could beat you up as hard as you are beating yourself up anyway. I read all the reports, all the evidence when it was prepped for court, and I still don't see what it is that you did so wrong?'

'I wasn't careful enough. I underestimated what we were dealing with and it nearly got you killed.'

'Then we both did.'

'I should have known better.'

'Fine, then. You can get the next two rounds in! But then we're back to normal, okay? Because I can't keep doing this.'

'This?'

'Turning up for these catch-ups and then sitting making shitty small talk just because you feel guilty. And now every time I go out on enquiries, I have some uniform chaperone stood next to me with his arms crossed. It can get in the way. Just yesterday I had to go out and speak to a sixteen-year-old girl who's definitely had a night out gone wrong and I had to make him wait at the bottom of the stairs. No way would she have spoken to me otherwise! I'm fine. I'm not so fragile that I need a bodyguard. I survived, don't forget!'

Maddie held her palms out. 'Okay, I get it! Do you feel better now?'

'I do, actually. Now, maybe we can go back to talking about nothing much and me taking the mick out of you about Vince. What's the latest with him anyway?'

'Latest? What do you mean *latest*?'

'Is he still endlessly pursuing you? I still say he'll wear you down one day.'

'I hear he has a girlfriend, actually. Someone out there has been naïve enough to let that man into their life.'

Rhiannon leaned forward and she dipped her head as if to force Maddie to make eye contact.

'What?' Maddie said.

'Are you okay with that? Because I think that's jealousy I hear . . .'

Maddie giggled. 'You know, I think I preferred the shitty small-talk phase!' She laughed fully now, Rhiannon too.

'It is jealousy, then?'

'I guess it must be. My last chance for happiness, all gone.'

'I'm not convinced he'll ever stop worshipping you.'

'We shall see.' Maddie picked up her coffee cup. She felt lighter. 'Work's okay, then? What's the story with this girl with the bad night out?'

'You tell me. She didn't! We get a seventeen-year-old lad found beaten unconscious in the small hours — his face was, like, twice the size it should be. I make a few enquiries and find out he was out with his girlfriend, Libby Battle. Great name, eh? So I go round to see our Libby and she's not so keen to tell me how her boyfriend was nearly beaten to death. She says he dropped her home in a taxi and he was just fine, but she wasn't telling me everything.'

'Her name's Libby?'

'Yeah.'

'I had a call from Custody this morning! There was a young girl at the bat phone. She said she'd spoken to a female officer about an assault and she wanted to talk to her again. She said her name was Libby.'

Rhiannon straightened up. 'When was this?'

'Early . . . like six a.m. early. I went down to have a look but she'd already left.'

'So maybe she wants to talk to me after all.'

'Maybe she does.'

Rhiannon glanced at her watch. 'I should . . .'

'I know. Go and see this Libby. Do you want company? And I'm not a bodyguard or a chaperone or anything — I'm just interested, if I'm honest.'

'Don't you have the car over the cliff to investigate?'

'Well yeah, but there's not much I can do this morning. In fact, Harry would have me write it off at this point if he had his way. Meaning it's either come out with you or go back to my desk and build a pointless case file that Harry keeps getting hassled about.'

'I imagine that hassle rolls downhill, though? Are you sure you're not better off going and getting that file done?'

'I would absolutely be better off. But I don't want Harry to think that I'm going to be doing what I'm told all of a sudden.'

'No, you need to keep him in his place. Do you not want to write this cliff thing off? Personally, I'm always happy to get rid of a case.'

'Me too if it's a waste of time — and Harry clearly thinks it is.'

'But you don't?'

'Actually, I'm at the point now where I think it probably is. I just don't want Harry to be right just yet. All that I have found out seems to point back towards some local criminal. Freddie Rickman — you know him?'

'No?'

'Me neither. He seems to be one of these people that anyone who has worked here for any length of time knows is up to no good but nothing ever sticks. There doesn't seem to be much of an appetite to find something that does, either.'

'But you want to?'

'I don't like him.'

'Did he like you?'

'I'm sure he would if he met me! It's just his reputation I don't like. Maybe I'm too fixed on finding something that isn't there. Like I said before, I'm not sure Harry is in the mood to give me too much freedom at the moment — certainly not enough to follow up on a hunch.'

'So you haven't even met this bloke yet and you've got it in for him?'

'I know. I want to. Maybe I'm being unfair. He might be a lovely fella.'

'Just misunderstood?'

'Exactly!' Both women laughed. Maddie dipped her head, suddenly aware of her surroundings. 'I might go and see some sex workers. There's not much to know about our taxi driver and I think we have all we're going to get about him. I've got very little on the female victim. Seems like a reasonable line of enquiry before I write it off.'

'And you know where to find sex workers, do you?'

'Nope. But there were some addresses in a book she had when she died. Seems like a good place to start.'

'Addresses? Is that all?'

'Pretty much.'

'And what do we know about them? From police systems, I mean.'

'Nothing recent. Land registry shows that they're all owned by one person. Can you guess who?'

'Give me a clue?'

'Okay . . . It's someone I'm not particularly keen on despite never meeting . . . someone who owns twelve properties and nothing is known about how he had the income to buy them . . .'

'And you're just going to turn up and knock the doors?'

'I was going to do a few. There's one building in particular that seems to have a few places he owns. Looks like there's a caretaker there who has called the police a few times and lives on the top floor. I thought I'd speak to him at least. There's not much else I can do. Harry's already convinced himself that they're just rooms for this Freddie's working girls to use.'

'But you're not?'

Maddie shrugged. 'I think he's probably right. It's the only thing that really makes any sense. But Holly Maguire can't tell me that for sure and I think I owe it to her to try and get a few more answers, seeing as how she seemed determined to take them to her grave.'

'Grim thought.'

'It is. Anyway, I planned that for early afternoon, as I don't reckon those places are in use much in the morning, so it means I have the time to come out and meet your Libby Battle.'

'Just so we're clear, no crossing your arms to accentuate your muscles and no steely looks. You're not a bodyguard.'

'Fine. Like I need to accentuate these!' Maddie gurned as she tensed both her arms then stood up. Rhiannon looked around, aware that she might be attracting attention. They both roared with laughter.

* * *

Kelly finally made it to the fourth floor. Her foot found the thin carpet of the corridor and she stopped to catch her breath. The lift was stopped on this level, the doors hanging clumsily open, one wider than the other with the *OUT OF ORDER* sign written in bold as if to mock her. She could barely remember a time when it had worked. She pushed through a heavy fire door that led back out into the open air. From here a length of walkway clung to the side of the building with identical front doors lined up on the left at equal distances from each other. On the right was a concrete wall at hip height that was then topped with a mesh of steel, which filled the space up to the concrete ceiling. Overall, the impression was of an oppressive grey rat-run — a cage for humans.

She had been planning on moving from the moment she had been given the place to live in. It was a council property; she had no valid reason to request a change so leaving would mean a private rent. She could afford it — a much nicer place, too — but for that she would need to prove her income, provide references and show bank statements for at least three months from a permanent employer. As long as she was being paid £500 a week in cash that was left on a chair in a dingy flat for her part in conducting adult performances in front of a live webcam, that was going to be a challenge. And even if she could secure a place, the monthly rent demands would serve to trap her tighter into her current employment. She and Holly had talked about saving up for a place together, about getting regular jobs to fund it. They would have had to have taken minimum wage jobs, and their pooled income would have been poor, they would have struggled to pay the rent and find extra for the odd night out. But that was just the sort of struggle couples in love were supposed to have, the sort of struggles that really didn't matter, because all you needed was each other.

It was something they had just kept putting off. Then Holly had suddenly announced that she had given her flat up and they were splitting up at the same time. She had said it didn't matter, that Kelly was at her mum's place a lot of the time anyway and still had her own place to go back to when she couldn't stay with her mum anymore. Kelly couldn't understand where it was all coming from, why they were splitting up. As far as she was concerned they had never been happier. Then Holly had repeated the same old line: that she wanted her to be *free*. Kelly had been so angry. She just couldn't understand where it was all coming from. She went to Holly's flat and it was as she had said: empty. A wooden pole was hammered into the small front garden announcing it was *TO LET*. Kelly had ripped it out in frustration, her eyes laden with tears, her hand stinging from a fresh splinter. She had never been so confused, so desperate, and it had all come from nowhere. With her mother's condition worsening, it felt like everything she loved was slipping away. She had tried calling, tried finding her, too, but she knew Holly wouldn't be found if she didn't want to be. She just wanted to know why — some sort of explanation.

She hadn't expected that it might come from Marlie Towers, two days after Holly's death.

Kelly had recovered enough from climbing the stairs to move forward but still she hesitated. She hadn't been here for around a month and even then it had just been a brief visit to get some more clothes to take back to her mother's. It took just a few steps along the walkway to form the impression that there was something different about her front door. It looked tired as usual and had the black scuffs from where her neighbour regularly dragged the handles of his bicycle against it, but the handle was hanging at an odd angle. It felt loose in her hand. The door was broken and it pushed in immediately. The sound of the creaking hinges was familiar, as was the musty smell that she couldn't get rid of, no matter what she did. Now the door's surround was revealed, she saw tool marks below the lock. A strip of wood yawned away as if it had been dug out with a chisel. The locking bolt on the door jutted out. She stepped in. The kitchen was to her right, her bedroom straight ahead. The living room was behind it, accessed via the kitchen, and on the other side of the small flat. The kitchen was untidy. She hadn't left it like that.

Kelly moved in, holding her breath. There was a tap at the window that caused her to catch her breath. Her heart was still thumping as she realised it was a broken blind, hanging in the breeze. She moved cautiously through the flat, taking in each room as she went. Drawers were pulled open, cupboards too, her bed upended. But there was no one there now. She made it back to the kitchen and her body slumped. A long breath came with it. She could see paperwork strewn all over the kitchen benches, laid out like as if it was flattened down, in a hurry to be read. She paced back through to her bedroom. She had some jewellery from her nan in the drawer at the bottom of a wardrobe. It was nothing special but the only thing of any value. The wardrobe door was open, the drawer, too. Her jewellery was still there.

She moved to her bedside cabinet. The top drawer had a couple of old mobile phones and an electronic tablet. They were all still in there. Nothing was missing. An opportunistic burglar would have taken the electronics, the jewellery, and the television that still sat on the low table in the living area. It would have only fetched someone a few quid on the black market but it would be enough to score a thief a hit of their drug of choice. This wasn't a burglary; this was someone looking for something. She couldn't think straight enough to even consider what. She was starting to panic, the crushing feeling on her chest and the shallow breathing that had started at her mother's house was back in spades. She had to get out. She didn't know where else to go, this was the only other place she thought she might be able to feel safe. She was back to searching the surfaces and furniture, seeing what she might need to take. She didn't want to have to come back.

Her anxiety had now increased to where it was all encompassing. It threatened to take her off her feet and she was genuinely scared that if she went down, she wouldn't be able to get up again. She didn't feel like she could go back to her mum's; it would surely prompt the same reaction. She knew where she could go. It was the only place she could think of, the only place where she might be able to feel a little closer to Holly — a little closer to being together again and feeling Holly's strength.

She stepped to the cupboard under the kitchen sink. Two bottles of vodka were right where she had left them, one unopened, the other half full. She scooped up the full one. When she stepped out of the door she pulled it closed. She didn't bother checking if it had locked shut; there was no point.

She had no intention of coming back.

CHAPTER 17

The weather was perfect. The sea lay out in front of her in a welcoming blanket of blue that sparkled brighter the further it reached out into the distance. The industrial landscape of Calais was clear today and the stretch of water separating the UK from mainland Europe seemed narrower as a result.

Kelly heard her taxi pull away. She pulled her mum's coat tighter around her and closed her eyes. Her heightened senses picked out a light breeze that pushed her gently in the back and ran across her fingertips. The clifftop was scented with cut grass and the sun was warm on her face. The calm, picture-perfect scenery was in stark contrast to her churning stomach, her short breaths and a constant battle to control her panic.

When she opened her eyes, she was on the edge of a flat piece of lawn and her feet trailed through the loose layer of trimmed grass as she moved towards the edge. There were benches ahead: one off to the right and one off to the left. She pulled the bottle of vodka out of her bag and walked straight down the middle, following the path she reckoned Holly had taken just a few days before. She could see a divot ahead, a clump of scuffed earth that must have marked the exact point where the car left the cliff. She made directly for it.

The breeze was stronger at the edge. She looked down at her feet and lined her toes up to finish where the land did. The scarring to the clifftop was more extensive here, where a chunk of cliff had been scraped and dragged away. The fresh white surface was so bright in the sunlight that she had to narrow her eyes to see it. She could see down to the bottom, down to a layer of thick brambles. From this height it looked like a brown carpet with glints of white poking through. There were no signs of any disturbance. It was as if the car and its occupants had just been swallowed up by the earth, leaving nothing.

She unscrewed the bottle and took a swig as deep as she could, until she balked at the taste and snatched her head forward where some dribbled out of her mouth and over the edge. She watched it separate into droplets as it was swept away by the breeze. She bared her teeth then took another long swig. This time she gagged. Her hands fell to her sides and she could feel the weight of the bottle pulling her down on one side. Her eyes fell back to her feet and she edged them forward so there was clear daylight under her toes. She rocked all her weight backwards onto her heels. Already, she could feel she was off balance. All she needed to do was shift her weight forwards and she would topple. Then this pain would end, this pressure, this constant nagging anxiety that seemed to have no antidote. And maybe they would be together again.

She closed her eyes to the warmth of the sun on her face. Now she just needed to shift her weight.

'It's a good place to come and think, up here.'

Kelly flung her eyes open, her weight was still on her heels. She edged back slightly, enough so she could turn towards the voice. An elderly lady smiled at her. She held a small dog like someone might hold a baby, its eyes peered out at her through a tangle of white fur, its nose a constant twitch.

'I don't want to think anymore.' Her own voice seemed to prompt her tears, which started to fall.

'I get that. It's hard isn't it? Life, I mean. I've seen other people come here before and they've said the same. Some people didn't make it away. That's okay, people make their choices but they all have had a cup of coffee with me first. Would you mind?' The woman moved her hand out from under the dog's head and Kelly could see she was clutching at a long, silver flask. She put the dog gently on the floor. It was on a short lead but it didn't pull against it. The lid of the flask doubled as a cup. She poured some out.

'Coffee?' Kelly almost chuckled. It just seemed so ridiculous. All of it. That she was here, that she was now totally alone, that she was standing on the edge with a sudden intention of these being her final moments and now some old woman with a dog was offering her coffee from a thermos.

'Oh, it's not so silly. Think of the things that have been done over a cup of coffee, conversations had, good decisions made. And then think of all the silly snap decisions we've made in our lives and how they might have turned out . . . how they might have been better if we had just taken the time to think about them over a cup of coffee. It's a failing of people, in my view. We never pause at the right places.'

'Or we pause too much,' Kelly whispered.

'The view from the bench there is quite beautiful.' The woman gestured towards the shuffling sea.

'The last thing I want is time to think.'

'Then use it to reflect. On all that you have, all that you've seen. If you're here to step off that edge then you have all the time in the world. Some things are too important to rush.' She sat on the bench with the dog on her lap and gestured with the steaming lid. 'Please, join me for a cup of coffee. Then I'll leave you alone. I don't want to see it. Please don't make me.'

'I'm not making you do anything! You can walk away — forget about me.'

'Is that what happened? Is that why you are here? Maybe it is time someone refused to. It has two sugars. I find coffee can be quite bitter otherwise.'

Kelly turned back to face out over the view. Her eyes dropped back to her feet. She was still close enough to be able to see over, to see the slipped chalk boulders mingling with the undergrowth. The breeze ruffled her hair against her face. A strand got stuck in her tears. She wiped it away. 'I'm sorry,' she breathed. She moved a little, enough to have to shift her weight again so she was rocked back on her heels. She turned back to the woman. 'You should look away.'

'Can't do that. I wish I could. I've seen it before and it haunts me every day. I always wonder if I could have done more but maybe some people just make a choice to hurt themselves. But please, don't hurt *me*. Don't make me watch it again. Have a coffee — over here on the bench and then I'll leave you to have a private moment. It's up to you what you do with it.'

Kelly scrunched her eyes shut. She stepped back. The breeze still moved her hair across her face. She focused on the sensation as it tickled her mouth and neck. When she opened her eyes and walked towards the bench she felt unsteady. She didn't think it was the vodka. Her eyes fell to the bottle that she still clung to in her right hand. She threw it to the grass and it glugged as it emptied. The woman held up the cup. Kelly took it and perched on the edge of the seat. She was turned away from the woman; she felt a rush of shame. She took a swig of the coffee. It was hot as hell and there was a strong aftertaste. 'Did you put something in this?'

'Of course I did! That's good whisky. I figured I might end up needing it.'

Kelly shook her head. She felt the dog nuzzle at her hand, it pushed its head under and she looked down to see just a button nose protruding. 'Hey,' she said.

'She likes you. She doesn't like many people.'

'Sounds like a sensible dog.'

'Oh she is. She doesn't like men in particular and I didn't even train that into her!' The woman chuckled. Kelly turned to the sound of pouring liquid. The woman had produced another plastic cup from somewhere and now filled it with hot coffee. 'It's a little early for this, really, but I suppose you won't be telling anyone now, will you?'

'Not likely.' Kelly managed a weak smile.

'What's your name? I'm Margaret.'

'Kelly.'

'Kelly . . . So what brings you here, Kelly? I'm always interested. The hardest thing about seeing this are the questions that are left. I hope you don't mind.'

'What brings me here? Now that's a question. I guess I've got nothing to keep me away. I lost it right here. I thought if I came here I could be a little closer to her.'

'Her?'

'My girlfriend.' She looked at the woman intently now. 'It's okay, you can disregard that if it makes you uncomfortable. I get it all the time.'

'Uncomfortable?'

'My mum . . . her friends . . . my nan, before she went . . . they all used to get uncomfortable. They never really wanted to hear it. You can't be in love with another woman — it's just a phase. Apparently. I'm *curious*. I'll *grow out of it*. That was all I used to hear. But, my God did I love her . . .' The emotion welled up in her again. She felt her mouth twitch but she managed to catch it in time.

'Doesn't make me uncomfortable in the slightest. The only thing that ever made me truly happy was being in love and being loved back. A man and a woman don't have exclusive rights to that. Not to shared happiness. No one does. I've never known pain like it when he left but, now that I'm a little calmer about the whole thing, I know I wouldn't change it. I had twenty years of happiness.'

'He left?'

'He did. I don't know what came over him. A case of the grass being greener, I think. But he didn't last long after.'

'Didn't last long?'

'Heart attack. I still don't know how to feel about it. He was everything, and we were together a long time. You get so intertwined in someone else it's like there are no joins anymore, so coming apart isn't possible without taking a lot of you with it.'

'I know exactly what you mean . . .' Kelly looked back out over the view. 'I feel like half of me is already over that edge. She took it with me when she went.'

'In a car?'

'Yes.' Kelly turned to the woman. 'You know about it?'

'The news. They're saying there was a man and a woman inside. She was your girlfriend?'

'She was.'

'I'm sorry. It must be a terrible time. It always is for those that are left.'

'It was because of me. That's why she did it. She thought she could set me free . . .'

'And did she?'

'I don't know what free is anymore but no. She started something, but I have to go the police. I have to tell them the rest. I have to tell them why she did it. That's what she meant.'

'And if you don't?'

Kelly turned back to the horizon. 'Then no one will know.'

'It's a waste of a life, when someone decides to take it for themselves. Always. If there's something you can do to make it less of a waste . . .'

'I can't. I just can't . . .'

'Not up here you can't. I can give you a lift — to the police station, I mean. If that's where you need to go?'

Kelly's mind had started to wander; the word 'police' snapped her back into focus. 'No, thank you. I really can't go . . . not now. I would have to talk to someone first.'

'Home, then? Or I can run you somewhere else?'

'No. I think I'll walk. I need to clear my head.' As she stood up, Kelly had to steady herself. She took one last glance towards the raised divot and the scarred cliff face. 'Thank you. For the coffee, I mean. You're very kind.' Kelly noticed the bottle she had discarded. She picked it up. There were still a few swigs left.

'I can take that. My bin will be closer.' The woman nodded encouragement.

Kelly tipped the rest of the vodka out then stuffed the bottle in her bag. 'I don't drink. Not anymore. The last time . . . something terrible happened. So I kept it, to remind me why I shouldn't drink I guess this is the last one now.'

'Ah, then you *should* keep it.'

'Thank you. Again.' Kelly started back across the grass towards the road.

'You're welcome!' the woman called out after her. 'Good luck!'

Kelly didn't turn back. The words registered but she was already lost in her thoughts.

CHAPTER 18

Maddie was aware that she had made for the front door first. When she stopped herself she already had her fist in the air to knock. She turned to a smiling Rhiannon and shrugged.

'Sorry. Force of habit! Your investigation.'

Rhiannon stepped past her and knocked the door. Wendy Battle opened it almost before she had time to remove her knuckles from the glass.

'Oh!' Rhiannon stepped back. 'Mrs Battle . . . are you just on your way out?'

'Do you have news? About my Elizabeth?'

'News?' Maddie could see that Rhiannon was caught out. The woman could see it too.

'You don't even know?'

'Know? I'm sorry, Mrs Battle, I think she might have come to see me this morning. At the police station—'

'She's missing! I called it in. Twenty minutes ago. They told me she wasn't missing yet, that I should call back later. But I still assumed that was why you were here?'

'Ah, okay. That call would have gone through to our control centre who would speak with my uniform colleagues first. I wasn't aware. But maybe I can take the details on their behalf?'

'Take details? They said they wouldn't do anything until she had been missing at least forty-eight hours! As soon as I mentioned that we had been arguing recently, they weren't interested. But you should be out looking for her, you all should . . .'

'I know they have their guidelines. Sometimes people aren't missing. They're just getting some space. When—'

'She's missing! A mother knows. She's not been right for the last few days — not since she came back on Saturday night. And she got worse after you came around yesterday. What *is* going on?'

Rhiannon glanced over to Maddie. 'Can we come in, Mrs Battle?' Maddie said. When the woman turned to her, she felt she should introduce herself. 'I'm Detective Sergeant Maddie Ives. I work with Rhiannon. You called the police because you need help, so let us help you. We just need some information first.' The woman still hesitated, but only for a moment. She moved back and the door swung open. Maddie gestured for Rhiannon to step in first.

They moved through to a lounge area. Wendy Battle stood in the middle. She made no attempt to sit or to invite the officers to do so. She was a picture of anxiety, made worse perhaps by her already frail build. Her posture was poor and she looked a little hunched. She kept shifting her hands from holding them in front of her, to her hips and then dropping them to her sides. She eventually settled on holding them across her front.

Rhiannon started. 'Okay . . . so Libby is missing?'

'*Elizabeth.* Yes, she wasn't in her room this morning when I got up. I'm always up early. I sleep light — if at all. I always take her in a tea when I hear her moving around, but this morning I checked on her because she still seemed so upset last night. She wasn't there!' She sniffed and dipped her head further forward.

'Have you tried phoning her?'

'Of course I have!' Her head snapped back, her tone suddenly short. Then she seemed to check herself. 'The phone she gave you . . .'

'It's okay, I know,' Rhiannon cut in. 'It's an old one. Maybe two years, at least. I have it here to give back. We wasted a few hours of police time downloading that. I intended on talking to Lib . . . *Elizabeth* about that.'

'I don't know what's got into her recently. I knew when she threw it to you that it was an old one. I didn't know what to say.'

'It's no problem. Really. So her phone — her *current* one — did it connect at all? Did it ring out? What happened?' Rhiannon's tone had softened. Maddie found herself biting her tongue, desperate to jump in. She would only have asked the same questions.

'It's switched off. I've never known her to have her phone off. Once she ran out of battery and it was like the world was coming to an end. She's sixteen — you know what they're like. The phone is their only window to the world these days, it seems.' Wendy sagged before them.

'Maybe we could sit?' Maddie couldn't keep quiet any longer. She knew the value of something simple like sitting down. It could change the whole mind-set of a person. Wendy Battle looked relieved to flop into the nearest seat. Both detectives followed her lead but they sat straighter, perched on the edge.

'Is this out of character?' Maddie asked.

Wendy waved her hand. 'Six months ago, definitely. Six weeks ago even. They change so quickly, you know? I can't keep up with it. Sometimes I convince myself that I can remember being sixteen, that I remember what it was like and maybe understand what is going on, but I'm just kidding myself. I have no idea! They change so quickly . . .' She seemed to run out of steam.

'Where do you think she would go?'

'I don't know. I really don't. All of her close friends, the people she spends some time with, I've spoken to and they haven't even heard from her. They sounded quite concerned. That was what prompted me to call it in. At first I thought with the way she had been acting that she had gone round a friend's house without telling me. She lied about Saturday night, after all. I didn't know where she was or who she was with then. But I've called everyone that I know of.'

'Have you checked with the hospital? To see if she has visited her boyfriend?'

'Boyfriend!' She shook her head. 'You mean the one I only just discovered existed? No. I mean, I don't even know his name.'

'Okay, well, that's something we can do straight away.'

'I didn't even think of that. I guess she could be by his bedside, couldn't she? That would make sense!' She was suddenly animated, her whole demeanour changing in front of them like they had already found her daughter. Maddie wasn't so sure. Rhiannon took her phone out and excused herself to step away and make the call. Wendy's eyes followed her. Maddie was drawn to the same door. A young boy had entered. He was wearing a blue dressing gown that had seen better days and furry slippers. His cheeks were flushed and his breathing loud as if through a blocked nose. Maddie guessed he was around twelve years old.

'Not now, Thomas,' Wendy sighed.

'Did you find Libby yet?' the boy said.

'Not now!'

'Mrs Battle, do you mind?' Maddie turned to the boy. 'Is Libby your sister?'

'Elizabeth!' Wendy snapped, then immediately backed down. 'Sorry, I'm fighting a losing battle with that, I guess. Thomas here is off school with a rotten cold. This is the last thing he needs.'

Maddie turned back to Thomas. 'Did your sister speak to you? Before she left the house?'

'She was crying.' Maddie noticed Wendy's head jerk; this was clearly news to her. The boy suddenly looked awkward.

'Do you know why?' Maddie said.

'Why didn't you say anything to me?' Wendy snapped.

'Mrs Battle, do you mind if we let him speak? He might know something important.' Maddie again addressed the boy directly. 'It's okay. Your mum's very worried. We all are. Do you know anything that might help? Why was she crying?'

'I don't know. Last night I wanted to use the toilet and I didn't want to come downstairs. The upstairs toilet is supposed to be for both of us. She was in the shower. She's always in there for ages but she was in there for like an hour. She wouldn't even answer. I mean, why should I go downstairs?'

'What happened then?'

'I opened the door. The shower was on. I could hear it. It had been running for ages. The room was all steamed up and she was still in there.'

'In the shower?'

'Yeah. I went in. I thought she would be angry. She gets really angry. But she wouldn't answer so I just went in there. She was sitting in the shower — just sitting down. I didn't look or anything!'

'It's okay. Did she talk to you?'

'She was crying. She didn't even shout at me. I thought she would.'

'What *did* she do?'

'I only opened the curtain. I put it straight back. She was all curled up anyway. She turned the shower off and she said she was sorry. She said she was just coming out. I asked her why she was crying and she said she couldn't talk to anyone about it. I said to talk to mum, but she said "even mum". I gave her a towel then I went back to my room. I heard her door go a little bit later so I thought she was back in her room.'

'She can talk to me about anything!' Wendy spat.

'Did you see her again?' Maddie said to Thomas. He shook his head. 'What time was that do you think?'

'After ten? It was late. I couldn't sleep 'cause my nose is all blocked up.'

'Okay. Thanks for that. Where do *you* think she is?'

Thomas shrugged and looked to his mum.

'He wouldn't know any more than me. Less, even.'

'She's a teenager, Mrs Battle. You would be surprised how little they share with the parents sometimes. All teenagers, that is. I wouldn't take it personally. But was she behaving like this before Saturday?'

'Not this badly. She's changing fast, like I said. But just disappearing like this? The Libby I thought I knew would never do that.'

'She's not been to the hospital as far as anyone knows.' Rhiannon stepped back into the room and took her seat next to Maddie. 'She hasn't made contact with James's family either. Apparently she sometimes messages his mother but there's been nothing since Saturday. The mother assumes she has been ignoring her and thinks she knows more about what went on.'

Wendy had her hand to her mouth. Her eyes were fixed wide and her focus seemed to flick between the two detectives. 'So where is she? My Elizabeth?'

Maddie was suddenly aware of her phone ringing. It was on silent but the noise of the vibrations was enough to drop all eyes to her pocket. She left Wendy's questions hanging in the air as she gestured at her phone and moved out into the hallway. It didn't matter who was left to speak with Wendy anyway — they had no answers for her right now.

The call was on her personal phone, and it was an anonymous number.

'Hello?' she said. Libby's brother came past her to go back up the stairs. He was carrying a plate of biscuits and he grinned like maybe he shouldn't be. Maddie smiled back.

'Mads.' Just one word. But it was enough. Her instant recognition was accompanied by a wave of emotion. She reached for the banister and swivelled to a sit on the bottom step. 'This a good time?' That voice again. She was going to have to reply, but she didn't know if she could.

'Adam?' she managed.

The last time she had spoken with Adam Yarwood he had been leaving her flat as her lover. Her secret lover. It had to be secret; he was so closely associated with an organised crime group based in the North West of the country that he had once been the target of an undercover policing operation. Maddie had been tasked with getting close to him, something she had taken a little too far.

When he last left her flat he was supposed to be taking her out to dinner later that night. She didn't know where. She never knew much where he was concerned. They had never made their reservation. From what she could piece together, Adam had been set upon by a number of angry men with baseball bats. The reason given was a dispute over a plastering contract but she had never been able to confirm that either, and she had come to accept that she might never find out what had happened. Adam suffered terrible head injuries and none of the medical staff had given out much information about his condition. She had tried to stay in the loop, find out what was going on through casual conversations with her colleagues in Greater Manchester about who was still active in running the drug scene up there. But it had been useless. It seemed that the Yarwoods had quickly been replaced not long after Adam sustained his injury. His brother had been the main player and he had fled to Spain to try and start again. He might have done, for all Maddie knew, but certainly his grip on the Greater Manchester drug scene was relinquished and, with it, any interest in the family. She had managed to find out that Adam was back at the family home and being looked after by his mother but that was about it. And now he was calling her direct.

'You remember, then?' he said.

Maddie let out a sound as she released her breath in a rush. She looked around, suddenly aware of her surroundings. She could hear Rhiannon's voice from the next room. It was raised and cheery where she was saying goodbye. She would be out in a moment.

'I can't talk.' Maddie got back to her feet. She paced a little then turned back, suddenly unsure what to do with herself.

'What now or never?' There was a subtle difference in his speech. It wasn't quite slurring, just more deliberate, perhaps — slower.

'Now, just now. Can you call me back?'

'Well you know, I get busy.'

'Midday.' Maddie had to end the call. Rhiannon was in the hall with her now. She pulled the door open and looked closely at Maddie.

'You okay?'

'Yeah!'

Rhiannon called out to say goodbye to Wendy again. Maddie didn't. She dipped her head and stepped out. Rhiannon waited for the door to close behind them before she spoke again. 'Did that call upset you?'

'No! Although it was about a case file, so it probably should have.'

'A case file?'

'Some bits missing. Nothing I can't sort but I am going to need to head back.'

'Well, okay then. Me too — seems I have a missing person report to file.'

CHAPTER 19

Maddie looked up to the sound of Harry crossing the floor. He was holding a small box that rattled as he walked. It looked to her as though he was trying to suppress the noise and conceal the box at the same time. He didn't look over as he slipped into his office. She left it a minute then padded across the floor, arcing out so he wouldn't see her approach. She leaned around his doorway. He was turned away from her, her voice made him jump.

'Are those dog treats?'

'DS Ives!' Her voice had made him jump. 'Can I help you with something?'

'Is there no dog food in the kennels?'

'There is.'

'So those *are* treats?'

Harry shrugged. 'Biscuits. The tins down there are just some bland supermarket's own stuff. I'm sure Jock is more accustomed to a bit of variety.'

'Jock?'

'Jock, yeah. That's his name.'

'I know. You told me. I just didn't realise you were on first name terms.'

'Was there something I can help you with?'

'You like him, don't you?'

Harry huffed. 'Contrary to popular opinion, I am aware of the feelings of others. He's had a bad few days. A box of biscuits is hardly going to fix it, but I was in a shop anyway . . .'

'He's a dog, Harry! Feelings of others?'

'I prefer dogs. They don't answer back.'

'That is true.' Maddie was still grinning.

'*Was* there something I could help you with?'

'No, I was just pleasantly surprised, is all. I thought I would come in and share it with you.'

'Well, thank you for that.'

Maddie turned to leave but was called back by Harry almost immediately.

'Maddie, how are you getting on with your cliff-fall case? Still taking up your time?'

'Some. I'm heading out this afternoon for some enquiries.'

'Enquiries?' Harry frowned.

'The address book we found in the bag. I gave it to Mitch. He's done some work around the contents. It's interesting, actually. All seven properties are registered to the same property company. Then he did voters and guess who lives in them?'

'Go on.'

'No one. According to that database there's no one living in any of them. DWP said the same — at least, no one living there is claiming benefits and they're generally at the lower end of the housing market. So, who do you think owns these seven properties without renting out a single one, thus missing out on thousands a month in income?'

'I'm sure I could guess.'

'Freddie Rickman. He owns the property company. Everywhere I look I see his name. I swear he will be invading my dreams before long.'

'Well, there you are then.'

'What do you mean *there you are, then*?'

'Freddie Rickman, the man linked to running drugs and sex workers — among other things. And a dead prostitute with seven of his addresses in her book. It's a list of addresses where she can take in-calls. It is good intel, so I assume you will be submitting it?'

'Good intel? That's it? So you're saying chuck a report on the system and then move on?'

'I didn't say that. I do appreciate that you need to follow things up, Maddie. I also think that you don't need to be taking too long. There are other things that may be a better use of your time.'

'Something isn't right here. I don't swallow the sex act on top of a cliff gone wrong theory, no pun intended. I mean, how badly wrong does it have to go to drive off a cliff?'

Harry shrugged. 'What else do we have? You can find no associations between the two, no motive for either to be unlawfully killed by an external source and no motivation for one to kill the other. There are two theories that make sense . . . sex act gone wrong or maybe this Holly had something over on the driver. Maybe she was extorting him or threatening him. He presented himself as a deeply religious man with a loving family. It would have been quite a fall from grace if he had been exposed as liaising with a sex worker. There might be a reason to drive her off that cliff in there somewhere. He had his belt off, didn't he?'

'Have you ever seen a taxi driver wearing a seatbelt?'

'No, but his belt was off. Maybe he was supposed to jump out and didn't quite make it in time.'

'I don't like it, Harry. I don't like not knowing.'

'We may never know what was going on in that car that led to it going over that drop.'

'I can't accept that. Surely the detective in you wants to know?'

Harry shrugged again. 'Sometimes you've got to let these things go. They can eat you up. Be choosy with that obsession you have for *knowing*, Maddie.'

'And Freddie Rickman? You think I should just let him go? We know he's a criminal.'

'We do. We have done for a long time, it seems. But there's nothing linking this event to him — or to anyone else. There's no real evidence of foul play, either. Rickman has been arrested five times previously and walked out of custody shortly after each time. I'd sooner not have any involvement in his sixth cameo.'

'The ashtray? It has bits of hair and blood on it. The CSI report says it could have been used as a weapon.'

'I was there when Charley talked about it. She also said that it was loose inside the car when it dropped six hundred feet in a second. It could have struck the passengers as part of the fall. Certainly she couldn't rule it out. That's not a clear pointer for foul play, nor does it link Freddie Rickman in any way. Maybe it even points away . . . When he took over that taxi firm he changed the name. You could argue that the ashtray points to whoever owned it before. And we've nothing that puts Rickman anywhere near that car. Instead we have a witness who saw the whole thing and confirms no one else was even on that clifftop.'

'Maybe it was supposed to point to *how* he took it over?'

'Is there any relevance in that?'

'Not that I've found yet.'

'You're clutching at straws.'

'Two people died, Harry. We owe it to them to know how.'

'We know how.'

'You know what I mean.'

'I know they're dead.'

'What does that mean?'

'What are you trying to achieve here?'

Maddie looked at the clock above where Harry was now sitting in his chair and started moving paperwork around as if his interest was already elsewhere. It was just a few minutes off midday. She wasn't going to convince him of anything while standing there and she certainly didn't have time to try. 'You know what? I was just trying to see if the dog downstairs had softened that exterior of yours. I see he hasn't. Don't worry, I won't be wasting much more time on this.' She felt her face flush as she stepped towards the door.

'This afternoon it is, Maddie. Unless you turn something up. Tell me you understand.' His growl was deeper than usual. He was angry. Maddie didn't care about upsetting him, but she would rather avoid him working against her.

'Understood,' she snapped. She kept moving. Right now she needed to get somewhere where she could talk openly and she didn't want to still be annoyed when she did it. She would put Harry out of her mind — the whole investigation, in fact — if only for a few minutes.

She walked out of the station and took a sharp right. There was a wall that was high enough to conceal her from anyone looking out of the window. She didn't know why she was being so careful; it wasn't like anyone would be able to tell that she was taking a call on her personal phone from a career criminal — and former lover. She ducked behind the wall just the same. 11:59 hours. Her phone went off.

'Hello.'

'Mads!'

The same wave of emotion swept through her. She leaned back against the wall. 'Sorry, I couldn't talk, I was with someone.'

'And now?'

'And now I'm not . . . Jesus, *Adam* . . .'

'I know. It's been a while.'

'How are you?'

'Slower!' Adam chuckled. Maddie laughed with him. 'I'm having speech therapy, would you believe. I forgot everything . . . how to walk . . . how to talk . . . but not you, Mads. I never forgot you.'

Maddie bit down hard. 'Okay then.'

'Okay, then?'

'I came to see you. When you were in hospital. Before your family came down. I managed to blag my way in. They thought I was your sister!'

'I know.'

'You know?'

'I mean, not at the time! And no one else does — don't worry. Someone told me a story about some confusion when they all turned up. The staff and the cops wouldn't let my actual sister in for quite a while. They ran her ID a couple of times.'

'I must have been more believable!'

'You did me a massive favour! She's a pain in the arse, Mads.'

'My pleasure.'

'Did you kiss me?'

'What?'

'Did you kiss me? When I was in hospital. Before you left?'

'Yes.'

'I knew it!'

'You were unconscious. How could you?'

'I just did. You're the type to take advantage. You never could keep your hands off me!'

Maddie laughed hard. She swiped tears that had welled up in her joy. It had been almost eighteen months. She had no real idea how he had been left from his injuries and here he was, remembering her, calling her and making her laugh. Just like he always could.

'How are you?' she managed eventually.

'I'm getting there. It's gradual. I've got my head around that now. I'm walking but I still have to think about it. My speech is still slow, you've probably noticed that.'

'Hardly,' Maddie lied.

'It's okay, I've got used to that too.'

'Where are you?'

'Home. Not far out of the city. My mum's looking after me. Still the same place but she's here a lot. She's all that's left.'

'I wish . . . it shouldn't be like that.'

'It has to be like this. There's no one else that can be here, everyone has their own lives to be getting on with.'

'You mean me?'

'You more than anyone. You did the right thing — distancing yourself, I mean. I'd never have forgiven myself if you had done something silly.'

'I would have got us both killed.'

'You would.'

'I still would.'

'It's not like it was but, yeah, we still need to be careful.'

'Can you come down? Like before?'

'No. Not yet at least.'

'I meant when you're stronger.'

'I don't know. I mean . . . yes.'

'But?'

'No buts. It will be a few months until I could even think about it. I'm starting to take trips out — short ones. I'll need to build up to a long trip down there, especially with all your counter-surveillance demands! But I will, if you want me too. I just wanted . . . I just wanted to call. To hear your voice. And to tell you that I know.'

'You know? You know what?'

'That you took advantage of me in my hospital bed!'

Maddie's laughter returned. 'I'd do it again.'

Adam was still laughing too. 'I'll bear that in mind. Thanks for talking to me.'

'Thanks for—'

The click told her he had gone. There was no number left to call him back even if she wanted to. That was a good thing. It would prevent her even having the option. But *he* had. She had no idea when he would call back or even if he would. Just like always.

She stretched as she walked back towards the police station. When she got close enough to the entrance door to catch her reflection, she was still smiling.

CHAPTER 20

Kelly saw Libby before she saw her. She was standing against a brick wall that fashioned a sort of square that housed the bins for the building. She stood facing her. Even from a distance she looked scared. She snatched her head up as Kelly approached.

'Hey.'

Libby looked almost frozen rigid against the wall. She slumped a little now. 'You came!'

Kelly smiled. 'Of course I came. I was the one telling you how important it was to be here. I could hardly do all that and not turn up!'

'And I have to do this again. There's no other way?'

'There isn't. But this is the last time. I have a plan to get us both away from this.'

'A plan?'

'Yes. I have a car round the corner. From here we go straight to the police station.'

'Police station?' Libby's eyes lit up. Her voice was louder too, and Kelly's attention flicked towards the building. Libby picked up on it.

'Sorry, I shouldn't be saying that out loud, right? You said we couldn't talk about the police around these people.'

'We should be okay here but, yeah, you don't want to be talking about that any closer. We just need to get this done.'

'So why can't we go now?' Her voice was whiny, pleading, and Kelly was reminded how young she was, how fragile. They'd had a rushed conversation yesterday when they were leaving the building. Libby had mentioned the police and Kelly had been quick to talk her out of it. Marlie's visit had changed everything, but they still had to be clever. Once they were done today, they wouldn't be expected back for at least twenty-four hours. That should be enough time for them both to get safe.

'We can't go now. There's no time. We are expected to work in a few minutes. Once we come back out we will have time to get far enough away. If we went now and didn't show up . . . It's not just you and me either. These people will go looking for us and they know my friends. They don't ask questions in a nice way. Everyone needs time to prepare.'

'Work?' Libby seemed to have only picked up on one word. 'That's what we're doing, is it?'

'You got your wage?' Kelly knew she had. She had seen her pick it up from the same table where she had scooped up her own. It was an identical envelope. Benny had told her what it was, he had given her the same spiel everyone got: *don't spend it all at once, don't start sticking it in the bank every week or flashing it around on social media or in front of your mum.* Basically it amounted to *don't do anything that shows up as earnings from something illicit.* She remembered when she first received money for her performances as a cam girl. She almost felt lucky. She wouldn't have argued if they had made her do it for free — she'd been so scared. But she soon realised why they paid: it was all part of the power Freddie had over you; it made it more difficult to argue but it also made you more dependant.

'Your wage?' Kelly repeated. 'The envelope?'

'Is that what it was?' Libby shuddered. 'I just threw it in the drawer.'

Kelly stepped in and took hold of her gently by the arms. 'It's going to be okay. This is it. We do the same as we did yesterday and then we're out. We keep our mouths shut and we go straight from here to speak to the people who can get us safe. That's it.'

'That's it.' Libby repeated back, again like a child taking in instructions. 'And we can't just go now?'

This time Kelly just wrapped her up in a hug. Partly to try and comfort her, partly to hide her frustrated scowl. As part of the embrace she caught an odour. Stale clothes perhaps, generally unwashed. She stepped back and looked at Libby closer. She looked dishevelled, a layer of grime on her face and hands, her hair unkempt.

'Have you been home?'

'For a little while, but I couldn't stay. I ended up sleeping out. I didn't want to wake up any of my mates . . . what would I tell them? And I can't be at home. My mum . . . I just can't!' Her voice was raised again like she was starting to panic. Kelly still held her by the shoulders.

'It's fine . . . it's okay. Later today we get this all sorted. You can tell the police everything and then we can work out what we do about your mum. But we need to get you cleaned up. Freddie . . . they won't like it.' Kelly opened the bag she had slung over her shoulder. She always kept a few make-up bits in there, a hairbrush, too. She had learned the hard way to keep something like that on her. She pulled out a small packet of wet wipes. Libby immediately recoiled.

'Why should I? Why should I clean myself up for them? For those pieces of shit on the other end of that computer? The things they ask . . . the things they want . . .'

'You shouldn't have to. I know that. But we just need to play this game once more and that means playing by their rules. Where did you stay last night?'

'Out. A bench for a bit, then a bus stop when it rained.'

'Do you have somewhere you can go later?' Kelly said and regretted it instantly. She was struggling to look after herself right now; the last thing she needed was someone else around.

'I don't know. I haven't thought about it, really. I just want to get this over with.'

'That sounds like a good idea.'

Kelly stepped away from the cover of the wall to peer up at the building. The curtains to Flat 12 were shut. A check of her watch showed that they had ten minutes. It was the earliest she had ever arrived and it was just as well; now they had time to get Libby cleaned up.

'Just follow my lead. One of the spare flats on the floor above has a shower we can use. I'll speak to Benny. You'll only have a few minutes but that's enough for a quick freshen up. It will make you feel better.'

'I don't want to shower in there. I don't want to go in there.'

'I know. Me neither. This is it, though — remember that. We play their game then we get ourselves safe and they get what they deserve as part of the deal. You have to trust me.'

Kelly moved out towards the entrance. She didn't look back, she didn't want to give any more opportunities to talk about the virtues of entering that building. They were going to have to. Both of them.

She stopped at the door. She saw movement the other side: Benny.

'You're early,' Benny said. The expected leering smile was missing. 'Both of you.'

Libby stepped in next to her. Kelly felt an arm pushed through hers where Libby held onto her.

'We need to use the shower. Libby, here, needs to freshen up.'

Benny stepped out of the doorway to allow the girls to step in. As soon as they did he moved behind them. 'No time,' he said.

'What do you mean? You just said yourself we're early.'

'So's the boss.'

'What?'

'Freddie needs to speak with you.'

'Freddie's here?'

'That's what I said, ain't it?'

Kelly took a moment. She didn't want to show she was rattled. 'Fine. I'll show Libby where to go. I can speak with him while she's in the shower. What does he want?'

'He has questions. For both of you.'

Kelly's anxiety was growing. It was already at the point where she was struggling to suppress the external signs. Benny was acting differently —pensive and fidgety as if he had been tasked with something in which he was terrified of failing. That could only be to bring the two women up to him. Kelly could not see how that could be a good thing.

'What's going on, Benny?'

Benny shrugged. 'You always tell me how I don't know nothing, how I just do what I'm told, ain't that right? Well, I've been told to bring you up. *Straight* up. That's all I know. So lead the way, yeah?' He gestured towards the steps.

Kelly felt the grip on her arm tighten. She'd taken a step forward but Libby hadn't. 'We have to go.' She nodded, try-ing to be reassuring, trying to communicate that everything was going to be okay. It was like coaxing a small child to a dentist's chair.

'What does he want with us?' Libby breathed.

'Let's go and find out, shall we? It's probably nothing much.' But Kelly knew Freddie Rickman. She knew he didn't come here unless he really had to, unless the message was one that only he could deliver. And she had heard rumours as to how he liked to do that.

She shook her arm loose and took hold of Libby's hand instead. It felt cold and clammy but Libby allowed herself to be led towards the stone steps. Benny followed too, hanging behind to block any exit.

'You're sweating,' Libby said. 'Your hands. Are you okay?' Kelly let go, she rubbed her hands together and real-ised it was *her* hands that were cold and clammy. She was suddenly aware of the pulse in her temple and her shortened breaths. She had been so busy trying to suppress Libby's fear that she hadn't realised her own.

When they reached the landing that led to Flat 12, she lifted her head to see a large figure standing halfway down. Immediately, the figure stepped into a room to the right. She knew which room and she knew who it was.

Freddie Rickman was waiting for them.

* * *

Parking was no issue, it seemed. The bays were numbered, probably correlating with the flats, but the vast majority sat empty. The sign warning of clamping in the area was so badly graffitied that Maddie could barely make out the words. It looked like it had been there a while; it certainly felt like an empty threat. She smiled to herself at the big black letters that made up the most prominent of the graffiti: *ACAB*. She had seen it enough times to know what it meant: *All Coppers Are Bastards*. As far as anti-police protests went, it had always struck her as one of the more half-arsed.

The communal door was made of a solid-looking wood. As she approached it, she was slowed by a feeling that she had been there before. She stopped a few metres short, still far enough away to be able to lean back and take in the whole of the frontage. It was largely featureless, a dull, brick building with slashes of faded orange that chased along the underside of the larger of the windows for each individual flat. The off-white letters making up 'Truro House' were stacked clumsily on top of each other to run down vertically down the wall by the door. She had seen this style all over the country; there must have been a time when councils were sharing templates for social housing. Maybe that was where the familiarity came from. It was hardly relevant. She stepped towards the entrance.

The door was not as heavy as it looked and Maddie over-compensated, bumping it so hard with her hip that it bounced off the solid wall. The sound boomed around what was an empty space with concrete the material of choice for the floor, walls and ceiling. As a result, the whole area was a drab grey, even the interior of the lift that stood idle to her left with its doors parted. Maddie opted for the stairs, despite heading for the top floor.

There were five floors accessed from a twisting flight of stairs that rose up in one corner of the building. Every landing gave a brief view out of large windows. The layer of filth was consistent, as was the smell of urine. Finally, she made the top landing. There were only three flats on this floor and also the first sign of carpet. It lined the corridor but was rucked up against the sides, roughly laid out rather than being cut and measured with any skill.

Maddie knocked on the door to Flat 59 then stepped back and stared up at the rather obvious camera angled down from the corner. A middle-aged man answered the door. Her first impression was dominated by thick glasses and a painfully thin build. She took a moment to take in the rest of him: a checked shirt tucked into once-smart trousers that had a protruding zip at the crotch, the shirt unbuttoned far enough to show a bony chest with wisps of grey hair.

'Help you?' he wheezed.

'Are you Mick?'

'Who's asking?'

Maddie lifted her warrant card. The man's eyes flickered to it momentarily. There was no reaction, certainly no surprise. A police visit did not appear to be out of the ordinary.

'I'm DS Ives from up the road in Canterbury. I just wanted to ask you a few questions about some of the places you have here. Is that okay?'

'Ask all you want. I don't know much. I don't ask no questions, myself. I just do my bit.'

'I'm sure you do.' Maddie reached into her bag and took out the photo of Holly Maguire from her last visit to police custody. It was a few years old and she looked a little worse for wear but it would be good enough for someone who knew her. 'Do you know this girl?'

'I don't know many people, really.'

'Now that doesn't answer my question, does it Mick?' She grinned. 'Do you know this person?'

'I don't want to get involved and I don't take no notice anyway.'

'You do recognise her, then? She visits the building?'

'I don't think I've seen her. I don't take much notice.'

'What *do* you do here, Mick?'

'Caretaker.'

Maddie bit down, trying to suppress her frustration. 'And what does that mean? Assume I've no idea. What's your day to day?'

'I look after the building. The grounds. Communal bits get a mopping three times a week. Any breakdowns from the boilers, water or gas coming in — that sort of thing.'

'So you go in every flat?'

'Some. I got a few landlords in here. Some of them just let me get on with it. They're glad I'm here so they don't get bothered. But others, they tell me not to get involved, they say they want to do it themselves. Makes no odds to me. They still pay towards my wages whether I go in there or not.'

'Who lives in Flats 12 and 14 on the second floor? Or 22 on the third floor?'

'I couldn't tell you.'

'Does anyone live in them?'

The man shrugged. 'Have you tried knocking?'

'I was hoping I could avoid doing that. You must know who *owns* those flats at least?'

'I don't get involved in that. There's a company what owns the building and they tell me what jobs I need to do and when. Some flats I don't get jobs for.'

'You don't get involved in much at all around here, do you?'

He shrugged again. 'It's that kind of place, lady. I get a job list and I work my way through it. I keep my head down apart from that. A few of the people in here don't appreciate me or anyone getting into their business. I get a flat and a bit of money coming in so I got a good thing going here.'

Maddie briefly peered past him to where the ill-fitting carpet seemed to continue. Behind him was a cluttered hallway. She made out a bike frame with an oily chain still attached and dragging along the floor. Just beyond that was a green jerry can, which was probably the source of the fuel smell that had been strong from the moment the door had opened.

'I can see that, Mick. Sorry to bother you, okay? I tell you what though, let me leave you my card. Just in case you think of anything or you hear anything that might be useful to me. Is that okay?'

The man's shrug this time was the most apathetic yet and Maddie tried to match it with the sarcasm in her *thank you* as she left.

* * *

Kelly didn't like this at all. Nothing felt normal. Benny was hanging back for the walk to the flat, when normally he would be right up with her, muttering into her ear and leering at her chest. He knew she didn't like being here and he liked to play on that, enjoying her discomfort. Libby's fear and suffering was more obvious than hers had ever been — he should be absolutely revelling in it.

When she checked over her shoulder again, Benny was looking back, too, as if he wanted to be sure that no one had followed them up. He had also dropped even further back. Kelly kept moving forward; she had no choice. She counted down the numbers, slowing as she passed No. 10 like she always did. She stopped on the threshold of No. 12, too. Just like she always did.

The door was wide open. Looking in, she could see the room was almost completely empty. No bed, no lighting rig, no laptop with a glowing screen or lines of text arriving with a chiming sound. Just two chairs tugged out into the middle of the room, their backs towards where she was standing.

And Freddie Rickman.

He was at the opposite end, filling the doorway that led through to a tiny bedroom. When he saw her he pushed off to swagger slowly across the room as if he had all the time in the world. Kelly stayed on the threshold. He continued past the door to crouch against the wall on the right side, down in the corner. She watched as he ran something dark through his hands. It looked like a cloth. There was another on the floor next to him.

'Come in and close the door.' His voice was deep, made deeper by the lack of soft furnishings in the room that might have otherwise absorbed his gravelly tones and she was sure that the floorboards themselves rumbled with his words.

'Okay, we can talk,' she said. 'But while we do that, I need to send Libby up to get a shower. She—'

'BOTH of you!' It was the loudest she had ever heard him. It made her jump. Her chest fluttered and her heart thumped. She glanced back to where Libby stood behind her. Benny was closer now, too. She fixed a look on him but he seemed to be avoiding eye contact.

Freddie had moved back out into the room to stand in front of the chairs. Whatever had been in his hands was back on the floor. He stared over at her, his gaze level with her mouth. She edged into the room, pulled in by his intensity.

'I got two seats,' he grumbled, 'and I got some questions for you.'

'Listen Freddie, I don't know—'

'SIT in them!' The power was back in his voice. The first word was delivered like a sucker punch that she could feel in her chest as well as through the floorboards. She did as she was told. She turned to a whimper from Libby who was now standing in the doorway.

'It's okay, Libby. We just need to talk to Freddie for a bit, that's all. We've got nothing to worry about. He's got a few questions.'

Libby was shaking her head, her unblinking eyes roamed round the room, settling on the black cloth Freddie had been toying with just a few moments earlier. She actually took a step back, her head shaking, slowly at first but quickly gaining in speed and intensity. She was starting to murmur too, Kelly knew she was close to trying something stupid.

'Libby!' Kelly called out — but it was too late. Libby turned away to where Benny was waiting. He grabbed her tightly by the arms, spinning her back around to face into the room.

'You need to understand something right from the off . . .' Freddie said, softly, his voice laden with menace. 'If you do not do as I ask, the punishment will be delivered to the other. Do you understand what that means?' He was looking beyond where Kelly had risen to a half-stand. Kelly glanced from Freddie to where Libby was being held so tightly that she grimaced in pain.

'SIT!' Kelly spun to the instruction. Freddie was a step closer and she did as she was told. The moment she touched the solid wood of the chair she felt the blow to the right side of her face. She saw a flash of white, heard her jaw slam shut and then she was aware she was on the floor, one of the chairs came with her, tipped on its side and lying on top of her. The pain came a moment later; it flashed across the side of her face and into her jaw. She stayed still, confused as to where she was, her hair had fallen over her eyes and she felt it move with her gasped breath.

'The next time you try and run, I break Kell's legs here, so she can't run after you.' The rumbling voice was some- where above Kelly and projected at the door. 'And if Kell here gets up and runs, it's your legs that get broken. You understand what I am saying?'

Kelly managed to throw her eyes upwards to where Libby was a blurred figure. She tried to speak, to tell her to stay calm, to stay where she was, to do what she was told. Her jaw shot with pain and no words came out.

'Let her go, Benny,' Freddie said. Kelly's vision cleared a little, enough for her to see that Benny's leering smile was back. He was deliberate in opening his hands to release his grip on Libby. He stepped to the side too, leaving a gap out into the corridor, back the way they had come. 'You can run. This is your chance. But then I'll have to take out my frustration on Kelly, here.'

Libby's chest was heaving as she looked down at where Kelly lay. They made eye contact. Kelly still couldn't speak, her jaw cracked as she tried. It sounded loud in her ears and an agonising pain was gone as quickly as it had come as if like her jaw had been knocked out of alignment and was now back in place. She opened and closed her mouth to test it. Libby looked up at Freddie and took a step back. Benny did too, as if to demonstrate that Libby was free to go if she wanted. Kelly knew better. Libby would never make it out of the building and it would be so much worse for both of them if she even tried. She still didn't speak. She didn't want to beg her to stay, she wasn't even sure she could manage the words. She closed her eyes instead.

'That's my girl!' Freddie spoke again, the low rumble back to his voice. Kelly opened her eyes to where Libby had moved closer to the chairs, her eyes now running with tears.

'Sit.' Freddie said, his tone at once warmer. The upended chair was lifted off Kelly. She was grabbed by her armpits and hauled up into it. She lifted a hand to her jaw. It still cracked and popped in her ears but there was no pain.

Behind her the door was pushed shut. For a few seconds no one said anything. For Kelly, it was enough time to catch her breath. Freddie was back, staring at her mouth. He broke away to run his right hand down the front of his smart jacket. The button popped open revealing more of the crisp white shirt he wore buttoned up to the top. He wore smart trousers, too, that finished at the perfect height to brush the tops of expensive- looking dress shoes — his trademark look.

He lifted his gaze to beyond her and nodded. A lock snapped. He slipped his jacket off. Benny moved into sight and took it from him. Freddie popped the buttons on his shirt and pulled it off to reveal a plain white t-shirt that hugged the contours of his body. Libby emitted a whine while Freddie handed his shirt to Benny, who then scurried back behind them. He took his trousers down, too. His boxer shorts were pristine white and when his shoes came off he was barefoot. He stepped towards the girls. Libby started moving enough to make the chair creak. He leaned forward, his muscular arms reaching between them to lean on the chair backs. They both tilted backwards.

'I need to ask some you some questions and you should know I'm only interested in the truth. The truth means I get to put my suit back on, no problem. Lies mean I have to go upstairs and take a shower first. Do you understand what I am saying?'

Kelly nodded. She didn't know if Libby did but she heard a whimper.

'Libby. Do you understand? Because that noise means nothing to me, girl?'

'She's just a kid, Freddie, give her a bit of slack.' Kelly spoke, her jaw flared a little. Freddie sighed. The blow to Libby's face followed almost instantly, a stinging slap; his hand swept so close to Kelly she could feel the draught.

'You SEE?' Freddie bellowed. He straightened up, tugged his t-shirt down and took a slow, deep breath. 'You see, Kell here spoke out of turn, so you get the slap. You see how this works? Are you both starting to understand what is going on here?'

'Okay, Freddie,' Kelly blurted, mostly on Libby's behalf, 'we understand. What do you want? Ask your questions, we'll answer. No problem.'

Freddie stepped forward. Both girls flinched. He then turned and stepped into the bedroom. He reappeared in a second, holding something concealed in his right hand as he moved back to stand in front of them. He let his hands fall to his sides. Kelly could make it out now: a cut-throat razor hanging from a loose grip. Libby whimpered again. Kelly swallowed. They needed to be clever now, calm and clever. She was keenly aware that this was not something Libby had been good at so far.

Freddie stepped forward. Libby flinched so hard Kelly could feel it through her chair. But his focus was on her. The blade flashed up and Kelly did her best to stay still but could do nothing to stop her eyes slamming shut. She waited for the pain, resigned to it. It didn't come. Instead she could feel something cold pushed against her bottom lip. She opened her eyes to see Freddie looming as close as he could, close enough for her to be able to see his nasal hair move in and out as he breathed. She could smell his aftershave too, sickly sweet, the same he always used.

'What do I *want*?' The cold metal blade moved. He dragged it, blunt edge down, up and across her top lip. He lingered there with it pushed over her whole mouth in a silencing gesture.

'You of all people know what men want! When they pay their money, when they fire up their screens and log on. It's all building up to the same thing. They all want their moment of release! Am I right?'

'What are you talking about?'

'That's what I want, too. But I'm not like those men. Those sad, pathetic men who have to get themselves off by thinking they have some sort of control over beautiful women a million miles away. That's not how I get my release. For my moment, I have to be here. I have to be right with you and I have to use a sharp blade. Do you understand?'

Kelly thought she did. She didn't reply. Her mind raced, but there was nothing to say that wouldn't put them in more danger. He was unpredictable at the best of times. The blade was still pressed over her mouth.

'My release comes with running this blade through *expendable* people like you. Through cutting off the bits that I don't need anymore, that's how I get *my* release.' She felt the blade turn so the soft skin of her lips folded around the sharp edge pushed into her skin. Suddenly he snatched back, taking the blade with him. She felt a sharp nick. Immediately she felt moisture and pressed a finger to it. It came back smeared red. Freddie paced in front of them, his attention now directed out of the window. He thrust his hands behind his back. He still clutched the razor. 'Someone has been talking to the police,' he said, quietly. What I *want* is to know who that person is and what has been said.'

'I don't know what you're talking about—' He turned on Kelly, the blade flashed again and ran straight across her eyes, millimetres from breaking her skin. She jerked back, her eyes snatching to the left where the blade now rested against Libby's cheek.

'You don't speak! Not until I tell you. I want to hear from this bitch first. The police had their time harassing me, but for the last few years there's been nothing at all. Now I hear things. I hear people telling me that someone out there is giving them little titbits, enough for them to be interested in me again. And that someone is talking to other people, trying to get in their ear, seeing if they'll speak to the cops too. A person like that might choose a dumb little bitch like this to speak to. Maybe she's ideal . . . a stupid little kid who thinks she's playing a game here? So, Libby . . . did anyone talk to you about speaking to the police?' He leaned in closer. The blade was still against her mouth, she turned away from it, towards Kelly. She only managed a whimper. Kelly stared right back, trying to suppress her own reaction. The next words out of her mouth could get them both killed. 'Or did *you* speak to the police, *Libby*?' The venom when he said her name was unmistakeable.

'I . . . I didn't say anything! There was no one there but I wasn't going to anyway!' Libby managed.

Freddie's left hand shot out to grab Libby high on her neck, his thumb reached round to dig so deep into her cheek that it flushed a deep red.

'What?'

'I . . . I went there . . . I didn't know what to do! But . . . I didn't stay, I left!'

Freddie shoved her head back. He stood straight to loom over her, his chest was tensed, his hands back at his sides. Kelly dared to look up at his face. All his attention was on Libby, his eyes glazed and unblinking. The grip on the blade was no longer loose; now both fists were gripped so tightly that his knuckles showed white.

'Look at you! *Pathetic!* Girls like you don't make decisions like that on their own Libby, do they? Someone has been talking to you about going to the police . . . *who?*'

Libby didn't answer.

'Did Kelly here talk to you about it? Did she say it was a good idea?'

Libby still didn't answer. Finally she snatched her head from side to side, a jerked shake of the head.

'Just you? Off your own bat?'

This time she managed a nod. Freddie stepped back. He rolled his shoulders like he was loosening himself up, his nose twitched above dimpled cheeks to where his jaw was clamped shut. Kelly held her breath.

'You would do well to watch this, Kell. You would do well to remember what happens to people that let me down, that think they can talk outside of this family and then lie to my face about it.' His voice was low and monotone. Kelly knew she should speak, that she should do something, but she couldn't; she was frozen in her seat. She couldn't look away either. He looked over the top of them both and nodded. The movement behind them was instant. Kelly didn't risk looking but she guessed that Benny had gone into the bedroom. Sure enough he appeared a few seconds later, sliding in the mattress that had once occupied the centre of the room. He pushed it up against the wall to her right.

'Sound deadening.' Freddie grinned. Benny's leering chuckle in the background made Kelly feel sick. Her eyes welled and her head started shaking; she had no way to control it. Benny stooped down in the corner of the room. When he stood back up he was holding the strips of material in his hand. Kelly could see that they were gags and it wasn't lost on her that there were two of them.

'Better safe than sorry, though!' Benny chuckled again as he handed them to Freddie.

* * *

'Hey, Harry.' Maddie stopped to answer the call. She'd only made it one floor down from the caretaker on her way out. She'd stopped on a small landing that gave her a view out over the car park. Idly, she watched a youth with his hood up leaning against one of the brick walls that defined the area where the bins were supposed to be stashed.

'Maddie, any update for me?'

'I didn't realise I was giving you one?'

'Is that a no?' He didn't sound in the mood to be challenged.

'I'm just coming away from Truro House.'

'Truro House? What are you doing there?'

'Freddie Rickman has three places here. They're all listed in Holly Maguire's address book.'

'And?'

'And it's a relevant line of enquiry.'

'I just got off the phone to CPS. They say they tried calling you direct a couple of times but you're not answering. Some of the work needed on that case file is now officially a few days overdue apparently? They said you knew about it, that you had discussed dates.'

Maddie paused. She was still peering out of the window. The hooded man with his foot up against the wall was now approached by another man. He stood away from the wall to greet him. 'Okay.'

'Okay? What do you mean, *okay*?'

'I do know what they want. I've told them I know what they want and we agreed a deadline. I'm not over that.'

'They say different. They also have the impression that you're now ignoring them.'

'No, they have the impression that I work one case at a time, so if I'm not working on that one then I'm not working at all. I have other cases, other enquiries. That's what I'm doing now. I missed a call around ten minutes ago when I was talking with a potential witness. That isn't ignoring someone, that is being busy.'

'I guess they didn't get that from their call being cut off.'

'I guess not. Maybe they could have given me half an hour or so to call them back before they went to my inspector — that sounds reasonable to me. Or maybe they should just stop wasting my time with phone calls at all. I know what they want.'

'They're concerned that you're not prioritising this case file like you should. You can't ignore calls from CPS because it's wasting your time because all they do is call me straight after and that wastes *my* time. And that is a different thing altogether.'

Maddie paused again. She still watched the two youths far below her who had now made their quick exchange and were both walking away in different directions.

'Fine. I'll call them and tell them again. I didn't know it was CPS. Like I said, my phone went off but I was talking to someone, that's all.'

'And you're done now?'

'I'm done here. Although I'm pretty sure I just saw a drug deal outside!' She laughed, trying to see if she could lighten her colleague's mood a little. She should have known better.

'Priorities, Maddie. That means this case file. That means securing a murder conviction at court with a real offender and with very real press interest. This needs to be absolutely airtight. Not chasing after bad reputations or street deals. Do you understand?'

'I think you've made it very clear.'

'So that investigation you're on now, what is the status? And think before you answer.'

'There are still some bits I need to bottom out.' Maddie waited for the explosion. It didn't come, but she quickly wished it had.

'Come and see me when you're back in,' he growled.

'I just—'

The call was cut and her expletives bounced around the concrete interior. She looked back down to the car park. The man who had been waiting in the area was now a speck in the distance, his customer already long gone. Maybe this was a fruitless exercise. She still wasn't entirely sure what she was hoping to achieve here. This wasn't an area where police questions were going to be answered readily. The caretaker had already proved that.

Her phone buzzed. It was a message telling her she had missed a call from a number she didn't recognise. She pressed to call it back. She considered she might be able to appease Harry a little if she could at least confirm she'd returned CPS's call. She stayed pressed up against the window, trying to muster the energy to sound genuinely apologetic. The call was answered quickly.

'Hello, this is DS Maddie Ives. I'm very sorry but I think I missed your call?'

'Ah yes, I did leave you a message — ten minutes ago, if that. Sorry to bother you . . . it's probably not relevant, really, but it's been playing on my mind . . .'

It wasn't CPS at all. Maddie recognised the voice of the woman she had met as a witness to the car going over the cliffs in Capel.

'Ms Thoroughgood. . . sorry, Margaret. Please, do tell me more?'

'A girl. This morning, I saw her standing on the edge. I did what I do . . . I took a walk out to speak with her. I know I said I wouldn't—'

'The edge? The cliff you mean?'

'Yes. The very same spot.'

'Are you okay? Did something happen?' The words were sinking in, Maddie suddenly realised that they might have another emergency on their hands. She started to move quickly down the stairs.

'I'm okay. And so is she. Seems I was able to convince her to sit down for a cup of coffee and to take some time to reflect. I'm not convinced she was one of the more serious ones. She had a bottle of something strong to give her a bit of courage for a start. I guess you don't need that when your mind is made up.'

'Oh, that's good.' Maddie slowed. 'Let me take a few details and we'll see if we can find out who she is so I can have my uniform colleagues do a welfare check. I don't suppose she gave you her name?' Maddie wished she hadn't given her card over; now this woman would be calling her every time someone walked past her house and cast so much as a look over the cliff edge.

'Kelly.'

Maddie had made it to another of the landings. She leant on the windowsill to write down the details.

'*Kelly*, you say. Did you get a surname or any other details?'

'Well this was the reason I called. I wasn't going to bother . . . only she said her girlfriend was in the car.'

'In the car?' Maddie shook her pen; the end seemed to have dried out.

'That went over. It was her partner. She was very cut up about it, no doubt about that. When she left she said she was going to the police. Her partner had told her to. She talked about how her partner took her own life so she could set this Kelly free. But she needed to tell you something first to make sure it all came right. I'm sorry . . . it all sounds a bit silly really, now that I'm saying it out loud. I guess I was hoping you had spoken to her.'

Maddie didn't have a reply, not an immediate one. She ran the words back through her mind, trying to catch up. 'Set her free?'

'That's what she said — a couple of times. I should have asked her for a bit more, really, but she said she was going to the police. She seemed set on it. I did offer to run her down to the station right away but she said she had something to do first. Did she come down?'

'Not as far as I'm aware.'

'I see. Maybe she'll come down later.'

'I am out of the office right now, Margaret. It's possible she's spoken to a colleague already. I'll have a look into that.'

'I see. I am sorry to bother you with this. I'm not sure it's too relevant for you. I just wanted you to know. She seemed very distraught. You will let me know she's okay, won't you?'

'Yes, yes of course I will.'

The call ended and still Maddie didn't move. So *Kelly* was Holly Maguire's girlfriend? And her death over the side of a cliff was designed to *set her free*? Yet why take a taxi driver with her? Nothing about him had revealed that he might have any hold over Holly or anyone associated with her — he'd only just moved to the area. There were still so many questions. But at least now there might be someone out there who had some answers.

'*Kelly* . . .' she said out loud. She had been through all of Holly's linked associates on the police system and there was no one she could recall by that name. 'Who the hell is Kelly?'

She started back down the stairs. She caught sight of *Floor 2* above a fire door. Freddie Rickman had a couple of flats on this floor and one more on the floor above. With Harry's words still ringing in her ears, she had intended on leaving without knocking, but her interest was stoked again now. She could try one of them at least. One thing she had learned about detective work was that you never knew where answers might come from. She pushed the door open to the second floor and started along the corridor, counting up the numbers as she went.

CHAPTER 21

It was the closest thing Kelly had ever seen to a genuine smile
from Freddie as he shuffled his feet to give himself a firm
base and moved the blade slowly towards Libby's face. She
was now gagged; Kelly wasn't. The black material had been
tied firmly around Libby's head to force its way between her
teeth, fixing her jaw open. Her eyes were fixed, too — wide
and full of panic. She was pressed back as far as she could
and Kelly watched as her eyes followed the blade, helpless as
it moved in slow motion towards her pretty face.

Kelly held her breath.

There was a knock at the door, solid and assertive
enough for Freddie to stop dead and twitch towards it. Benny
was already close to the door. He shrugged at Freddie. They
obviously weren't expecting anyone.

Freddie inclined his head irritably towards the door and
Benny edged hesitantly to the peephole, approaching it like
it might somehow be a two-way. Eventually he pressed up
against it just as it thumped again to make him flinch.

'Police!' The voice was female, urgent and somewhat
muffled. Kelly made a sound from her throat and Freddie
jerked to it. He pushed his hand over her mouth, no doubt
wishing that he'd gagged her, too.

'I just want to ask a few questions!' the voice called out.

No one moved. Benny was back to peering back over at his boss, waiting for some sort of direction. It didn't come.

'A neighbour said there was someone in here? You're not in any trouble.'

The third knock was even louder. Again, Benny reacted like he had been prodded in the ribs. He looked a little panicked as he waited for an instruction.

Freddie snatched the second strip of black material from the floor and applied it roughly and tightly between Kelly's teeth. Then he walked over to the door. He transferred the razor to his left hand and pushed against the door with his right.

'I'm worried now,' came the voice. 'I've been told someone is in here but I'm not getting a response. Do I need to force entry to make sure everyone's okay in there?'

Freddie and Benny exchanged glances. Something was whispered between them.

'I'm not decent!' Benny called out. His voice was strained.

'I can wait,' came a delayed reply.

'I'm fine.'

'I can wait!'

Benny shook his head then exchanged another whispered word with Freddie. Freddie turned back to the two girls. The blade was back in his right hand as he motioned at them to stand then hustled them towards the bedroom. At least Kelly understood this to be what he meant; Libby didn't move and Freddie grabbed her roughly. She grunted as she was pushed through the doorway. Behind her, Kelly could hear a front door being opened slowly. She strained to listen but she was pushed further into the room. There was a clump of material under a far window that she recognised as the floral bedding and Libby was pushed to collapse onto it. Kelly's bag had been tossed in here too and was lying on its side.

Kelly was allowed to stay on her feet at least but that just meant she was closer to Freddie. And the blade he held tightly under her throat.

* * *

'So you're the decorator?' Maddie said. The man seemed to have struggled telling her, as if the word *decorator* was too long and made up of more syllables that he was used to using. He was sweating, a layer of moisture clear on his forehead. His skin in general was a washed-out and clammy white and his lips were pulled back in a sort of tense sneer.

'Yeah.'

'You paint naked?' Maddie smiled playfully.

'Naked?'

'A moment ago you weren't decent?'

'Top off. Hot in here.'

'How very thoughtful of you to cover your nipples for me. You've made a start, then?' Maddie leaned to see round him, she was conscious that he seemed to lean with her. The small area she could see was barren, no furniture or personal belongings at all. She could see one wall on the right side and it did look like it had been stripped back to the plaster, even if it didn't appear to have been done recently. The floor had a carpet that looked worn and tired. The place certainly needed a decorator.

'Not really. I keep getting interrupted.' His face was still a sneer and he leaned forward a few inches to get closer. His chest puffed up as if he was trying to make himself bigger.

'Just you in there?' Maddie held her ground and persisted.

The man stepped forward now, he pulled the door shut behind him as he went and Maddie was forced to step back. His movement had caught her out and she cursed herself for letting him shut the door.

'Not even me, now. I'm done.'

He was too close for comfort but Maddie didn't want to give any more ground.

'It doesn't look done . . .'

'Just popped in for a bit of measuring. So I guess you got all the answers you need?'

'Not even close. Is that your flat?'

The man moved first. He stepped past her and started down the hallway. Maddie watched him go for a few steps, her mind swirling with options. His head was turned slightly to one side, just enough to make sure she was following. She stayed still, her focus flicked back to the closed door.

'You staying there?' he called out while continuing to walk away. More than anything she wanted to know what was in that flat, what it was he was so obviously trying to lead her away from. But there was nothing she could do; she had no power to be kicking in doors, she never had. Her only chance to get anything at all was to find out what she could about this man. She walked after him.

'What did you say your name was?' she called out.

'I didn't.' His pace quickened. Maddie's did too.

* * *

Kelly rested her hand gently on Libby's shoulder. Libby lay on her side, her eyes held tightly shut. All the while, she sobbed through the thick material of the gag. Kelly needed to present herself as calm; if she was seen to be panicking, too, it would only make Libby worse. She wondered how Holly had always been able to stay calm and assured, no matter what was going on. Perhaps it had all been an act, like what she was doing now, projecting a calm exterior for the benefit of others while her mind was in turmoil.

Freddie had stepped out of the bedroom but she could still see him. He was at the large window in the living room, staring intently out. His phone was upturned in his right hand as if he was waiting for it to ring. The razor was on the windowsill, still within his reach but he seemed distracted. Kelly's self-imposed calmness had her thinking straight, almost logically. Freddie was here to kill Libby, to torture her and extract the information he needed, but then to kill her. Libby would tell him of Kelly's plan to go to the police straight from here and then neither of them would leave the building alive. Freddie was just waiting for the police officer to leave and for Benny to report back what she wanted. That could all be resolved within a couple of minutes.

She turned back to survey the room. There was hardly anything in there. The bed frame was propped up under a small window with some of the bedding draped over it. She could see enough of it to tell that it was still largely complete — too bulky to be of any use. Then her eyes rested on her bag. It was on its side and some of her make-up items had spilled out. The neck of an empty vodka bottle protruded from inside.

Freddie's phone rang for a split second. He snatched it to his ear.

'She gone?' His voice was rasping, laden with tension. 'Okay, fine. What did you tell her?' He paced as he listened, his attention still out of the window.

It was now or never.

Kelly stretched for her bag. She could just reach the edge of it but enough to pull it gently towards her. She met Libby's now open and panicked eyes as she did so. She got enough of a handful of the canvas to turn the mouth of the bag towards her. Now she could grip the vodka bottle by the neck, leaving most of it still hidden in the bag. She made eye contact with Libby again. Libby jerked a nod. Even in a glance she had been able to communicate her thoughts. This was it. It was their only chance.

Kelly stood up and started forward in the same movement. Freddie was facing away, the phone still pressed to his ear. He started to turn when Kelly's foot scuffed on a rucked-up bit of carpet. Her grip tightened on the bottle. As he turned she swung it with everything she had.

The bottle struck him with a sickening thud. He grunted and stumbled away from her. His phone dropped to the floor with a clatter. A few more seconds passed and he dropped to one knee. She swung the bottle again, this time bringing it downwards on top of his head. The bottle smashed. The noise was tremendous and the sounds of scattering glass seemed to be all around her. Freddie slumped forward, groaning, and his palms slapped on the ground as they took his weight. His face hung close to the floor and his head shook as if he was trying to clear it. He pushed back off his palms, struggling to get back up.

Kelly discarded the bottle and scooped up the razor from the windowsill then ducked back into the bedroom where Libby was standing at the back, her face a mask of horror, her eyes seemingly staring beyond Kelly to where Freddie's groans were getting louder and closer to words. Kelly grabbed Libby's wrist. She led her to the front door and held her breath as she spun the handle.

The door opened.

They dashed out into the corridor and broke instantly into a run. Kelly still led Libby by the wrist and they burst through the fire door at the end. The sunlight was bright here, despite the filthy window. She turned to Libby and lifted the blade in front of her eyes. Libby recoiled but then realised that Kelly was hacking at her own gag. Once it fell away she set to work on Libby's.

'You okay?' Kelly stammered.

Libby managed a rushed nod.

'We need to go.'

Kelly took a hold of her wrist again but after only two steps forward she froze in her tracks. A familiar cough reverberated up the stairwell — Benny was coming back up. His strides sounded stronger than normal, like he was taking two stairs at a time. Kelly pulled Libby desperately towards the lift. She would normally avoid them at all costs but now she pressed the button over and over. A mechanism clunked into action high above them but it sounded laboured. The call button was lit but flickering. It was taking too long. She spun back towards the corridor. A figure was moving clumsily along it with a steadying arm pushed out. It was some way off but, dressed in a bright white t-shirt and underwear, it stood out from the gloom. It was coming closer. It had to be Freddie. The footsteps on the stairwell were getting louder. In just a few seconds Benny would emerge and they would be hemmed in.

'We need to go up!' Kelly hissed.

'Up?' Libby exclaimed.

'Up.' She grabbed Libby's wrists again and they started up the stairs. After just two flights, she could feel the burning in her thighs. They made the landing of the third floor and she pushed through the door to the corridor. They sprinted along it, past the first few doors. Kelly headed instinctively for the flat she knew on this level then slowed suddenly. Freddie and Benny knew it too! Of course they couldn't hide in there. Kelly dragged Libby past it and thumped the next door she came to. She only waited a second before she moved to the next. She thumped again, using the bottom of a fist, trying to communicate the urgency while not being too loud in the process. There was no answer. She knew this building; she knew the cloud of fear hanging over it that Freddie had deliberately fostered. No one got involved in other people's business. No one answered panicked knocks either.

She moved to the next door. Libby was still with her, she was hitting the doors on the other side of the corridor. Kelly tried a lighter knock. The door opened quickly and an elderly woman filled it. She scowled out into the dim corridor through thick glasses.

'That you, Janey?'

'Janey . . .' Kelly bowled towards her, stepping through the door, 'Janey yeah, it's me!' Libby followed her in. The woman moved back into the room too and Kelly stepped back past her to close the door.

'You're not Janey! Get out of my house!'

'Please, lady! My name is Kelly. This is Libby. She's sixteen! There are men that are trying to find us. They've already hurt us. They'll do far worse if they find us again. Please . . . we need to stay in here for just a few minutes. We'll just stand here and be quiet — we *all* need to be quiet!' Kelly reached into her pocket and wrenched out the piece of material that had been covering her mouth. She held it up as if it might back up her point.

'I don't know about that!' But the woman was looking intently at Kelly's cheek and jawline on the side where she had taken Freddie's blow.

'I don't usually get involved. You just looked like my Janey through the peephole. She's due here. I don't normally open up.'

'Just a few minutes, that's all! Please?'

The hammering on the door silenced them all. The woman's thick lenses spun to the door then back to the two girls.

'Don't answer it,' Kelly whispered. 'He won't just hurt us.'

'I know who you mean. I bet I know. It's that bully. It's that bully from downstairs. People talk about him. They say to stay away and if you can't stay away, just do as he says. Don't cross him!' The woman was whispering too but the panic was clear in her voice. She seemed to be thinking out loud, but the more she spoke the more panicked she sounded. The door beat again. Louder this time.

'Please . . .' Kelly said. Libby whimpered. Kelly moved across the floor to the windows. She parted the curtains to peer out. She already knew they were too high. The window had stopped being an option the moment they had gone up instead of down.

'I don't want to be involved.'

'You're not in!' Kelly hissed. But it was no good; the woman had already stepped to the door.

'He's got no reason to hurt me,' she said.

'Please!' It was too late. Kelly grabbed Libby and pushed her roughly into the bedroom, instinctively trying to get out of sight. It was small. There was a fitted wardrobe where they might both fit. Kelly pulled the door open but changed her mind. It would be no use hiding. She was back to searching the flat frantically, the kitchen area was on the other side of the room. There would be knives in there, some sort of weapon at least. She heard the woman's voice — there was no time. She ducked back into the room and grasped Libby gently by the shoulders.

'It's okay,' she said, then pressed a finger to her lips. Libby was shaking so hard. Kelly sat on the bed, patted the space next to her and smiled, a sudden calm taking her over. She didn't expect Freddie to ask many questions — maybe not any. In a few seconds he would just barge in. There was nothing they could do but wait. They both took up the end of the bed and faced the bedroom door.

Kelly balled her fists. She wanted to see him coming at least and she would go down fighting.

'You want what, now?' The elderly occupant's voice was distinctive.

'Sorry to bother you.' *It was a woman's voice!* 'I just want to speak with you for a moment.'

Kelly reckoned it was the same voice that had called through the door upstairs. The *police* officer. She stood up, pressed her finger to her lips again and got closer to the door as the conversation outside continued.

'Do you know anything about the flat a couple down? Does anyone live in it?'

'Oh . . . I don't really know much about what goes on round here.'

'Sorry, are you okay? You seem upset?'

'I'm fine, love. I was waiting for my Janey is all. You caught me in a bit of a tiz. I don't know about other flats. I keep myself to myself. Sorry I can't help.'

'No problem. Do you ever see anyone going there? Or maybe you hear people in there? I'm just trying to work out if it's in use.'

'I hear people, sure. Why are you interested in that place? I haven't seen you in the building before?'

'Oh, no. I hear it might be coming up for sale is all. I was thinking it might be a good investment place. What do you think?'

'Oh, well, I don't know about any of that. I just keep myself to myself.'

'So you said. Are you sure you're okay? When is Janey due back?'

'I'm fine. Any minute — so don't be getting no ideas! She'll be back and she's got a key and a mobile phone. If you're after seeing what you can get out of me you're wasting your time!'

'No! No, please, you misunderstand. I was just a little concerned about you is all. I think I may have caused you distress. I really didn't mean to.'

'Well, okay then.'

'There's a caretaker, right? I guess he might know more.'

'I guess he might. Top floor. He's in one of the only flats up there. Can't miss him.'

'Does he go in Number 22?'

'I really can't help you, love. Go up to the caretaker. Good idea.'

The door pushed back closed. Kelly let out a sigh. She was holding onto Libby firmly, she had grabbed her when she had tried pushing past her.

'What are you doing?' Libby said. 'That's the police officer! Why don't we just tell her?'

'Then why didn't she say she was a police officer? Even if it was, I think she's on her own. She wouldn't even get us out of the building.'

'How *are* we going to get out of the building? Surely she would have had a better chance than we do?'

'Freddie and Benny will want to be as far away from here as possible. They probably left while she was talking.'

'But what about us? How do we get out?'

'We walk out.'

The elderly woman appeared. 'You need to go. I can't have strange people knocking on the door. That was some woman but I guess she's something to do with *him*, is he? I didn't like her. She asks a lot of questions.'

'We're leaving — don't worry. And thank you.' Kelly walked to the front door. She opened it gently, trying to make as little noise as possible. She leaned out slowly to take in the corridor in both directions. Nothing moved. The woman who had knocked was gone and there was no sign of Freddie either. She stepped out, looked back at Libby and beckoned for her to follow.

'I'm going to find her,' Libby said.

'Who?'

'The policewoman. She's knocking doors, said she was going up to the caretaker. I heard that. I'll go up there.'

'The top floor! That's further away from the exit, from getting the hell out of here! You can't. If Freddie's still in here he'll kill you. This is your chance to get away.'

'I can. How am I safer with you than the police?'

'You don't know Freddie. He won't care that there's a copper here — not a woman on her own. He'll go through her if that's what it takes. She won't know what's hit her. He can make people disappear. Coppers *and* silly little sixteen-year-olds who run straight back to him.'

Libby jutted out her lip. 'I'm not some silly little sixteen-year-old. I'm going to find her. You don't need to worry about me . . . I can take care of myself.'

'You're coming with me. We're running down the stairs and we're not looking back. Kelly glanced towards the end of the corridor where a fire escape led to steel steps bolted to the side. She had seen the doors chained shut before. She couldn't rely on it. The only way out was the main stairwell. She turned back to the sound of the front door shutting. Libby must have closed it. Kelly swore. She tapped it lightly. She was starting to lose her patience.

'Libby! Open up!' She was back to hissing. Her head flicked left and right, half expecting Freddie to appear at any moment.

'Go away!' Libby called out. 'Run if you want to. I'm going to find the police officer!' There was no way of telling how far Libby's voice would travel.

'Libby . . . I can't look after you. Not if you don't come now.' There was a pause. Kelly held her breath for the reply, her left hand making a spider shape on the wood with her fingertips.

'No one asked you to!'

Kelly considered beating again on the door. Maybe even shouting back but Libby's sentence cut through a haze of growing panic. *No one asked you to!* She was right. This wasn't her and Holly. Libby was not her responsibility.

'Last chance, Libby. I gotta go.'

'Go! I'm staying here until it's calm. A few more minutes then I'll go and find the policewoman. I'll be fine!'

'Take my number — just let me know you're okay when you get clear.'

'Leave me alone! You're not my mother.'

'Fine. Then take it for the police to call me. She's going to want to speak to us both.'

'Then come find her with me.'

'I have to go. You should, too, trust me on that.' There was no answer this time. She waited as long as she could. When she considered she had already waited too long, she started pacing away. She stopped after a few steps and almost doubled back.

But then she shook her head and continued for the stairs.

CHAPTER 22

'You made it back okay, then.' Maddie spun to the gruff voice of Harry Blaker.

'Just about!' She chanced a grin and it got her nowhere. She leant back in her desk chair.

'And then you came to see me straight away, just like I asked.'

'Oh. I didn't realise it was *that* sort of request. I got a little distracted.'

'This whole investigation is a distraction. Why are you still looking at Freddie Rickman?' Harry gestured at her screen. Freddie Rickman's mugshot filled half of it. It was the custody photo from his last arrest, a cannabis cultivation job that never stuck. It was the latest of five arrests, all for different offences, all hinting at serious criminality and nothing had ever stuck. If police systems were anything to go by, Freddie Rickman had never done a bad thing in his life. Maddie didn't believe that for one second.

'I wasn't actually. I was looking at his associates.' Maddie clicked to bring another screen to the front. This man had a much longer rap sheet, which included successful convictions at court, mainly for drugs — some possession and some with intent to supply. There were intel links to prostitution on there, too, but as so often with that sort of crime, it was nothing more than that. 'Shane Porter. *Benny,* as he's known on the streets — who knows why. Do you recognise him?'

Harry shrugged. 'Should I?'

'There's a lot of local intel around him. Links to organised crime and prostitution and of course our friend Freddie Rickman.'

'And I hope, to your murder case involving the Harnett brothers? You know, the one that CPS need to be able to prosecute in less than seven days? The one they keep calling me about because they've given up calling you.'

'There's something going on with this Shane Porter. I met this guy today at one of the addresses listed in Holly Maguire's book. His reaction to me, Harry . . . he didn't want me there. It was *so* clear. He literally stepped out of the flat the moment he knew I was a cop and then walked me out of the building. I let him. But I walked straight back in the moment he turned his back, I wanted to knock the other add—'

'After our conversation? You did this after we spoke?'

Maddie was a little taken aback. Harry wasn't listening and he seemed to be working himself up.

'I know what we talked about, okay? I will stay on to get it done if that's what it takes but—'

''It's not okay. What do you mean *there's something going on?* There's always been *something going on* with Freddie Rickman. He's a career criminal. You're telling me that you think he is involved in prostitution and that a dead girl in a car might have been working for him. Now you have an address she had on her that's occupied by a known associate who also has links to prostitution and who didn't want you to come into his flat? Where are you going here? Why are you insisting on wasting your time on this?'

'You didn't let me finish. I got a call. From the woman who saw the car go over the cliff with Holly in it. Her girlfriend appeared, back on top of the cliff. She got into a conversation with her, she was talking about how she was supposed to go to the police, how she had something she needed to tell us, something about what Holly had died for and that she needed to give us the rest of the story.'

'Okay,' Harry was still angry, there was no hiding it. 'And who is she?'

'All she could say was *Kelly*. But I came back and I had another look through Holly's property, the stuff that was in her rucksack. And this, Harry . . . I can't ignore this . . .'

Maddie swept her desk to bunch up the paperwork. In the space she had created she laid out three photos. She ignored Harry's huff to continue.

'These are the three photos that were in Holly's rucksack. At that building today I got the feeling that it seemed familiar, like I had been there before. I haven't, I'd just seen these photos!' She pointed at the one laid closest to her. 'This is the entrance.' Her finger moved along the row. 'This one is the door that leads to the second floor — you can see the corridor behind it. And this last one . . . this is the inside of a flat. I only saw a snippet of the inside but it could well be the same flat!' Maddie spun to take in Harry's reaction. He was leaning forward now, poring over the photos. He pushed off the table to straighten back up.

'Okay?' His standard growl was present and correct. He wasn't impressed but he didn't seem quite so angry either.

'And then there's this. Also from her rucksack.' She reached down to her bottom drawer and pulled out an evidence bag that clunked as she dropped it on the table. She flipped it over to reveal the item inside, a worn metal number. The number 12.

'No prizes for guessing which door number our weasel-faced *Benny* was behind. What do you think?'

'Number twelve?'

'Boom! It's true what they say about you, Harry. A great detective!'

'So what is this saying to you?'

'I don't know. Not a great deal in isolation, I'll admit. But that phone call, Harry . . . this Holly . . . what if she was trying to tell us something? What else *could* it be?'

'Okay . . . So she drives a car over a cliff, killing herself and murdering a taxi driver to tell us to go to a flat where people are engaged in prostitution? Why not just come to us and we could sit down with a coffee and a pen. It's all a bit much isn't it?'

'Yes. I see that, of course I do. I had a look at Holly. She's got quite the record . . . petty theft . . . drugs . . . accosting. Nothing recent, but a chequered past. And five years ago she did sit down with us — our colleagues here at least — and she told them how she was raped by a punter. The investigation was closed pretty quickly, and from the notes I didn't see much evidence of an investigation. I know times were different even then. I know we're better now. But Holly Maguire doesn't — *didn't.*'

'So she didn't think she would have been listened to?'

'Sex workers, Harry. I've worked with them before when I was undercover. I heard a lot of talk about the police, none of it was positive. The general consensus is that police see sex workers as fair game who are asking to be victims. I don't know any of this for sure but it would make sense.'

'What else was in that rucksack?"

'Relevant lines of enquiry Harry! That's what.' She reached down for another evidence bag. This one contained a lined page from a notebook laid out face up and visible through the plastic. It was a list of names. The page was headed *Ugly Mugs.*

'Ugly mugs?' Harry said.

'Yeah. A common term on the street. We had the same system in the North West. If a girl had a bad client, if they got beat on or the client was particularly depraved, the client's name was added to this list. They were known as *ugly mugs.* The list got shared so the other girls knew, sometimes with other houses, too.'

Harry's eyes lingered on Maddie long enough for her to sense an enquiry.

'What?'

'*We* had a system?'

'I was good at it, Harry. Undercover work, I mean. That doesn't mean I had sex for money! There are other roles you can perform without blowing cover.'

'I assume blowing cover wasn't one of them?'

'A Harry Blaker joke! And a crude one! I should start documenting these — each one feels like a breakthrough.' It felt even more like a breakthrough in that moment. Harry seemed calm again — interested maybe.

'I surprise myself sometimes.'

'I much prefer you joking to how you were when you came in here. You're not angry with me anymore, then?'

Harry sighed. 'Is there any point? You have that excitement about you. I've seen it before. I might as well see where it goes and stay involved. If I tell you to leave it you're just going to carry on in private, as it would appear you have already. You have your teeth in this.'

'There is something here to get my teeth into. Something more than just a career criminal running girls. I just need to find it.'

'Fine. You have twenty-four hours to make headway. If you haven't, if there's nothing more you can tell me you're going to have to move back to your case file. And I mean grounded at the nick until it is done.'

'Headway?'

'Headway. Right now all we have is a career criminal running sex workers. Even if you *could* get any of the workers to talk to you, it's pretty much decriminalised. Headway means getting something Major Crime might be interested in.'

'I think Major Crime are already interested . . .' Maddie studied him intently.

His nose twitched upwards.

'Tell me you're not!'

Harry turned away. 'I'm always interested in catching criminals, Maddie. We just need to make sure we're focusing our efforts on the right ones. This is *Major* Crime.' He started moving away now. Maddie had to call after him.

'So you keep saying! What are you going to do? If CPS call you again, I mean?'

'Same as you. I'll be ignoring my phone.'

'What if they miss you out and go to the Chief Inspector?'

Harry didn't stop or turn to answer. 'Very likely. You have twenty-four hours as far as *I'm* concerned, but Mr Lowe might have different ideas if he gets a sniffy prosecution lawyer on the end of the phone. I suggest you start making your *headway* as soon as possible.' He reached the door and he was gone.

Maddie looked back down at the contents of Holly Maguire's bag. The items were strewn across her desk and floor in clear plastic evidence bags. In isolation they were a mishmash of nonsense: an address book, a metal door number, some out-of-focus photos, a solid ashtray — totally unrelated. But Maddie was certain they were pieces of a puzzle and the hidden message was so important that a young woman had ended her life to deliver it. Harry might need some convincing, but Maddie was very much there already. Whatever picture these pieces of puzzle made, it was *very much* of interest to Major Crime.

* * *

'Fuck!' Kelly stepped back from the kitchen drawer. The paperwork that had been in her hand fell to the floor and a little drop of blood fell on top of it. She shoved her finger into her mouth and sucked.

She was back at her flat. She didn't think he would come here first. She'd hardly spent any time there — always at Holly's. But she hadn't thought he knew her mum's address at all and yet he'd walked right up to the door. She had to assume he knew her better than she thought. Surely he would be looking for her right now. And she knew what it would mean if they found her.

She just needed a few items. She was convinced her passport was in the kitchen drawer, she could remember putting it in there when she moved in. There had been no reason to move it since. It wasn't there. The drawers were untidy. She had been grabbing stacks of old letters and documents to clear the drawer out completely and, in her haste, she had stabbed her finger on a discarded bottle opener.

The prick of pain had distracted her from the panic a little. She focused on her breathing, but this merely quelled the panic to a niggling anxiety. She needed to get out of there.

The thud against the door made her jump so hard she expelled air in a whimper. She was frozen to the spot. It was a single thud, not a knock, and it was accompanied by a clink of glass as if someone had bumped a sack of jars against it. She paced over to the door. The spyhole showed the wall opposite and nothing else. She listened. There was no sound. It was impossible to move through the stone walkways without being heard. She waited a full minute or more, her eye pressed against the spyhole the whole time. Nothing.

She felt for the handle. To her heightened senses the metal was cold and the sound of the mechanism was deafening as she turned it. She stepped back, her body so rigid that it made her neck ache. She pulled the door quickly.

A black sack yawned inwards, the top layer of its contents spilling out. Two glass bottles thudded onto the thin carpet.

'What the hell?' She pushed out with her foot and nudged one of the bottles. A label for some cheap vodka rolled into view. She expelled a breath. It had to be some lazy neighbour who couldn't be bothered to walk the two flights down to the bins. She stepped to the door. She stuck her head out enough to check both ways. The corridor was empty.

She dropped the two errant bottles back in the sack and pulled the sack together to tie it. She caught a glimpse of something white. It was on the other side of the sack. She leaned forward. Something was written on a stapled piece of paper in messy writing. She moved around to see it.

Put this in your bin. Do it now.

You have work tomorrow.

You will be told where.

Do it now.

Kelly felt the air leave her lungs again. She stepped right out into the corridor this time to view the whole length of it. There was still no one in sight. She stared over dumbly at the black sack, not knowing what to do. She moved back inside and leant on her front door to hold it closed.

'Think!' she said to herself in a voice that didn't sound like her own. She looked around her flat, not knowing what for. Her gaze lingered on the knife drawer.

She yanked it open too hard, the cutlery inside made a metallic *clang* and she spun back to face her front door like someone the other side might now know what she was doing. She shook her head. Most of her knives were near useless; the good ones had all been at Holly's. The only one that looked sharp was a small, stubby thing she had used for peeling fruit. She pushed it into her pocket and moved back to the front door, tugging it open. The bag was still there. She bunched it up and tied off the neck. She felt her pocket for her keys and pulled the door shut.

She read the note again, this time she seemed to absorb the words a little better. *You have work tomorrow.* She read that sentence a couple of times. If someone was coaxing her out of her flat to hurt her, why write that? And why coax her out at all? The doors here were easy to force; she was pretty certain that hers would just push open and then someone would be able to confront her away from prying eyes.

She felt a little more assured, enough to be able to move forward. Still, she tiptoed along the corridor to the stairs. She stopped at the top. The layout was different to Truro House, the stairs more enclosed, and she couldn't see down the middle. She stopped to listen. Silence.

The air outside of the block was still. She rucked up the doormat so that it would stop the communal door on the ground floor from latching behind her. She had a fob but it would make a second or two's difference and that might be time she needed. The confidence she had gained from reading back the note was all but gone now as she stepped away from the building and out into the open. She felt exposed and vulnerable. The bins were all stored together. The block had a wide tunnel for cars that looked like it had been gauged through the middle of the building as an afterthought. The road itself was only just wide enough to allow access to the car park behind. The bins were kept in a recess on the right, half way along.

She took a sharp turn left. The tunnel was formed by huge concrete posts that were intermittent along its length with a steel mesh bolted to them to create storage areas behind. These stone posts wore a layer of grime and the staining continued onto the ceiling. There was a reddish brown staining on the floor, too, where rivulets of rusty water from the cage had formed shallow puddles. The daylight was vastly diminished as she moved under the building and it took a moment for her eyes to adjust. She waited for it, her heightened senses picking out the rustle of something near the bins. It sounded like a rodent — hardly unexpected but it still slowed her pace.

Her bin was marked with her flat number daubed on the front. Normally she would have to go hunting for it, spinning each filthy bin until she found hers. She wasn't here enough to use it much, so it would get pushed to the back. Yet, today, it was near the front and clear to see, just a couple of steps past a couple of the other bins, one of which was on its side as if it had been swept out of the way in a hurry. She moved towards it, conscious that the other bins and the shadows provided plenty of places for someone to hide in wait. She dropped the bag when she got to the bin and pushed her hand into her pocket to feel the handle of the knife. She looked around and her attention was caught by the sound of a car passing the front of the building. The strains of a couple arguing leaked from an open window in one of the flats somewhere above her.

She turned back to her bin and lifted the lid, swinging the sack at the same time to drop it in. She caught sight of something and her swing halted, the sack clinking as it collided with the lip. She didn't drop it in. instead, she stared down into the foul-smelling depths. She gasped. She couldn't scream. The lid crashed back down and she stumbled backwards dropping the sack. She stumbled over a low kerb that unsettled her balance. She felt the pain in her left forearm before she realised she was on the ground, lying in a puddle. Her back was instantly soaked and a rank smell filled her nostrils. A shadow moved to her right, she jerked towards it. Freddie Rickman stood over her, his dark suit seeming to merge with the blackened ceiling. Livid red scratches on his face were the only source of colour. His eyes fidgeted over her body, finally resting on her mouth.

'I thought long and hard about what you did.' His voice was a growl, low in volume but laden with menace. 'About how I make amends for that and about how I get some control. You're out of control, Kell.'

'I . . ..' She stammered, 'I—'

'You don't SPEAK!' His roar seemed to come from everywhere, reverberating off the walls and ceiling as if he was all around her, part of every shadow. It pushed her head back down so far she felt the stinking puddle in her hair. 'The easiest thing to do would have been to kill you. And I still might. But not yet. I have a better use for you. You will work tomorrow. This is how you will know where.' She heard something clatter to the floor and slide towards her. A mobile phone. She didn't reach out for it. 'Where is yours?'

She reached into her pocket then held her phone out mutely. She was in no position to argue. He snatched it from her.

'Tomorrow you might find that the work is different, but I think you know your place now, Kell. I think I've showed you what I'm capable of. I think you will get on with it. What do you say?'

She jerked a nod. Her mind flashed with the image of that bin, of what she had seen inside it. A tear sprang from her right eye and her neck pulsed with pain as she moved slightly. Her back flashed cold from her soaking hair.

'Keep that phone on. Start following instructions — no questions.' He stepped away and gestured with his hand. An engine surged behind her and she turned to see a flat-fronted van moving quickly towards her. The bumper dipped as it braked hard, stopping just short of where she still leant back on her forearms. She kicked out, trying to find some grip on the floor, finally dragging herself backwards and out of the way. She was barely clear when the van surged forward a few metres. She heard the back doors pop open. Her vision was now blurred with tears but she was aware of a bin being wrenched free, knocking others over as it was pulled towards the van. It was her bin. She turned away; she couldn't even bear to see the outside.

One of the felled bins rolled to rest against the van's front bumper. She managed to pick out a figure moving around to drag it away. She heard doors close and then the engine surged again. The van turned a corner hard to disappear out of sight and the noise of its engine was sucked away into the distance a few moments later. Kelly was left alone.

CHAPTER 23

Tuesday

Maddie leant back in her chair and ran her hand firmly down her face, pulling her skin taut as she did so. Her view of the ceiling was replaced by one of PC Vince Arnold, who was now standing in front of her desk.

'Shit, love, you've got a lot going for you but don't be pulling that face again. It's enough to make me look elsewhere and I know how devastated that would make you!' Vince's grin was as big as everything else about him. His uniform clung to broad shoulders, his load vest with baton, radio and cuffs jutting out of it at different points, making him look bigger still, pushed out as it was by the stab vest underneath. The stubble of a few days before was now starting to take shape as an established beard.

'Strange that you should come to me talking about looks. What's with the beard, Vince? It's starting to look like you've done that on purpose. You look like a hipster.'

'Hipster, I'll take. *Action Man* was what the lads on section said.'

Maddie clicked her fingers. 'Action Man! I don't see it. Give it a bit more growth and you might get to sweaty biker?'

'Like I said, Mads . . . I could go off you!'

'I heard you were seeing someone, anyway. Is that true? Has your hopeless flirting with me become all the more inappropriate?'

'Did you? I'm sorry, Mads, I didn't want you to hear about it this way. I was going to tell you myself only you get to the point where you just don't want to be breaking no more hearts, you know what I mean?'

Maddie laughed hard and Vince joined in, his laughter booming around Major Crime's empty office. It was still early morning, too early for any of her detective colleagues.

'I very rarely know what you mean, Vince.' Maddie said.

'Anyway, you wanted to see me? I got your text. Is that what this is all about? You just wanted to check for yourself that I was off the market?'

'Well yeah, I mean that was the main reason. I had some other stuff I planned to ask you about, too, though. You know . . . to make it seem like I didn't care. I guess I might as well still ask you. See if I can keep up the façade.'

'To save face?'

'Exactly. So, tell me what you know about Freddie Rickman?'

Vince's face flickered in surprise. 'Freddie Rickman!' He licked his lips and seemed to be considering it carefully. 'Official or unofficial?'

'I've checked the systems. I know all the official stuff. Do you think I would be asking you if I wanted that?'

'I suppose not. And you're right, there isn't much known about him officially, not when you consider that he has to be one of the biggest players round here. Freddie Rickman has got his fingers in a lot of pies. Some we know about and there's probably some we don't. I remember when he was involved in the drug supply for the area — that was a while ago now. He was fair game for a while, but then he got a bit bigger and we all had to back off him. I thought the powers that be were building something against him, giving him enough rope and all that. Turns out he was one of those who just fall between the cracks.'

'Between the cracks? How does a known criminal do that?'

'Simple, Mads. We see it a lot. You just have to get to be the right size. He got too big for the likes of me doing anything worthwhile by stopping him in his car, but not big enough for the drug squads out of headquarters to be bothered with him. The man's made a career out of it. You know as well as I do that the management here are only interested in the criminals that are visible. Freddie Rickman runs all his stuff quietly. Girls is his thing now. I've not heard his name linked to drugs for a while. He might have packed that up. It's a lot less risk, I suppose. No one carries anything illegal and you don't get no one talking to you about it.'

'Why is that?'

'The girls who work for him need to make a living. Some of them enjoy what they do but they need to be switched on. It's a tough world on your own. A man like Freddie could easily add a bit of security, maybe even get the clients. I've no doubt he deals with the payment side, taking his cut first, of course. So the girls just need to go where they're told and they're onto a good thing. I know a few. They don't walk the street. They work out of sight. He's not stupid.'

'Do you know where?'

'Where they work? Not officially. We used to have a few of the local hotels hosting them. That's what I'm talking about when I say *visible*. We had a few calls and did some enforcement work — well it was more like disruption. No one got nicked that I saw. I guess Freddie learned from that. I've not heard anything about hotels since.'

'I had a look into him. He owns a lot of property in the area, most of it is showing up as unoccupied. They're not just sitting empty though, are they?'

'No. That'll be where they're working then. But the girls have wised up. They know the law. You'll find they'll work in a place one at a time and they'll move it around to save drawing any attention to the place.'

'One at a time?'

'Yeah. There was a law change recently. One prozzy on her own ain't going to get her collar felt but you get two together and then it becomes a *brothel*. You can get nicked for that.'

'So there aren't any brothels anymore?'

'There never has been officially. It's not like you put something out on TripAdvisor when you're done.'

'I know that, Vince. Help me out a little, though, will you? Prostitution legislation isn't exactly my strongpoint. Do you know any girls?'

Vince grinned. 'I know a lot of girls, Maddie, I'm a popular guy!'

'Is that why you grew the beard? To get rid of all the attention?'

Vince's hand lifted to pat his facial hair. 'You really don't like it?'

'I really don't care! The girls, Vince — the working girls . . . who do you know?'

Vince eyed her. 'Come on, Mads . . .'

Maddie waved him away. 'I get it, they don't like coppers. I'm not about to go knocking on their doors and ruining their day. I just need to find out something about Holly Maguire. Right now I've got nothing.'

'Holly, yeah . . . She was one of them.' Vince's smile was all gone.

'One that you knew?'

'Yeah. She's been around a while so most of us old sweats do. I met her a couple of times when we did some drug warrants a few years back. Since then I've met her a fair few times. I stopped her a few times in the dead of night when she was the only thing moving. Then I helped her out when a trick got a bit heavy. She always called me *Big Vince*. It stuck with some of the others too. You can imagine I had to explain to crewmates a few times why a known sex worker was referring to me as *Big Vince*!' His smile was back; it was genuine, too. 'She was a nice girl, a good heart and doing what she needed to survive — just like we all are. A bit messed up.'

'What about her girlfriend? Did you know her?'

'Girlfriend? Nah, I knew she batted for the other side—'

'Vince, Jesus!'

'What?'

'Is that the politically correct term?'

'Is it not? I ain't got no issue! Live and let live I say! But no, I know she was mates with another girl who was running one of the houses but I didn't get that they were a couple. They had a big falling out anyway. I don't know the ins and outs. Probably over money.'

'A madam?'

'Yeah, that's what you call them, innit? The head prozzy?'

'I think they prefer madam. So there *was* a brothel?'

Vince reacted; Maddie could read it instantly.

'There still is, isn't there?'

'Come on Mads, I dunno . . . these girls . . . they're spot on for info. I use them a lot. There's not much about the street they don't know. My first call if someone's wanted and playing hard to get is one of the girls. I don't wanna risk—'

'I get it. Do you have a change of clothes?'

'A change . . . You mean do I have something a bit more comfortable to slip into?'

'No. Something that doesn't have *police* written on it?'

'Jeans and a t-shirt.'

'Perfect. Fancy giving me an introduction?'

'Introduction? You mean to the head prozzy?'

'To the *madam*. I promise I'll be careful with her. I just want to ask a few questions. I'm not looking to cause her any issues.'

'I dunno, Mads. She won't like a knock on the door. We're not supposed to know it's a knocking shop. It's like an unofficial standoff, you know, unless they call us.'

'But if we were just knocking on all the doors in the area because we've had a few burglaries and we needed to offer security advice? See if any residents have seen anything sus?'

'She'll see straight through that. Don't underestimate these girls. They read people. It's like some sorcery shit.'

'Of course she will. So then she'll know that we're not there to cause her any issues, that we're trying to keep her off the radar.'

Vince huffed. Maddie could see he was weakening. 'You want to go now, don't you? I'll have to check with my skipper, Mads. He had taskings for me this morning.'

'Tim Betts, right? I'll go see him now and let him know that I need you. It should only be half an hour.'

'I've heard that before! Fine, then. Get your coat, Maddie Ives, and be prepared for the jealous stares. It'll look like you've pulled a cracker!'

'Really? With that beard I reckon I'll look like I'm moving on the homeless.'

* * *

The woman took so much time answering the door that Maddie had to snatch her arm back from a follow-up knock. She stepped back too, from a door that was pulled inwards. It was only a few inches. A young, timid-looking face peered out.

'Can I help you?' the girl said. Maddie reckoned she couldn't be much older than eighteen.

'I'm DS Maddie Ives and this is PC Arnold. We're knocking some doors in the area due to a spate of burglaries. We're offering security advice and we wanted to ask if any residents had seen anything suspicious.'

The girl glanced from her to Vince. There was no reaction in him. Maddie was pretty certain this was not one of the women Vince knew.

'Is Marlie about?' Vince said.

'Marlie?' The girl's anxiety seemed to increase.

'It's okay. I know her. Maybe you could let her know that Vince is at the door and would like to talk to her. Tell her it's nothing to worry about but I wouldn't be here if it wasn't important.'

'She isn't here.'

'Okay. When are you expecting her back?'

'I don't know. She should be here. I don't know where she is. She never came back after . . .'

'After? After what?' Maddie tried to keep her tone comforting, encouraging the girl that it was fine to speak to her.

'It doesn't matter. She isn't here.'

'But you're worried about her?' Maddie had read it into her expression. 'Maybe I can help. Off the record, if you like? Just tell me what's happened.'

'It's fine. I'm not worried. She's her own woman.'

'It's out of character, though, right? She runs a tight ship and she isn't here. You would have tried her phone and she didn't answer. And she always answers. Am I right? How long will you leave it before you call the police? And what then? Uniform officers, maybe a marked car parked outside. That will cause all sorts of issues.' Maddie stopped. The young woman was visibly shrinking in front of her under the pressure. She seemed to check behind her. Her face appeared back at the door.

'I need to take her dog out for a dump. She goes to the grass on top of the viaduct.'

'I know it,' Vince said.

'I'll leave in a minute.' The door pushed shut. Maddie stepped back. Vince was already walking away.

'She's worried about something,' Maddie said.

'I saw that. I have a number for Marlie. I'll give it a go.' Vince was holding his phone to his ear when they got back to the car. By the time she found her place in the passenger seat he was already pushing it back into his pocket. 'No answer.'

When the young woman appeared, it was in a coat that didn't look like it belonged to her. It was two sizes too big at least. The sleeves covered her hands and she had just pulled the middle together rather than attempted the zip. Slim, bare legs showed from under it and her pedicured feet were pushed into flip-flops. The dog was small, a terrier of some sort, and it quickly set about cocking its leg against anything upright. It suddenly looked smaller still as it took on a thick-trunked tree that jutted from a grassy expanse and held them all in its shade.

Maddie smiled. 'Thanks for agreeing to talk to us.'

'I didn't agree to anything.' She wasn't so timid now. It seemed she had used the time since closing the door to harden her resolve.

'That's right, you didn't. And you don't have to talk to us. But I can tell you're worried. When did you last see Marlie?'

'Lunchtime yesterday. The others . . . they're out looking. I shouldn't be talking to you. What you said about how long we would leave it before we called the police . . . we would never call you.'

'Maybe we can help?'

'If you wanted to.'

'You think I'm just here to enjoy the view over the town and the faint smell of dog shit?'

The girl's eyes hardened and her tone was now laden with sass. 'You came to the house because you knew she was missing, did you? Because you wanted to help us find her?'

'No. I came here because of Holly Maguire. I thought Marlie might know something about her because right now there's just a black hole where her life and memories should be and I don't think anyone deserves that. Did you know Holly?'

'No. I've heard people talk about what happened a few days back.'

'And what was that?'

'She threw herself off a cliff.'

'And what do they think about that? The girls who were talking about it?'

The girl shrugged. 'Shit happens. In this job it's more likely. Someone had some stats about it. Cheerful stuff.'

'She didn't work with you, then?'

'No. She worked with some of the girls before, but they said she ain't been part of the scene for years. What's this about? No one reckoned you lot would give a shit about all this. Some working girl throws herself off a cliff? Ain't nothing to you lot.'

'Well, I think she died for something and I want to know what that was. I care about her and I care about Marlie. If you want, I can care about you, too. But you need to be a bit more open about what's going on.'

The girl shrugged and her eyes fell back to watching the dog.

Maddie didn't say anything. She was aware of Vince off to her right, clearing his throat as if feeling awkward. Maddie wasn't, she knew she needed to let this woman be the next to speak and silence was often the most effective pressure — especially on the young. A breeze blew across them and roused the surrounding trees to a chorus of white noise. They were high up, elevated over the town of Langthorne on a path that ran alongside the viaduct. Trains still rattled regularly between its ancient walls. Maddie had been told it was the oldest viaduct in the country, a national treasure. From here she could barely see a piece of wall or fence that wasn't daubed with some sort of graffiti. If it really was a national treasure, it didn't appear that the locals were giving it the respect it deserved.

'She went out. Some guy turned up. Before you ask, I don't know who he was, but the other girls — the older ones, at least — they all seemed to. They were proper scared. Not of him, though. They said it was of who he worked for . . . the guy who owns the house. Marlie went with him.'

'He worked for the guy who owns the house we just came from?'

'Yeah. That's what I said,' she snapped.

'I just want to be clear.'

'Anyway, this guy was only at the house, like, two minutes. Not much else I can tell you.'

'So this is unusual?'

'I ain't been there long. Not long enough to talk about what's usual.'

'The other girls . . . you said they were talking. They said it was unusual, right?'

'Marlie, she don't leave. She runs it tight there. Sometimes she don't give you room to breathe, you know? It can be a bit much.'

'And when she isn't there, she's quick to answer the phone.'

'Always. It's a standing joke. She'll go out to cash in at the bank and we have bets on how soon she'll call someone. It's never more than, like, twenty minutes.'

'How did she look?'

'Look?'

'Yeah, was she joking and laughing when she left? Was it like she was leaving with a mate?'

The girl hesitated now. She took a moment to fix on the dog. Maddie waited. 'She looked scared, okay. And she never does. Someone asked her if she was okay and she didn't even look at them. She picked up her coat and a bag and just left.'

'And this was yesterday lunchtime?'

The girl shrugged again, her bottom lip now jutting out like she was sulking at being spoken to sternly. It served to remind Maddie of just how young this girl was. She didn't want to ask her age; that might start a line of questioning that could put the barriers up completely.

'Lunchtime, yeah. We hadn't had no work in so it must have been early.'

'What time does that start?'

'Eleven-ish some days. Usually midday though.'

'And the girls are still trying to get hold of her?'

'Yeah. We've all tried what we have. The girls are out at her haunts, but we've done texts, Instagram, WhatsApp— the lot. She's not replied. We've put word out and no one's seen her. One of the girls has a number for the guy she left with. They tried calling him, too. There was a bit of a drama about that . . . some of the girls said not to. They're all shit scared. He didn't answer anyway.'

'And no one said a name? For this guy, I mean? Even a nickname?'

The girl shrugged. 'No. And I don't know people. I've not been here long. That's why they left me here to watch the dog go toilet while they all went out to see what they can find. I don't know no one.'

'And did you see this guy?' Maddie pressed her.

'Briefly.'

'What did he look like?'

'Dunno.' Again there was a sulky lift of the shoulders.

'You know how important that is right? This guy she left with holds the key to finding her — you get that, right? Why wouldn't you tell me what you know?'

'The girls . . . they all said not to. They said they would sort it.'

'But here you are. You've told me this much and it's obvious why. You're worried and you know that your mates should have found her by now. Or at least had contact.'

'You don't talk about these people — they all said that. I shouldn't be here. I had to bring the dog out. I can't help who talks to me but I ain't talking to you no more.'

'Until when?'

'What do you mean?'

'You won't talk about this guy. You won't talk to us any-more today. Until when? Until Marlie's missing for a day? Two days? A week? Or maybe until someone gets hurt? Or turns up dead — would that be enough?'

'Well she ain't, has she?'

'Turned up? No, she hasn't. Isn't that why we're all worried?'

Vince stepped forward. 'I know Marlie well. She's always been good with me and I've returned the favour. I'm the rea-son we knocked right on your door today because Marlie likes for me to know where she lives and works. She's moved a couple of times and she always tells me where in case she ever needs me to know. I think you know what I mean by that. We're not here to cause a problem, we're not writing anything down or reporting back. We're just worried. I'm worried. Just like Marlie would want me to be. Who was this guy she left with?'

The girl chewed her lip. She seemed to take Vince in, her eyes dropping to his feet and then slowly lifting up his bulk. They seemed to linger on the Velcro nametag that read: 'PC Vince Arnold: Response.'

'You're *Big Vince*,' she said, eventually. It made Vince break out in a smile.

'I have been told that!' he chuckled. Maddie rolled her eyes. Even now in this situation, he couldn't resist. The girl didn't return his smile.

'You're in the manual. Says you're alright. For a copper.'

Maddie knew what *the manual* meant. It was more street slang that she had heard before. Brothels kept a book of visiting clients. The examples she had seen had been meticulous. Each client would have notes that included what they liked, who they liked and how they treated the workers. It was a key part of making sure that clients were treated right and regulars were looked after. The turnover of staff in a brothel could be high, girls were often moved about and it was an important part of the fantasy that a new girl could still treat a regular client like an old friend on their first meeting — and she would already know what he wanted. The manual made this possible.

'You have ugly mugs in there too?' Maddie rushed her question; she couldn't hide the sudden excitement in her voice.

'What?' The girl had heard her; she was stalling.

'Ugly mugs. The list. Is it in the manual? They were always kept in there when I worked one in Manchester.'

'You worked a house?' The woman now looked Maddie up and down.

'I was sent undercover. Someone was going around the different houses in the North West beating on the girls bad. I was there to protect them.'

'Yeah, the manual's got the ugly mugs in there.'

'Can I see it? The list I mean?'

The girl shook her head vehemently. It seemed to have prompted her to make a decision. 'I shouldn't even be up here! I can't tell you what happens if I was to show the manual to a copper!'

Maddie plunged her hand into her inside pocket where she kept her cards. 'Put this number in your phone. Just take a picture of the ugly mugs page. *Please.* I don't need the list of initials — I have that. I need the names. I know they will be in there too. It might really help your friend.'

'Initials . . . ? How would you know that?'

'I told you . . . I used to work in a house. Sometimes we had them listed as initials in case someone was taking them out of the door. But I know there'll be names, too — somewhere. I could really do with them. Please, think about it. It might really help your friend.'

The girl took her card. 'I can't promise anything.'

'Please try. Like Big Vince said, none of this is on record and you can trust him. Your manual says that!'

'It don't say *trust!* It don't go that far.'

'Who was this guy?' Vince tried again. The girl was squatting down now, trying to reattach the leash on the dog. She straightened up and dragged the dog towards the same steps from which she had emerged. She stopped at the top of them. Her shoulders dropped like she had sighed.

'I think someone said *Benny.* I don't know no more and I didn't see what he looked like.' She continued towards the steps, walking quickly. Maddie watched her until she was out of sight.

'*Benny* is another name I keep hearing. An associate of Freddie. They've been stopped together a few times. I met him yesterday and he did all he could to get me away from a flat in Truro House — one of Freddie's. You don't think she was in there, do you? This Marlie?'

'She could have been,' Vince said. 'But she'd probably have wanted you to go away just as much as this Benny fella did.'

'I knew I needed to get in there, I just couldn't. They're worried, to be out looking. This has to be out of character. Girls like that are a tight group. They know when something isn't right.'

'So where do we go from here?'

'This whole time I've been wanting to meet this Freddie. I think that's become my next priority.'

'You can't talk to him about any of this. You have to—'

'It's okay, Vince! This isn't my first day. You really care about these girls, don't you? I'm seeing a whole other side to you.'

They walked back towards the car and Maddie looked over and smiled at him. She was sure Vince would have sensed it, but he kept looking forward.

'They're the most vulnerable people we have in our community. I've heard some horrible things, Mads, but never official. Some of these girls get a real shit deal and we never hear about it. Instead it's left to people like Freddie Rickman to sort.'

'Maybe that's the best way sometimes? If a client gets out of hand, I imagine that street justice is a bit more satisfying than what we can manage at times.'

'Maybe. But what if it's not a client? Who polices Freddie? Officially or unofficially, he's a violent piece of shit. A real short fuse, too, I've heard.'

'I guess that's us, then.' Maddie said. 'We'll head back in and do some subtle digging. I need to meet this Freddie. We'll find your friend, too.'

Vince was still looking forward but a faint smile flickered across his lips. 'I know you will,' he said.

CHAPTER 24

'Still ignoring your phone, DS Ives?'

Maddie lifted her head to Harry Blaker's growl. She was back at her desk on the Major Crime floor. She had spread out even more; exhibits and paperwork were now on at least four desks as well as the floor. Harry was casting a look over it all. He didn't seem impressed.

'Did CPS call you again?' she asked.

'Well, yes, actually. They wanted some sort of commitment to getting an update by the end of today, but that—'

'What did you tell them?' Maddie cut in. Then took a breath. She was frustrated with them, not Harry.

His reply was deliberate. 'That they're asking the wrong person. That trying to tie Maddie Ives down to one investigation at a time is like trying to herd cats.'

'And what did they say to that?'

'I didn't give them much of a chance to continue the conversation.'

'Sorry. I wish they wouldn't call you.'

'They probably won't again. Now's the time they might start going higher up the chain.'

'Understood.'

'Well I can see you're no closer to wrapping this up. You've spread out further?'

'Do you remember this?' She lifted an exhibit bag with a piece of lined paper in it and he took it from her.

'*Ugly mugs,*' he read the handwritten title on the page. 'Sure, these are the initials of bad clients.'

'Right. I went down to a brothel in Langthorne, somewhere Vince knew. The madam there knows the street scene well. I was going to ask her about Holly.'

'A brothel? And we know about this, do we?'

'Well, off the record we do. There's an agreement in place. We don't bother them, they don't bother us type thing.'

'Is there? The last thing the police need is anything kept *off the record* in my opinion. Do you know who sanctioned that?'

'Please, Harry, don't focus on that. We need them talking to us, the last thing I need is to upset them. For now at least.'

'Was going to?'

'What?'

'You said you were *going to* ask this madam about Holly?'

'She wasn't there. There was only a young girl, new to the house I think. She sent me this.' Maddie clicked her mouse to wake her computer. A mobile phone screenshot of a piece of lined paper was enlarged in its centre.

'It's the same.' Harry said, referencing the exhibit he still held in his hand.

'Identical. I didn't look at it too closely before, but now it's easy to see that what we have is a photocopy. And then she sent me the next page.' Maddie clicked the mouse to reveal a list of names. The handwriting looked the same, as was the lined paper.

'Am I missing something?' Harry said. 'So what?'

'Why take the time to write a list of initials on one page, then have the full names on the next?'

Harry shrugged. 'You've got me.'

Maddie slumped a little in her seat. 'I don't know either. But Holly wants us to know, or at least she wants us to go looking. What are we supposed to be finding, Harry?'

'You think it's Freddie Rickman.'

Maddie shrugged. 'I do. His name does keep cropping up. This brothel today, Freddie Rickman owns the building. When we went down to the house the girl there said she left this morning with a man called Benny, the same guy I met at another flat owned by Rickman. And our madam is still missing.'

'Missing?'

'Well, not reported. But it was made very clear that the girls would never report her missing. Seems prostitutes don't have a very high opinion of us — not enough to ask for our help, at least.'

'Do we have anything other than the fact that a man linked to the landlord turns up at a house and leaves with one of the residents? And in full sight of other people there. What is it that makes them so worried?'

'She's not back. She's not contactable. And, according to the girls, they never see anything of anyone linked to Freddie. Unless that is, something is very wrong. We know he distances himself from his *enterprises*.'

'But this wasn't him. We don't know he sent this Benny to do anything on his behalf?'

'We don't. But I think he did. I think something drastic must have happened for this Benny to turn up and knock at that door.'

'Like a car going over a cliff?'

'Maybe. We've been to his business and I've knocked on a few of his doors. Word will have got back to him that we're sniffing around. Maybe he wants to make sure that no one is talking to us about him. That makes sense to me.'

'It's all conjecture, though, Maddie. I mean, yes, it could make sense, but what evidence do we have to support it?'

She gestured at the exhibits stacked around her. 'It's here, Harry, I know it is.'

'It might be. Or this is just a collection of items that a known sex worker had in her possession when she died in an unforeseen incident. She also happened to have a list of bad clients in her bag that she copied from the local brothel. Maybe they all carry one when they go out for calls. That would make sense to me.'

'She wasn't a prostitute. Not at this house, anyway. They know of her from old but she's not a prostitute. Hasn't been for ages, apparently.'

'The intelligence on our systems says different. And, again, what do we have? So she doesn't work there? Someone at the house knows her from back in the day and is looking out for her, sharing the list of bad clients in case she gets booked by someone particularly undesirable.' Harry gestured at another piece of paper that was sealed up in a bag on the desk. 'She also has a few addresses where she meets clients on her . . . what else do we have?'

'I can't shake this gut feeling, Harry.'

'I know that. I can see that. And I know what that's like. But it can only take you so far.'

'I need to speak with this Freddie.'

'Then let's go and speak with him.'

'I would, but no one seems to know where he is.'

Harry grinned. 'If you would have let me speak when I first came over here, I would have told you that he's at the front counter. They've called your desk phone, your mobile phone and sent you an email. Do you have any idea how overpaid I am to be your PA?'

'He's here? You've got him here?'

'He just turned up. He has a solicitor apparently. Asked for you by name. You said that he would know you were looking for him. Seems he wants to offer you some answers.'

'And you tell me now! Why didn't you interrupt me?' Maddie stood up and searched the mess around her, tried to work out what was relevant enough to take with her. 'There's so much here. I need time to prep, to work out what I should take down . . .'

Harry held up his hands. 'Pen and paper, that's all you need. And I wouldn't recommend you get that out to start with. He's come in to see *you*. My bet, he's trying to work out what you know, so give him nothing. And take your time. He can sit and stew in a police station for a while. That was one of the reasons why I didn't interrupt you.'

Maddie took a long gulp of air. She felt calmer, instantly. Harry had that knack when it suited him. 'One of the reasons?' she said.

'Yeah. The second is that you don't interrupt Maddie Ives when she's got her teeth into something.'

Maddie smiled. 'Okay. And there's a third?

'I wanted you to bring me up to speed a bit, so I could come down with you.'

* * *

Maddie immediately felt like she had met Freddie Rickman before. She hadn't of course, not in person, but she had certainly met his *type* before. The expensive, fitted suit, the solid gold watch that moved freely about his wrist and the handshake designed to intimidate rather than greet. He was the carbon copy of heads of crime gangs and the numerous wannabes she had met in her time working close to criminals when she was undercover. The arrogance was present and correct too, as was his attention on Harry; his expectation was already set that the male officer would be the one doing the talking, despite Harry sitting himself back from the table and flicking idly through his phone.

Freddie Rickman was a big man. He shifted his bulk in his seat to lean forward and his watch dragged against the surface as he did. He was wearing a flat cap that loosely matched his suit but Maddie thought it looked ridiculous. Finally, Rickman seemed resigned that he was going to be speaking with the woman and he turned his attention to her. She felt as if his eyes were scouring her body until, finally, his gaze seemed to settle just below her eyes. It made her feel uncomfortable.

She glanced away to take in the man who had followed him in and now sat next to him. His build was far slimmer, his suit a little cheaper. At least he was looking her in the eye, albeit over the top of a pair of glasses. He introduced himself as Darren Harvey and described himself as a 'solicitor of law'. He hadn't needed to; everything about him had already told her that.

'Detective Sergeant Maddie Ives . . .' Harvey spoke first. He slid his glasses off his face and gestured with them. The use of her name and rank was classic solicitor. 'My client made contact with me and requested that we attend your police station this day to discuss matters with you directly.' He sat back, his attention moving to a briefcase that rested on the floor. He pushed his glasses back on his nose. A notebook appeared and then a fountain pen that scratched out fervently across the page: *Detective Sergeant Maddie Ives.* The whole room watched it: classic power play. Harvey was taking the time to remind her that he was here as formal protection and that, should anything step out of the framework provided by UK law, there would only be one person to blame. He underlined her name firmly. Twice.

'These places are all the same, no matter where you go!' He flashed Maddie a yellowed smile. She waited for it to fall away and for him to continue. 'Yes, well, the matter in hand . . . My client is aware that efforts are being made to speak with him. As a result of this and to save you all time and effort he has graciously appeared here today to answer any questions that you may have.

'Very gracious.' Maddie said.

'Indeed. We are all for saving you time, you see, and you can be sure that any pursuit of my client *is* a waste of your time. Mr Rickman is a prominent businessman in this area and has assisted police before when activities have been alleged at one of his numerous properties that were considered to be overstepping the mark of legality without his knowledge. Are we to assume this is a similar matter on this occasion?'

'I wouldn't call it a *pursuit*. I have a dead girl that worked for Mr Rickman and, seeing as no one else seems to know much about her, I thought it would be a good place to start.' Freddie had been staring at her the whole time. She could feel it. She turned to him when she mentioned his name. His only reaction was to lick his lips.

'Worked for?' Harvey said.

'Does he speak?' Maddie still looked directly at Freddie. It prompted a response.

'I speak.' There was aggression in those two words.

'Holly Maguire?' Maddie said.

'Now, Mr Rickman,' Harvey said, 'you will remember our conversation before we came in here. You're not under any caution right now, so anything you say right here is just conversational. I would advise you not to talk about anyone else specifically, just about yourself. You've done nothing wrong. I'm sure the officer here will caution you and remind you that you have the right to leave, that you don't have to answer her questions?'

His words were to his client but it was clear they were for Maddie's benefit. She leaned back and crossed her arms.

'That doesn't sound like advice to someone who has done nothing wrong, Darren.'

'Surely *Mr Harvey* is a more suitable level of formality? Or have standards slipped since I was ACC? I would have ensured my officers addressed fellow professionals correctly in this context.'

Maddie couldn't help but smirk. It was right at Darren Harvey, too. Now he had made sure she was aware he was ex-police, and a former senior officer, too. She made sure she ignored that completely.

'Well, Darren, my understanding of this *context* is that you and your man here walked in unannounced and expected me to drop everything to come down and speak to you. A formal interview where I remind everyone of their rights and use formal names . . . that's for people who are being talked to with regard to a possible offence. It's a little odd to come in here telling me how your man here has done nothing wrong and is an honest businessman and yet you wish for him to be cautioned like someone being investigated? Should I be investigating him?'

'Well, no . . . I mean there is a protocol—'

'Was it *honest businessman*? Were those your words?' Maddie had her own notebook out now, she had written *Freddie RICKMAN — honest businessman* at the top. She underlined it.

'Well, I think I said *prominent*, but—'

'So *not* honest.' She crossed out the word and looked over at Freddie. His mouth was curled up in a grin. She spoke to him directly.

'Mr Rickman, I have an impression of you, that you are a direct man who does not appreciate playing games. *Prominent* businessmen are very busy, I'm sure. Your solicitor here would have us playing games all day. The fact he has made sure I know he was previously a senior police officer causes me more concern, as one thing I know about some senior officers is that they are very good at getting nothing achieved from long meetings.' Maddie paused for just a second. She was desperate to look over for the solicitor's reaction but she stayed fixed on Rickman. 'Holly Maguire . . . tell me about her.'

Freddie sniffed. 'She worked for me, sure.'

'Now Mr Rickman, I will remind you—' Harvey was rattled, his cheeks suddenly a shade of red, he stumbled over his words as if he wasn't used to being spoken to like that. Maddie had attacked him on purpose; if you let solicitors walk all over you, their clients think they can do the same.

'She's right and I ain't got all day to be playing no games on notepads. She worked for me, okay? Holly did. Sure.'

'As a prostitute?' Maddie said.

'Prostitute? You lot think I'm some sort of pimp?' His chuckle caught her out. He moved away from her to look over at Harry.

'So what did she do for you?' Maddie said.

'She was a cam girl. All above board, okay? I run a few and they're all very happy.'

'Cam girl? Tell me what that is.' Maddie said.

'A cam girl gets up in front of a webcam and she gives the men what they want, you know what I mean?'

'Humour me. What men?'

'Subscribers. I provide videos to a website. People — mostly men — pay their money and they get access to a members' area. From there they can watch live webcams of my girls or they can access the archive of snipped videos. Those are just the best bits,' he was watching her closer now, desperate for a reaction maybe. She gave him nothing. 'When they watch it live, though, they get to interact. So they'll type something out on the screen and the girls see it. Normally it's a request, or a compliment. Or both. Sometimes you need to be nice to get what you want.'

'And what do these men ask for?'

Freddie leaned forward, his face beaming. His bottom lip was trapped by his teeth before he released it to speak. 'They might ask her to slow it down a bit, you know? Or a different position. Or maybe even speed it up, we're all on the clock.'

'So she strips?'

'Sometimes it's a strip, sure.'

'On her own?'

'Sometimes. Holly liked to work with other women, too.'

'So your girls are doing sex shows, too?'

'Sex shows can happen. They react to the requests from our members — the ones they want to react to. No one's forced to do anything they don't want to do.'

'Who did Holly work with?'

Freddie's grin was back. He straightened up and his watch scraped the table again as he did. 'Mr Harvey, here, tells me that I don't need to be giving any details out about no other girls. Not without some DPA thing, he said. Is that right?'

Harvey pounced as if he had been waiting for this moment. 'Yes of course. But the officer here knows about the Data Protection Act only too well. We can't blame her for chancing her arm now, can we?' He seemed to have gathered himself again. His expression was so smug that Maddie had a sudden urge to beat on his face until it was gone.

'Quoting DPA legislation? Again, I didn't think we were at that point. I thought we were helping each other out? I just need a few questions answered then I can look elsewhere, rather than at Mr Rickman and his prominent businesses. I guess I just thought you would prefer that?'

'My client will answer any questions about him but he cannot talk for other people. I am sure you can appreciate that some of the people in this industry do not wish for their details to be discussed in open forum.'

'That's right.' Freddie's grin was back. It dropped away as he leaned back in but his eyes were still alight as if he was enjoying himself. 'We get all sorts, you know. A lot of the girls are just topping up a salary. They do straight jobs in the day . . . magistrates, estate agents and some who work for the law. Not just because the money's good either but because they *love* it! Ain't nothing a beautiful woman wants more than to be told they're beautiful. There's always room on the books.' His eyes flickered over her again.

'So tell me about Holly.' Maddie said.

Freddie sat back. 'She always just turned up for work, did her thing and left. She was a dream, actually. A good worker. I wish they were all like her.'

'And was she *topping up*?'

'I don't know if she was doing something else. Nothing that I know of. Some of the girls will do once a week or like a couple of times in a month for their pocket money. She was five times a week. Full time, I guess you could say!'

'And what does that mean?'

'Mean?'

'What were her full-time hours?'

'You asking for a friend, sarge?' His grin widened. 'She does five one-hour shows. Normally goes out live early or mid-afternoon. It can vary.'

'Afternoon?'

'You sound surprised.'

'I assumed it would be a later shift.'

'Ah yes, because people only like to get wild when it's dark outside. Actually, I don't deal much in the UK. The market for this is stronger elsewhere. That's the joy of the *world* wide web. So you've got to consider time zones.'

'So you don't have any UK members?'

'I got money coming in. I don't run surveys on where from. But the market's worldwide.'

'What's the site address?'

'I'm not sure my client needs to be sharing information of private business ventures . . .' Harvey fizzled out as his client leant across him to take hold of Maddie's notepad and pen. His writing was oversized and messy. He spun it back to her.

'And this is your site?'

'Nope. I just provide some material. Someone else owns the site. They monitor the traffic that goes through the links to my videos. That's how I get paid.'

'Who hosts it?'

Rickman shrugged. He lifted the flat cap by the peak and rubbed his closely cropped head underneath in one movement. When he replaced it. the peak fell at an angle.

'Have a look. And remember what I said . . . it's good, easy money.'

'Holly ever come with anyone? Anyone drop her off?' Maddie said.

'I set up the business, I sort the rooms and the equipment but I don't get involved with the workers. I have people who do that for me.'

'So I would need to speak to them?'

'I guess you would.'

Maddie picked up the pen he had discarded in the middle of the table. 'So who do I need to call?'

Freddie shrugged. 'Like he said, I'm here talking about me. You want a list of employees and what they do, you need to go through this DPA thing. Then Mr Harvey here needs to agree it and then I got ninety days to provide the information. Like he said, I'm happy to help.'

'I'll be sure to get that document in.'

'You will need justification as to why you need that of course,' Harvey said. 'That would normally include the offence for which my client is under investigation — or any of his employees, for that matter. Right now I can't see how you might pass that particular test.'

'Does Holly have a next of kin that you know of? Friends or family?' Maddie still ignored Darren Harvey.

'Like I said, I rarely see the girls. I only met Holly a handful of times, really. In all the years she worked for me, I rarely had reason to see her.' Rickman lifted his cap to scratch his head again.

'Who did you buy the taxi firm from?' The question was quick, an attempt to blindside him.

'The taxi firm?'

'You run a taxi firm. I understand it was already established and you bought it?'

'I didn't realise the taxi firm was up for discussion?' Harvey cut in.

'Is there a problem answering that?' Maddie said.

Rickman was still leaning back, trying his best to appear apathetic. 'Nope. A fella called Neil Henners.'

'Tell me about him.'

'Maybe he'll tell you about him. I can't say I know enough to tell.'

'Is he still local?'

Harvey cut in: 'I think Mr Rickman has answered all he can about the previous owner of a firm he has now owned for a good five years or more. Unless you want to inform us all of the relevance, I don't think we need to be answering any more questions about that. In fact, I would suggest we have come to a natural point of conclusion, would you agree, Freddie?'

Freddie sniffed. 'Yeah, I think I'm done. I got some business this afternoon. Unless there's anything more you need to ask? I can't have you turning up at my places, see. The cops . . . they spook the girls. I need them nice and relaxed for their work.'

'What do you think happened?' Maddie persisted. 'To Holly, I mean.'

'I heard all about it. It was in the news. She went over that cliff up in Capel. Nasty business. I was sorry when I heard about it. She was a good girl. A good earner, too. The punters liked her.'

'How do you think that happened?'

Freddie stood up. His bulk nudged the table so it scraped away from him as he did. 'You obviously know that she's got a bit of a history for doing a trick or two. I heard maybe she was up there with some punter. I guess it got all hot and heavy and she didn't see it coming. Or he was some psycho who got his rocks off taking her out with him. Like I said, I didn't know the girl.'

'He worked for you, too, didn't he?'

'The fella? He worked for my firm. I never met the guy. We did all the checks. He was licensed and done the job before, up the road a bit. You can see it all if you put in the right stuff.'

'The DPA stuff . . . yeah, I get it.'

'Well, thank you for speaking with us,' Harvey said. 'We were keen to come in here and assist.' He proffered his hand. His smugness now seemed to be a permanent fixture.

'Of course you were,' Maddie said. 'Just not too much.'

Harvey made a show of putting his notepad and pen back in his briefcase. Maddie used the time for one final question.

'You don't look comfortable in that hat, Mr Rickman? I hope you didn't just wear it for our benefit.'

'Your benefit?'

'It looks brand new is all.'

'I like to make the effort for the coppers. Look me up on your system and you'll see that.'

Maddie did manage a smile now. Harvey was finally done and standing in the door, holding it open for his client.

'I have, don't worry,' she said. She waited for the door to click back closed after they had both left. 'I need a coffee. And out of here.'

Kelly halted her quick stride to take the phone out of her pocket. She ran her fingers down the side, over the fresh scrapes that were caused when it had been thrown to the floor next to her. It still worked okay; she'd received a solitary message that had given her a time and a place.

She knew the road well enough. It was not far from Langthorne's central train station. She opened the message to check the house number. It would be the fourth time she had checked. She pushed the phone back into the inside pocket of her coat and set off again. She walked past a walk-in hospital on her right and a pond with some hardy anglers and waddling ducks to her left. The sunlight was freckled on the wide pavement through tall, mature trees that rose up close to the kerb. She took a left and continued for fifty metres. The house to which she had been summoned came up on the right.

Her first impressions were dominated by its impressive size. It was a large townhouse, as wide as it was tall, with a double-sized front door at the top of some steps. There was a more standard-sized door leading to the basement and, as she got closer, she saw an arrow pointing to the side labelled: *Flat C*. She moved up the driveway to the steps. Slowed by a sense of foreboding, her foot caught on the first step. It was as if every part of her mind and body was imploring her to turn back. But she couldn't. She knew that. She'd been given a first-hand demonstration of how few options she had. She checked the message for a final time. There was no mention of a flat number. Even that little problem made her breathing quicken and the knot in her stomach contracted so tightly that she felt like she might be sick then and there.

'You're early!' Benny's voice called out from below. She looked down to see him at the foot of the steps peering up. His face had the familiar sneer that she had come to despise so much and he was pointing towards the lower door.

She walked back down and followed his instructions in silence. The door hung open, exposing a hallway that was decorated in a way that might have been welcoming in another context: earthy colours and a carpet thick enough for her to feel the give through her shoes. It smelled new, too. There were pictures on the walls that all seemed to be seaside references. It had the feeling of someone's home. She didn't quite know what to make of that. She slowed, waiting for an instruction.

'The door to the right,' Benny said.

She did what she was told. The door opened up to a living room. The carpet was the same in there. The walls looked freshly painted and there were more homely touches. She couldn't see anything too personal, no pictures of actual people on the wall. The living room was long and narrow. The far end had a large window but there was a clear line of daylight two-thirds up to remind her she was in the basement. In front of that and pointing back out into the room was a camera on a familiar-looking tripod. The usual laptop was over to the right. The sofas were arranged so that the longer one was in front of where the camera was pointing while the shorter one, a double seater, was pushed out of the way entirely. The lighting was set up but the rig was scaled down. There was another monitor too. She hadn't seen that before. Benny seemed to make a beeline for it. The screen flashed white when he turned it on and he turned his leering smile towards her.

'He's on his way.'

Kelly knew what that meant. She felt her heart quicken and her chest tighten at the same time. Those few words pushed her closer to a panic attack. She shouldn't have come here. She should have gone to the police, not cared about the other people who might have got hurt. She needed to look after herself.

It was too late now.

She heard a noise behind her, the door pushing open. She didn't turn to it. She didn't have to. She already knew who it was.

Freddie swept in front of her. His attention seemed forward as if he was looking towards Benny or the screens. He carried what looked like a tradesman's bag, the sort that carried tools and opened out. He turned so that he was facing her and dropped the bag onto the soft carpet. It made a metallic thud and fell open. Kelly waited for him to speak. He stared at her and a few seconds passed.

'I worked out that there needed to be some changes.' Freddie's voice was low, but both more menacing and more assured than she had ever heard before.

'Changes?' Kelly had to swallow first, before she could find her voice.

'You don't get to speak.' Freddie's reply was instant. 'I took some time to think and it seems you have given me an opportunity. More money — that's important. But the really important thing is an opportunity for you to understand that you *DO NOT* cross me.' His shout was so sudden and laden with such venom it was like a punch in the throat. Then he looked like he was composing himself. He took his time.

'The bin . . . I . . .' The words fell out of Kelly's mouth before she really knew what she wanted to say.

Freddie's hand flashed down to reach into the bag, he was on her in a few steps and something swung at her while she was frozen to the spot. There was a huge thud next to her. She opened her tightly shut eyes to a hammer embedded in a wooden table beside her, claw end first.

'I SAID . . . you don't get to speak unless I ask you a question. The next time I don't miss. Do you understand?'

Kelly's gaze lingered on the hammer, her mouth filling quickly with saliva as if she was going to be sick. She turned away and heaved but nothing came up. She couldn't swallow; her throat was too tight. She spat in a tissue. Freddie seemed satisfied. He walked back to the monitor, leaving the hammer in place. Kelly took a step away from it. Freddie moved to the shorter sofa that had been pushed back against the wall. He sat straight, adjusting his clothing so it wouldn't crease, his back rigid as if he had been told to sit up by a headmaster. He stared forward, breathing deeply like he was trying to calm himself down.

Finally he stood back up. 'This is all you need to worry about from now on.' Freddie walked the length of the living room to gesture at the monitor. Kelly was too far away to make it out and she was struggling to focus. 'Come over here,' Freddie growled. 'I need to show you.'

She moved forward, each step heavier than the next. She stopped when she was close enough to see the monitor, chancing a look to the left where Benny stared at her, his face still twisted into a sneer.

'Closer.' Freddie almost whispered.

She shuffled forward. She could make it out now — all of it. The monitor was divided into four different camera images. The top left showed a live feed of her and the two men, angled down from one of the corners of the room. She looked up and couldn't see it immediately. It didn't matter any-way. She could see the movement of her head on the screen with only a second of lag. Next to that was the view from a camera set up under the window and focused on the long sofa. The bottom left screen showed a different room entirely. It was similar to the one Kelly was in but the furnishing was different. The view was also towards a sofa and there was an elevated view with a wider angle of a carpeted area.

'What is this?' Kelly whispered. Even as she spoke there was movement in the images on the bottom row. She leaned in a little. A female figure walked in and stopped near the sofa. She looked tiny, she was shivering and she kept looking over her shoulder as if there was someone behind her. It was Libby.

'What *is* this?' Kelly said louder. The blow came as she turned towards Freddie. It caught her out, knocking her to the ground. She looked up to see a blurred image of Freddie looming over her, a hammer lifted above his head. She threw up her hands. 'Okay! Nothing! I say nothing! I get it!' She shut her eyes firmly, her hands still reaching up, scrabbling in the air.

'Get the fuck up!' Freddie hissed. She opened her eyes. He still held the hammer high, his nostrils flared, his stare seeming to have no focus. She did as she was told. Her hand lifted to where her cheek stung.

'Your little friend never made it to the copper,' Freddie continued through a clenched jaw. 'She got damned close. Then we had a little *conversation* and now she understands. You need to understand the same. You are alive because I have decided you *can be*. You are now in my debt and I don't trust you. That means I need to be sure you're doing as you're told and that ain't something you're good at, now, is it?'

Kelly looked back to the screen. Libby was still standing in the middle of the room shaking her head and facing away as if reacting to a voice behind her. There was a blur of movement and she was grabbed and thrown onto the sofa. Kelly could now see a man with his back to both cameras, gesturing as if agitated. Libby covered her face and pulled up her legs, making her look even smaller. Freddie moved to obstruct Kelly's view of the screen. She was frozen to the spot, her hand covering her mouth.

'I'm only going to give you these instructions once,' Freddie said, 'so you need to listen. You will work every day until you pay off your debt. Do you understand?'

Kelly nodded.

'You will do as you are told. Refuse, and Libby takes your place. Understand?'

Kelly didn't. She tried to make sense of it. Her mind was fuzzy with confusion. There was a rustle behind her and she turned to see two men fill the doorway. Both stood in their underwear, one of them she recognised from before. Her body sagged. A tear fell and ran onto her bottom lip that was trapped between her teeth.

'You got what you wanted,' Freddie continued. He moved to stand next to the monitor, to where Libby had started a wobbly dance for the camera. 'You wanted her left alone — just a solo dance, you said. You got that. But we have her now and she does whatever you won't. I got you worked out, just like I had your whore girlfriend. It seems that threatening you — even beating on you or whatever — don't cut it. A worthless whore knows when they're a worthless whore. You don't care what happens to you. We could beat on you all day and it would hardly make your day worse would it? But her . . .' Freddie gestured at the screen. 'She still thinks she's something and she'll have people that think it, too. It's gonna take a bit longer to break her down. Look at you, Kell. Who have you got now? Even Holly jumped off a cliff so she didn't have to be with you no more. I mean I've heard of some pretty drastic measures but that takes all the biscuits!' His snorting laughter cut through her like a scalpel and her eyes leaked more tears. She didn't even wipe them. 'No one cares about you. You don't care about yourself. All you are is a camera whore and we're going to show it to the *world,* Kell!'

He stepped in closer. Close enough that she could smell his odour and feel the heat from his body. She looked down, lacking the energy or spirit to lift her head.

'You're going out on the dark web, Kell. There's no limit on there. Nothing you can't do and people pay the big money to see it. So there you are! You've finally made the big time!' He snorted again then he stepped back and addressed the back of the room. 'Remember what we talked about, lads. Take what you want and be rough doing it? Oh and try and wind her up a bit, first — see if she's got some fight left. It's good for the show!'

Kelly didn't hear any response. She looked back to the monitor where Libby had started to shed some of her clothes. Freddie leaned forward to speak softly.

'You're a broken whore, but I know you've a little bit of fight left. Our viewers will appreciate that.'

He nodded at Benny who suddenly burst to life. He leaned into the laptop. The top half of the monitor that had been showing images of her in the room went black. He fidgeted with the keyboard, his grin still in place, his eyes darting over the screen. Finally he straightened up and nodded.

'All set.' Freddie said. 'The dark web's a bit different, Kell, a bit riskier. You don't want to be beaming your stuff out to the weirdos for too long, you never know who's trying to find out who you are. So we have a twenty-minute window. Now that isn't long, not for you and your two co-stars, but don't worry . . . they should be able to make the most of it!'

Freddie paced to the rear of the room. He stopped by the door.

'Every day you will work in a different place, so keep your phone on. If you don't want to come back, don't. But then it's all on Libby. I'll be watching.' Freddie stepped out. Benny gave her one last leer and followed him. He patted one of the men on the chest as he passed.

Kelly couldn't manage any response. Her body still sagged. All the energy, all the life, all the fight had left it. There was nothing more she could do. She had no contact with Libby and no idea where she might be. It was hopeless.

She turned back to the screen where Libby's tiny form shook in a nervous dance. The two screens covering her room were back on. She could see herself from two angles, still and silent. From the raised camera she could see the two men were moving towards her now. Their faces and outlines blurred as more hot tears plunged down her cheek. She heard the distant sound of the front door being pulled shut.

She closed her eyes to the sound of the lock being bolted.

CHAPTER 26

'What did you think?' Maddie put the coffees down. It was their regular place and their preferred table. She had hurried along a young lad who looked like he might have been considering packing up his laptop to leave. The table was right at the back but with a good view down the middle. She always liked to see who was coming in.

'You feel better now you've met him?' Harry said.

Maddie still fussed over her drink. 'Not really. Terrible aftershave.'

'Aftershave?'

'Freddie Rickman. He smelt like a week-old wine bottle. Too sickly for me.'

'Is that a key part of his character?'

'It can tell you a lot.'

'He didn't tell us much else.'

'I don't like him, Harry.'

'Which isn't a crime unfortunately.'

'It isn't. Dig enough around a man like that, though, and it's only a matter of time before the crimes show up.'

'You might be right.'

'There's a *but* coming . . .'

'You know my thoughts. That meeting needed to move us along. It didn't.'

'You said I had twenty-four hours. By my reckoning I still have a lot of that left.'

'He only came in here to find out what you know, which is very little.'

'I didn't tell him *all* that we know. And the fact he turned up at all and with his brief means we have him rattled.'

'Maybe we did.'

'So what are you saying? That I should just leave it there? Give it up?'

'Give what up?'

Maddie went to say something but it left her. She tried again but only managed the start of a word.

'And there you are. You still can't answer that question, why you are spending your time pursuing this man.'

'I just want answers.'

'There's a whole police force out there looking for answers to questions. Some are looking at who nicked a Mars bar from the local shop . . . others are specifically assigned robberies or domestic burglaries. We have our work. This isn't for us, not anymore. I think now is the time to hand this over to CID.'

'This is hardly the theft of a Mars bar, Harry. Two people died. We still can't rule out foul play.'

'You just needed to prove that any offences were committed by the persons involved only — with no one outstanding. I think you've done that.'

'Who was the murderer?'

Harry's face wore an expression that she had come to recognise as a warning — that she should back away. She wasn't going to today.

'If it wasn't an accident,' Harry said, 'if there *was* a murderer then you have done a very thorough job of building a clear picture of our suspects. Holly Maguire was a known sex worker with previous for suicide attempts, drug and alcohol abuse and mental health issues. The taxi driver has a clean record, a young family and was making positive plans. He'd no history of mental health issues or suicidal tendencies. So we could write this up right now if we wanted to. Holly forced that car over the cliff. I don't know why and we may never. Maybe she couldn't jump? If that were true then using a car would make sense — it does the hard bit for you. She doesn't have a car so a taxi was the only option? But you seem to have this refusal to believe what your investigation is pointing directly at.'

'What about the backpack? The messages?'

'Messages? Photos and addresses of where she took clients, a list of clients who *may* have treated sex workers badly and a tentative link to how Freddie Rickman bought out a business five years ago. It's a passing shot maybe? Holly didn't want to go without having her final say. You didn't like Freddie Rickman after five minutes in a room with him, so it's not difficult to see how someone who worked for him would dislike him too.'

'Perhaps.'

'Perhaps? What else is there?'

'Something more. Her girlfriend, the woman who appeared on the top of the cliff — what she said to the informant . . . that stuff about how she was supposed to come and see us, that she has something she needs to tell us about Holly — about Freddie maybe.'

'Maybe? But she hasn't, has she?'

'And what about this Marlie? She's missing from the brothel. The girls saw her leave with someone we know to be a close associate of Freddie's.'

'We don't actually *know* who she left with. We have a nick-name and no description and no likelihood of a statement.'

'Okay. But a missing person with foul play suspected — that's Major Crime territory right there!'

'She's missing, is she? Reported? On our system and with the witnesses giving full support and information?'

'You know that won't happen.'

Harry sighed. 'Nothing's happened until it's reported. We have to work like that. We can't just go chasing down everything that piques our interest. There are other jobs, other case files that need work done on them. Pass this over to CID. Rhiannon can run it, maybe. I know you two have a bond. She'll keep you well informed.'

Maddie swigged her drink. It was too hot but it was effective at stopping her first response. She used the moment to think again. Harry always came from a place of logic, of black and white, and she was struggling to argue with that. All she really had was a gut feeling. But it was strong, here, stronger even since she had met Rickman.

'The list of ugly mugs. I gave it to Mitch. All the names had hits. Some show as associated with Rickman, either directly or indirectly. Some of them are taxi drivers . . . some are linked to enforcement work for Rickman when he was peddling drugs — assuming he's stopped doing that, of course.'

'Okay?' Harry said. His tone gruffer, his patience wearing thin. He was not a man who liked to be challenged on the same subject for long.

'I'm just thinking out loud, Harry. I can't argue with you, but there are lines of enquiry still. His website . . . I want to have a look at that.'

'Hand it over, Maddie. That's me meeting you in the middle. And speak to CID — don't go straight to Rhiannon. You'll need to speak with the guv'nor in there and you'll need to *sell it*. They're just as busy as we are — busier even.'

'And if I can't? Sell it, I mean?'

'Then I think that tells you what you need to know.'

* * *

When Maddie returned to her desk, she was glad she found an instant excuse to leave it again. It was a mess of property and paperwork and unlocking her screen showed a number of unread emails and a to-do list that had been unchanged for days. The excuse was stuck to her keyboard in the form of a handwritten post-it note. It said simply:

See me.

Rob.

She knew it to be from Rob Ford. She had sent him a scanned copy of one of the pages from Holly's address book. To her it was two jumbled up lines of letters, numbers and symbols but one of them started 'HTTP' and, even with her limited knowledge of the connected world she knew that to be a website. She snatched the note and took it with her.

Rob Ford was one of the Forensic Media Technicians. His was a role that was becoming more and more essential in modern policing. He had a talent for finding information about people of interest from their social media presence or records held with any number of public domain databases, most of which Maddie hadn't even known existed. Even more important than his knowledge was his ability to present this in a format that would be accepted as evidence. This was a far more difficult task than Maddie had first realised but he had been able to explain it in a way that made sense.

'Effectively, Maddie, the internet is never still. It changes every second of every day. Picture the sea and imagine you see someone drop a cup of water into it down at Langthorne beach. Tomorrow, if you were to check again it could be almost anywhere in the world, separated into a million droplets and you would have no way of proving it had ever been where you saw it, let alone who tipped it in.'

It made sense to her. The internet was just like the ocean, constantly moving and changing, and utterly terrifying.

'Hey, Rob. I got your note.' She held it up to prove her point.

Rob looked up from his monitor. Due to the nature of the work they did and the things they had to view, the windows were constantly covered. This was despite them being on the fourth floor. The door also had a combination lock on it for when they were working on sensitive material. Today it was wide open. The working environment was oppressive, not only dark and stuffy but cluttered and noisy. There was a large number of laptops, computer towers and monitors dotted around, some with their innards hanging out. A large flat screen TV on a wall silently played the game show *Countdown* and it seemed to be the main source of light for the room. Rob's desk had a small lamp that was angled to point down at what looked like his main keyboard among several.

'So I see. I should thank you, that was one of the more interesting tasks I've been given recently.'

'Interesting?'

'Sure. A couple of free strip shows on company time? I've had worse days.'

'Strip shows?'

'Yup.' Rob clicked a mouse on his desk and looked up. The large television changed to mirror a computer desktop. Maddie watched the cursor chase across it as he moved the mouse to bring up the force's internet home page. From here he copied over the first of the links she had sent him. The screen changed instantly to divert to a website. It was instantly obvious what sort of site it was.

'Okay then.' Maddie had her daybook. She opened it up to the last page, to where Freddie Rickman had written KAMGIRLS.COM in his oversized writing. It matched with what was written up on the screen. It was misspelt so the *K* could be fashioned to look like a pair of legs in tights. 'It's all very classy, I see.'

'It is indeed. And for just fifteen pounds a month you can get yourself access to the members' lounge. I love the way they've called it a lounge. Sounds exclusive.'

'And what do you get in this lounge?'

'It's a little unclear. Most of the pages are in Russian. You'd need it translated properly but it seems that a member can take advantage of regular live shows as well as watch an archive of older ones. The site caters for a lot of tastes.'

'Tastes?'

'Yeah, there are a lot of categories. You can choose to watch singles, couples — a group, I think but that wasn't clear — and any combination of male and female, male and male . . . You get the point. I didn't click around too much. I can't be seen to be having too much fun.'

'No, I don't blame you. It's pretty much as he said anyway. Can you tell me anything about the background? He said someone else was hosting it and he just provides the feeds. I didn't want to come across as an idiot, but I can't say I know too much about what that means.'

'Okay. So, yeah, from what is publicly available, this site is registered and hosted in Russia. You can take that with a pinch of salt, however. I can set up a site now and register it just about anywhere in the world from this chair. Means nothing. Porn sites that are making good money will usually claim to be operating from the country that has the best tax conditions, or sometimes the country that has the right attitude towards those sort of sites, if you know what I mean.'

'You mean licensing?'

'There's no licensing for porn. There are the usual laws around age of the model, etc. but there's no other regulation. Not for your common site anyway.'

'Jesus!'

'I know. It's terrifying, really. It's easy money, too, from what I can see. I suggest your friend will have a simple webcam set up with a secured Skype connection that will have been provided by whoever hosts this site. That will provide the member access to the feed and both ends will get traffic information.'

'Traffic information?'

'How many men you have holding their dicks at any one time.'

'Thanks. A little too much information.'

'That will be how your man gets paid.'

'So the more punters, the more money.'

'Simple as that.'

'And the other? You said there might be two sites listed on there?'

'Yeah, I was right, too. That wasn't quite so exciting for me but potentially it is more exciting for you.' Rob was clicking again. He copied over the second jumble of text she had sent.

'It is a web address, then?' It didn't look like it to Maddie.

'It is but for the dark web. They look very different because they don't have to follow the rules that are in place for search engines. Here we are.'

Maddie's attention was back on the flat screen. '*UKamgirls*' she read out. 'Suddenly the misspelling makes more sense.' This time the word was in a simple, flat font. There was no accompanying graphics or half-naked females designed to tempt you in. just the word and then an underlined word underneath that said *ENTER*.

'So it's the same thing, just on the dark web?'

Rob shrugged. 'The same theme for sure but the content will be more specialist, it has to be.'

'Specialist?'

'Why bother otherwise? If you have a viable porn site on www, why bother doing it again in a far more difficult place? Taking payment on the dark web is far from simple, people only do it if it's really worth it.'

'So what do you mean by specialist?'

'Something that doesn't have to abide by the law. You're talking underage, bestiality, forced . . . the nasty categories basically. There will be stuff neither of us have the imagination for, even.'

'Jesus . . . and assuming it's the same concept we're talking about, someone beaming this out *live* and for entertainment purposes?' Maddie shuddered at the thought.

'Exactly. I can't tell you much more, though — we've hit the standard dark web brick wall.' Rob clicked on *ENTER*. The screen changed, now there was a small box in the middle with words next to it: *Host passcode*.

'Passcode?' Maddie said.

'Yeah. I've seen it a lot with indecent images of children cases. Someone will upload their whole collection to the dark web and then they give out their passcode in forums to other users, people they think they can trust, usually someone who has shared images with them first.'

'And without that passcode?'

'Even with that passcode there are likely to be other layers and checks. Then you're going to need some sort of digital currency. In summary, we ain't getting in.'

'Even you!' Maddie smiled and patted him on the shoulder. 'Thanks though, that helps massively.'

'Does it? I wish I could tell you what was behind that link. Or who. That's another thing . . . I can't tell you anything about who set that link up or is running the content behind the passcode. Sorry, Maddie.'

'Oh, don't worry about that, I'm pretty sure I know that part already. Proving it, however . . . I don't suppose you can get details of any of the girls on the site we can see?' Maddie said.

'I can get screenshots of what they look like. The site also lists name, age and nationality — no promises of the accuracy, though. I can get you a document with them all listed but it'll take a while.'

'That would be great — if you're sure you have the time? It might not take me any further. It's a bit of a fishing trip, to be honest.'

'Don't worry. I'm sure I can fit in a few hours of watching strip shows, you know, if it's *essential* for your work. I think I can isolate the feed so I will know only the girls your friend is supplying.'

'That would be great. And try not to enjoy it too much, Rob. These girls are very likely being exploited.' Maddie still managed a smile but there was an edge to her voice she couldn't help.

Rob's expression turned serious. 'Sorry, Maddie, I get that. Good luck with getting this bastard.'

Maddie felt a vibration in her pocket where her phone was going off. She pulled it out just in time for its chirp to fill the room. She silenced it.

'Thanks again for your time.'

'No problem. I'll put it all in a summary document, just in case anyone does ask me why I was sat watching a strip show over my lunch. I'll have to put you down as the OIC and send you a copy. Protocol.'

'Perfect. Thank you.'

'What about Harry? I usually just send things to you both now?'

'No!' Maddie was aware she was a little too keen. She came back softer. 'No need. He's got other bits going on. This is something I'm running.'

Rob smiled and tapped his nose. 'I get it. Every couple has their rough patches. No problem.' His grin was back. Maddie turned her attention to her phone and saw she had silenced a call from Vince. She pressed to call him back. The phone held to her ear was the perfect way to signal that she had to leave.

Vince's voice boomed down the phone immediately. 'Seems they finally got scared enough to call Big Vince!'

Maddie moved the handset away from her ear to scowl at it and turn it down a couple of notches.

'What? Who?'

'Big Vince. I'm in their book, remember? If in doubt, call Big Vince. He's the good guy.' Vince chuckled but he sounded tense.

'Who called?'

'She didn't say her name, just that she was from the house on London Road. She said she had called the number from the book. Said she knew I was a copper and was insistent it was all off record. Then she said that Marlie was missing and that they were all worried about her. I didn't tell her that I knew that already.'

'You didn't mention the girl we spoke to?'

'No and nor did she. I didn't want to stitch her up. This was a different girl. She sounded terrified — like proper scared. Whatever's going on down there, they've all got a bad feeling about it.'

'She said that?'

'Pretty much. It was frustrating, Mads. She called me up to say they needed help but she weren't about to give me anything that I could use. She only wanted to talk about one thing, really.'

'What was that?'

'Kelly Dale. She said I needed to speak to her. That was all she would say. That ain't someone I've heard of. I was just calling to see if that name had come up with you yet?'

'Dale? Someone else told me about a Kelly but they didn't have a surname. It *must* be the same! Did this girl say anything more about this Kelly Dale? Like how we might get to speak to her?'

'They don't know where she lives. The girl said this Kelly has just lost her mum apparently, like in the last day or so. She also said that Marlie went to see her and that this Kelly's scared — really scared. Apparently she don't like to go home. Someone else from the house has seen her hanging about any place she can in the evening so she don't have to.'

'What else?'

'Nothing from her but I got the FCR to put *Kelly Dale* through PNC. She's not known to us. The bloke doing the checks didn't sound like he knew what he was doing, though. I was going to have a look myself when I got back in.'

'Don't worry, I'm still at the nick now. I'll have a look. Did this girl tell you where she's been seen hanging about?'

'I asked her that. She just said the town 'til late. I guess there won't be too many places that are open. You probably wouldn't hang in the pubs . . . there's a bingo hall and a twenty-four-seven McDonald's or she might just be finding a bench. No guarantee she goes there every night either.'

'When are there ever guarantees in policing? Where are you now? I could do with using your desk.'

'*My* desk? You know I work response, right Mads? I don't get no desk. I can see if there's one spare in the report writing room. Why can't we use the nice big space you got up in Major Crime? There's normally a cup of tea up there too!'

'Not right now. The boss . . . he doesn't want me working on this at the moment. I just want to stay out of his way until we know what we've got. In case it's nothing.'

'It didn't feel like nothing, Mads. This girl was proper scared.'

'So you said. But Harry's going to need something more solid than a scared voice on a phone.'

'Alright then, let's see what else we can get. I'm worried, too, Mads. Don't get me wrong, Marlie's a tough old bird. But she's got her girls scampering around and calling the Old Bill. Even off the record they don't do that lightly.'

'I know that. Call me when you're back in. This Kelly Dale has all the answers for us, Vince. I'm sure of it.'

Wendy Battle's expression and demeanour was not what Rhiannon had been expecting. She had called Rhiannon directly just an hour or so earlier to say that her daughter had returned. Libby Battle's missing episode had been assigned to her uniform colleagues but she was glad Wendy had called her first. Rhiannon was still dealing with the assault on her boyfriend, an investigation that was going nowhere right now and this would be a good excuse to go back over that.

'I'm so glad you came!' Wendy breathed. She stepped back and her front door opened wider. Rhiannon could see the same carpeted steps behind her that she knew led up to Libby's bedroom. There was no sign of Libby herself. Wendy was furtive. She half turned towards the stairs then changed her mind. Then she started to speak but seemed to stumble over what she was going to say.

'Is everything okay, Mrs Battle? You said Libby had returned home. Is she okay?'

'She's not okay!' Wendy's voice came out like a rushed breath, her face creased with it like a silent sob and Rhiannon had to give her a moment to recover.

'Is she in her room?' Rhiannon had ditched her chaperone to come out on her own this time. After her conversation with Maddie earlier, she felt like she had permission. Now she wished she hadn't. She could do with a colleague to stay with Wendy while she went to speak with her daughter. Her mother had seemed keen on making a drama out of the situation from the moment they had met and this could only be counter-productive. As it happened, Rhiannon didn't have to worry. Wendy was gesturing at the stairs. Rhiannon checked behind her when she was half way up. Wendy had stayed on the ground floor.

'I'll make some tea,' she said. And then she was gone. Rhiannon's sense of déjà vu was strong as she knocked on the door. This time however, she didn't wait for a reply. She pushed the door open. There was instantly a scurrying sound to the right. Libby Battle was at her wardrobe, partly concealed by one of the open doors. A bundle of clothes spilled out of the bottom and onto her feet as she froze to stare at her visitor.

'Hey,' Rhiannon said. 'I did knock.' Libby's gaze switched back to the wardrobe and her attention with it. More clothes tumbled out. Suddenly she stepped back and pushed the doors. They wouldn't close right up; they still caught on the material hanging out of the bottom. She turned away with a handful of clothes, some dropping onto the floor as she piled the rest onto the bed. She reached down to pull a bag out from under.

'Going somewhere?' Rhiannon asked.

Libby stopped what she was doing and turned half back. Rhiannon was expecting a volley from a petulant teenager, anger at least. But straight away she could see a face close to breaking. Her eyes were wide with a red rash underneath. She had been crying a lot. She was gripping her bottom lip in her teeth as if trying to hold it still. Rhiannon stepped further into the room and closed the door carefully behind her.

'Maybe I can give you a lift somewhere?' Rhiannon said.

'No. Thank you.' Libby spoke. She was packing. There was no care taken. The clothes she had bundled on her bed were now simply bundled into a bag.

'You missed a sock.' Rhiannon pointed at the floor with a grin.

Libby scooped it up and didn't return the smile.

'I can help, you know. Sometimes we all need it.' Rhiannon was careful with her words, desperate not to be condescending. She was sure Libby's mother downstairs had that as her speciality.

'Thank you,' Libby said. She still wasn't looking back over.

'I can see you're upset. I would really like to help.'

'There's nothing you can do.' She stopped what she was doing. Her left hand stayed resting on top of the bag; her right gripped the zip that still hung open. For a moment she looked like she was considering her options. Rhiannon waited, trying to give her some space. Libby jerked back to life, she pulled the zip hastily across and threw the bag to the floor.

'I have to go out,' she said.

'Okay. You were reported missing, your mother—'

'I wasn't missing. I told her that. I just can't be here with her sometimes. You must understand that, surely.'

'I do.'

'Then I have to go out.'

'When someone is reported missing we have a process. We like to talk to the person when they return. Just to make sure they didn't come to any harm.'

'I'm fine.'

'Okay, Libby. But that's an answer to a different question.'

'I don't have to answer your questions!' The petulance had returned.

'You're right . . .' Rhiannon said. Libby was a blur of movement now. She stomped across the floor and pulled a jacket roughly out of the wardrobe. The hanger came with it and clanged against the radiator as it dropped. Rhiannon waited for her moment. Then she spoke again. 'He's awake, by the way.'

Libby stopped for just an instant, just long enough for Rhiannon to know she had heard her. Rhiannon waited her out. Thirty more seconds passed.

'That's good.'

'It is. They think he's going to be fine. I went to see him but I wasn't allowed to be there for a long time. He asked after you.'

'What did you tell him?'

'I told him you were missing. He was very worried about you. He still will be.'

'You should tell him I'm not missing anymore. Maybe tell him I never was. He knows what my mum's like.'

'Why don't you come and tell him? I'll take you. I need to speak to his consultant anyway. He wasn't around earlier. James can't remember much about that night. I wondered if getting you both together might help.'

Libby had pulled on her jacket roughly and gathered up the handles on the bag, ready to leave. Now she flopped to a sitting position on the bed and she dropped the bag between her feet. 'I can't.'

'Why not, Libby? Don't you want to?'

'I do!'

'But you can't?'

'You wouldn't understand.'

'I don't understand. Help me out. Did he do something to you? Something bad? You don't have to protect him, you know. Maybe you told someone else what he did and they got hold of him? That wouldn't be your fault. I just need answers, Libby. I'm sure you understand that.'

'No! I told you, he dropped me back. He was fine. He would never hurt me. I never realised . . . *how* nice he was. I wish I'd stayed with him . . .'

Rhiannon stiffened. Libby's reaction was genuine enough to have her cursing mentally. Her best theory had just been blown out of the water.

'Stay with him? What do you mean?'

Libby picked up her bag and took a step towards where Rhiannon was in the way of the door.

'I just mean something happened to him after he dropped me off. You told me that, didn't you? If I had stayed with him I might have been able to help him out.'

'Or maybe you would have been hurt too and lying in the hospital bed next to him? He still has some recovery. It'll take time but he will recover. If there's a still a threat towards you or him I can help.'

'Are you going to let me past?' Libby hadn't looked Rhiannon in the eye the whole time she had been there. She did now. Her eyes were tinged red. She looked exhausted. Rhiannon stepped to one side for her to walk past but she turned to follow her down the stairs. Immediately her mother's voice was shrill.

'You're leaving again? Where are you going? Are you going to let this happen?' Libby made the bottom step and moved to the door. Her mother did her best to block it.

'You've packed?'

'I'm just going to the charity shop, Mum. I don't want these clothes — any of them. I need to start again. Please . . .' She was still looking at the floor.

'Your clothes? You're just getting rid of all your clothes? Why would you do that?'

'Please Mum. Please . . .'

'Well then, I'll drive you.' Wendy was plainly fighting to keep herself under control.

'No. Please, just leave me alone. I'm fine, I just need some space.'

'You're sixteen years old, Libby. Of course I'm going to worry about you when you're not here, when you don't tell me what you're doing, when your new phone's switched off, when you're ditching your clothes?'

When Wendy didn't get a reply she looked over to Rhiannon for an answer. Libby took the opportunity to tug open the door, it bounced into her mother's hip but it was enough for Libby to squeeze through the gap.

'You're just going to let her leave?' Wendy said to Rhiannon. 'What did she say to you?'

'I can't stop her, Mrs Battle, she's free to go.'

'What can you do, then? Nothing at all from where I'm standing!'

Wendy strode out of the door and stopped at the end of her drive. Rhiannon moved to stand next to her and both of them watched the tiny form of Libby walking off into the distance.

'So what now if she doesn't come back?' Wendy snapped.

'Then report her missing.'

'Fat lot of good that will do. The last time I called I was told she needed to be missing for twenty-four hours! She's sixteen years old and your lot would have her on the street for twenty-four hours?'

'I understand, but sixteen-year-old girls go out, they need space. She came back, that's a positive. If we hassle her too much she might stop doing that.'

'And then what? You might start taking this seriously?' Wendy Battle's last word was a shriek. She turned quickly and Rhiannon watched her walk back into the house.

CHAPTER 28

Kelly leaned her weight forward onto her hands and felt the
solid cold metal through her palms. She felt tired. Maybe
it was the fact she was standing close to the door, close to
where a ceiling heater was blowing warm, dry air downwards
over double doors that were fixed permanently open. It had
to be broken, surely; the evening was almost as warm as the
day had been and certainly more humid. Over the last few
weeks, the late summer warmth had regularly been building
during the day to conjure up storms in the evenings and the
latest was a torrential rainstorm, with heightened winds as an
accompaniment. She was dry at least.

She turned away from the white noise of the beating rain
to follow the smooth movement of mechanised arms as they
slid in and out, cajoling the pile of two-pence pieces that hung
over the edge with intentional promise. She glanced furtively
at everyone who walked past. Any moment she was expecting
the manager of the amusement arcade to come over and tell
her that she had leant on that same machine for almost an
hour, that she had barely spent anything and that she couldn't
just stay in there as a place to shelter from the rain.

She looked down at her plastic pot. She had changed up
enough two-pence pieces to just about cover the bottom and

it needed to last. The employees all wore mustard-coloured polo shirts with their name written in red. One was not too far in front of her and visible through the smeared glass. She couldn't see his face but, from the overhanging stomach, she knew it to be the same man who had spoken to her the previous night when she had also needed shelter from a brief rain shower. He had been friendly but it had been a warning and tonight the rain looked more set in. She pushed some coins into the machine as noisily as she could. There was nowhere else to go and she couldn't go home. She couldn't face even catching a sight of the bin area under her building or, even worse, sitting in her upturned flat waiting for the sound of bottles clinking against her door. She had slept at her mum's the previous night, finally getting there at around 1am after spending an hour nursing a cup of coffee at a twenty-four-hour petrol station on the outskirts of the town. She didn't want to go there either and it wasn't just the painful memories of her mother and of happier times; she was sure Freddie Rickman's sickly sweet aftershave still lingered, despite knowing that to be impossible. She couldn't feel safe.

'Penny for your thoughts!' A woman had sidled up to her and was now dragging a stool to sit down at the next slot along. Kelly didn't recognise her. She carried her own pot and it jangled as if it was a lot fuller than hers. She started feeding coins into the slot instantly. 'Shit joke, right?' the woman said. 'Sorry. You just looked like you've got a lot on your mind.'

'You been watching me for long?' Kelly looked past the woman but couldn't see anyone else. She looked back over her shoulder, too, through the door to where the rain was still coming down hard. The bit of the street she could see was deserted save for shiny cobbles. The whole of the doorway flickered briefly and the rumble of thunder was quick to follow. The woman was feeding in the coins as if she was in some sort of race.

'Watching you? Don't be soft. I just came in here to get out of the rain. Then I thought, you can never have enough two-pence pieces! You on your way somewhere?'

'No.'

'Well, that told me!' The woman laughed. 'Sorry okay, I talk a lot. People always tell me that. I can see you want to be left alone.' Her stool scraped again. She stood up to the sound of coins hitting the floor where they tipped out of her pot. The woman cussed and bent to retrieve them. With her attention elsewhere, Kelly took the opportunity to get a better look at the woman. She was older than her, mid-thirties maybe — a similar age to Holly. Attractive, too, with her jet-black hair that was long and straight, despite the weather. She had a white vest top that was wet round the shoulders from the rain and tight, black jeans that ran into flat shoes.

'It's okay,' Kelly said. 'I'm not the most talkative at the moment. Actually, you're helping me out. Fat boy, over there, already gave me a warning about spending too much time in here without spending the money. It's not like it's any skin off his nose. Jobsworth.' Kelly decided that getting into a conversation with someone might not be a bad thing. She didn't reckon the manager would have the balls to take on both of them.

'I'll say. Why would he give a shit? You're spending money anyway.' The woman leaned over to look into her pot. 'There must be like sixteen pence in there!'

Kelly laughed. She wasn't sure where it came from. The ridiculousness of the situation might have helped as she found herself in the kid's section of an amusement arcade, trying to make a fiver last the rest of the night.

'You eaten?' The woman was back to forcing as many coins into the slot as she could. Kelly watched her for a few more seconds.

'You're not here for the two-pence pieces, are you?' Kelly's laughter had died and she was back to looking around, trying to see who else was with the woman.

'I couldn't care less about them, Kelly. I just want to make sure you're okay. You can't react, though, okay? Just play your game. Did you know someone was watching you?'

'So you have been watching me?'

'I didn't mean me. Someone else.'

Kelly stared at her. 'How do you know my name?'

'Play your game, Kelly. Then we talk.'

Kelly did as she was told. She plunged her hand into her pot and picked out a coin. She pushed it into the slot but she wasn't watching where it fell. She glanced to the door, plotting her move out if she needed it. 'Who are you?'

'My name's Maddie Ives. I'm here to help you — and not just you. Marlie too. But you have to help me.'

'Who says I need help?'

'I know you're scared, Kelly, I just don't know why. Same as I know someone's been watching you for a while. I don't know why that is either.'

'What's it to do with you?'

'You don't seem surprised?'

'I won't ask again but I will leave,' Kelly said.

'I'm a copper, a detective. I'm investigating a local man called Freddie Rickman. I think you're involved with him. I think the man doing a bad impression of playing the slots over there might be involved with him, too, and I think you may be in danger. Am I anywhere near the money?' She was still looking forward, still feeding coins into the slot.

'I could see it was a wig. I thought you were a hooker. I didn't get copper from you straight away.'

The detective jangled her pot of copper coins. She pushed another couple in. 'Well, that was the look I was going for. I used to be good at it so I'm delighted I've still got it.'

'What do you want from me?'

'To take you to dinner. Somewhere quiet so he can't get too close. When you're asked why, you can tell them that I'm new to the area. I'm looking for a house to work from and I heard about you. You're offering to introduce me to Marlie, maybe. But I need to talk to you. Off the record.'

'What about?'

Though her head stayed forward, the detective's eyes kept darting to the man on the slots. She pushed more coins in as she continued. 'I talked to a woman who lives on Capel's clifftop. I think you met her, too. She said you were going to talk to us about something. About Holly. She died so she could force the pieces of a puzzle on me. I think the final piece was supposed to be you.'

'You don't know anything.'

'Then tell me.'

Kelly was drawn to movement. Two men walked in; one stopped next to her to shake rain from a black jacket. She couldn't see his face. She didn't think he was taking any notice of her but she couldn't be sure. She waited for him to keep walking. He said something to a man he was walking behind, they both laughed and continued through to the same wall of fruit machines that the other man was sat at. She looked them over. 'I can't. I don't know what you're talking about.'

'Then it will be a silent dinner but dinner all the same. Somewhere dry and where you can feel safe for an hour. I'm not the only police officer here. No one can get to you. I can make that permanent if you'll give me a chance.'

'Permanent?'

'We can protect you, Kelly. I just need you to tell me what I'm protecting you from.'

Kelly reacted to the use of her name again. Again she looked around, trying to pick out any other coppers that might be hiding in the shadows. She didn't trust them, never had, not their motivations and not their abilities either. She couldn't afford to be seen with a police officer, not if Freddie did have someone out watching her. Not until she had control of Libby.

'I can't.'

'Do you know where Marlie is?' the detective persisted. 'A lot of people are really worried about her. Her girls . . . they seem to think you might know.'

Just the mention of that name had Kelly sucking in a breath of rushed air. She knew the woman would have seen her reaction and she was worried someone else might have too. She had to get out of there. She didn't want any more questions. She didn't know this woman was who she said she was; Freddie could have sent her to test her. 'I have to go!' she said, with a sudden intensity.

'Are you okay? You seem upset.' That phrase . . . the voice that accompanied it . . . Suddenly Kelly recognised it as the woman who had come to the door when they were running through Truro House, expecting it to be Freddie. She had said she was a copper then, too. She had to be. Kelly hesitated. For a second, she considered changing her mind, taking the dinner invite and pushing all this stress and pressure onto her. Then her mind flashed to a scenario where she might have to lie. If she was being watched she would be asked who she met with. Right now, she didn't think she had the strength to lie, not when she knew that Libby's life would depend on it.

'I'm fine. I've got to go . . . There's a problem at home. My . . . my bin's missing.'

The detective stared at her as if she was mad but she didn't stop her from getting up. She heard her call out after her, though. She was loud and sounded angry.

'FINE! I don't need your help anyway! I can find my own tricks! Maybe start up my own house, yeah? THANKS FOR NOTHING!'

Kelly didn't look back.

* * *

Maddie finished her bucket of two-pence pieces. The next few after Kelly left were pushed angrily into the machine to keep up her charade. The man who had been playing the slots soon got up and walked right past her. He took a good look at her as he passed but she kept facing forward, slapping the glass to add to the effect. She gave him enough time to get clear then spun on her chair and made for the exit, waving a dismissive hand at an employee who had crossed the floor to remonstrate with her.

The rain immediately lashed her in the face and soaked her to the skin. Kelly Dale had turned left but there was no sign of her on the slick cobbles. The man who had been her shadow was gone, too. The only sign of life was a man huddled in a doorway with a hood up who stepped out and turned towards her.

'Did you get it?' she said.

'Of course I got it,' Vince said. He was grinning. He threw a crumpled jacket at her and then thrust his hands into his pockets.

'And he didn't see you?'

'Give me some credit, Mads! It ain't just you with the softer skills, you know.'

'I just know that subtlety might not be your strongest point.' She wrapped herself up against the rain but that horse had bolted; the water was already running freely down her back and chest.

'What are you talking about! I've been copping a look all my life! Ain't often I get caught these days. Fine art it is!'

Vince turned the lit screen of his phone towards her. She bent in to look at the image. It was good enough. He had captured the man in full stride, walking right past him. There was enough of his face for comparison.

'Okay, good.'

'What do you need it for anyway?'

'I'm going to run it against the associates for our friend Rickman, see if I can find out who he is.'

'You think Rickman sent him?'

'I do. He's rattled.'

'You think she might come to some harm?'

'She's scared of something. *Really* scared.' Maddie shivered, the rain wasn't quite as torrential but she could still feel the water spreading down her back. 'We should get out of this rain.'

'We should. So what now, then? A nice dinner somewhere, maybe? Just the two of us? Or we go for a different sort of night and find somewhere hosting a wet t-shirt competition? I reckon you'd storm it, sarge!'

'I don't think so, Vince. It's been a long day already without having to feign interest for another hour. Anyway we might get spotted. I wouldn't want you to get in trouble over something so totally unattainable.'

Vince boomed out with laughter. 'Unattainable?'

'Just drive the car, Vince. We still have a couple of stops before I head back in.'

Vince shrugged. 'Whatever. You're paying my overtime bill!'

'Overtime? You mean you're not just doing this for the love?'

'You just told me that was unattainable!'

'The love of the job, Vince.'

'Definitely not for that.'

* * *

The caretaker did nothing to hide his displeasure at Maddie's second visit and she did nothing to apologise.

'Still raining?' The man grinned as Maddie swept damp hair from her forehead. She was already aware that the removal of the wig had left it squashed down and frizzy and she was in no mood for small talk.

'Spitting.' His smile dropped away when he took the time to observe Vince. He was standing just off her shoulder.

'I know 'im,' the caretaker gestured.

'Of course you do, Mick! I used to be here a lot. You were gonna sort me a room at one point. Nothing recent though?' Vince spoke with his usual lack of volume control.

'Well, no. I been keeping a lid on the place. Just like I told you I could if you lot just left me alone.'

'We always leave you alone, Mick. It's the drug dealers you keep letting in that we come here to bother.'

'I don't let in no drug dealers! The last four have been crashing with someone else. I put it on their tenancy that they can't have no one staying. I do what I can.'

'The *last* four! Tells you all you need to know about this place, Mick! And you wonder why we keep coming back.'

'It's always about something I got no idea about. I told the pretty lady that last time. What you back for? And at this time of the night!'

'I need your keys,' Maddie said. 'Flats ten, twelve and twenty-two. I've been knocking the doors — no one's answering.'

'That ain't against the law last time I checked? People don't need to answer you lot and I can't just be letting you in just 'cause they don't.'

'You're right. I just wanted to give you the option.' Maddie started moving away.

'What you mean by that?' Mick called after her.

'Vince, here, is going to kick the doors off their hinges. He's looking forward to it — I think that's a man thing. I told him we would come and try and get it done the simple way but I understand what you're saying.'

'Those ain't my flats! I ain't got access or nothing to do with them!'

'I checked the tenancy agreement. One of your residents was very happy to share it. Turns out the flats might not be yours, but the doors are. It's a little unusual that, but Vince here says it happens a lot down here in these types of places. You have to ensure the building meets fire regulations. That means all communal doors, corridors and *fire* doors — which includes all the front doors to the flats — are your responsibility. So any damage is yours to deal with.'

'Don't mean I got access — just that I got to clean up your mess.'

'That means you installed them. Am I to believe you installed the doors and didn't keep a spare key? You'd have every right to. You have the responsibility to repair and inspect them. You can't do that if they're locked. The resident I spoke to was certainly under the impression that you had a key to her place. She wasn't happy about it either — I wasn't detecting a lot of trust for their caretaker.'

'Trust! You leave that at the door at a place like this. I've
been here a long time so you can *trust* me on that.'

'Another reason why I know you have access is—'

'You got a warrant?'

'Nope. I've got a missing person with links to those
flats. I am concerned for life and limb. Section seventeen of
PACE tells me I can kick the door in to make sure she isn't
dead behind it.' Maddie turned away to add some pressure,
to force a snap reaction. She was fibbing. Section 17 *was* a
power utilised by police to gain access, but she would need
a lot more to invoke it; a tentative link to a woman who had
no auditable links to the abode in question would never be
enough. And she was never going to be able to kick those
doors in. 'Vince is dying to kick something.' She kept walking.
She could hear Vince close behind her.

'Hold up, yeah?' Mick called after them. 'I'll open the
door. You can have a look but I'll be with you, so no snoop-
ing. You get to make sure there's no one dead in there. There
ain't — I can tell you that for nothing. But if you lot are going
to do what you want anyway, I might as well save myself the
clear-up job.'

Maddie stopped and smiled back at Mick. 'You're unusual, you know that?'

'What, 'cause I'm helping you lot out?'

'No. Because you tell us bits for nothing!'

Flat 22 was the first one they came to. Mick made a show
of knocking and shouting loudly, taking his time. Maddie
hung back with her arms crossed, happy for him to hold
them up a few minutes and play out his little protest. Finally
he pushed the door open and gestured instantly.

'See — nothing!'

He was right, too. There was literally nothing. The walls
were stripped bare and the thinning carpet was the only sign of
colour. It had track lines, suggesting that it had been hoovered
recently. There wasn't a scrap of furniture, not a single personal
belonging. Maddie stepped in, ignoring Mick's protestations.
The kitchen was around a sharp corner and the sparse theme

continued. There was a smell at least: bleach. It was unmistakeable. She pulled open a cupboard to find her first items: a discarded sponge in a small plastic basket. In the bathroom she found a few crumpled bottles of shower gel. But that was it.

The bathroom smelled of bleach, too. The metal taps and edges of the shower surround were scrubbed so hard she could see herself.

'Do your occupants usually leave like this?'

'I said I would let you in. I don't need to be answering no more questions.'

'Okay then. I suggest you let me into the other two.'

Mick fell silent but he was dutiful. He led them down a level to the two rooms that were right next to each other. It was the same story in both: stripped walls and scrubbed floors. There were two items of furniture in total. Both were in Flat 12: matching dining room chairs with cracked plastic tops pulled out into the middle of one of the rooms. The chairs also smelled of bleach and had dried watermarks on them from where they looked to have been cleaned.

'Someone really scrubbed these places. It's almost like they were worried the police might turn up for a look round?'

Mick shrugged. 'You get good leavers and bad leavers.'

'He's left, then? Freddie I mean? Or at least his decorator has. Without decorating, I might add.'

'I told you before . . . these ain't my flats. You'll have to ask the management who they belong to and what they are doing with them.'

'Of course, I forgot. Thanks for the reminder. I guess I've wasted enough of your time. I've certainly wasted enough of mine.'

'I'll lock up, then.' Mick's face flickered a smile. Maddie turned away from it to make her way out.

* * *

The Major Crime office was just a dark block through the glass in the double doors as Maddie approached. She pulled the door open and sensors clunked a greeting, then bright, white lights flickered on overhead. Maddie had to narrow her eyes as she made for her desk. Vince was behind her.

'You can head off, Vince. I really appreciate you staying on.'

'Are you getting off too?'

She sighed. 'Soon.'

'That means no!'

'I told the boss I was staying on to get some stuff done on a case file. I'll need to do something on it. There might be some good news on my email, too. I had people looking for any social media stuff on Kelly Dale and I want to have another look through Holly's stuff. If it turns out I missed something . . . well, I don't know what I'll do.'

'You want a coffee?'

'Don't just make me one. You should go . . . you said you had something to do yourself tonight?'

'I can stay for a quickie!'

Maddie met his twinkling eyes. They both laughed.

'I was going to do a door-knock is all,' Vince said. 'London Road. On the way home.'

'The same address we went to earlier?' Maddie was intrigued.

'I wanted to see if there was any update. The girl we talked to didn't leave a number.'

'And you don't think she would have called if there was something more to know?'

'She did say she would. Marlie would herself — especially if she knew someone had spoken to me and they didn't need to — she'd be on the phone pretty quick. If she's trying to deal with something down there, I might be the last bloke she wants knocking on the door. I'm just worried she's got herself involved with someone she *can't* deal with. I don't just want to drive home and do nothing.'

'We could have dropped in on the way back here,' Maddie chanced. She already knew that he was keeping her away on purpose. He obviously felt he might have more joy on his own.

'I didn't even think of it to be honest. It's on my way home so I was just gonna knock the door.'

'No problem.' Maddie didn't see the need to challenge him. He might even be right. 'I can't help but think that it's all tied up somehow. And I'm pretty sure the answers are here somewhere. Amongst all this shit. Maybe I should have just dragged Kelly Dale down here tonight. Sat her down, shone a light in her eyes, locked her up even. She'd be safe then at least.'

'Dragging her here might not be the best way to keep her safe, Mads. Sometimes the best thing we can do is stay away. As much as that hurts.'

'I know that. That's why I tried not to pressure her too much. I just wanted her to know that she can come to us.'

'She knows that by now.'

Maddie tugged a plastic box out from under her desk. Holly's yellow rucksack was on top, sealed in a clear bag. She lifted it out to get to the rest of the items underneath. She laid them out like she had before, mixing up the order, seeing if that made any difference to how she interpreted them. Vince picked up the rucksack.

'Grim,' he said.

'Grim?'

Vince was still looking at the bag. 'The bloodstaining. I assume that's what it is?'

'Oh, yeah. Sorry, I forgot you knew her. I should have given you a warning.'

'Don't matter to me, Mads. I never knew her well. I know Marlie better.' He was still eyeing the bag, his jaw clamped shut, tight enough for it to make ripple marks on his cheeks.

'It's not nice seeing it on a kid's bag either. This is a kid's bag, ain't it?'

'Looks like it to me. No telling why a thirty-four-year-old sex worker was holding onto it when she died.'

'And it's definitely hers?'

'She was holding it tight when she died and from the stuff inside it's definitely hers.'

'And she doesn't have any kids?'

'She doesn't. And from a historic intel report, we know that she couldn't have them. I think she had a rough start in life, to say the least.'

'Seems to be a pattern. I get the impression Marlie was the same.'

'She's going to be okay, you know,' Maddie said. 'I don't see someone walking her out of a house full of her mates as witnesses if they wanted to harm her. That wouldn't make any sense.'

'I would agree with you in the normal world, Mads. But this ain't normal. It certainly ain't the world me and you occupy on a daily basis. It's all about power plays and control. We've had some pretty shocking violence on us before and no one says nothing. You suddenly find a girl hospitalised or we've even had a girl dead before and you know it happened in a house full of people but no one saw nothing. Prostitutes and gangs are the same. They see it all but they don't *witness* nothing.'

'You think Freddie is trying to scare those girls?'

'They're already scared of him. Something's got them terrified. I can't tell you how big a thing it is that they called me up.'

'It's here,' she said. 'The *answer*. Or at least where to look for it. Mixed up in an address book . . . in a couple of website addresses . . . piss-poor photography . . . a metal door number . . . maybe even the crumpled leaflet for Airbnb that was in the bottom of the bag . . . something in here holds the answer. And just when we might have been starting to get close to Freddie, he's shut everything down.'

Vince frowned. 'Airbnb?'

'Eh?'

'Airbnb you said?'

'There was a leaflet in the bag. It looks old, the sort of thing you find at the bottom of a bag from years ago. Looked the sort to be dropped through people's doors.'

'A few years back we had a problem with a woman — one of these dominatrix types. She booked up a couple of holiday homes for a few days at a time — a week even. Then she advertised for blokes to pop along to get their nuts stood on. She had to keep moving because of the neighbour complaints. It was probably the noise. I would give it a right good holler if someone stood on my bits! Short-term lets suited her. By the time that someone came out, she was gone.'

Maddie scrabbled around in the box until she found the leaflet. It was as crumpled as she remembered. It wasn't even bagged; she hadn't seen the point. She had been told there was no point bagging any of it up but it all felt significant to her, like it was part of something bigger. But she hadn't even considered the leaflet. She considered it now. It was just a brief appeal to those looking to make extra money from an extra room or a holiday home. She threw it back down on the desk. 'You think Freddie Rickman might be using Airbnb lets?'

Vince shrugged. 'I reckon he's a man to keep his options open.'

Maddie was already waking up her computer monitor. She typed out her search term: *Airbnb lets, Langthorne.* It directed her to an official-looking site where she had to type out her area again. She swore and rubbed at her eyes.

'I'll put the coffee on,' Vince said.

'I don't think this is going to help anyway. It gives pictures and descriptions but no addresses. There's loads of them . . .' Maddie swore again.

'So we just need to get a list of all the Airbnb properties available in the town and their addresses, then details of who has booked them. Simple!'

'Not quick, though, Vince. There'll be a few hoops to jump through. And do we just do the town or go further afield?' Maddie rubbed at her eyes again. 'There's nothing I can do tonight and I'm too tired for this damned case file. I'll just send Mitch an email to see what he can rustle up around your Airbnb theory. He's the best I know at this sort of thing.'

'Sounds like a plan.'

'And scrap the coffee. I'm going to get home and try and get some sleep. I think I need a fresh look at all this tomorrow.'

'So not even time for a quickie?' Vince grinned of course.

''Fraid not. And if the boss asks, I was working all night on my case file.'

'Got it. And you definitely did not have a quickie.'

CHAPTER 29

Wednesday

'You got my message, then.' Harry's growl was deeper and harsher than usual. It resonated even out here, in the wide woods that loomed over and around. It was a cacophony of movement and noise, of swirling, shushing trees, green and browns blending then separating, caught in a constant cycle. The storm had continued for most of the night and Maddie had watched a lot of it pressed up against her window at home. Storms just seemed more dramatic on the coast, where the wind was unabated, the lightning seemed to have more sky to play with and the thunder seemed to roll in with the waves, building in pace and power to roar at the land. She loved it.

At 7 a.m., there was only some of the wind left. The ground was sodden, the rain had been incredible, still unrelenting when she had finally turned in and she had lain awake listening to it.

Now they were gathered under thick trees and the worst of the wind was held out by the canopy, leaving just a pleasant breeze and the occasional drop of water shaken from the leaves above.

'I did. I appreciate it.' Maddie had taken Harry's call at around six thirty. She was still confused when she answered and it took her a few moments to work out what was going on. By the time she had deciphered *I've been called out. You're needed at work*, he had already hung up. Maddie had then received a text message almost immediately with a postcode and another short instruction: *bring wellies*. She had managed to find a CAD on the system that had been tagged for Major Crime overnight and read it on the way as best she could. It seemed that a hardy dog-walker had been up in the Forestry Commission land known as Farthing Common between Langthorne and Canterbury at first light. Here they had seen a van parked up deep in the woods rather than in the open parking area. It was described at the time as 'smoking'. The call had been categorised initially as a stolen vehicle and uniform police had attended in the first instance. The only detail on the CAD from that point was welfare related, with a note added for the attending officer to be sent to a service that provided counselling following attendance at particularly traumatic scenes.

The final entry was of a record of the call going into the on-call Major Crime Inspector and Harry hadn't updated anything since.

Maddie could see the van from their position well within the cordon. The back doors were towards her and open but the sun was still struggling to penetrate the canopy and she could only see darkness inside. Then Charley Mace emerged from between the doors. She was in a full white forensics suit, complete with hood up and a blue mask covering most of her face. The white of her suit stood out against the streak of black staining up her arms and across some of her chest. Her knees and shins were similarly stained. She made eye contact with Maddie and moved towards her. She was well away before she lifted her mask over her head and pulled her gloves off. She took a deep breath of the fresh air. 'Just arrived?' she said to Maddie.

'This second. I think you need a new suit.'

'I think I need a new job.' Charley pulled her hood down and a run of sweat came down her cheek. She had a packet of wipes and she ran one over her face. She looked rattled. Maddie had seen her at any number of scenes and couldn't recall seeing her quite so pensive.

'You okay?' Maddie said.

'Has the boss here got you up to speed?'

'I think it's best we just take a look,' came Harry's voice from behind her. She turned to see his legs already in a forensic suit like Charley's. He held out a sealed suit towards her and she took it. 'Then she'll know just about all that we do.'

They got dressed in silence. Maddie had always enjoyed turning up to a scene where Charley was the CSI on duty, as she could always be sure of a little bit of banter. Often Charley would pick on Harry and they might even gang up on the old man. Charley was just about the only person she could do that with. But today there was just the sound of rustling paper suits and tugging at zips. Charley even looked to have stepped back a few paces away from Maddie, a conscious effort to stop her asking questions perhaps.

Maddie slipped on her mask and tucked her hair into her hood. Training told her to always put on the gloves last — two pairs, as per new guidelines. Charley ran her eyes over them both, head to toe. She seemed satisfied. She was back in her full suit and held some big squares of cardboard in her hand. She turned towards the van and Harry gestured for Maddie to follow. It was already starting to warm up and she was walking directly towards the sun. Maddie fixated on the back of the van. It still looked dark inside. Maddie had assumed it was due to the position of the sun but now she was closer she could see the scorched white paint of the doors and surround. She could also see a black shadow pushing out of the van and upwards, coating the top of the doorframe in a pattern that looked to her like spindly fingers of ash reaching out from within. It added to the tugging feeling in her gut. There was evil here.

The inside of the van was white too, or at least, it was supposed to be. The floor was still largely white but the sides were a dark grey and the roof was coated entirely black. Stood in the middle was a clump of black. A standing lamp was set up in the far corner, Maddie didn't notice it until Charley stepped up into the back and turned it on, where it shone back at her. Charley had put the cardboard down before stepping up, giving her something to stand on that didn't mess up anything that was already on the floor. She now looked back out expectedly. Maddie took the hint and stepped up into the van.

The smell was overwhelming and sufficiently distinctive to be the first thing she could make sense of: burning. A fire had been set in the back of the van and its source was the container that was dead centre. It stood up just above hip height and was charred black. She leaned forward and Charley tilted the light so that Maddie could see what was inside.

'Shit!' She stumbled back and her foot stepped onto Harry's. She moved off it and took a moment before she stepped forward again. This time she was a little better prepared.

'You guys could have warned me.' She tried a grim chuckle but it all came out distorted from beneath her mask. She could hear her own breathing, too, and it added to the claustrophobic feel. The dark roof and sides felt like they were closing in all the time. She forced herself closer still.

The container held a body. A woman's body. Maddie could tell that from the shape of her legs and some of her chest was showing. She was sitting on her bottom, her legs bent up so she could fit in the cylinder with her knees almost against her chest. Her head was tilted back as if she had been peering upwards when the final blow had come. Maddie already knew what the final blow was; the killer had left it for them to see.

A metal handle stuck out from the woman's collapsed face. Maddie was still holding her breath as she leaned in a little more. The weapon used was a solid steel hammer and the blow looked to have collapsed her skull to such a point that it had absorbed the claw end entirely. Anything recognisable as being part of a face seemed to have fallen in around it and any identifiable features were missing almost entirely. Maddie focused on what she could see, on picking out features as a way of keeping calm. She wanted to snatch away from it, to push everything away and step back out into that beautiful woodland scene with the shushing noises of the leaves above and the fresh breeze filling her nostrils.

Instead she continued looking down. The victim was reaching up with one of her arms and the other was across her lap. Both her arms ended in a charred stump where her hands should have been. It was the final detail for her. Maddie did now turn for the light, already scrabbling to get her mask away from her mouth. She stepped out the back of the van and kept moving until the air she was gulping wasn't tainted with the acrid smell of burning. And death.

Harry wasn't far behind her.

'Well, okay then,' Maddie managed. 'So that's our day set.'

Harry pulled away his own mask. 'Looks that way.' Charley was next to appear. She clutched two bottles of water and both officers took one.

'Thanks,' Maddie said.

'I knew you would want to see the scene but I'll capture the rest in photos and whatnot. I've got a colleague on the way from the north of the county. We'll be here for a while I would imagine. There's no need for you to spend any more time in there. It's not exactly pleasant.'

'I just needed some air,' Maddie said. 'Is there anything specific you wanted to show us?'

'Nothing I can't talk you through,' said Charley. 'I would rather you stayed out of that van anyway. I had to step away, too. Some scenes give you that initial shock. You take a moment and go back and it's just like work again.'

'You okay?' Harry said.

'Yeah,' Maddie nodded.

'Glad you are, kid. I'm not sure I could go back in there.' Maddie flashed him a smile. She didn't believe him for a moment but she appreciated the sentiment.

'I wasn't expecting that.'

Charley shrugged. 'I could have warned you. I could have said, beware of the woman with the hammer sunk into her skull but I figured I had to pull open those doors. No one warned me.' She chuckled, and it seemed to break through the tension.

'It could have been worse.' Charley continued. 'Someone tried to set a fire.'

'It didn't take.' Harry said.

'Definitely not like they would have wanted to. She's badly burned on her lower half. She's sat in the accelerant I would say. The blistering suggests she was getting up to temperature too but that temperature dissipated — and quickly.'

'Someone put her out?'

'Maybe. Or something.'

'Something?'

'The storm. It had to be. The witness who found the van said that one of the back doors was wide open. I think that was what drew his attention to the van in the first place. Luckily for him he didn't check inside. The wind was stronger overnight. I reckon someone didn't close the door properly and it blew wide open. The floor in the back is soaked, the rain was sideways last night and the van is actually in a small clearing.'

'I could feel the water,' Maddie said. 'That cardboard was soaked straightaway. I guessed someone had put her out.'

'Nope. The fire brigade are tucked up. They haven't even been out. We're not supposed to go in there until they've made it safe but I always try and beat them. The fire brigade are a CSI's worst nightmare. They're all big boots and squirty water!' Her grin was back and Maddie couldn't help but mirror it. She was certainly feeling better. 'I've cancelled them now. They might still come out. Technically they should. I've just asked that they keep their forensic guys running.'

'Forensics?'

'Yeah, when it comes to fires we tend to take a step back for part of it. Their forensic people can tell you a lot more about what was started, where and what was used. We're just here for the *who*.'

'You shouldn't feel bad,' Maddie said. 'That's the bit I'm really interested in.'

'I imagine you are. I reckon they'll tell you a similar story to what I can anyway. They set our woman alight in an upright container. She would have gone up big and bright, too, once the fat caught. Humans are an excellent source of combustion. Think of a barbecue when you prick a sausage.'

'Jesus, Charley . . .' Harry growled.

'What? You don't normally need the dumbed-down version.'

'We get the picture.'

'Okay then. So out here in the middle of the night it would have been as dark as a witch's cat. Lighting her up would be like lighting a beacon. They would want to get out of here pretty quick — come and see this . . .' Charley's usual enthusiasm appeared to be back. She led them on a short walk that took them closer to the van but at an angle. She pointed down at the disturbed earth. Two fresh-looking gullies, now levelled out with rainwater.

'Tyre tracks,' Harry said.

'Not just tracks. You see how they are much wider and deeper at that end? Those are the tracks of someone in a bit of a panic. I reckon they very nearly got stuck. Looks to me like these idiots pulled their getaway vehicle right in here, too. Probably worried that they might get seen from the road if they didn't tuck it right in. But the rain was heavy, the ground was cutting up and it was getting worse all the time. Those tracks are from something rear-wheel drive, too — just about the worst thing you can have in these conditions. They panicked and floored it. Can you imagine the relief when they got free?'

'So you think they made a mistake? They left the door open and the storm put their fire out?'

'That wasn't their mistake. They would probably have opened the door on purpose to get some air in to feed the fire. Their mistake was leaving before it had properly caught. They could have just pulled the car forward, back into the car park where the surface is much better but I reckon they decided that the big fire burning behind them was about to attract a lot of attention and they just wanted out of there. The door probably blew right open in the wind and the rain did the rest. The back of the van still smells like accelerant. Whatever they had planned, it didn't take.'

'So we're not looking for professionals.' Harry's tone was a grumble, almost as if he was unimpressed with the amateurish nature of the crime.

'I don't know. There is a clear demonstration of forensic awareness. The hands have been cut off, the emphasis on removing the face and putting her in a container that bunches her up — that should have ensured the intensity of the heat was on her. On another night this could have been a perfect job.'

'What about the hammer? Why leave the murder weapon?' Maddie was essentially thinking out loud. Charley answered anyway.

'Why not? We would be able to tell she had suffered blunt force trauma to the skull. Anything linking the weapon to the person holding it would be completely destroyed in the fire.'

'So why the hands? Is that just about prints?'

'Yeah, I've seen hands removed before. No hands means no quick way to ID the victim. You don't normally get prints from badly burned victims anyway but maybe they were making sure. The lips . . . that one I haven't seen before.'

'The lips?' Maddie said.

'Sorry, did I not say? The lips have been cut off, too. It's very early on, but I'd say that happened before she was killed too.'

'Lips . . . Jesus . . . there's no forensic significance to the lips is there?'

'Not especially. Obviously in sex offences the mouth of the victim can be very significant if there has been contact but the lips are just about the first thing to go in a fire. They're basically two clumps of fat . . . I won't use the sausage thing again, but you get the picture.'

'Cutting off the lips . . . that has to be symbolic.' Harry seemed to be thinking out loud now. 'So why do that and then burn her for no one to see?'

Charley had her palms up. 'Another example of when I'm rather delighted to be *just* the CSI. I can tell you something about what happened and the order it happened in. *Why* is always the question I like to leave for you guys. You always seem to be pretty good at it, to be fair.' Charley was back to chuckling again.

'From what I saw we can get an approximate age now. We can say she's a white female, dark hair . . . I couldn't make out much more.' The shock was clear in Harry's voice.

'She looks to me like she's wearing a black dress. I'd put her mid to late thirties, maybe. She could be younger but . . . without a face . . .'

Maddie actually stepped back. She saw Harry react, too.

'I know you'll have a search team out, but may I suggest a cadaver dog?' Charley said.

'Cadaver dog?' Harry turned to Charley quickly. 'Are you expecting someone else to be out there?'

'No. The case I mentioned before, where the hands were cut off . . . that was also in woodland and the killer threw the hands close by. The animals get them pretty quick and you don't have the worry of driving around with them in your glove box. In that particular case, they carried them off but we were able to get one of them back.'

Harry was shaking his head. 'Point taken.'

Maddie stepped suddenly away and pulled her phone from her pocket. She pressed at the screen and lifted it to her ear. 'Come on, come on!' she muttered.

Harry was looking over at her. 'You got something urgent?'

'Probably not.' The phone rung out. She was just pressing to redial when her intended recipient called back.

'You just can't leave me alone can you, Mads!' Vince Arnold was instantly full of himself.

'Your friend, Marlie. What's her description?' Maddie scrunched her eyes shut and told herself to slow down.

'Description? Why?'

'She's missing, isn't she?'

'She is, but we're not putting anything official on. No one's told us anything official. You remember that, right? That's very important.'

'I do. I'm not trying to compromise anyone. I'm out rattling cages is all and I don't know who I might come across. Just in case I see her . . .'

'Before seven in the morning? Do you ever sleep, Ives?'

'I guess not.'

'Okay then . . .' Vince didn't sound sure, no doubt picking up on her voice. 'She's white, she'll be late thirties, I guess. But she looks a little older without her get-up on. Wears a lot of make-up. I've never seen her anything other than proper glammed up, heels, a dress always, you know the sort.'

'What colour hair?'

'Varies. Last time I saw her she was a dark red. I think she's dark, naturally. Her hair's normally some sort of variation of that at least.'

'Any tattoos, marks or scars?'

'Sure sounds like the list of questions that make up our misper form, Mads. You ain't stitching me up now and putting nothing formal in, are you?'

'I wouldn't do that Vince, not without telling you.'

'She has a few. She showed me one. Between her shoulders. A dove with its wings out. I stopped her coming out of the tattoo place actually. It was still raw. A few years back, that was. That one sticks in the mind, I can't remember any others.'

'Okay, that's great. Thanks Vince.'

There wasn't an immediate reply but when it did come it caught her out a little. 'You wanna tell me why you're lying to me now?'

'Lying?'

'What's this about, Maddie? If you know something about her—'

'I don't, Vince. Soon as I do, I'll call you first — I swear.'

The call ended. Maddie turned back to where Harry was still talking with Charley. She was only a few steps away but it was far enough for the sound of the shushing trees to drown them out completely.

'I need to have another look!' Maddie was close to shouting. 'Just quickly.'

Charley's expression was one of surprise. 'Any reason?'

Maddie lifted her mask back over her face. She pulled her hood up and fiddled with a clear packet containing fresh gloves. She pulled on a base layer and fiddled to get another two on. 'I just love this sort of thing!'

Charley's smile was back but it was a little more unsure. She pulled her own mask up.

'You don't need to come with me.' Maddie had to raise her voice from behind her mask.

'I know. I like this sort of thing, too. And I like to make sure you're not messing about with my crime scene.'

'I need to see her back. The top of her back. Hopefully it's not too badly burned?'

'It shouldn't be. The top half is pretty good.' Charley led the way to where she pulled the back door open and stepped up first. She moved around their victim and clicked on the light. She grunted as she lifted it up, it wasn't designed to be mobile. Maddie took more in this time. The handle of the murder weapon was pointing almost directly at her. At the business end, the blunt head glinted in the direct light of the torch while the curved claws weren't visible at all. Around it was a black and red mass of the woman's face. There was some white too that Maddie guessed to be pieces of exposed skull. The force of the blow had been such that her eyes were turned inwards and among the mess of the lower part she could make out a couple of teeth at obtuse angles.

Maddie shifted her attention from the face to her hair. It was long. Some of it was pushed forward, the ends clearly scorched shorter on one side where the flames must have been higher. The direct light revealed the roots as dark brown but there was a red tinge to the rest. She leaned over to see her shoulders. The tub she was sitting in was higher at the back; the front was more warped from the heat.

'I need to move her.' Maddie said.

'Move her?'

'Just lean her forward. Just for a second.'

Maddie could only see Charley's eyes, but they were enough to show that she was scowling. 'Okay, but just for a second. Do you want me to do it?'

Maddie shook her head and then regretted it immediately. She put her hands on the woman's shoulders. Instantly there was that coldness that you only get from dead flesh. It leaked through both layers of gloves to caress her fingertips. She had to forage with her hands down the victim's back to try and get a grip. She pulled the woman towards her and the hammer knocked lightly against Maddie's midriff. It made her jump so violently that she let the cadaver go; it thudded back against the side of the container.

'I'll do it!' Charley had a nervous giggle in her voice.

'It's fine.' Maddie reached for the shoulders again but was rougher this time. She pulled the body forward firmly, a string of fat pulled between the lower back and the side of the container. Maddie swallowed down a gag. She had to lean forward a little more. It would just take a second.

The light drenched the woman's back. The skin was charred black at the bottom then it merged into a pinky-red and the top was a shocking white. There were scraps of black material stuck to the skin at various points. And clear for her to see was the black ink of a dove with its wings unfurled.

'Okay then!' Charley said. 'I'll need to get a photo of that! I'll do it later.'

Maddie put the dead woman down as gently as she could. She was careful not to touch the hammer when she shifted her grip and pulled the arms back.

'I assume that was what you were looking for?' Charley had her thumb up as part of her question.

'Yeah.'

'That's good then. Makes my job a lot easier. Yours too.'

Maddie had that same, sudden urge to get back out into the fresh air. This time she was desperate to rip off the gloves with which she had touched the body. She moved out the back door of the van. Harry stood a short distance away. She walked a few paces past him, far enough that she felt like she could breathe.

'Her name's Marlie. I don't know her surname but Vince knows her. She runs a brothel down in Langthorne.' She could sense Harry on her shoulder.

'You know this for sure?'

'She's the woman I talked about — the one who went missing yesterday after she left with a man linked to Freddie Rickman. And Rickman owns that house — she works for him.'

'Freddie Rickman . . .'

'Yes. And I know what you're going to say . . . that name again and always from me, but—' She stopped.

He had his hand firmly raised and was shaking his head. 'I said you had to make headway. I think this counts as that, don't you? Have we got enough to get him in?'

'We need to head back. Speak to Vince. I didn't have the chance to have a look at her yet, I don't even know if Freddie and Marlie are associates on our systems. As it stands, we have hearsay. Someone saw something and told Vince off the record. I mean, yeah, that's enough for me, but I don't want to be bringing this fella in if it means I'm going to have to let him go again. And I promised Vince I would keep those girls safe. I don't know how we do that right now. We can't just be rushing in and arresting people.'

'I agree. But we need to consider searches, forensic capture, etc. The earlier the better for all that.'

Maddie turned back towards the van. 'Judging by what I've heard about him, what *you* told me about him, I'm not convinced he would have been up here wheel-spinning his car in the mud. Are you? Much more likely he got some of his grunts to do the dirty work.'

'He might have been the one hitting her with a hammer and dumping her in a container, though.'

Maddie looked over towards the van. 'Container . . . or a bin!' She spun back to Harry. 'A bin! Kelly Dale said her bin was missing!'

'Kelly Dale? What are you talking about now?'

'Last night, I found her. Kelly Dale. I managed to get to speak to her. She didn't want to talk, I thought I got nothing out of her at all but she said she had to go — said *her bin was missing!* It made no sense at the time, like it was out of nowhere, but it wasn't at all. She was trying to tell me something . . . We need to find her, Harry. We need to find her — she has all the answers.'

'You were working on your case file last night? I know that because you told me.'

Maddie was tearing at her suit. She was so hasty she nearly lost her balance trying to get her foot out. 'We need to go, Harry. I fibbed, okay? I was out trying to work out why a woman and a taxi driver ended up over a cliff edge. But all this is linked — I just don't know how. But there's something at the centre of it all, *someone!* Freddie Rickman. And that *is* headway.'

CHAPTER 30

Vince had none of his strut and thunder as he paced across the floor to Maddie's desk. She stood up to greet him. Her work area was much as it was when he'd left her the night before, with exhibits still scattered across her desk and on the floor. Harry was with her, he had been standing over her while she wheeled around on her chair, pointing at exhibits and talking out her theories. She was doing her best to bring Harry up to speed.

'What shit is going down in Major Crime, then? I got a message to report in. You got something heavy you need moving?'

Vince's standard jokes couldn't hide his agitation overall. His eyes flickered around the items on the floor then settled on Maddie, eyeing her warily. He obviously knew there was something for him to know. Maddie didn't hold back.

'We have a body. I think it's Marlie.'

He shifted a little on the spot and sniffed. 'Okay, then. You need me to identify her?'

'The circumstances, Vince . . . I don't think you can.'

'Circumst— what did that piece of shit do to her?' Vince's anger consumed him all at once, puffed his chest bigger and stood him straighter. His voice was deeper and louder and it rumbled around the open office. The general hubbub stopped. Everyone looked over to see what was going on.

'It doesn't matter. You just need to know—'

'It *matters*.' He puffed up bigger still, his cheeks and neck flushed.

'Okay, Vince. You wanna take a seat?'

'I'm not some IP, Maddie, some vulnerable witness. What did he do?'

'There was a call, late last night. Suspected stolen vehicle. It was a van up at Farthing Common. Marlie was found in the back. We think she was dead already. Someone tried to set a fire that didn't really take. The murder weapon was still in situ . . .' Maddie ran out of words.

Harry stepped in. 'She was beaten to death with a hammer. The claw end was left lodged in her skull. It was brutal but it would have been instant.' The big man's eyes glazed and he took a step backwards to steady himself. He dragged a seat roughly out from under a desk. It banged and clanked as he fell into it heavily. Maddie waited for him to speak. His voice came back quieter.

'Takes a brave man to beat a woman with a hammer.' He forced his words through a clenched jaw. 'I assume you need help bringing this *brave* man in?'

'We're still going over what we have,' Harry said. 'There aren't any offenders yet to—'

'You're joking, right? This is Freddie Rickman. We know that. Me and Maddie knew that last night. We sure as hell know it standing here. And her with a hammer in her skull. She was probably already dead when we sat here last night tossing it off about whether to have a coffee or not.'

'I agree, Vince. I don't need any more convincing. What I do need is to make sure something sticks. I can't be bringing this man in to release him. I met him and his arrogant lawyer. Freddie will have been careful. He'll have distanced himself from whatever has happened. I've been going through his record this morning. We know he's been arrested five times but do you know how many victim or witness statements have been submitted as evidence for those arrests combined? *None.* Not one. If we go rushing in now it will happen again and he'll walk.'

'So what? We do nothing?'

'We certainly don't do that. I need your help, if you're up for it.'

Vince was back to standing before Harry had finished his sentence. 'What do you need?'

'We need to go back to London Road,' Maddie took over talking. 'We need to speak to those girls again. Hopefully to a few of them this time. Someone has to tell us something official about who Marlie left with.'

'Someone will if we can go down there and tell them that we've got him in,' Vince said. 'That Freddie Rickman is in a cell and he ain't going nowhere. Then they can all talk freely.'

'I know that, but then what? My point is that without anything solid he'd be released, and he'd know he was in our sights. I'm not sure what he'd do next. We can't guarantee their safety if we do that. But if they'll talk to us now . . .'

Vince rubbed his face. 'We can try. I don't really know anyone down there now. I knew Holly enough to say hello, I knew Marlie enough that she trusted me but with them gone. I don't know, Mads. I don't know what they'll say.'

Harry stood up. 'Let's go and find out.'

Vince didn't move. 'No disrespect boss, you might want to sit this one out.'

'Sit it out?'

'I know these girls. At least, I know their type. Our badges will put up a big enough wall as it is, but I've got an in. I turn up with some miserable old sweat with a scowl and I'll be lucky to get a word. Mads knows a bit about these places and she has a set of tits. We should at least get through the door. With you there, I don't think we will. No offence.'

'*No offence?* I literally do not know where to start with—'

'I think Vince is only suggesting that we tread lightly.' Maddie wished she had cut in earlier. 'They may recognise Vince as someone they can trust and they may respond better to a female officer. That's all.'

'Except his version included a part of your anatomy. Know your audience, Vince. I know all this isn't pleasant and there's some emotion involved but we're still professionals here.'

'Sorry, boss. Sometimes I'm not good at professional. I'm good at this, though . . . at finding people that beat on women. I'll find him and I'll bring him in. Me and Mads have got this.'

Harry waved them away. 'I still need to get a grip on this investigation anyway. Seems a lot of work has been going on without me. Missing another visit can't hurt. I suppose I should just be glad I'm aware that this one is going on.' He fixed a glance on Maddie. She couldn't tell if it was hurt or anger. Whatever it was, she took it as her cue to leave.

* * *

If Maddie had been unsure of how they'd be received by the occupants of 118 London Road, she got a good idea of it in the first seconds of the door being opened. The woman in the doorway sneered as she looked them up and down and took another few chews on her piece of gum.

'Help you?'

'Are you running the house?' Vince spoke quickly, too quickly. He paused as if waiting for confirmation, some sort of reaction, at least. He got nothing but a dead-eyed stare. 'With Marlie not home?'

'Who?'

'Marlie. Don't mess me about, I can tell you now I'm not in the mood for games. I need to talk to you, to *someone*, about Marlie. It's important.'

'Ain't no *Marlie* here, mate.'

'I know that. That's what I need to talk to you about. I had a call. Someone from here called me to ask for my help.

I'm in your book . . . Marlie wrote my name in there in case you lot ever needed a copper to help? Big Vince?'

'There ain't no one calling you from here, love. You must have the wrong house.' The door shifted, she went to close it. Vince's palm met it with a slap and he shuffled his feet to get a firmer base. 'You wanna let me close this door?' she said, her gum-chewing suddenly a lot more animated.

'No. I want to come in and talk to you. I know you're worried about her. I've got some information.'

The woman was leaning on the door now. There was a voice behind her, too low to make out what was said. The woman at the door turned and said something back. When she turned forward again, she spat the gum on the ground between the two officers. 'I don't know what you're talking about. No one here knows you. You say your number's in here somewhere if we need you, so I guess we can call that.'

'You don't want to know? About Marlie?' Vince said.

'You already do, don't you?' Maddie spoke over where Vince still leaned forward against the door. 'How do you know? Do you have any idea how important it is that you talk to us?'

'I don't even know what you're talking about. There's no Marlie here. I've heard her name but she ain't been here for some time.'

Maddie stepped forward a little bit, now. Close enough to be at Vince's side as he held the door. She tried to see behind the woman, to see if there was anyone else she could appeal to. The woman in front of her was mid-thirties, maybe later — the same sort of age as Marlie. It would make sense that she took over the running of the house. She wasn't going to help, but there might be someone in there who would.

'I think you know what happened.' Maddie spoke loudly, loud enough for her voice to travel through that door and into that home. 'If I'm right, then you're all scared, scared that you might be next, even. I can keep you safe. If you want that, you can call me or Vince. I'm DS Maddie Ives. I can only help people who are willing to help themselves. Talk to me and I'll keep my promise. Don't talk to me and I don't know what happens next.'

'You done?' The woman looked from her to Vince.

'I guess so.'

'Then you can leave now. Maybe *Big Vince* here can take his hand off my door.'

'*Your* door now, is it?' Maddie snapped. 'That's a big responsibility. It means that those girls in there are yours, too, and you need to keep them safe. The next person that knocks on that door might not be quite so quick to leave when you tell them. You follow?'

'We're all about letting people *in* here, darling. And if you don't mind, we go online soon.'

Maddie stepped back and Vince turned to her. She nodded for him to remove his hand. The slamming of the door was instant.

'Seems they don't want to speak to ol' Big Vince,' Maddie said.

Vince was shaking his head. 'They're idiots. We can get in there though, Mads, now we have a murder. This was the last place she was seen. It's a crime scene, isn't it?'

'It is. We would still need a warrant. I thought they would talk to us. I thought they would be scared enough. The problem with turning up with a warrant is that they could all keep quiet and then they scatter to the wind the moment they get the chance. I want someone to *want* to talk to me.'

'We don't need them thrown out,' Vince said. 'We just need to get in so we can talk to them. That cheery bitch may have acted like she was talking for the house, but I bet there's at least one girl in there who'll talk.'

'They won't. I've seen it. These houses are like a family. They have to want to talk to us. Enforcement is certainly not going to help with that.'

'So what do we do?'

'We have to pull away. They know where we are. Maybe someone will make contact. I think we've put enough pressure on for one day. Marlie was walked out of this location. I can't see there being anything of major use in there. We know she wasn't killed here and that's the place we need.' She pulled out her phone as they walked away. 'I've missed a call from Harry.' She waited until they were back in the car to call him back. Vince started it up but left it ticking over until being told where to go next.

'DS Ives,' Harry said.

'You called. Sorry I missed it. I was talking with our friendly brothel residents.'

'What did they tell you?'

'Absolutely nothing. We need to pull away for now and let them think their situation through a little. I think we'll get something from there eventually, but nothing if we push. Are you up to speed yet?'

'Oh I think so. I was looking through your notes and I took a little trip out. I'm currently under a sign that says *No fly tipping, CCTV in operation.*'

'Okay?'

'It's in the underpass at Kelly Dale's home address. I called Mitch and had him run this location through. Four reports where this venue is listed as a location of crime — all fly tipping. The first two, nothing ever came of it. The third and fourth time there was a conviction both times. You know why?'

'CCTV!' Maddie breathed.

'A sofa, car batteries and a fridge by all accounts. All dumped by the bins for someone else to clear up. Makes my blood boil, fly tipping. Is there anything worse?'

'Yes, Harry. There's murder, for a start. What does that mean?'

'It means the CCTV covers the bins under Kelly Dale's building. Which might not mean much, except all the bins here all have numbers on the front. Can you guess which one is missing?'

'Kelly Dale's. Harry, I could kiss you.'

'Don't be kissing anyone just yet. The caretaker's on his way. He covers a few buildings.'

'You want me to come to you?'

'No. Why would I want you to do that? Seems I'm capable of investigating crime too. Not bad for a surly old sweat with no tits.'

The call was cut. Maddie was left initially confused and then grinning hopelessly at a blackened phone screen.

Vince peered over at her. 'What was all that about?'

'We need to head back to the nick and wait for Harry.'

'And that made you grin like a Cheshire did it?'

'No. I think Harry Blaker just said *tits*!'

CHAPTER 31

'Ah excellent! My message arrived, then?' Harry breezed into Major Crime with his expression matching the smugness in his voice.

'Yes. Get my reply?' Maddie wasn't smiling anymore. Ten minutes earlier, she had a text from Harry saying *put the kettle on*. Of course she had replied, asking if anything had come from his CCTV enquiries. The evidence from that might be massive and he knew it. She'd tried calling but gave up when the phone rang out for the third time. Then she did get a message from Harry — she'd snatched at her phone and nearly dropped it on the floor — it simply said: *Black, extra strong, no sugar.*

His coffee was steaming on the desk. He took a maddeningly long swig and Maddie stayed silent, accepting that he was going to have his moment no matter what.

He put his mug back delicately on the table and walked into a briefing room leading off the main Major Crime area. There was a big, flat screen television on the wall. He took a data stick out of his pocket, inspected it, then slotted it into the side of the television. It clicked on. Maddie raised her own coffee to her lips to stop herself shouting at Harry. She made eye contact with Vince who was clearly struggling too. He was leaning on the edge of a table, fidgeting.

Harry silently operated the remote control. The screen was on but almost completely black. A white squiggle appeared through the middle where the footage was sped up. There was a timer in the top corner and it was the only thing she could see moving. Finally Harry paused it. He moved to a chair at the side of the room where he took another swig of his coffee. Maddie's rage was just about to fall out of her mouth in a series of profanities when he pointed the remote to start the footage.

It was clearer now. The screen showed the view from a camera that was elevated and looked to be tucked in a corner. She could see a blurred wall either side of the screen and another above. She could make out solid shapes but everything was either dark or light grey and nothing was very clear. She could see an area in the centre of the screen with a smattering of untidy bins. Either side of the bins was a mesh cage that butted up against thick posts, which seemed to get darker in colour the closer they were to the ceiling. The lightest shade of grey was reserved for the road that ran through the shot at an angle. It was punctured with black smudges that were either puddles or potholes.

A female appeared on the right side of the screen. Maddie stiffened. She heard the table shift where Vince pushed off. He moved to stand next to her. She leaned closer to the screen.

'She's carrying something,' Maddie breathed. She couldn't make out too many details, just enough to identify a female form walking slowly with what looked like a black sack in her right hand. Whatever was in it, her gait suggested it was heavy.

The woman hesitated at the edge of the bins for a moment before moving through them down a cleared path between them and stopped. Her back was to the camera now and Maddie could just see the lid of one of the bins being lifted.

Suddenly the woman jerked backwards as if pulled by an invisible force. She only stayed on her feet for a few paces before stumbling over a low kerb and into a puddle.

'What happened there?' Maddie said.

No one answered.

There was more movement on screen. Kelly was half way to the bottom of the screen now. Someone was over to her right but almost completely out of shot. Maddie could just see an arm flicking in and out of the view as if the person was gesturing. A small object landed on the ground, close to the woman. It had come from the direction of the gesturing figure.

'Dammit!' Vince leaned even closer. 'We can't see who that is!' The woman was still looking up to her right. A foot appeared by her leg. Then the figure leaned forward and the peak of a flat cap appeared over her.

'A flat cap! Freddie wore a flat cap when he came in!' Maddie breathed.

Vince clapped. 'We've got you, son!'

Maddie glanced over at Harry. He was still silent, his attention on the screen, his coffee rested against his lips. She turned back to the footage. The woman scuttled suddenly backwards across the floor, moving to the bottom edge of the screen and just in time for a van to cut across from right to left to stop where she'd been sprawled. The van braked hard, its position now blocking the view of the bins. The woman was facing the van and she didn't try to get up. Maddie could only see it from the side — she tried to peer through the passenger window at the front to make out any occupants. There was no chance of seeing a registration plate. More movement caught her eye as a bin appeared on its side. It rolled in an arc and came to rest against the front bumper. Someone was quick to bend down and move it out of the way and Maddie got another flash of a flat cap. A few more seconds ticked by and then the van pulled away in a hurry.

Finally Maddie felt like she could take a breath. The woman in the footage looked to be the only one left. She took her time getting to her feet. She was shaky and she struggled to walk at all to start with but then exited the screen back the direction from which she had first appeared.

'Can we see it again?' Maddie turned to Harry.

'Of course. That's the fifth time I've seen it. The monitor at the building was actually clearer. You can see some very interesting things.'

'Interesting?'

'Interesting. Like a bin is not there when the van leaves. You can also see the number on the bin that goes missing and you can make out the number on the bin someone pushed out of the way of the van.'

'Why is that important?'

'Because you can also see that our friend in the flat cap does not appear to be wearing gloves when he did it.'

Maddie gasped. 'Tell me you got prints?'

'Charley should be done by now. She's going to update me as soon as there's something to say. But even if we get Freddie Rickman on that bin, it's a moveable object in a communal area. We can't put him there beyond reasonable doubt — the CCTV isn't good enough. But if the woman sat in a puddle tells us a story . . .'

'Kelly Dale,' Maddie said.

Harry shrugged. 'It's her building. You would think it has to be. Unless you can identify her from that footage she will need to tell us that, and of course she needs to tell us what she saw.'

Maddie was shaking her head, 'right build, right size, approximate age and hair but you can only see her from behind. I couldn't identify her from that.'

'As I thought. I also seized the black sack. I can't say for sure it was the same one, but Charley said they're okay for prints and even better for DNA capture. Judging by how scared she looked, she'll have shed sweat all over it. It should prove she was there, at least, even if she won't admit it.'

'Something else to put to Rickman. It's enough to get him in now, surely?'

'We're beyond inviting him in for a chat. He needs arresting, which means you get to say you told me so. Just get it over and done with quickly.'

Maddie ran her fingers through her hair. 'I don't think it's quite the time to be gloating yet. It's still a mess. We're not much further on. What are we putting to him in interview? Before forensics we have nothing evidential to link him to Marlie — or Holly, for that matter. Still no one is talking to us and we have no idea where Kelly Dale is.' She snapped her fingers suddenly at Harry. 'Her address! That was her building. Did you get in?'

'The front door was pretty much hanging open. The place is a tip. There's a search team en route and a patrol stood on the door until they get there. I had a bit of a look around. It looked like someone else had, too. There was nothing I could see that might help us find her. I knocked on neighbours' doors. The few that answered said they'd seen a young girl come and go before but were under the impression she'd moved out. No one seems to have seen her recently. She definitely isn't living there.'

Maddie was up and pacing now. 'Okay. So what else? Holly, I never did get a home address for her. We think they were together. Maybe they lived together in Holly's place.'

'Holly's address is already a live action. One of the team is on that. They'll be doing checks with DWP, Land Registry, letting agents, voters and anything else they can think of. We should have that soon.'

'We should chase that up. What else do we know?'

'We now know that the van with the body in the back was stolen overnight from outside a carpet place on the Park Farm Industrial Estate It was their delivery vehicle. The keys are still in their office. There's CCTV but it wasn't covering the van. The van type matches with the one we just saw, but we didn't get a registration from the footage so we can't say for certain it's the same one.'

'But is it?'

Harry shrugged. 'Of course it is. But, just like everything else so far, we know things that we can't quite prove. That won't be enough when we're building a case.'

'It won't.' Maddie pictured the weasel-like solicitor beside Freddie Rickman, peering over the top of his glasses with that smug and superior air. He would rub his hands at holes in the evidence like that.

'I'll go and get him in.' Vince tugged firmly on the zip to his load vest, which had been hanging open for comfort.

'We have a problem there, Vince,' Maddie said. 'We have eight addresses linked to him. Some residential, some listed as commercial premises. We don't know where he is.'

'Give me the list and I'll start knocking doors and rattling cages. I'll get him.' Vince had stood up and was patting himself, checking his baton and cuffs were present and correct.

'Sit back down, Vince,' Harry said.

'Sit down?' Vince stopped dead to stare hard at the inspector.

'We need to think this through.'

'*Think?* What the fuck is there to *think* about?'

'You're angry. I get that. But at him, not at me.' Harry got to his feet. 'You swear like that in my presence again and I will stick you on, you understand?' For a moment, Harry and Vince were almost squared up. But there was only ever going to be one winner. Vince backed down.

'Fine,' he said. 'Let's have a *think.*'

'We need to be clever.' Harry sat himself back down and Vince reluctantly followed suit. 'We know Rickman's been arrested five times and released five times. He's never been anywhere near a charge because no one will ever speak out against him. The intelligence around him says he gets his loyalty through violence or threats of violence. Right now he probably thinks he's untouchable and I think that's reflected in what we know. Rickman sends a known associate of his to pick up a woman he intends on never returning. He does a poor job of burning out a van after she is killed. He then ignores or just doesn't see a CCTV sign when he talks to Kelly Dale. This is a man who isn't even considering that we are as close to him as we are. And we wouldn't be, we would never have gone to that building, had Maddie not identified Kelly Dale as being important.'

'And when he turned up at the police station, that was a fishing trip?' Maddie said.

'It was. He wanted to see what we knew. This is not a man who doesn't like *not* knowing.'

'We knocked on a couple of doors that belonged to him, visited his taxi firm and asked for him by name and it drew him out. He wants to know why and how we have linked him to Holly.'

'He doesn't know about the rucksack?'

'He can't do. And it's the only source of information that he can't control, that he can't silence.'

'You think he thought Marlie was talking to us?'

'He thinks someone is. Why not her? Either that or she's just been around a long time and she knows the scene — and everyone knows her.'

'So she was a message.'

'Of course she was. Beaten to death with a hammer and left in a bin for Holly's girlfriend to find — and with her lips cut off? She was a reminder and it worked. No one's going to talk to us now. He's back in control.'

'What about Kelly Dale?'

'That's where we have the advantage. He can't know how close we are or he would be more careful. She's the most important person to find right now.'

'More important than Freddie Rickman?' Vince's tone was aggressive. Maddie could understand why, but there was a bigger picture here.

'The boss is right, Vince. Freddie needs to come in — of course he does. But without Kelly this will just be his sixth arrest and his sixth release . . .'

Vince was on his feet again and striding to the door. He tugged it open so roughly that it clattered off the wall. Again, people outside the meeting room stopped and stared over. Maddie gestured to let them know it was nothing to worry about.

'I'll give him a moment,' she said to Harry.

'Good idea. Then you need to talk to him. I'll call Freddie's solicitor and invite him back in. I'll tell him we need to clarify something from our meeting yesterday. I don't want to spook him. I don't think we should be out hammering doors just yet. We don't know how he'll react and we might be putting other people at risk. Best to keep it low key for now.'

Maddie nodded. 'And when he turns up we send someone other than Vince to take him to a cell.'

'Which is a shame. I think it would be good for everyone if it was Vince slapping on the irons — just not good for the case.'

Maddie thought for a moment. 'Do you think she's still alive, Harry? Kelly Dale, I mean? I was sitting right next to her. We had a conversation. If she had believed me . . . if she had come with me then.'

'Yes, I think she's alive. If they were going to kill her they would probably have loaded her in that van we just saw. They must have other plans for her.'

'For now at least.'

CHAPTER 32

Kelly had kept her head down for as long as she could manage. The woman wasn't moving. Kelly looked up, making sure she sipped from her cup as she did, then moved it away to project a questioning look.

'Can I help?' The woman had a large build; the brown material of her McDonald's uniform looked to be gripping her tight. Kelly had seen her buzzing around, cleaning up tables as people left. Kelly had tried not to make eye contact with her. The restaurant had been getting steadily busier and the woman's cheeks were now flushed from the exertion of keeping up. She now stepped out of the way of a family that seemed intent on pushing through without using any words. This put her directly opposite Kelly. Her eyes followed the family for a couple of seconds before she turned back.

'Sorry, did you want me to get out of the booth for the families?' Kelly felt like she needed to speak. 'I know I've been in here a while.'

'Nah, you're alright. The thing about families is that they've got each other. You don't look like you got no one.'

Kelly gestured at the table. 'Well, no one's hiding under here.'

The woman laughed, her whole body shook with it. 'I mean you look like you ain't got no one in the world. Work here long enough you pick up on it.'

'In McDonald's?' Kelly said, finding a smile herself.

'Honey, this is a busy place — a lot of coming and going and we don't got the time to be waiting on tables. What did you pay for your tea, there? One pound ten? You can sit in here for two hours with a tea, put the lid on it like there's still some left and ain't nobody gonna bother you. That's fifty-five pence an hour to be warm, safe and surrounded by people. Don't think you're the first person to take advantage of it.'

Kelly looked down at her cup, complete with lid. It had been empty a long time. 'I suppose not. I'm sorry, okay? I should go.'

'Go? I was just gonna see if you needed another one? No charge now, honey, I don't like seeing people sad.' She lingered on Kelly. 'Or bruised.' She bit her tongue as if she considered she might have said too much.

Kelly's hand rose up to where her face was a little swollen. She knew there was dark shading under her right eye that she'd mostly covered with make-up. It was nothing compared to the purple bruising that stretched up her right side.

'I won't charge you nothing love. That one must be long gone by now?' She plucked Kelly's cup from the table and shook it to prove her point then made for the counter, disappearing among the queues of hungry patrons.

Kelly waited for her to disappear completely then reached into her pocket. She lifted out the crumpled piece of paper that she must have read a hundred times. *Maddie. Call me. Maybe we can help each other.* A mobile number was written beneath in large numbers. Her mind whirled with what she had seen, with what Freddie might do if she called that number. She hadn't even realised she had the note. This Maddie must have slipped it in her pocket while sat next to her. There was no mention of her being a police officer. Kelly appreciated that; it showed she was thinking of her safety. But this wasn't just about her. There were so many others at risk. Her immediate instinct on finding the note had been to throw it away, but it kept going back into her pocket. She was either going to have to call or ditch it. She couldn't risk it being found on her.

The phone ringing in Kelly's pocket made her jump, breaking her from her thoughts. The subsequent jolt of pain in her side made her exhale a hiss through her teeth. The screen showed *No Number.* She pressed it against her ear, struggling over what to say long enough for the person calling to speak first.

'Kell! Nice to see you've been waiting by your phone.' It was Benny. The voice and the laughter were instantly distinctive.

'What do you want?'

'Oh, you know, just to chat. I wanted to thank you for the show last night. I watched it all. You looked like you were having fun, though, to be honest. Maybe you should be thanking me.'

'What do you want?'

'No need to be like that! It ain't about what I want. You're working again tonight. Eight p.m. I suggest you be early. It's Canterbury so you need to get your arse over there.'

'Eight? Why so late?'

'You lost the right to ask questions, Kell. Don't forget that.' Benny's tone was noticeably different. There was no more laughter.

'Why so late? It's never been so late.'

'What did I just say?' Benny hissed. 'Just fucking be there or God help you, Kell — you *and* that little bitch you're so attached to.'

The phone was silenced. Kelly couldn't drop it on the table fast enough. A shadow appeared over it and a McDonald's cup next to it.

'You be careful now, honey. This cup is hot. Just like that phone, eh?' The large woman chuckled again. Kelly turned her attention to the handwritten note that was still lying on the table. She ripped it twice then screwed it up in a tight fist. She'd known the phone was going to ring, known she was going to be asked to work again, but now she had a place and a time. It was real. And so was the threat. Kelly's eye scanned the restaurant to find a bin. She suddenly felt a desperate need to distance herself from the police officer's phone number in her hand.

The woman sat down opposite her, her bulk nudging the table and she waited in silence. Finally Kelly acknowledged her.

'Hey.'

'Sugar?' The woman gestured at the tea and Kelly shook her head. 'There someone I can call? Family? Friends, maybe?'

Kelly sucked in a breath and waited for it to steady enough to speak without breaking down. 'You know what, I don't think there is. They're all gone.'

'Gone?' The woman leaned in like she was trying to hold onto Kelly's attention. She was looking at her intently, her face a picture of concern.

'Just gone.' Kelly managed finally.

'Why would they just go and leave you like that?'

Kelly flickered a smile now. She could taste a hint of salt on her lips. She hadn't felt the tear run down her swollen face. 'So I could be free,' she said. 'So I could be happy.'

* * *

Maddie hesitated at the door. She looked back to her left, to where she could see Harry a short distance away. He was just outside, still holding the communal door open while he faced towards the window of the flat registered to Kelly Dale's mother. He looked back at her and gave a thumbs up. He had it covered. Maddie didn't think Kelly would go out of the window — she didn't really know what to expect — but the last thing she wanted was to get this close and lose her. She was already kicking herself for not doing more the previous night when she had been sitting right next to her.

She knocked on the door and waited. Nothing. She knocked again, this time stepping forward to push her ear against the wood before sliding her hand down the door as she bent to try and see through the letterbox.

'Can I help you?' A woman's voice — instantly bolshy.

'Ah, I'm looking for someone. She was living here until recently, I wondered if she still was.'

'No one lives here now. He with you?' The woman was in her sixties maybe. She gestured towards Harry.

'Yes. That's Detective Inspector Harry Blaker. I'm Detective Sergeant Maddie Ives. Are you a neighbour here?'

'The police?' Her tone softened.

'The police. We're looking for Kelly. I know she was here, I know her mother—'

'She's dead.'

'I saw that. Some of my colleagues came out. I read their notes. That's how I know Kelly was here at the time.'

'She was. I saw your lot come and go. They left just after they took Eileen away. I went to see Kelly the next morning, took her some breakfast. Saw to it she had a meal at least. We were good friends, her mother and me. A bit of a part-nership, really! We liked to cause trouble.'

'I bet.'

'She's a good girl. Kelly, I mean. This has been difficult, as you can imagine. She's had a rough few days.'

'She has. She's not in any trouble. We're more worried about her, really. Have you seen her?'

'Seen her? No. I've been worried about her, too. I like to make sure people are okay. You know, you've got to look out for each other round here. I've knocked on the door a couple of times, but nothing. I think she might have been in there one of the times at least. She obviously wants her space. Can't complain about that.'

'Do you think she's in there now?'

The woman shrugged. 'I've not heard anything. She might be with her . . . girlfriend? I think that's what she would call her.'

'Girlfriend?' Maddie played dumb.

'Older woman. Me and Eileen, we thought it was all just a phase, you know. It's all very much *in* these days. Young people think it's cool, you know what I mean?'

'I'm not sure I do? Do you mean same-sex relationships? You think someone does that to be cool?'

The woman flushed. 'No! I mean . . . each to their own of course. There's no harm in it. But Kelly . . . her friend's older — quite a bit, I think. You just worry about them. Kelly's only twenty-two, this woman's in her thirties, I think, and with a bit of a record, too — so Eil was telling me. She'd be known to you, I suppose. I don't know what she did, though — or her name or where she lives for that matter. I don't suppose that helps you very much. But I bet that's where Kelly is.'

'Okay then, we'll bear that in mind.' Maddie turned back to the door.

'Her mum . . . when she was getting worse she gave me a key. Before Kelly moved in. I've still got it. It's one of the reasons I've been trying to get hold of Kelly. I need to give it back, really. Do you want to try it?'

Harry appeared. He was shaking his head. 'No sign of any movement in there.'

'Nothing from here, either. Our friend, here, has heard her coming and going a few times. She's tried knocking but not got any answer and she has a key. I think we should at least do a welfare check while we're here.'

Harry nodded. The woman produced a bunch of keys from her pocket. She isolated one and fiddled to remove it.

'Better give it one more go.' Harry's growl added to a suddenly tense atmosphere. Maddie hit the door harder this time but she didn't wait anywhere near as long. She had already put the key in the lock. She pushed the door open.

'Police!' Maddie called out. She stayed on the threshold, her eyes scanning what she could see for a few moments before moving forward. Harry stepped in directly behind her. He mumbled a promise to the neighbour to return the keys and pulled the door shut.

Maddie smiled at him. 'Poor woman was desperate to get in here.'

'Of course she was.'

'Pain in the arse.'

'She had a key at least.'

The door had opened straight into a small living area. A few kitchen units were built into an alcove on the right. Beyond the kitchen and on the same side of the room, a bed was pushed against the wall. It faced the window that streamed sunlight from the opposite side. There were more kitchen units and a small sink fitted around the window. The room didn't have the size or the layout for a bed to make sense; it looked clumsy in a room where everything else seemed to have its place.

There were signs of recent habitation: a cereal bowl was next to the sink; the water in the washing up bowl still had a wisp of white suds. Maddie dipped a finger; it was cold. A letter was laid out on the bench top as if it had been left where it was read. It was addressed to Eileen Dale. Eileen was how Maddie had found this address. Vince had been told that Kelly might have lost her mother within the last couple of days and Maddie knew that police attended the majority of deaths. She had someone at the control centre send her all the attended calls that matched the description in the area. From there, the surname was easy to spot, and she just needed to speak to the officers who had attended. One of them had had taken an account from Kelly Dale; it was only a few lines but enough to see that her mother's death had been coming for some time.

Maddie scanned the letter for Eileen. It was from the local housing association. They had got wind of Eileen's demise and already sent their standard letter. The content looked generic, certainly lacking any human empathy. It stated how *Langthorne District Council are aware that the tenant Eileen Dale has now vacated the property* . . . It then went on to give a seven-day notice for keys to be returned and the property emptied before stating that the registered account would be charged for any outstanding rent owed to that date.

It was all very cold, a stark reminder that for those on social housing, death was purely part of the process.

She found more paperwork in kitchen drawers, but it all related to Eileen. She made one last scan, her frustration increasing. When Harry appeared back from a hall at the far end, she had fixed on a cheery duck in yellow welly boots on the windowsill and resisted a sudden urge to knock its beak off.

'One bedroom and a tiny bathroom. Looks like Kelly has some clothes here still. Bed looks slept in. I think she's living here for now.'

'Would make sense. If I was her I wouldn't go back to my own building.'

'And the only other place she stayed was Holly's?'

'It was. And we know she gave that up a week ago. I got a message from the team. The letting agent said she just turned up with her keys and the place was empty.' Maddie cast another look around. 'Poor girl probably doesn't know what to do with herself.'

'Is it worth leaving a note asking her to call?'

'She should have my number. I left it in her pocket for her to find. If I leave a note she will know we were here, then we run the risk of scaring her away. This is just about the only place we have left to look for her.'

'You don't think the nosey neighbour over the hall will pass on news of our visit the instant she returns?'

'Fair point,' Maddie conceded. 'Asking her not to would just be wasting our breath. I'll leave my number again. Maybe she doesn't check her pockets.'

'I'll get a CAD put on with a tasking for regular door knocks from any passing patrol. We need to speak to her — to see her, at least. I want a welfare check done.'

'Okay . . .'

'You don't sound sure?'

'I just want to be the next officer who speaks to her. A uniform cop turning up here might be the last straw. I think I can get her to talk to me.'

'You're certainly the best person for her to see next, but we've got little choice. You can't stay here on the off-chance. The response teams have a much better chance.'

Maddie nodded. She turned over a torn envelope to write on. She checked her work phone for the right time so Kelly would know when she was here. She left it brief, just asked for Kelly to call to let her know she was okay.

Maddie kept her phone in her hand until she was sitting back in the car, then she scrolled through her new emails. She skipped past two from CPS, both labelled *Urgent tasking*, knowing that it would be another enquiry that would eat into time she didn't have.

Her thumb stopped at an email from Mitch Evans. She clicked it open.

Maddie,

Regards your email for DPA checks with Airbnb. They're a typical web-based firm — took me ages to get to speak to an actual person!

I got there in the end. I had to send the standard form — Harry Blaker is authorising. (I'll let you tell him!)

Please find attached a list of the addresses of Airbnbs that are currently rented. I didn't know how far to cast the net so I went big. It covers most of the county. Not sure how much this helps. I asked for booking details but they would only provide full names of the lead person for the booking against the full address of the property booked. Without dates of birth or any other information, I'm not sure it's of much use. I went back to them and they will give me the full details for individual properties, but I get the impression it'll be one at a time. So you'll have to let me know if any one booking stands out.

Kind regards,
Mitch.

Maddie clicked to open the attachment. It came up small on her phone, so small that she instantly knew that this was a job for back at the office. It was a simple spreadsheet, listed alphabetically with surname first. There looked to be hundreds. She sighed her dismay. She scrolled down with the faintest of hopes that *Rickman* would be listed. Unsurprisingly, it wasn't — nothing even like it. It was a dead end, a fishing trip with no real idea of what she was even hoping to find. She pushed her phone back into her pocket and huffed again.

'You okay Maddie? I'm hearing a lot of sighing.'

'Not really. I'm still missing something.'

'Missing something?'

'I just can't shake the feeling that we have everything we need to nail this right in front of our faces.'

'We'll head back in and go through all that we know about Kelly Dale. That missing something you're talking about? It's her. You've been saying it from the start and I think you're right. We need to find her.'

'We do. I don't think she'll call me just because I left her a note asking her to. I should have just nicked her, Harry . . . I've thought about it since someone at that house said that Kelly knew something about Marlie. I could have just brought her in for the murder.'

'You think that counts as *reasonable suspicion?*'

'No. It might have been enough to get her through the door, though. And then we would have had control of her, locked in a room while we ask her questions.'

'She doesn't seem keen to be answering questions so far. That could just push her further away.'

Maddie peered out of the window. Her eyes blurred to the passing scenery as they picked up speed. 'It could. Right now I don't feel like she could be much further away. She was *supposed* to come and speak to us, Harry, why hasn't she?'

'That's the missing something.'

CHAPTER 33

'I'm impressed with the commitment, Maddie. You're really getting on with that case file?' Harry caught her out and she was hasty in her movements to minimise the document on her screen. She didn't bother to bring up the Harnett case file that she'd assured him she was staying late to work on; she didn't see the point.

'Well, I like to keep on top of these things.' She looked at the clock on her desk phone: nearly 5 p.m. She should have finished at four.

'Nice of you to get CPS off my back. I appreciate that.'

'You know me, Harry. I just do what you ask me to.'

'I do know you. That's how I know you don't.'

'I'm actually not doing much of anything. You caught me staring at a list of names and going back over the same things.'

'Maybe you should call it a day. You're not going to make a big impact on anything in that state of mind.' Maddie couldn't tell if he was humoured or if his tone carried genuine frustration. 'We need to be fresh for tomorrow. We might get something back from forensics or the post-mortem. But however much or little we get, we're going to have to change tack.'

'Change tack?'

'I was talking with the boss. We're swearing out a warrant for the house on London Road. The night duty DC will be tasked with getting it sorted out of hours so it's ready to go first thing. We have enough to suspect that something in there might link to whoever killed Marlie Towers.'

'Do we have a formal ID yet?'

'No, but we're well beyond reasonable suspicion. It's her. In any case, I'm hoping the magistrate won't ask about the finer details. I'll be sending night duty to go out and knock the door after midnight. I'm thinking a bleary-eyed magistrate just hears the word *murder* and signs the paperwork to get back to their bed.'

'We don't usually get too much resistance out of hours.' Maddie grinned. 'I'm seeing a devious side to you, Mr Blaker. Did you mention that bit to the Chief Inspector?'

'He knows we're getting the warrant.'

'Just not how.'

'I made sure he knows as much as he needs to.'

'We all do that.' Maddie smiled. 'With the next rank up, I mean.'

Harry smiled, too. 'Don't I know it.'

In UK law, warrants were granted by magistrates. In office hours this was a formal affair, with three magistrates in courtroom surroundings and a trained legal advisor assisting with any decision. Out of hours and with the timing right it would be a single magistrate hurriedly wrapped in a dressing gown in the small hours of the morning. In this scenario, an argument was a lot less likely.

'Early start tomorrow, then?'

'I've asked for the tactical team to go through the door at 7 a.m. That should be early enough to guarantee a full house and we'll have the whole day to talk to whoever they scoop up.'

'Are they getting arrested?'

'We'll ask them to speak to us under caution. Anyone who refuses is putting themselves forward to get arrested. We'll see what we get.'

'Assuming there are girls there.' When Maddie had spent some time in a brothel, only a couple of the rooms had actually been occupied, the rest were for girls coming in from elsewhere to do a shift. There were often good reasons to keep their work away from home: neighbours, children or just a desire to keep the things separate. A brothel gave that separation, as well as security.

'Nothing we can do about that. That will be part of our questioning to find out who's missing.'

'And you think they'll talk to us?'

Harry shrugged. 'They had their chance to talk to you on their terms and they didn't take it. I can't see any other way. They might be expecting it — maybe even waiting for it to happen so they can talk to us where they know they'll be safe. You never know your luck.'

'That would be nice.'

'So it'll be an early start. I suggest you give it a rest for today. All this will still be here tomorrow.'

'That's what I'm worried about.' But Maddie knew he was right. She was tired — too tired to make a difference. She had a sudden craving for something hot, bad for her and cooked by someone else.

'Don't suppose you fancy a takeaway do you, Harry?'

'A takeaway?' He looked a little perplexed.

'Sure. You know what one of those is, right?'

'They're not really my thing. I can't tonight, anyway, Maddie. Sorry.'

Maddie nodded, even a little relieved. She had blurted it out without thinking. She couldn't imagine an evening of small talk and hot food with Harry Blaker.

'Suit yourself!' She feigned hurt but she could sense his relief too.

* * *

Once the idea of comfort food and a sofa had got into Maddie's head she couldn't shake it. Her home was half an hour's drive away and the daylight was seeming to fade the closer she got to home. She sorted her food order on the way up to her apartment. There were some elements of modern technology she enjoyed and the ability to order and pay for a takeaway using an app on her phone without speaking to a soul was one of them. It suited her tonight more than usual. She now just needed to mumble a *thank you* in exchange for the delivery and she was done communicating with the world for the night. She had considered calling Rhiannon to see if she wanted to join her but even that thought had been fleeting. She was ready for a night on her own.

She kicked her shoes off and flicked on the kettle. Her phone screen dimmed with confirmation of her order and a thirty-minute wait still showing on her screen. She slid the phone along the work surface, followed by her bag. It hung open a little, enough for her to see the stapled document she had printed off to bring home. It was the list of Airbnb rentals Mitch had sent through. She pulled it out and laid it flat on the table. She had printed it to bring it home without ever really intending on spending any time looking at it. It was just a list of names against addresses. She had run all of the addresses shown in Langthorne through the local intel system and some had people associated with them but, as Harry had pointed out, the likelihood was that anyone hiring out Airbnb accommodation would be from out of the county or even overseas. What she had was potentially just a list of holidaymakers. It was another dead end, printed out in desperation that *something* might stand out.

And then something did.

Maddie was flicking the pages, almost idly. The list was alphabetical with surname first and the third side of A4 showed a block booking. Five apartments all booked by the same person.

'Victoria Long?' Maddie said. The only answer was her kettle clicking off, the steam loitering under her kitchen unit. She picked the sheet up to study the name closer. She reached back for her phone, clearing the screen of her food order to open a new web page. She typed in the first address of five listed as booked by *Victoria Long* and typed it into Google followed by *Airbnb*. The top hit was a review from TripAdvisor from a couple of weeks before. She opened the review.

A little sceptical at first. The website shows it as being a few of the university halls available in the summer break before new students go in. I was a student myself and I remember how basic the halls were. Actually they seem to have improved! The room was clean and tidy with (basic) amenities but it's a decent enough place from which to explore Canterbury. It's quite a walk to get off the grounds to the nearest bus stop, as the bus doesn't come through the uni grounds in the summer. That's reflected in the price and a taxi into town was around £5. Overall a quiet night's sleep and soooooo much cheaper than the city centre hotels!

And a very clever way for the uni to earn some extra cash I might add!

Chantelle, Weymouth.

University halls. Maddie put the phone back on the bench, her mind racing. She knew the Canterbury campus, the part where the accommodation was, at least. It was on the outskirts of the city and would be deserted this time of the year. The students weren't due back for a week at least. The review said that a few of the rooms were available. If it was five that would mean Victoria Long had booked every one. Either she was catering for a large party or she was assuring the use of the rooms with no neighbours to be concerned about.

Maddie had already dropped her phone into her pocket and was gathering her shoes back up from where she had flung them. She stopped, her mind suddenly running with doubt. Five student rooms was probably just ten people — a standard-sized hen-do. Perfectly reasonable. But on a Wednesday night? She shook her head and got back to getting her shoes on. Whatever it was, she wasn't happy to leave it until the morning. The booking was for tonight only.

She bustled out of the flat, pulled her door shut then bumped into a young lad whose yelp could be heard even through his crash helmet.

'Sorry!' Drawn by some wonderful smells, she noticed the bag he was carrying with a receipt stapled to the top.

'This is for in there?' His voice was muffled as he pointed at her door.

'Oh, yeah! It said half an hour!'

The boy shrugged. 'It always says that.'

'Can you . . . I'll just . . .' She snatched it from him. 'I'll take it with me!' She grinned and turned away before he could reply.

When he emerged from her building to get back on his bike she was already in her car waiting for her phone to pair. She watched him. He was still shaking his head — probably for his lack of tip. She felt a pang of guilt; it hadn't even crossed her mind.

'Maddie . . . how did I know that it would be you?' Harry answered the call when it was close to ringing out.

'Because you saw my name come up on your phone?' The darkness of the night was almost set in now, enough for her to see the beams of her headlights as she moved out onto Sandgate High Street.

'Even before that. What do you want, Maddie?' Harry sounded grumpy. That was perfectly normal, but there was something else.

'Did I interrupt a workout or something? You sound a little out of breath.'

'About as much of a workout as I get these days. I took a walk is all. Now, what do you want?'

'A walk? Are you alone?'

'What? Yes, I'm alone.'

'Not even a four-legged friend with you? Maybe one that likes biscuits and was last seen in the police station kennel all alone?'

The hesitation was long enough for Maddie to know the answer already. 'That was no good for him. Too small. He was due to go to a charity kennel.'

'You mean the sort where he gets adopted by a nice family?'

'He's old, Maddie. Old and set in his ways, those places are for younger dogs, no one's going to choose an old dog like him.'

'And I suppose you can relate to that!' Maddie chuckled.

'They don't get long in those places. There's a turna-round. He'd sit in a cage for a month and then . . .'

'Then what Harry?'

'Then they free up his cage. He was everything to some-one once. It's not his fault he isn't anymore.'

'And now he's everything to you. Why are you being so coy about it? I think it's great, Harry. You have a wonderful home. You should share it with a wonderful dog.'

'What did you want, DS Ives?'

'You only call me that when you're angry with me.'

'I'm off duty.'

'You're never off duty. And even if you were, I'm head-ing back in so I thought my boss should know that.'

'Back in? What for?'

'Victoria Long.'

There was another pause. 'Is that a name I should know?'

'It might help massively if you did. But, no. I took the list of Airbnb bookings home. I don't know why. I was just glancing through it. Victoria Long has booked out five student flats at Canterbury Uni, the halls they have there. They're booked out for tonight and I bet that's all of them that are available.'

'Okay . . .'

'That's odd isn't it?'

'Odd? On its own I don't see it?'

'Vince . . . He said that he had known sex workers to use Airbnb addresses. It suits their—'

'I get that, Maddie.'

'Right . . . so we scared Rickman off from using his own places so maybe he booked out a block of student halls. I know that campus. It's right out of the way. You wouldn't be disturbed there.'

'Is Victoria Long a known sex worker?'

'That's what I'm going in to check. Holly's address book had some names in it. I don't recall that one, but I want to check again.'

'Then what?'

'What do you mean?'

'You know what I mean, Maddie. Are you about to go knocking on doors four hours after our shift finished?'

'I don't know.'

'That means yes.'

'It means I don't know. If I open up that address book and she's listed then of course I will. But I'm pretty certain I didn't see it.'

'But you're still going in.'

'I wouldn't sleep if I didn't.'

'Fine . . . I'm five minutes from home. I'll meet you in the office.'

'Oh don't do that! That wasn't why I was calling. It's a shot in the dark. The name will probably come up with nothing. Should I get lucky, I can get the night duty DC to come out with me — or a response car. There's no need for you to come back to work.'

'Then why did you call me?'

'I don't know, actually. I guess I just wanted to run it past you.'

'You wanted my permission. You wanted to be able to say that I okayed it when you turn up at some hen party preparing for a night out and get a complaint for accusing them all of being prostitutes. You don't have my permission, Maddie. You need to find something pretty hard and fast linking this address to something in this case before we turn out. This *is* a shot in the dark — even for you.'

'I thought of the hen thing and I agree with you, believe it or not! I guess I wanted to talk it through and now I've said it out loud I can see there's a number of plausible reasons. It just stood out. I can't not check that name, though.'

'I'm five minutes from home, then it's twenty-five minutes to get to you.'

'I'll be wasting your time, the more I think about it . . . Harry?'

There was no response; he'd already hung up. Now she was worried. She never minded wasting her own time on a likely spurious lead but now she was bringing her inspector in, too. And she was still trying to build up his confidence in her. *So what*, she shrugged, she had told him not to come out and conceded that it was tenuous. It might not all be a complete waste anyway. She had ordered far too much Chinese food.

* * *

University Hill in Canterbury was as steep as its name suggested, meaning that Kelly's car very quickly started to struggle. A mechanic had told her what it was, something about the fuel line maybe moving or pinching when the car was at an angle so that it choked the fuel supply. That was certainly a good fit for the sound; it was as if someone was wringing its neck, leaving room for just an occasional splutter to jerk the car forward. She was thankful that the turning for the campus was only half way up the hill. Had it been much further, she was certain the car wouldn't have made it.

The nights were really starting to draw in. It was just before 8 p.m. and already as dark as it was going to get. The clocks would go back in a few weeks and British Summer Time would be over — not that you would think it from the warm air blowing in through her open window.

The university's campus grounds were expansive. She hadn't been here before and it was nothing like what she had expected. The uni buildings in the city were modern, with aggressive edges and darkened glass, at odds with the medieval walkways they pushed up against. Here, all she could see were flat lawns punctured by clumps of trees. She narrowed her eyes and leaned forward to try and see as far ahead as she could. Grey tarmac snaked away into the distance with the green of the lawns turning black the instant they moved beyond the reach of the white street lamps that peppered the raised pavements. Her headlights were of little help, reaching out with a weak, off-white beam and flickering as the car threatened to stall again when she slowed for every speed hump. The gradient was increasing again and the whole car seemed to rattle and shake as she pushed harder on the accelerator, trying to get enough momentum to be able to coast the rest. She dipped the clutch just before it cut out completely.

'Come on! Come on!' She just made the brow and the road levelled out. She let the breath she'd been holding out in one go.

Buildings started appearing: black outlines at first; then came black outlines with lit windows and communal doors. She had instructions to follow signs for *Gulbenkian Theatre* and the block she needed would come up on her right.

She passed square, featureless buildings that were labelled as *Student Accommodation*, then more interesting buildings, with inspiring quotes and designs, clearly places of learning. The road continued on to a square of buildings that had the feel of the hub of the campus. She drove around it. There was a bus station, a large building that looked like a nightclub and a cash machine that seemed to blink in hope rather than expectation. Everything was empty and silent. It had the atmosphere of a town that had been evacuated in a hurry. And of course it had. Term had ended almost three months before; a new one would start in just over a week. Though life was due to rush back in, for now at least, it felt like it was just her.

She came to a mini roundabout. *Gulbenkian Theatre* was signposted right. This seemed to take her away from the main buildings, away from the cafes and nightclubs and away from the main clump of accommodation blocks. Even the street lighting ran out and lawns either side were now nothing but blackness. Her headlights picked out a white sign that pointed right and stated: *Block J*. She turned towards it. This building stood on its own. The entrance door was in the centre of the ground floor and lit in warm orange with a bright green sign announcing it as an exit. The parking area was empty.

The car spluttered for a final time when she killed the engine. She stepped out and the silence was instant to the point of being oppressive. The humidity added to the feeling overall. After the storms of the night before, the air was now heavy and eerily still. She had seen silent flashes of lightning on the way over but there were no other signs of a storm. She shut her door, snuffing the interior light and the night was darker still.

She walked towards the entrance on the south side of the building. The brief message had given her a time and address and nothing much else. She still took the phone out from her coat pocket to check it again. She was wearing her mother's coat tonight, despite the warmth. She had doubled back to get it, a sudden need for the extra security she felt when wearing it perhaps. It didn't seem to be having the effect tonight. Walking was uncomfortable, her thighs and her side still causing her pain, while a couple of strong pain-killers had only softened the edges of the discomfort from her swollen face and head. All her injuries had been sustained the night before. She didn't think she could take another one like it. She was halfway to the door when she stopped. She could feel a layer of sweat clinging to her back and she knew it wasn't just the humidity. She tapped her pocket then spun back towards the car, striding back with more purpose to the driver's door. She tugged it open and reached for the fruit knife she had abandoned in the side pocket. She held it so that it ran up her forearm, concealing it in case she was being watched, then pushing it into the pocket of her jeans. She had heard horror stories from girls who had carried knives for protection, about how clients had got hold of them and turned them on the carrier. She knew a knife was no guarantee of safety but she felt a little better as she crossed the car park back to the entrance.

The communal door was open. A fallen branch had been dragged in place to stop it swinging shut. She stepped over it as she entered. Now she could be sure someone else was there. She hesitated at the start of a corridor. It wasn't lit beyond the entrance hall. She assumed the lights overhead would come on as they detected her movement. Either side of her were message boards with smiling students under bold headlines offering opportunities for new starters. She swept past them, instantly hating their warm colours and carefree tone.

Block J was three floors. The message she had received had just said *ground floor corridor*. She continued along it, noting that the lights stayed off, her pace slowed as she moved further away from the light. She moved past shut doors on the left and right. Even in the diminishing light she could see they were all the same shade of yellow with peepholes above door numbers that had a decimal point. She passed 1.1 on her left while 1.2 was staggered and next on her right. 1.5 was ajar. The room beyond was also in darkness. She stopped to peer into the gloom.

'Come in.' It was Freddie's voice, distant, as if it had come from the back of the room. Kelly reached out to push the door open further, trying to see where he stood. She felt her wrist gripped tightly and then she was jerked into the room, her head colliding with the door as she went. A light came on — instantly blinding and Kelly had to narrow her eyes. Her head throbbed with the new injury caused by the door and the old one agitated. Freddie was in front of her, leaning against a radiator that ran under a long window. The curtains were pulled tightly shut. She sensed someone off her right shoulder and turned to Benny's standard grin. Her eyes struggled to adjust to the bright light.

'What the fuck?' Kelly managed.

'Save your potty mouth for the show,' Benny said. 'They like it when you talk dirty.' He chuckled at his own humour. Kelly looked over at Freddie. He wasn't smiling or talking. The camera was set up over to her right, with the sofa pushed aside and a mattress laid out instead. She snatched her eyes away from it, doing her best to hold herself together.

'I can't do . . . not like last night, not so soon. It's too painful . . .'

'It was a good performance,' Freddie growled quietly. 'Have you any idea what people are paying to see that sort of stuff? You can get forced stuff on most sites but it's all staged and the punters can tell. They want the real thing! There was nothing staged about last night. You put up a good fight, Kell. It's almost a shame that this is to be your last performance.'

'Last?' Kelly felt a sudden flush of hope. 'And Libby, too?'

The radiator clunked where Freddie pushed off it. He paced in front of her. 'Ain't that typical. Always thinking of others. It's almost nice.'

Kelly felt a rush of emotion, she had to suppress it. 'But, why? You just said you were making good money?'

'Be careful now, Kell! You might talk me out of it!' Freddie grinned. He stopped for a moment to linger on her mouth. He licked his own lips and continued his pacing, his hands thrust behind his back to push his broad chest out. 'It's risky, all this. The authorities take very badly to this sort of thing. They might call it *rape*. Personally I don't see how you can rape a whore. There's no such thing as consent with you, is there? I could see you were enjoying yourself. I saw your eyes light up when those two men walked in. You might have tried to fight them off, Kell, but you weren't fooling anyone.' He rounded on her and stepped close enough to push his lips almost against hers. 'You ain't fooling me.'

Kelly recoiled and turned her head sideways, away from his hot breath that smelt like an energy drink. It mingled with his sickly aftershave.

'Am I right?' His breath was against her ear now. He leaned closer still, close enough to take her lobe between his lips in a sort of embrace. She gritted her teeth as his hot tongue flicked out and he ran it up the side of her face. She finally pulled away, heedless of any consequences.

'Jesus, Freddie!'

He laughed hard. Then he was back to pacing. 'I'm right, though, aren't I? Maybe that's why I realised I had to let you go. These punters are paying top dollar. They want to see real fear. They want to see a hot young thing fighting for all she's worth — not some washed-up old skank who thinks it's all foreplay. They don't want to see you anymore. You're no fucking use to me, Kell. Libby, on the other hand . . .'

'Come on Freddie! You know she's not right. You talk about risks? About getting caught? You know I won't say nothing. But that girl will roll the second the cops get a hold of her. And she's a kid! They'll *really* throw the book at you for that stuff—'

'At *WHO*?' The power of his shout almost knocked her off her feet. He was back close now, his breathing heavy and all over her face. His eyes fixed on her mouth. She felt his hand on her cheek and he caressed her face, his thumb running over her bottom lip, and he leaned in like he might kiss it. He snatched away, pushing her head as he did. 'No one talks to no one about me. You don't think I just made sure of that? You just need to do what you're told, Kell. I know that ain't something you're too good at but just do as you're told and that's it. Once more. Then you're done. And there's no point worrying about Libby either. I'll look after her.' He turned away to face out the window. There were a few steps between them now. There was a long pause, during which she could hear Benny shuffling to her right.

'Do we have a deal, then?' Freddie said.

Kelly's head dropped. Her mind rushed over what she could do, what she could say. There was nothing. Not here, not now. One more show and she was out. She could work on getting Libby out later. She didn't know how yet; she just needed time.

'Can I take my coat off,' she whispered. 'Before, I mean.'

'What?' Freddie rounded back on her. Kelly's shoulders were slumped forward. She felt totally drained, like he had sucked every ounce of fight out of her. He wasn't here to negotiate and she knew she couldn't refuse.

'The coat . . . it was my mum's. The only thing I got from her. I just don't want . . . no one else touches it and I don't want it . . . messed up.'

'Sure! Do what the fuck you want, Kell. But don't be taking no more off! Let's leave a few layers as part of the show, shall we?'

Kelly slipped the coat from one shoulder at a time. She gathered it up in her hand and moved to a desk that was against the wall. She lifted it to linger on her mother's scent before bunching it up gently and putting it down. Freddie seemed happy to wait before he continued.

'That's better, Kell. See? You do as you're told and we can get along. You seem to forget that I know how to play this game. I've done this a million times, with a million other girls. Or did you think it's just you and her? Of course you did! And do you know how I do this? Do you know how I keep my business in order? It's very simple and it's all about what you're feeling now . . . *fear*. That's all I need. The police, they came to talk to me. Someone got stupid. They must have mentioned something to the cops. So I took action, I took back control of my business.'

'Marlie. . . What you did was because of me?'

'Fucking right it was! The hammer in her skull was for *you*, Kell.' He licked his lips. Kelly didn't think she had ever seen him so animated. 'And I gave you the freedom to make sure the word got out. And it did, didn't it? You went out like a good little messenger, making sure the rest of the girls knew not to fuck with me, that it wasn't worth the risk to even breathe in the direction of the fucking pigs. And do you think they've been back to see me since? Of course they haven't. They know *nothing*, Kell. I worked that out when I sat in their grubby little station while they fished for information. As for Libby, she won't talk to the cops, even if she might have thought about it once, she won't after tonight. I've arranged a little demonstration of what happens to people who think they can talk about me. You got to see our friend Marlie after I threw her in the bin like the fucking worthless whore she was. And here you are, Kell, just the same. And now you get to be the demonstration for Libby.'

He moved past her and she turned to watch him. His attention was directed at the floor. He stopped where a line of tape had been stuck to the carpet. There was another under the radiator on the opposite side of the room. She had vaguely noticed it but it hadn't registered until now. Benny moved to an internal door, staying the far side of this same line. He thumped on the door twice then turned back towards Kelly, his face a picture of glee. He was struggling to contain himself, even emitting an excited little whimper. The door opened and two men entered. Both wore balaclavas and jeans and had broad, exposed chests. The lead man carried a hammer; the one at the back was dragging something big behind him. She already knew what it was: a big, black bin.

Kelly moved instantly towards the door. She ran into Benny, who struck her hard enough to send her sprawling back into the middle of the room where she crumpled to the floor. For a moment she didn't know which way was up. She could hear a voice now, it sounded distant. Her vision was mostly black, just a small square of white in the middle that was only gradually expanding.

'Can you hear me, whore?' Freddie's voice sounded muffled as she lifted herself up onto her forearms.

'Please, Freddie, you don't have to do this!' She could now see that Freddie had also pulled on a balaclava. He was now looming over her.

'You've just gone live, Kell, and your public are expecting your final show to be a good one!'

'Please!'

'Just be sure to stay in the marked square now, won't you? We don't want the camera to miss your best bits.'

'Freddie . . . please . . . I've always been good for you. I've always done what you wanted.'

There was movement in her peripheral vision. The men were closer, and so was the bin. Freddie gestured to them and they stopped. Freddie moved away, out of the square marked off by the tape. He pulled off his balaclava and sucked in enough air to bloat his chest. The movement drew her attention to the brown leather gloves on his hands. She didn't know if he had been wearing them the whole time.

'It's like I said from the start. It's you — or it's Libby there.'

Freddie pointed over to a monitor on the floor next to the laptop. As before, it was divided up into four separate screens. Libby was already dancing in the top two, as seen from different angles. Her terrified and awkward shuffle was already familiar.

'She's not far from here,' Freddie said, his voice louder in his excitement. 'I can just get her in here, swap you over and put you in there for a solo like the good old days. But Libby then gets to take over your performance and I think you know what that means. Is that what you want? Just say the word!' Freddie's face was a picture of delight. He licked his lips again.

Kelly couldn't find the words for an answer. The men were now either side of her. She scrabbled a little to move backwards so she could see them better.

'I thought as much. Now then, you take what's coming like a good little slut. You might enjoy the first half. You won't enjoy the second. I want you to know that I'm going to go sit in with Libby, just to give a bit of moral support. But I'll have you up on the monitor for us both to see in there. Now, the punters . . . they like a bit of sound — it helps with getting them off, see. So I'm going to have Benny, here, turn the mics on in just a moment. You might be thinking about saying silly things — shouting out names. Before you do that, think about me sitting next to Libby. I just want to hear two types of screams, that's it. Ecstasy and pain. Or maybe just ecstasy? We both know you're pretty messed up. Who knows . . . this might be your biggest fantasy coming true.'

Freddie stepped away, closer to the front door. He pulled it open to reveal the darkness of the corridor beyond. 'And if I see even the slightest attempt to open this door, Libby's next performance is also with these two blokes. You don't *both* have to die tonight, do you understand me?'

Freddie didn't wait for a reply. He knew he didn't have to. He moved away from the door, leaving it tantalisingly open. Benny was at the back of the room fiddling with a second laptop. Kelly could make the door easily but the fact that she even had the opportunity told her all she needed to know. She wouldn't make it any further. Maybe they even wanted her to try as a way to start the performance. Benny turned back into the room, his grin part-obscured by the finger on his lips as he walked towards her. He was careful to stay outside the taped square until he made the open door. He gave one last look back into the room and then closed it behind him.

Kelly turned to the two men. The one on the left still held the hammer casually by his right side. He was the more muscular of the two, but both looked strong — stronger than her, for sure. The second man was holding nothing but was breathing heavier, his eyes wider. He spoke first.

'This don't have to be hard. We fuck you first then we make it quick. That's the plan. You go easy and quick or you play about and we take our time. Those are your only choices, so get anything else out of your little head, you understand?' His chest was rising harder and faster now, his excitement growing. His veins would be flushing with adrenaline.

Kelly, on the other hand, could feel her own strength sapping. She had already accepted that this was hopeless. Her eyes were dragged to movement on the monitor beyond the two men: Libby was now down to her underwear as her morose dance continued. A heavyset man in a balaclava stepped into view next to Libby. He stopped to stare right up at the camera and lingered for just a second. Kelly knew that was for her, a message: she had to accept her fate or Libby would share it.

Either way, she was supposed to die tonight.

CHAPTER 34

Harry grunted as Maddie gestured at the coffee cup next to her. He scooped it up instantly and slurped at it. 'Don't think this makes up for it.'

'I told you not to come in. Would Chinese food help? You hungry?'

'No. I ate already.'

The food was still wrapped up. Maddie had told herself she was leaving it packaged so it stayed hot for Harry's arrival, but in reality she had lost her appetite. She had booted up her machine as quickly as she could, stumbling over her passwords in her excitement to run the name *Victoria Long* through every database she could think of. There were hits for that name but none of them stood out as likely. Then she'd checked the address book that Holly took over the cliff with her and drew another blank. Her excitement had quickly diminished and it was with some effort that she was now running each of the names listed on the *Ugly Mugs* list through the police system to see if any of them had associations with anyone close to a *Victoria Long*. Her frustration gnawed at her.

'I can't find any links. Nothing on our systems, nothing open source. Just nothing. I mean, I found a million social media accounts linked to that name but no reason to think any of them are currently booked into university accommodation in Canterbury. Or linked to Freddie Rickman. I could be looking right at her.'

'At who?' Harry growled.

'Victoria Long.'

'And who is she?'

'The booking? The name the booking was in over at Canterbury Uni.'

'I know, I get that. I just mean who *is* she? In all this? If we don't have any links on the system or in what Holly left us to find, we don't have anything. That address has nothing to do with all this.'

Maddie huffed. She had the urge to argue with him, to stand her ground, but she had nothing to offer. He was right. 'I was hoping I would run that name and doors would open.'

'I get it. I'd have done the same.'

'I had a look through the address book and the paper, the name doesn't appear. Her phone, maybe — but that wouldn't make sense . . .'

'Her phone? Who's phone?'

'Holly's phone. It was still in her pocket. It was pretty smashed up but they still got something off it — enough to show that it was back to its original settings. Someone had given it a factory reset.'

'Holly wiped it?'

'I don't know. That's what's eating away at me here. I just got the email through today. I need to go back to Rob to see if he can find out when that happened. If it was after her death it will be very significant but . . .' She slumped, her energy leaving her all at once. 'I don't think that's likely. I saw where she was found. She *must* have wiped it herself.'

'It might have given us too many answers too quickly. She wanted us to have to look for ourselves. To speak to people and to have to find them first.'

'She did. I hate her for that!' Maddie managed a weak chuckle.

Harry sighed, perched on the edge of her desk and fixed her with a look that suggested he felt bad for her. She braced herself to be patronised.

'But she didn't and here we are. This *Victoria Long* could have been everything. You were right to come in and bottom it out. At least now you know.'

Maddie pushed away from her desk to lean back in her chair. Her eyes chased over the exhibits still laid out over her desk and floor. 'But I still don't. I don't *know* anything. I could have just called the control room and had them run the name. I didn't need to be driving up here to do it myself. I just feel like *I'm* missing something and I guess I want to be the one that spots it. You sure you're not hungry? It might all go to waste. Suddenly I don't fancy it.'

'I'm sure. Take it home with you. I'm sure you'll want it later.'

'Are you heading off?' Maddie hoped he wouldn't detect that she was hoping he would. She wanted to be on her own.

'Are you?'

'Yeah. I'm just going to run through that rucksack one more time. Just to be sure.'

Harry looked down to where it lay on the floor. He held his breath for a moment. 'Okay then, how about you talk me through it. Every item.'

'Go home, Harry. I'm sure you have better things to be doing with your evening.'

'Just humour me. At least I get to feel like I came up here for a reason. Let's take them out of the exhibit bags and give them a thorough look. Then, if anything's been missed, then we both missed it. Anything to help you sleep better at night.' Harry picked out a pair of scissors from a pot on the desk he was sitting on. He held them out to Maddie.

'You sure you don't have to get back to Jock? Seeing as how you two are an item now?'

'He can wait.'

Maddie giggled, feeling a little better. She reached down for the rucksack as the obvious place to start. She read from the label while she slit open the top.

'So . . . Exhibit CM/5 . . . a child's yellow rucksack.'

* * *

Kelly's head was spinning. Previously when she had been knocked down there had been time to recover a little, at least to the point where she could defend herself from the next blow. This time she had been grabbed almost instantly and dragged to the mattress. She could hear heavy breathing and grunts through the material of the balaclava; the man's mouth had to be close to her ear. The mattress made a crackly sound and it was cold to the touch as if the top layer was plastic — *wipe clean*, she thought.

She looked up. The man who had dragged her now loomed over her while the second man squatted down over her feet. He looked beyond her to where the screen was, checking her position on the camera no doubt. Then he began tugging on the bottom of her jeans. This was it. This was the point where they stopped toying with her, where they moved the show on. She could only imagine the punters at the other end of that webcam. They would be leaning in close to their screens, baying for her pants to come off, for the show to step up.

The man who had been looming over her head had moved a step to the right. He pulled his belt off quick enough for it to emit a high-pitched whoosh. She heard the buckle clang on the floor behind her. He pulled his pants down at the same time as the tugging stopped on her jeans. They had barely budged; they were too tight. The man at her feet got on top of her. She felt hands at her waistband, pulling at the buttons and zip. She moved her head up to remonstrate and moved her hands to hamper him. The blow was instant. She felt her nose crack and her head was suddenly too heavy to hold up. She fixed on a spotlight above her, refusing to let her eyes close; she couldn't lose consciousness — not now.

She felt her jeans being tugged again. They started to give. Soon they would pull off and her one chance would be gone.

She shook her head, her focus switching to her right hand. She forced it firmly down into her jeans pocket. Instantly she could feel the solid handle of the knife. She rolled on her side as she pulled it out, concealing it as best she could.

'That's it, *bitch*!' one of the men spoke, his voice still muffled. 'But don't make it too easy. Play up for the camera!'

She was pushed roughly onto her back. She pushed the knife under her leg to conceal it. Her jeans had come down a little and now he was trying to jerk them past her buttocks. The man behind her had knelt down so he was over her. She felt him lightly slap her face as he spoke to her.

'You know what you have to do now!' He sounded excited. She could just see a blur of skin above her; he was so close.

She edged her right hand under her leg until she could grip the knife in her fist. The man leaned forward above her. He couldn't get any closer. It was now or never.

She threw her right fist backwards with everything she had left in a movement that was like chucking the knife over her right shoulder — only with no intention of letting go. Her fist smashed into his stomach with an audible thud right above her head and he instantly expelled air with a grunt and a wheeze. Then she felt the hot fluid slip out of him, falling onto her face, stinking instantly of blood. She jerked up to a sit, clawing at her face, temporarily blinded by the sheer volume of blood. The man at her feet shouted something and she felt him move his weight off her. He stumbled over her leg and she heard him crash to the floor. The man behind her now uttered panicked gasps.

Kelly had smeared the worst of the blood out of her eyes and she forced one open just in time to see the man in front scrabbling for the hammer while on his knees. It fell out of his grip in his haste to pick it up and clattered back to the floor. By the time he stooped again, she was on him.

The knife was still firmly in her hand. She thrust it at his back. The first blow struck something hard and gristly and seemed to bounce off him. She pulled it back and stuck him a second time and this time it went fully into the small of his back. He reared up and roared. The hammer clanged to the floor for a second time but now he was making no effort to pick it back up. The knife was still in him. She felt him try to twist around so she yanked it back out before he took it with him. He half twisted and she stabbed again. She could feel the strikes but she had no idea where they were going. The man roared for a second time and she kept stabbing until he flopped to the floor in front of her and fell silent. She pushed herself away, turning to where the man had been behind her. He lay on the floor in a foetal position, whimpering, his back to her, his legs twitching. She didn't assess any threat. That only lasted a second.

Someone beat on the door.

She knew who it had to be. She tensed back up. The man's moaning seemed louder suddenly but all her attention was aimed at the door. The handle was dipping and jerking like someone was trying to open it in a hurry while fumbling over the mechanism. She pushed herself back and lifted to her haunches. She glanced over the monitor. The bottom row was black. Someone had stopped her live stream. Libby's room was still showing but there was no one in view of the camera.

She fixed back on the door, the knife still gripped tightly in her hand, her jaw locked shut, her mind racing with thoughts of Holly, with thoughts of freedom. Freddie would have seen what had happened; he would know what she did. The element of surprise would be lost and he was going to come in. But maybe he expected her to run, to be already trying to force herself through the window. She was done running. This was maybe her only chance to catch him off guard. But it needed to be the instant that door pushed in.

She wiped her face with her free hand, trying to clear her vision. It made it worse, smudging more blood into her eyes. She lifted her hand to wipe them again. There was no time. The handle dipped again, then the door flew in and a blurred and broad shape filled it instantly.

Kelly propelled herself forward, hand raised, the blade pointing in front and a scream forcing its way through her clenched jaw. She heard a shout — she had no idea if it was words. She made the door before anyone stepped in, thrusting the knife at the shape. But it moved faster than she expected and she missed. Her momentum took her out into the darkened corridor where she crashed into the wall on the far side. More shouts came but she couldn't make anyone out. She felt a blow to her right arm, close to where she still gripped the knife. She tightened her fist around it and backed away from the direction of the blow. She could sense movement all around her. There was more than one person in the corridor. *Of course Benny would be here, too!* She slashed out with the knife, aiming for the shadows and movement, her eyes still stinging. Someone grabbed her right arm firmly. She reacted by swinging with her left and missed. Almost instantly she felt a strong blow to her chest and a grip to her throat like a vice. She threw another punch with her left and felt it hit something but it was weak and had no effect. Her ability to breathe was gone, her ability to fight gone with it.

She felt a tugging at her right arm, then the sound of the knife dropping to the floor. There was more shouting but it was quickly becoming distant. She was starting to shut down. She squinted in the darkness. The light from the room she had just left leaked out in a bright sliver across the forearm that held her. She could make out a jagged scar going up the wrist until it was hidden by a sleeve. She focused on it and, in a moment of clarity and acceptance, she realised it was to be the last thing she would ever see. A shrill voice penetrated her darkening haze.

'You're going to kill her, Harry!'

Another hand appeared, this one rested on the scarred forearm and was more slender. And then she was falling. The darkness seemed to close in again as she hit the floor. She could still hear the shrill voice sounding just as urgent.

'Kelly! Kelly Dale! Can you hear me! It's the police, Kelly!' A cheek appeared. 'She's still breathing. Can you hear me!'

Kelly tried to speak. Her lips moved and bumped but it sounded like her voice was only coming out inside her head.

'Police?'

'Police, yes! It's Maddie. We met last night. It's okay now. You're safe.'

'Libby . . .'

'Libby? Who's Libby? Are there more here?'

'They'll kill her.' Words were agony. Kelly swallowed a couple of times — she had to force the words. 'In . . . another room. Saw her.' She heard movement almost instantly. It sounded like something big moving away, and the corridor echoed. The woman called Maddie spoke again but sounded scared.

'Be careful, Harry!'

* * *

Harry grunted and moved away from the door. His eyes were pretty well adjusted. He'd looked for a light switch on the way in and couldn't find one. The lights in this sort of place would normally be automatic and the fact they didn't work meant they were either faulty or someone had disabled them. The moment he and Maddie had stepped through the communal entrance from the car park he had felt uncomfortable. The darkened corridor had only added to the discomfort.

He paced to the next door. He had racked his baton when they had heard the shouts from behind the door where they had found Kelly. He had tucked it back in his belt to get hold of her but he pulled it back out now. His arm, chest and shoulder flared in pain. He knew he was bleeding. It was only a slash; he didn't think it was too deep.

He pushed himself up against the next door he came to. He couldn't hear anything.

'POLICE!' He bellowed at the surface as if his voice alone might force it in. There was no reaction at all. He tried the handle. The door was locked. He stepped back to get a firmer base to push off from. The door took two kicks to go in this time. The room behind was pitch black. He reached in to flick on a light that revealed a university dorm that was untouched. He moved on to bellow at the next door. There was no reaction from this one either and it took three kicks to put in. It was on the other side of the corridor and, as before, the light revealed a made-up room waiting for new guests. There was no sign of anything untoward and it had the smell and feel of a room undisturbed.

The next door moved inwards an inch. He pulled it closed, leaning back with all his weight to keep it closed. He peered back towards the block of light from Kelly's room. The hall was empty now. Maddie must have gone in. Kelly, too. He had to go in.

'POLICE!' he roared at the door, pushing it firmly inwards as he did, his baton raised to rest on his shoulder, his whole body tensed.

This room was brightly lit. A young woman stood in the middle in just her underwear. She was sobbing quietly. She looked over at him with mascara smeared down her cheeks. Her feet were pushed into black boots that looked far too big.

'You Libby?' Harry demanded, his throat tight, the words squeezed out.

She jerked a nod.

'Anyone else in here with you?'

She shook her head.

'Where did they go?'

She nodded over towards a window. A long radiator ran underneath a net curtain that fluttered in the lightest of breezes. He moved further into the room, his gaze swinging left then right, his baton still raised and ready. He could see no one else. He paced to the window. It was sufficiently wide open for anyone to climb out. He snapped a radio from his belt, pressing his emergency button to interrupt whoever else was talking on the airwaves.

'Whisky Alpha one-one, this is a call for assistance. We have persons making off on the Canterbury University grounds. We are just short of the Gulbenkian Theatre in accommodation block J. I need search officers, a dog and a helicopter.' Harry lowered his radio. The girl was staring at him with eyes so wide it didn't look like she would ever blink again.

'Did Freddie do this?' he said. 'Was he here?' She jerked another nod. Harry was back on the radio. 'Male is believed to be Freddie Rickman. Please circulate his last custody image to all attending officers. And, Control, we're going to need ambulances on the hurry up.' He looked back over at the girl as excited voices were already streaming back through his handset. He twisted to turn them down.

'Come with me.'

* * *

Maddie pulled her finger away from the man's neck. She had lingered longer than she needed. She already knew he was dead. His mate was faring better. She could tell that from the moaning. She had handcuffed him to a thick, metal pipe that fed the radiator. She had needed to drag him a metre or so to manage it. There had been no blood on the carpet when she had secured him. Now it was pooling round his hip. He was lying on his side and facing away. She squatted down over him.

'Can you hear me?' She only got a moan in response. He didn't resist when she rolled him onto his back. It was easy enough to survey him for injuries, given that he was naked. There was an obvious puncture wound in his gut but nothing else that she could see. She had picked the knife up off the floor when Harry had forced Kelly to drop it. It had a four-inch blade, more than enough to kill someone if you knew where to aim, or if you got lucky. This man would certainly die if he was left for long enough but sadly that wasn't an option. The blood still oozed from the wound and his skin was pale. She pushed his free hand over the wound.

'Press down as hard as you can. You need to stem the bleeding or you'll die.' The man's eyes told her he had understood. Maddie stood up to look over at where Kelly was pushed up against the wall on the opposite side of the room. She jerked suddenly as Harry bowled through the door.

'Libby!' Kelly exclaimed as a young woman stepped in behind him. She had her head bent, her bare legs sticking out from a waxed jacket that Maddie recognised as Harry's.

'She's okay.' His growl filled the space. The young woman fell onto the seated Kelly and they hugged each other tightly, both sobbing openly. Harry walked over to where Maddie stood. 'What about them?'

'One's gone. This one's going to be okay. He's got a nasty nick but it looks to me like a flesh wound. His mate's a bit of a pin cushion. I think the one in the back of the neck did it.'

'She did all this?' Harry peered around. There didn't seem to be a surface that wasn't splattered in claret.

Maddie shrugged. 'You saw what she was like when we opened that door. She was fighting for her life, Harry.'

'We know why?'

Maddie looked over to where the two girls were still embracing. 'No idea what happened. Not yet. But maybe someone will talk to me now.'

'Rickman was here. The girl told me that much at least. I think he went out through the window. I have every search resource on the way but he's got quite a head start.'

'He has. But we'll get him now. He messed up.'

CHAPTER 35

Thursday

Maddie pushed through the door to the women's toilet on the first floor and sucked in air that reeked of strong bleach and spent perfume. No one else was in there; she was so glad of that. She moved into a cubicle and bent forward so her face was hanging over the toilet bowl, stretching her arms out to rest her palms flat against the wall behind. The feeling of nausea had been sudden but seemed to have gone away just as quickly. She moved out to where three sinks lined up under a smeared mirror and again let her palms take her weight, this time via a damp counter. One of the taps dripped. It was the only sound.

She raised her eyes to take in her reflection. She looked pale — gaunt, even. Despite it being close to the middle of the day, the lighting was poor. The window to her right was frosted to the point where it was verging on opaque. It was still light enough for her to see that she looked like shit. She pressed the tap and cupped her hands under it. It stopped almost immediately. She got just enough to rub it on her face, concentrating on under her eyes, hoping the cold sensation on her skin might take away the knot of rage that only seemed to subside when her nagging exhaustion crept in.

She hadn't slept the previous night. She had dozed, maybe, but only for fifteen minutes at a time when she had managed to get her breathing under control. Even then she had been disturbed constantly by the words she had come to dread: *sorry to bother you, sarge, but someone else has just called in asking to speak to you.*

Her exhaustion was so much more than physical. She felt like she had been chipped away at through the night as she had listened to stories that seemed to be repeating themselves, each time probing for the sort of detail that had her almost living the horror herself. Now it was done, she felt largely empty, but the rage still came, together with a sudden anxiety to do something — and then went away, leaving her feeling sick.

Rickman was still at large. And now she knew what he had done.

She didn't feel that anyone was safe while he was still out there and they had been so close, *she* had been so close. She reckoned he must have been running out the building as they had stepped into it.

There was a knock at the door.

'Maddie . . . you in there?' Harry's growl leaked through a door pushed open a few inches.

'I'm nearly done.'

'You coming out?'

'In a minute, Harry. Jesus.' The door was still pushed open. She knew he wasn't finished.

'He's in.'

'Rickman?' She was aware that her voice now had a squeak.

'Yeah. They just got him at one of the addresses. It wasn't Vince that got him. I only had a quick update, but it went fine.'

She snatched at the sheets of paper towel and dabbed her face as she strode for the door. She pulled it open hard. Harry was just the other side. 'I want to speak to him.'

'I know that. And we will.'

'Now.'

Harry stepped back to put a little more distance between them. 'He hasn't even made it to custody yet. Then he needs to be booked in and then we have twenty-four hours. We've a team downstairs full of fresh detectives who want to speak to us, with a full list of witnesses. We still need to go through the accounts we took overnight and we'll be adding more as the day goes on. We should use this time well. I'm here to send you home for a few hours. Then we can come back in after some rest and see what we have to prep our interview. I've already started the ball rolling in case we need the extra twelve hours. Anyone can see this is already a big case with a lot of material.'

'I want to speak to him now, Harry.' She was aware her teeth were gritted as she spoke. There was nothing she could do about that. She tried to keep the emotion from falling out of her but the knot in her stomach had tightened its grip. She considered she might have to go back and lean over the toilet bowl again.

Harry sighed. 'It's been a tough night, I know that. But if we—'

'Don't patronise me! Even before you start going down that line, Harry. I'm ready to talk to him now. I know enough. I've been listening to it all night. We can still talk to him again later.'

Harry took a moment. Maddie was expecting him to come back angry. He surprised her with a softened tone.

'You need sleep. That's not patronising you. I do too. I've just spent most of the night at the hospital getting my chest glued shut. They had to work around the phone I was holding to my ear the whole time. I'm exhausted and we're both tied up in the emotion of the whole thing. Neither of us is in the right frame of mind to do this now. We can come back fresh and it still happens today.'

'We can make it happen now. I'm ready.'

'Maddie, think about it. If I pull his solicitor in now to give him disclosure when we're still talking to potential victims and witnesses and we're still putting our case together, we'll get nothing more than a *no comment*. Any brief would advise that. For Rickman to answer any questions now would be idiotic.'

'I know that.'

'So why waste your time and energy?'

'Because right after I talk to him, I take him back to his cell and I close that door. And then all he has to do is to sit there and think about what we know and what more we might be finding out. He sits and he stews.'

'You don't think he's doing that already?'

'No.'

'Okay, or he has time to come up with excuses — a defence even, for everything we've talked to him about. Or, as is even more likely, we then have to get him out again and we get a second *no comment* interview and waste our time on two interviews rather than one. Come on, Maddie . . . Go home and get some rest. You still get to sit in a room with him later today.' Harry left a gap for Maddie to respond. When she didn't, his tone was noticeably firmer. 'Ultimately this decision lies with me anyway. We need to work together on this. We both need to be ready, there'll be a lot of new material that neither of us can have foreseen.'

'Work together?' She couldn't help but rear up. 'I know the decision is yours. I know you're in charge — goodness knows I do! You've been quick to remind me at every opportunity. *Now* you want to work together? I've had to resort to sneaking around, trying to make sense of what I could all week behind your back and now you want to step up and remind me that you're leading the investigation? It took a dead woman for us to get to this point and, who knows, maybe we could have avoided that!'

Harry took a breath. Even through her growing rage, Maddie knew she had overstepped the mark. She couldn't back down now, however. She stared him out instead. His face was a mask of fury. She waited for it to bellow at her. He was far more controlled. 'You're exhausted and you're not angry with me. Remember that.'

'Please, Harry, just trust me on this. I'm ready. He needs to start accounting for what he has done. Help me with this bit at least.'

Harry's face shifted to one of anger again. 'Okay then. We run this your way. I'll make arrangements in custody and see if his solicitor is available. I suggest you use the short time we have to get yourself ready.'

'I've just spent the last two hours listening to what Kelly Dale and Libby Battle had to tell me. I've never felt more ready.'

'And that's exactly why you're not.' Harry moved away. Maddie detected a flinch of discomfort as he lifted his arm to push open the door. Her mind flashed with something to say — not an apology, but a step down maybe. She suddenly realised that she hadn't even asked him about his injuries. No words made her lips and the doors fell roughly shut behind him. She moved back in the toilet as the feeling of nausea swept through her again.

* * *

'Good afternoon,' Maddie said.

Harry had seated Rickman in the largest of the interview rooms but it was still an oppressive place. There were no windows for natural light and the walls and ceiling were different shades of mottled white, giving the overall impression of a padded cell. Rickman sat on a solid wooden chair that was bolted to the floor — all of the furniture was. He was leaned forward over the table, his head down enough for Maddie to see a partially healed cut on the back of his head. He wasn't wearing his flat cap today; it had been taken off him when he was booked into custody. He took his time to sit up and stretched out a yawn. Darren Harvey, his defence solicitor, had answered Harry's call promptly and now filed in behind him. Rickman stood up to shake his hand and muttered, 'Sorry to waste your time,' before taking up his seat again. Harvey sat on a long bench that ran along the wall closest to the door where Maddie had entered. Harry had a seat on the door side of the table with the recording facilities behind him. Her seat was next to his and she moved to hover over it.

'I have to say, this is all rather extraordinary,' Harvey said. 'An early call for my assistance today. I appreciate your desire for an expeditious investigation, of course, but I do not get the usual feeling of readiness that accompanies a major crime investigation.' He was staring over at the inspector. Maddie didn't know if it was Harry's gender or his rank that meant Harvey seemed insistent on addressing him. She decided it was probably a little of both.

'You have had disclosure Mr Harvey, is that correct?' Harry said, ignoring the point made completely.

'I have. Detective Sergeant Ives, here, was diligent and succinct. I did not feel the need to write anything down, however, and I quickly formed the opinion that this may be a rather short conversation this afternoon.'

'Okay, then,' Harry said.

Maddie felt like the silence that followed was for her to break. 'Can I get anyone a drink?' There were shaking heads around the room. 'I'll get some water then, if you don't mind.'

When she came back, it wasn't water she was dragging behind her but a large plastic box of exhibits. Rickman leaned forward to peer down at the floor then exclaimed as he sat back, 'Fucking joke!'

Maddie ignored him to go back into the corridor. Rickman slapped the table and chuckled as she dragged the second box over the lip of the door. She also put a laptop onto the desk and then she went back for the water.

'Finished?' Rickman said when she finally settled in the seat opposite him. Harvey had taken out the same notepad and ornate fountain pen from the last time they had all met and was now occupied with wiping his glasses. There was a distinct atmosphere of disinterest in the room. She would have to do something to puncture that.

'I have all I need,' Maddie said. 'Shall we make a start?'

Harvey balanced his glasses back on his nose then looked down it to speak. 'Good idea, I think. I would like to remind you that my client is a very busy man and of course self-employed, hence his time is highly valuable. And as I explained to him immediately after your disclosure, this is now the last requirement before we can process his release. He does not want to miss any more of his working day than is strictly necessary.'

'I'll bear that in mind,' Maddie said.

The interview commenced at 13:20 hours. Maddie stated as such as soon as the recording equipment had finished its long beep to confirm that sound and vision were now being captured from a couple of angles. Maddie moved through the rest of the formal bits, ensuring every point was covered in detail and checking Rickman's understanding each time. He was still rolling his eyes, still stretching and yawning. He didn't look like a man under any pressure at all. His attitude fed her anger.

Finished with the formal elements, she took a swig of her drink while Rickman complained again to Harvey about the time it was taking. Her drink allowed her to take a moment to silence the voices in her mind. Her first question was designed to silence the voices in the room.

'Marlie Towers is dead. She was murdered. Did you kill her?'

'No!' Rickman laughed after a shocked pause. He moved forward to lean on the table where previously he had been lounging back, doing his best impression of being bored. He bit down on his bottom lip while appearing to study hers. 'Does the prosecution rest now?' he said, finally. He roared with laughter and Maddie let him die down before another exclamation: 'What a fucking joke!'

'Do you know how she died?'

'I didn't even know she was dead. No one tells me nothing, it seems.'

Harvey shuffled along his bench to get closer to his client, close enough to rest his hand on Rickman's shoulder in mild restraint. When he spoke he watched Maddie the whole time.

'Mr Rickman, you will remember the advice we discussed prior to your interview? You're confused and troubled that you have been brought in here under arrest for no apparent reason for a very serious offence and as such you will not be making any comment at this time.'

Rickman nodded. 'Ah yeah. Like the man here, says . . . I won't be making any comment at this time. Which is a bit of a shame, 'cause we could have some fun!'

Maddie seized on him. 'You think the murder of a woman is fun?'

'No comment.' Rickman threw his hands out and tutted as if he was disappointed he couldn't engage.

'Did you know Marlie Towers?'

'No comment.'

'Did she work for you?'

'No comment.'

'People are telling me that she did, that she worked for you and that you knew her well. Very well, too. Is that right?'

'Are you saying these allegations have been submitted as statements?' Harvey interjected. 'As part of evidence of an offence, I mean, or is this just rumour and hearsay?'

'They will be,' Maddie said.

'But they haven't yet?' Harvey pushed.

'How long have you known her for?' Maddie's questioning was back at Rickman.

'You have a beautiful mouth, Detective Sergeant. Not all women are blessed with that. Maybe you missed your calling?'

'Do you like women's mouths, Freddie?'

'I like everything about women.'

'Mr Rickman, don't be drawn into a conversation,' Harvey said. 'Remember what we talked about.' He put his hand back on his client's shoulder.

Rickman sat back. 'Yeah. No comment. Do I have to keep saying that? Only it's gonna get a bit tedious if you're going to keep asking me stupid questions.'

'This is my interview. I can ask as many questions as I want.'

'No comment then, yeah? No comment.'

'I am going to keep asking questions and I want it recorded in here. Then, you see, when we're all in a courtroom together, a jury will know that I gave you every opportunity to tell me straightaway how innocent you are, how it couldn't be you that killed Marlie and why that's the case. And the fact that you're not telling me? Maybe they'll look at that and think it odd. Why wouldn't an innocent man explain to me at the first opportunity what he knows and give me his alibi? Unless he doesn't have one, of course.'

'Yes, thank you,' said Harvey. 'It's called *inference* and I discussed this with my client prior to your coming in here. He is fully aware of this rather oppressive tactic where it is suggested that a man not answering questions is *always* lying when we know full well that a defendant has the right not to incriminate himself when he is confused about how he has even ended up here in the first place. Previous miscarriages of justice have proven this to be correct. Juries will be understanding of this, of course, that is assuming a courtroom is relevant. And from what you have revealed so far it is most certainly not.'

'Are you going to keep answering for your client, *Darren*?'

'I will continue to act as a buffer to oppressive tactics, yes. I am here to ensure the fair treatment of my client. We are both as concerned as you are that the correct person be brought to justice, *DS Ives*.'

'When was the last time you saw Marlie, Freddie?'

'No comment.'

'No comment . . .' Maddie repeated back. She could feel she was starting to lose control of that rage. She had known that Rickman wouldn't answer any questions and had even told herself that this was the best outcome, but only if she could hold it together. She took a swig of her water to give herself a few more seconds, but the anger was still there, stuck in her throat. She was going to have to use it.

'Are you alright, Detective Sergeant?' Harvey looked amused as he spoke.

'Not really, Darren. If I'm honest I'm fucking appalled at this whole charade. That your client comes in here, sits down with a grin on his face and offers not a word of explanation, not a single word of assistance.'

'In all my time . . .' Harvey's reaction was dramatic, but Maddie wasn't in the mood for *faux-appalled*. 'You *cannot* sit a man down and lambast him with *foul* language simply because he is not giving you the full and frank admission for which you are so clearly desperate! *Inspector* Blaker, I suggest you take control of your officer, of this entire interview in fact, since it seems clear to me that DS Ives here it too emotionally involved to conduct herself properly. This is an innocent man until you have proven him to be—'

'Except he isn't.' Maddie cut back in before Harry could. She could see that he had his palms raised as if about to appease the two men. That was the last thing she wanted. 'You're not innocent are you, Freddie? I *know* what happened.'

'Just saying you know something is not evidence of anything!' Harvey was laughing now, doing his best *incredulous*.

Maddie pushed her book completely over to one side then lifted a bagged item onto the table. It was a yellow rucksack still in a sealed evidence bag.

'Okay then. Seeing as you don't seem too keen to answer any of my questions, allow me to tell you a story of an incredibly brave young woman. I suggest you concentrate. Her name is Holly Maguire. And just four days ago, she took her own life by forcing the taxi she was travelling in over a cliff. She took a driver with her. Both were killed. Two lives lost. She did this because she was so desperate that she believed there was no other way out, no other way for you to relinquish the grip you had on her and on her girlfriend.'

Rickman bridled. 'What the f—'

'*When* she went over that cliff, she was clutching onto this bag.' She pushed it towards Rickman who huffed and sat back. His face was now contorted into a half-smile. There seemed to be an increased intensity in his stare however, which still focused on her mouth. It had been awkward before, but now Maddie was delighted. She wanted him to *see* every word as well as hear it. That way he wouldn't miss a single one.

'In this bag she had a number of items that were meant for me to find, to prompt me to question them. They all seemed to point to one man. Specifically . . . Freddie Rickman. And it wasn't just the bag and its contents. The taxi driver was chosen on purpose, another lead for me to follow right back to *Freddie Rickman*. I didn't know why at the time. But now I do. This was a man who was forcing girls as young as sixteen to perform sex acts on live camera feeds against their will, who was arranging for these same girls to be systematically raped for the pleasure of subscribers all over the world and who ensured this remained a source of income through threats and demonstrations of appalling violence. Including the murder of Marlie Towers.'

'Well, that is a wonderful—'

'*First* there were these.' Maddie cut Harvey off this time. 'These are photographs of Truro House, a building where you own three properties. No need for you to confirm that — we have the open source evidence. The photos are of the front, then some interior shots that are designed to map out how to get to your flats. The focus is on numbers ten and twelve, but number twelve was the source of much of Holly's misery, as was signified by this.'

Maddie threw the metal door number *12* onto the desk. Even through its see-through bag, it clanged on the solid table. She waited for Rickman to look at it.

'The caretaker has given a statement detailing regular access to these flats by both Holly and Kelly. He also names you personally and *Benny*, who I now know to be an associate of yours called Shane Porter, a man that I can have identified from my own brief meeting. Not that I *need* to identify him as all the girls suddenly seem willing to name him as your accomplice.' Next she lifted out a plastic fob. 'This is access to Truro House. I guess you gave this to Holly so she could come and go and you could continue with your general business model of staying away. You do this because you mistakenly think that distance makes you safe. That wasn't your only mistake, but I'll come onto the others.' Maddie paused for a reaction. She didn't get one. She lifted a small book out of the box, labelled *Addresses*. She put it on the table.

'This is a list of all the properties you own. This was very useful. We sent police out to knock the doors of each of these addresses and while we didn't find you, we found plenty more people claiming to be victims. I'll come on to how we *did* find you in just a moment, Freddie — you're going to like that. Any comment yet?'

Rickman's bored expression persisted. He had crossed his arms and was leaning back, his eyes lifted to the ceiling. Maddie continued.

'Ugly mugs.' Maddie lifted two sheets of paper. She pushed the one showing a list of initials in front of him. 'A lot of brothels keep a list that they refer to as *ugly mugs*. Generally these are clients who can't behave themselves, who beat on the women or who have demands that make the women feel uncomfortable. It's unusual to have them as initials. Why not write the name out in full? This is a secret journal after all.' Maddie leaned forward. 'Now then, because initials made no sense I had to go to the brothel and ask for the list of full names. Holly wanted me to do that, she wanted me to go to that brothel, to work out that you owned the building and to make myself known to the girls that work from there. And the names? The girls have cleared up the mystery behind them for me now, just like they were supposed to. This is the list of people that you call on when you need something done. This is like your *crew* isn't it? Some of them you use for enforcement, some of them, like SP, here — *Shane Porter* — manage the girls giving camera shows. Some of the other men on this list we now know are taxi drivers. They drive for your firm but that's not all they do, is it? They also identify vulnerable young women they can bring to you for the whole recruitment process to begin. If any of this is wrong in any way, feel free to tell me?'

Rickman spoke to the ceiling. 'No comment, love.'

'I spoke to the man you bought the taxi firm from — very briefly this morning. I think I got him out of bed. But he will come down. Seems he's only too keen to stick his boot in. It was a partnership to start with, but then you wanted to use the cars to drive girls around for sex. He challenged you about it and you fell out. Then you started employing the sort of people as drivers that he didn't agree with. He challenged you again and from that moment you bullied him into selling his share of the business for a lot less than it was worth. You threatened him, told him you knew where he lived with his kids. Holly made sure I dug that up by leaving me this.' Maddie dropped the ashtray onto the table to make the loudest thud yet. It drew all eyes to it and Darren Harvey tutted. '*NH Cars*. That's what it was called when you bought into it, right? You told me you bought it outright when you came in before, but I reckon Neil Henner's account is much more accurate. What do you think?'

'You couldn't make it up!' Rickman chuckled.

'So he walked when you had taxi drivers starting to recruit girls to become prostitutes for you. But it's changed recently, hasn't it? It's young girls now, underage and manip-ulated into sex acts on camera — usually when they're drunk — and then you blackmail them into performing again, threatening to release the footage to their social media con-tacts. All of them get told that the footage is streamed abroad so no one here will ever know, as long as they do as you ask. And once you have them you can do whatever you want with them. Am I right?'

'No comment.' Rickman's face was still a leer. If she was rattling his cage, he was doing a good job of hiding it.

'Another name on this list is AM. This list tells me that is Andrew Miles. Last night Andrew Miles was stabbed in the gut by a desperate woman who was fighting for her life while you made off from the building via a window. Andrew Miles and another male were sent by you to rape and murder Kelly Dale. Andrew's going to be just fine, by the way, and I'm looking forward to interviewing him very soon. What do you think he will say to me, Freddie? He's in a lot of trouble, after all. Do you think he'll take it on the chin and make no mention of the man who sent him there, even if it might reduce his own sentence?'

'No . . .' Rickman leaned further forward, leaving a pause just long enough that Maddie was about to follow up her question. '. . . comment!' He grinned as if enjoying himself.

Maddie grinned back. 'You know what . . . I could do with a break from talking at you. How about we watch a short video?' She flipped open the laptop. The login screen appeared almost immediately. She had left the media player ready to go. She clicked *PLAY*. The CCTV footage Harry had seized started immediately. Maddie would normally use CCTV as a basis for questions, pausing when someone appeared, asking if the person in the footage was the defendant, asking if they knew where this footage was from. This time she said nothing. Rickman flopped back against his seat, his arms still crossed, almost watching out of the corner of his eye. But he was watching.

Harvey was more obvious. He leaned forward, his nose scrunched to stop his glasses sliding off. 'You did not show me this footage in disclosure, officer.'

'I don't have to,' Maddie snapped.

'In the spirit of giving me the opportunity to best advise my client?' Darren fixed on her over the top of his glasses.

'And why would I want to do that?' Maddie snapped again.

Harvey's gaze flicked to where Harry shuffled next to her. She waited for him to intervene. He didn't. She knew she was pushing it. Harvey's attention moved back to the grainy footage on the laptop. The quality was worse than when it had been on the big screen upstairs. She watched Rickman closely as it played, trying to pick out any reaction at all. There was none.

'What was that?' Rickman said when it finished.

'You tell me.'

'No idea! Oh, sorry . . .' He grinned again. 'No comment!'

'Okay then, let me help. That was you in the van there, along with an associate who is unknown at this time — maybe even two associates. Marlie Towers was dumped in the bin you could see in that footage. The intention was to show Kelly Dale how Marlie had met her end. You were trying to terrify her, to get her compliance, but also the compliance of everyone else. I think you were pretty sure it had worked.'

'Maddie . . .' Harry's growl did now cut through the tension in the room. 'Maybe we should leave some details out, let Mr Rickman here have the opportunity to fill in the gaps.'

Harvey's instant delight was painfully obvious. To him, Maddie had just been shown up as an amateur. She knew the rules: you didn't reveal what was in a bin, you asked. But she was building to something and there was still a lot of detail that Rickman was going to fill in. Just as soon as she could make him realise that it was in his interest.

'Am I correct?' Maddie said to Rickman.

'No comment. And did you just get told off there?'

Rickman's solicitor beamed next to him.

Maddie took a moment. She moved the laptop to one side to rest her hands on the table, her fingers meeting to make a bridge. She leaned forward until she could be sure she had Rickman's attention.

'And there it is. Another example of your biggest flaw . . . *arrogance.* It was always going to get you in the end, Freddie. I read the arresting officer's statement from this morning. You came quietly. Your response to caution he recorded as *here we go again!* You've been here before, in one of these rooms, responding to questions. And every time you've walked. But I think that's made you sloppy. You've convinced yourself that no one will ever talk to the police about Freddie Rickman — they wouldn't *dare!* That arrogance was what led Holly Maguire to do what she did, that allowed her to get all the information she needed for us to look at you in the first place. That arrogance is the reason the van containing Marlie Towers's body didn't catch — so none of the forensic evidence was destroyed in the fire. That arrogance is what had you demonstrating what you had done, to Kelly Dale under a CCTV camera *and* moving a bin out of the way with no gloves on and that arrogance had you underestimating Kelly, had you thinking that she would never sit down and give us a statement that she would then follow to court. So, stick to your guns . . . show me your arrogance one more time. I want to fucking *see* it once more, Freddie Rickman — keep telling me *no comment!*'

Freddie was still grinning. His solicitor gasped, then tutted. Harry was fidgeting again, too. Maddie had risen off her seat a little. She could feel the burn in her legs.

'Well . . . that is quite a story, DS Ives,' Harvey said. 'And all conjecture! Every word of it. Still not a shred of *actual* evidence. You talk of forensics and lack of gloves etcetera, etcetera . . . Do you actually have any forensics? And a statement is just the word of one person against another unless you have *some* corroboration at least?'

Maddie lowered herself back into her seat. She took a moment to get control of her breathing. She stared at Rickman, who still seemed fixated by her mouth, still not making eye contact. She didn't think he could.

'No comment then!' He chuckled, his head shaking subtly.

'You might be right.' Maddie came back quieter, concentrating on her breathing and her words. 'The DNA work is ongoing but I *will* be able to put you in that van, Freddie, you can be sure of that. I have a fingerprint hit on the discarded bin, too. Can you explain how your fingerprint got on that?'

'No comment.' Rickman now huffed like he was starting to get frustrated.

'A moveable object in a communal bin area,' Harvey said. 'And you haven't even told us where.'

'I'm done telling you anything,' Maddie sighed. 'We still have a scene from last night at an accommodation block at Canterbury University. Have you ever been to Canterbury University before, Freddie?'

'No comment.'

'Why would you go there?'

'No comment.'

'If I find forensic evidence linking you to the Canterbury University campus, can you explain how that might have got there?'

'No comment.'

'No comment,' Maddie repeated. She leaned back as she spoke, her words drifting out in a sigh. She moved back to the laptop. She brought the media player back up. 'You remember I talked about your arrogance Freddie? You were so convinced that you had control over Kelly that when you took her phone off her to cut her off — to isolate her. You provided her with a replacement of course so you could still get in touch. We just saw that transaction take place in the CCTV footage. That phone, Freddie . . . it has a recording function.' She paused.

Rickman's only reaction was to lick his lips.

'You were in a room with her last night, weren't you?'

This time there was no answer.

'I know that. Kelly's told us, of course, but you also licked her face and bit her ear, didn't you Freddie? We've swabbed that for analysis. How do you explain how your DNA is on her cheek and ear Freddie? Let me guess . . . no comment? But that wasn't even your worst mistake, not by a long shot. This phone, with the recording facility . . . do you remember you let Kelly take her coat off — her mother's coat, she told you?' Maddie waited again, desperate for something. Freddie was back to looking up at the ceiling. 'She took it off when you let her and she also found the time to point that phone out from under it and start it recording.

She thought she might be able to get the audio at least, but you know what? She fluked it. She got *more* than we needed.'

Maddie clicked *play*. She spun the laptop to a position where the whole room could see. Rickman uncrossed his arms and leaned in, his attention dragged to the screen, his face suddenly pale. Harry too shuffled in his seat to get a position to see. He made eye contact with Maddie very briefly, his gaze questioning; this was new to him, too.

The audio kicked in. *'That's better, Kell, see? You do as you're told. You seem to forget that I know how to play this game. I've done this a million times, with a million other girls . . .'* The voice was tinny, distant-sounding, and there was a loud hiss where the speakers were struggling to play on full volume. The screen was flared bright white where a spotlight in the ceiling was pointed towards the lens. Maddie clicked to pause it, enjoying dragging this moment out.

'Is that you, Freddie?' she said.

'I . . . It's—'

'You don't have to comment on this!' Harvey cut in with some urgency. 'We have no idea what this is or where it has come from. That could be anyone's voice! You are reminded of my advice, Mr Rickman. *Nothing* has changed. This was not shown to me in disclosure, I have not had suitable time to discuss this matter with my client.'

Maddie moved her hand right back from the laptop. 'Would you like more time now?'

'I don't want to see it!' Rickman shouted. 'Take it the fuck away — this is all bullshit! You're stitching me up!' His emotional lock had suddenly given way. Maddie had him backed into a corner and she had him angry; she couldn't let that advantage go.

'I'm going to play it — *all* of it. That way you can point out how it *isn't* you in the footage.'

'This is bullshit!' Rickman said again.

She clicked to restart the footage. The camera seemed to be focusing better the longer it went on. The angle wasn't ideal; the screen was part-blocked by a triangular shadow that took out much of the left side and she guessed to be part of the coat hanging over the lens. But the phone's cheap camera was compensating for the light and forms were starting to appear out of the flared whiteness. Already it was good enough to make out Rickman. The camera was angled upwards, capturing his torso and, most importantly, a good enough shot of his face. Good enough for *beyond reasonable doubt* at least.

Harvey moved his hand to cover his mouth. He lifted his glasses with his finger and thumb as he rubbed his face.

'The police, they came to talk to me. Someone got stupid. They must have mentioned something to the cops, so I took action. I took back control of my business.'

Maddie watched Rickman closely as the voice changed and Kelly spoke. She was quieter. Darren Harvey leaned towards the laptop.

'Marlie . . . What you did was because of me?'

Freddie's voice cut back in loud and brash: *'Fucking right I did! The hammer in her skull was for you, Kell!'*

Maddie paused it again. 'You killed Marlie Towers with a hammer in her skull, didn't you Mr Rickman?'

The paused screen and the question broke the spell. The two men opposite had been leaning in together; they broke away together, too. Rickman's eyes were still aimed at her lips but they looked unfocused, glazed almost. He shook his head, his lips pushed out like he was running his tongue over his gums and he grimaced.

Maddie started the footage again.

'And I gave you the freedom to make sure the word got out. And it did, didn't it? You went out like a little messenger, making sure the rest of the girls knew not to fuck with me — that it wasn't worth the risk to even breathe in the direction of the fucking pigs. And do you think they've been back to see me since? Of course they haven't. They know nothing, Kell. I worked that out when I sat in their grubby little station. As for Libby . . . she won't talk to the cops. Not after tonight. I've arranged a little demonstration of what happens to people who think they can talk about me. You got to see our friend Marlie after I threw

The room's attention was still on the tiny laptop screen. Rickman looked away as his image moved off the screen and he walked to another part of the room. Now the footage just showed a white ceiling with the yellow flare of the spotlight in the middle.

Maddie let it play. She knew what was coming next. She sipped at her water, her focus still on Freddie Rickman, on every flicker of his face. He couldn't pull away from the footage, his head jerked like he wanted to but his eyes stayed locked on that screen. A scuffling sound came through the speakers, a woman screamed. It was Kelly Dale. She appeared in the screen briefly too, so did Shane Porter — *Benny,* when he blocked her efforts to make for the door by throwing his fist. There was a loud thud where she struck the floor. It was perfect. Maddie chose this moment to pause it.

'I want you to think, Freddie. I want you to consider, when we show Shane Porter this footage in his own interview, when he sits accused of murder, false imprisonment and rape — facing the rest of his life behind bars . . . what do you think he'll say? Who do you think he'll point the finger at? And what else do you think he'll tell us if he thinks he can save his own skin — reduce his own sentence? And that might be a possibility, Freddie. He's already shown an appetite to strike a deal.'

'I don't know no Shane Porter!' Rickman mumbled.

'Oh dear . . .' Maddie shook her head. 'That's the thing with *no comment* . . . that's why people like Darren, here, like it so much. I can't challenge *no comment,* but I can prove a lie. We know you and Shane work together.' She gestured at the screen. 'Here you are in the same room for a start! Besides that, where do you think we got the address where you were found this morning from? That place wasn't linked to you, Freddie. It's not one of yours. People are already starting to turn. I want you to think about that. And you'll have plenty of time to do some thinking over the next day or so, I can promise you that.'

Maddie didn't give him a chance to respond. She clicked for the footage to start back up. Kelly's voice was instantly shrill, she was begging for her life now. Maddie took a deep breath at this point, just as she had the first time she saw it. The footage portrayed Freddie as enjoying his moment; he was toying with Kelly. Maddie knew he had done the same with Marlie Towers. She must have been so terrified.

Freddie appeared back on the screen and pulled a piece of black material from over his face. It wasn't clear but Maddie knew from Kelly's account that it was a balaclava.

'It's like I said from the start. It's you — or it's Libby, there!' Rickman's shoulder raised into the shot then his head turned to give the clearest image of his face yet. Maddie took another swig of her water while Freddie's final exchange with Kelly played out, his final sentence was delivered with particular glee: *'You don't both have to die tonight. Do you understand me?'*

Rickman's head fell into his hands. He was no longer looking at the screen. It didn't matter. He would still be able to hear the two men he had left in that room as they told Kelly what she could expect.

'This don't have to be hard. We fuck you first, then we make it quick. That's the plan. You go easy and quick or you play about and we take our time. Those are your only choices, so get everything else out of your little head, you understand?' Maddie paused it again.

'That pleasant individual is Andrew Miles. We've talked about him already. He is currently handcuffed to a hospital bed while doctors patch up his stomach injuries. It's still touch and go if he'll be wearing a bag for the rest of his life. Which may well be in prison — for, you see, Kelly is about to personify everything you dismissed in your arrogance, Freddie. She's about to fight back.' Maddie allowed more time for a reaction. Rickman's head was shaking — subtle, almost unnoticeable, but Maddie noticed. She slid from her chair and stood up.

'Kelly was trying to hold them up until Libby was done, maybe even gone. She was trying to drag it out until you came back in so she could be sure Libby was safe. But Kelly was exhausted and the men you ordered to rape her and then kill her live on camera, they were about to remove her jeans so at that point she had no choice. The knife was in her trouser pocket, see. It had been there all the time. Arrogance *again* Freddie! You never considered searching her, did you? It never even crossed your mind that someone like Kelly might stand up to you. Well, she did, Freddie, just like Holly and Marlie did.' Maddie could feel herself leaning forward until she was right over Rickman, her palms flat on the table and taking her weight. He was still holding his head in his hands. Darren Harvey had no more protestations about how his client was being treated. She leaned right forward until she was as close to his ear as the table would allow.

'You got any comment yet?' she hissed. She waited, lingering over him, close enough for his sickly sweet aftershave to fill her nostrils. But it was mixed with something else now: fear.

Maddie fell back into her seat. She clicked play again. There were immediate sounds of fighting. Kelly's shrill voice stood out against the more bassy grunts and threats from the two men. She begged for them to stop, she begged for them to leave her alone. *'Please don't!'*

The phone's battery cut the footage short. Maddie worked out that it had cut off just a few minutes before Harry had kicked that door in. She left the room silent for as long as she could.

'When did you run, Freddie?' she said, finally. Her voice was breaking as she spoke. A sign of her anger, perhaps, excitement more like. She could smell blood. Freddie Rickman was on the ropes in front of her. He finally looked up, his eyes still glazed, his forehead beaded with sweat. 'When you saw us arrive or when you saw Kelly fight back? I bet it was Kelly that made you run — the first sign of someone standing up to you. Am I right?' She leaned in, desperate for a rise — not for the case; she didn't need any reaction from him; she had enough already — but she wanted to see it.

He was beaten, however. His head fell forward, dragging his shoulders with it. His face hung just a few inches from the table. Maddie left the room silent again. Her next question snapped his head back straight.

'Tell me about Victoria.'

His focus was back on her lips. His nose twitched. She knew she had provoked him with the question. 'I don't have nothing to say to you,' he managed, finally.

'We had an idea that we had scared you away from using your own places. We were sniffing around and you couldn't risk it. Not if you wanted time and space to be able to murder Kelly — maybe Libby too. A colleague of mine has known sex workers to use Airbnb. Do you know what that is?'

'I've got *nothing* to say to you!' His anger was returning. Maddie was delighted.

'It's a web-based thing. People can rent out spare rooms or whole houses to travellers. We were a little desperate. We got a list of all the rented accommodation across the county. It was a bit of a needle in a hay stack. But one booking stood out. *Victoria Long* had booked out five rooms at Canterbury Uni. Which, as we both know, is in the middle of nowhere. And in the middle of the week? We dismissed it as nothing — we couldn't find anything to link it to any of this. But then we had another look at Holly's largest and most outstanding item. When we opened it up we were able to get a proper look and there was the final piece of the puzzle, the final *fuck you* from Holly, the one that would bring you down.'

She reached back down to the exhibits. She lifted the rucksack from where she had put it back in the box and slid it back onto the table. 'It's not easy to see, not when it's back in an exhibit bag, so let me help.' Maddie angled the bag, pushing the top towards Freddie. She pointed under a flap that held the teeth where the main zip bit. There was a slim, white strip of material with the name of the bag's owner stitched into it: *Victoria Long*.

'You see that?' Maddie said. She didn't wait for a reply. She left the bag on the table. 'A name tag. This is Victoria Long's school bag, isn't it? That's why we couldn't find a social media presence for her, because she's seven years old. And we couldn't find a mention of her on any police systems for the same reason. Except there would have been something on there had we known she was your daughter.' Maddie sat back, again allowing for a reaction.

'You do have a daughter called Victoria, right?' Maddie didn't wait long for him to answer. 'Of course you won't answer that. You've kept her to yourself this long. She's in foster care. But her mother still saw her when she was allowed, because she was taken off her some time ago. She wanted her back permanently, of course. But social services were never going to give her back all the while she was reported to be running a brothel, were they? Did Marlie Towers consent to that relationship or did you just take what you wanted? And you wouldn't let her quit, would you? Not to get her daughter back. She had to keep running that brothel, *your* brothel, because you thought you could keep control over her if she still worked for you. And then when we started sniffing around, asking questions that seemed like they could only have been prompted by what Marlie knew, you killed her, using it to take back control of who was left. Am I anywhere near right?'

There was still no answer, still no expectation of one.

'Marlie only ever talked to one other person about you. About her past with you, about your daughter. Holly Maguire. Holly did what she did because it was the only way they could all be free. Kelly for sure, but Marlie was going to get her daughter back, too. Marlie knew about the underage girls on the webcams and what you were forcing them to do. She knew that you were demanding more and more of them. She knew that you had found that there was big money in forced sex, bigger even than having kids strip. And she told Holly. And that was it, the final straw that prompted Holly to give the only thing she considered she had valuable enough to make the police listen to her — to make everyone listen: her life.' Maddie paused again, this one wasn't for effect; this was to stop her emotion boiling over. She took a moment before she could continue.

'Do you have any comment now?'

'Much has been disclosed that was not previously advised, DS Ives. Harvey's voice had made Maddie jump, despite it coming in softly. 'I think my client and I would appreciate a break. We have been in here an hour or more. And perhaps I wasn't given all the information I required from my client either.'

'I think you're absolutely right, Darren. Fine, then. But I can do better than your break. You see, I'm done. You can request another interview if you think of anything you want to tell us. But, so you know, it might not be me and the boss here that come back in if you do decide to answer some questions. We have some rookie detectives who could do with the experience of being involved in a murder investigation. Seeing as how this is pretty cut and dried, I might give them the experience. I have a lot of work to do, see. The last I heard we had at least five underage girls sat at home with their parents, ready to tell us their story, which I imagine will be very similar to Libby's. I also have a number of your client's associates to interview. They'll all get to see this same footage and then they will know that this empire has collapsed, that they can finally talk freely about Freddie Rickman because he is never coming back out of jail. I want them all to know that there is nothing left . . . not even the arrogance. So, yeah, you let the custody sergeant know when you are ready.' Maddie stood up again. 'Unless you want to say anything now?'

Freddie's head was still down, his hands over it, gently rubbing back and forth over his head.

'I'll take that as a *no comment,* then.'

* * *

The door out of the custody area was the heaviest in the building, made of solid steel and with a mechanism that clunked shut with a drama that suited its purpose. Harry waited for the clunk before he spoke.

'That was a new approach. Maybe in the future you could let me into your interview plan.'

Maddie was getting better at reading him, but at that point she had no idea if he was delighted with her or boiling with anger. 'I'm sorry I didn't tell you about the video. I only knew about it an hour before we started. Kelly didn't offer it up straightaway. She almost didn't show me it at all. Just goes to show the levels of fear and control that man was able to hold over those girls.'

'I might have had a different opinion about interviewing him straightaway.'

'You wouldn't. You would have wanted to see it first. It would have taken up more time. I just needed to get in there — it was burning me up inside.'

'Of course I would. And then I might have understood your conduct in that interview room a little better. Not that it would have excused it.'

'I knew you would see the footage in the interview. I'm sorry, I was angry going in there. I knew that. I thought I could use that to my advantage.'

'You were on the edge. Had it not been massively undermining I would have pulled you out half way through. Your conduct reflects directly on me, Maddie. Don't ever forget that.'

'I lost sight of everything but getting the job home. I know that. I spent all night listening to what that man did...' Maddie stopped. She had left all her anger in that interview room. All that was left now was exhaustion. She didn't have the energy to defend herself. Not when she knew she was in the wrong. Harry's cheeks rippled where his jaw was clamped shut. She waited for his reprimand to continue.

'It could have turned out worse, I suppose. I do think we have him now.' Harry kept a straight face for just a few second before releasing a subtle grin.

'I'm quietly confident,' she chanced.

'I was watching him closely. You could see the exact moment he realised you'd been playing him along the whole time. That will stay with me for some time.'

'I think I saw it, too. Maybe we should take the still from the interview tapes for the office wall. As a reminder.'

'A reminder? Of what? That time when you were entirely right and I was wrong?' Harry's grin dropped away. Again Maddie was finding him difficult to read.

'That wasn't what I meant at all. But now you mention it . . .'

Harry was back to looking humoured. 'Good job Maddie. No one ever got anywhere near that man. It wasn't just the women who worked for him that thought he was untouchable. I think a lot of us thought the same. We didn't reckon on you. He certainly didn't.'

Maddie didn't take compliments well, even less so when they were coming from Harry. She never knew quite how to react. She smiled dumbly and the moment turned quickly awkward. Harry turned for the stairs back to the office.

'You didn't really mean it, did you?' he called back. 'When you said that we would send some rookie detective down there to finish off the interview?'

'I didn't at the time, Harry. I was just trying to send him a message, kick him while he was down. But right now it doesn't seem like a bad idea. I seem to have just realised how tired I am.'

Harry stopped on the stairs to face back down. 'It was a long night. I don't see him wanting to talk to anyone for quite some time anyway, and even if he does, he can wait. I'll get the team to go to CPS with what we have. We'll get a holding charge, no problem. That gets him into prison while we work out the rest. The last I saw, there were nine charges being investigated — ten if you include the attempted murder of

Libby's boyfriend. I don't think anyone's considered that yet. To be honest, we still don't really know how many victims might come out of the woodwork. We'll remand him tonight. I don't see him ever coming back out.'

'And that's just him, boss. We need to do the same with Benny and we have a stabbed man cuffed to a hospital bed whose day isn't about to improve . . . And there's the whole ugly mugs list . . . Jesus, there's so much to do . . .'

'There is. And it will get done. But you chopped off the head of the snake, Maddie. Those girls are safe now. We'll come back to it this evening feeling a lot fresher than we do right now. Go home. Get some rest.'

Maddie nodded. She had been running on adrenaline in that interview, quite literally fuelled by her hatred for the piece of shit sitting opposite. Both of them. But her day wasn't done yet. Not quite.

'Sounds wonderful. I just have one last visit to do before I can go home.'

'Visit? What visit?'

'Taruc's wife. Our taxi driver. I can't forget about him, about his wife. I need to talk to her. I need to tell her that he was completely blameless — wrong place, wrong time.'

Harry sighed. 'I thought the same. We can offer her a few more answers now at least. It doesn't have to be you though, does it?'

'It does. I think it does, at least.'

'It's not going to make a difference, it won't be some magical cure to the pain that family is feeling. You know that, right?'

'I do. But when this is finished, when it is confirmed that Freddie Rickman is never coming out of prison I'm going to go back and give her every detail, if she can stand it. And if she can't, I'll wait until she can. There's a bigger picture. Taruc was part of that. It doesn't make it right but he didn't die for nothing.'

Harry seemed to hold back his first response. 'You're right, he didn't,' he said eventually. 'That's a difficult message to deliver at any time, but when you're exhausted . . .'

'It has to be now. There's already enough keeping me awake without this hanging over me too.'

'What else? This is done, Maddie. For now at least. Building the casefile and securing—'

'Adam called,' Maddie blurted out. She regretted it instantly. She had wanted to tell him but now wasn't the time.

'Adam Yarwood?' Harry said. Maddie didn't reply. 'He's okay, then?'

'Enough to speak over the phone.'

'And what did he say?'

'That he would like to see me.'

'Tonight?'

'No! Who knows when — weeks, months.'

'Then you've got nothing to stay awake for. Go home and get some sleep, for goodness' sake.'

'That's it! No stern advice or words of wisdom about staying away from people like Adam Yarwood?'

Harry started moving up the steps again. He lingered on the last one before he would turn out of sight. He looked slightly humoured.

'Advice? Wisdom? Since when have you listened to any of that DS Ives?'

Harry did now step out of sight. Maddie heard the beep as he passed through another security door. She still lingered on the stairs, already picturing Mrs Taruc Mardin standing in front of her while she tried to give a clear explanation of how she had come to lose her husband. She owed her that. She couldn't finish her day until it was done.

And Harry was right about Adam Yarwood too. He was a consideration for another day.

CHAPTER 36

Friday

The breeze was stronger that morning, the view of France clearer. White wisps of cloud seemed to move so quickly over her head that the sky was like a time-lapse video as she stood on the edge of the grassy verge.

Kelly Dale moved forward. There was still some of the cut grass left, it was brown and brittle and it floated backwards in the wind when she disturbed it with her feet. She could see the woman's back as she sat on a bench that stood out as looking brand new, the wood showing none of the weathering of the neighbouring benches. Beyond it she could now see more of the flat ocean. It looked to be made up of horizontal lines of differing blues and greens. It was beautiful.

Kelly ran her hand slowly over the back of the bench. The woman was over to the right, her long hair was down and the breeze was delighting in moving it in every direction as it caught in the swirls rising up and over the lip of the cliff. The edge was further away than it had looked from the road. The woman had a small dog on her lap. Its nose twitched, flitting between millions of moving scents.

'You got my message, then?' The seated woman had a voice. Still she looked away. The breeze seemed to move the words around. The woman lifted a flask into view and Kelly smiled at the back of her head. She moved around to sit next to her. She kept her back straight, her eyes still forward over the shuffling colour chart laid out in front. The dog pushed its wet nose under her arm and it made her flinch.

'I did.'

'I'm glad you came.'

'I wasn't going to.'

'I didn't know if you would. Not yet anyways.'

Kelly didn't reply, she didn't know what to say. Maybe she was just done talking.

'I introduced myself the last time we met but you weren't listening so well. You had a lot on your mind. My name is Margaret. Margaret Throughgood — and this, of course, is Molly. She's my Bichon Frise and she has a cold nose and a good aim!'

Kelly smiled but she still didn't speak.

'I know that you're Kelly Dale. The nice detective told me that. She also said that you're an extraordinary woman and that you've had an extraordinary couple of days.'

'I'm nothing of the sort, I can tell you that. I was backed into a corner and I fought my way out. Anyone can do that. What's extraordinary is someone who wasn't backed into a corner, someone who planned for a long time to do something amazing. To sacrifice themselves for the good of a lot of people. For me.'

'Now that does sound extraordinary. Did you want some coffee?' Margaret poured some of the steaming liquid into the cup. The breeze forced the scent on Kelly. It smelled delicious. Her smile got wider, still directed out towards the sea.

'You remember what I told you about bad things happening when I drink?' Kelly said. 'I don't want to tempt fate.'

'Drink? What sort of a lush do you think I am? This is just coffee, I'll have you know. I do remember what you said. You also said that you like to carry around the empty of the last thing you drank from — to remind you of how it always ends badly. Well, I rather like this flask!'

'Okay then.' Kelly took the drink. She brought it just close enough to her lips to realise it was molten hot. She moved it away again.

'Have you seen it?' the woman said.

'No.' Kelly's grin dropped away a little. 'I almost don't want to. I know it's going to sound silly but . . . it was the last thing . . . the last thing she did for me. That's it, then.'

'I don't agree. You're a very young woman. I have a few . . . well, a lot of years on you. They come with experience. You have no idea how much she's done for you. Extraordinary people have that about them. Much later you'll be doing something in your life, going through something and suddenly you'll realise that you're better prepared because of them. Your girlfriend . . . she sounds like the sort of person that will never leave your side, one way or another. I have an ex-husband like that, for all his faults. I wouldn't see this as the last thing she did, more a reminder that you're a better person because of your time with her. And now you can have a better life.'

Kelly leaned forward. She took a breath and turned. The bronze plaque was right in the middle of the highest slat, between the two women. It looked brand new to the point of being out of place. The letters were embossed, a trick of the light made them look black in places. She ran her fingers over them, absorbing the words. She had promised herself she wouldn't cry, but a tear escaped to be buffeted by the breeze.

I'LL BE THE SKY
AND YOU BE THE BIRD.
HM 4 KD.

'Perfect!' Kelly sniffed. 'We used to come up here just to watch the birds. The sky just seems bigger here and the birds seem free to go where they please. She used to write some poetry. She was good, I mean she would never have me say it.

She wrote one for me. She said she wanted to be the sky for me . . .' Another tear fell to the wind. 'So I could be the bird.'

'Well . . .' Margaret grunted as she got to her feet. 'These are private times. Do you want me to leave the coffee with you? I'm only over the road? You can take as long as you like.'

'No, thank you. I have to be going myself. I have an appointment. I have a funeral to arrange. I just wanted to come up here first, to see it for myself. I'll be back, though, whenever I need to.'

Margaret beamed. 'It seemed to just appear! But she'll always be here now. I might not be but, all the time I am, you feel free to knock on my door for a coffee, you hear me?'

'Thanks again . . . *Margaret.*'

She waved Kelly away. 'Don't mention it. I hope the funeral stuff goes well. Not something you should have to be arranging for your partner. Not at your age.'

'Actually, this one's for my mum.'

'Your mum! My goodness, you have had a rough time.'

Kelly's smile was still genuine, her eyes followed a gull as it rode an upsurge of warm air.

'A rough week, maybe. But the rest of my life doesn't look so bad now does it? Now I get to be the bird.'

THE END

ALSO BY CHARLIE GALLAGHER

MADDIE IVES
Book 1: HE IS WATCHING YOU
Book 2: HE WILL KILL YOU
Book 3: HE WILL FIND YOU
Book 4: HE KNOWS YOUR SECRETS

LANGTHORNE POLICE SERIES
Book 1: BODILY HARM
Book 2: PANIC BUTTON
Book 3: BLOOD MONEY
Book 4: END GAME

STANDALONE NOVELS
MISSING
THEN SHE RAN
HER LAST BREATH
RUTHLESS

FREE KINDLE BOOKS

Please join our mailing list for free Kindle books
and new releases, including crime thrillers, mysteries,
romance and more.

www.joffebooks.com

Thank you for reading this book. If you enjoyed it please
leave feedback on Amazon or Goodreads, and if there
is anything we missed or you have a question about then
please get in touch. The author and publishing team
appreciate your feedback and time reading this book.

We're very grateful to eagle-eyed readers who take the
time to contact us. Please send any errors you find to
corrections@joffebooks.com

Made in United States
North Haven, CT
23 May 2023